Samantha drew the bolt shut behind her

Feeling tense, she tidied the living room, washing the coffee cups and putting them away. In her bedroom, she opened her window, pausing when she heard the crisp tread of feet on the sidewalk. Holding her breath, she waited.

A moment later she exhaled. A bobby, his arms swinging at his side, was treading his beat. Obviously Inspector Allen's orders to keep an eye on the building were being carried out.

She showered and changed, going back to the bathroom to brush her teeth. But when she pressed the soap dispenser to wash her hands, she was horrified. A stickly crimson liquid oozed over her fingers and dripping into the sink. Blood.

ABOUT THE AUTHOR

Tina Vasilos has successfully written romantic suspense for many years. She has traveled widely around the world, and she uses her trips to research her novels. Tina and her husband live with their teenage son in Clearbrook, British Columbia.

Past Tense
Tina Vasilos

Harlequin Books

TORONTO • NEW YORK • LONDON
AMSTERDAM • PARIS • SYDNEY • HAMBURG
STOCKHOLM • ATHENS • TOKYO • MILAN

To John and George with love

Harlequin Intrigue edition published February 1990

ISBN 0-373-22132-0

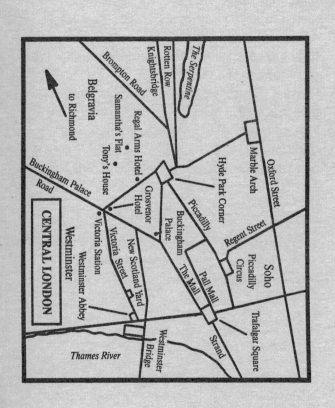

CENTRAL LONDON

Westminster

Thames River

to Richmond

Belgravia

Brompton Road

Knightsbridge

Rotten Row

The Serpentine

Regal Arms Hotel

Samantha's Flat

Tony's House

Buckingham Palace
Road

Grosvenor
Hotel

Victoria Station

Victoria Street

New Scotland Yard

Westminster Abbey

Westminster
Bridge

Buckingham
Palace

Hyde Park Corner

Marble Arch

Oxford Street

Piccadilly

Regent Street

Piccadilly
Circus

Soho

The Mall

Pall Mall

Trafalgar Square

Strand

CAST OF CHARACTERS

Samantha Smith—She had rotten luck with men, and now her former fiancé was stalking her.

Tony Theopoulos—A brilliant hotelier, he was a patsy for a woman in distress.

Michael Dubray—A prominent minister, was he alive or dead?

Bennett Price—Fast-track Canadian mogul or swine?

Jason Wheeler—He rented down the hall and showed up in the oddest places.

Miss Hunnicutt—The hapless gossip was fated for a fall.

Aunt Olivia—Daffy but sophisticated, she lured her beloved niece into *dangerous* situations.

Maurice St. Clair—A wealthy financier, he wanted the upcoming trade conference to go on without a hitch.

Chapter One

Samantha Smith hummed a little to herself as she stepped through the glass doors of the Regal Arms Hotel. The chandelier, a carefully preserved antique, winked at her as she walked briskly across the lobby, her shoes silent on the plush carpet.

The newsstand was at the far side, near the elevators—correction, the lifts. Her low humming died in mid-note and she frowned at the slip. This time it had been only in her mind, but it showed she was getting complacent, careless. At first it had been hard to think in British, but she'd practiced meticulously and had learned how. She shrugged lightly, her shoulders flexing under the thin sweater she wore.

Perhaps complacency was no longer dangerous. Maybe it was time she stopped looking over her shoulder, fearing pursuit. She'd been in London for nearly six months, with no sign that anyone either knew or cared about her whereabouts. She was increasingly inclined to rationalize the incident that had precipitated her flight from Montreal. The highly emotional state she'd been in at the time must have colored her interpretation of what she'd seen, exaggerated the danger.

In any case, she'd covered her tracks well. She'd bought bus and train tickets with cash. She had ridden on a lumbering Greyhound to Toronto, then taken a train to New York, then boarded an airbus to Paris. Another train had carried her to Nice, where she had made arrangements with an eccentric artist friend, Amelia Fontaine, to send postcards at regular intervals to friends at home. The long, often tedious journey had given Samantha plenty of time to prepare the cards in advance. Amelia, who had little use for marriage, had been only too ready to accept and applaud Samantha's broken engagement and fall in with her request.

Besides Amelia, only Mr. Collins knew she was in London. Mr. Collins was her solicitor and she'd just had lunch with him in a dark, smoky pub. Their usual meeting grounds.

A stuffy little man, and the only other person Samantha had taken partially into her confidence, he'd handled her financial affairs, so far without a glitch. He'd transferred funds from Montreal to London to pay for her tiny flat and provide her with a safe cushion in case of emergencies. She saw him once a month to discuss her investments and other private matters.

Mr. Collins would maintain lawyer-client confidentiality under torture. Samantha would have staked her life on it. If anyone asked him, she was in the south of France and he had correspondence to prove it.

A mirror on one of the columns that supported the lofty ceiling briefly reflected her image as she walked by. After all these months she still felt a momentary start when she caught an unexpected glimpse of her new self. Her best friends were unlikely to recognize her. Blond again, she'd gone back to her natural color after years as a dramatic redhead. The glasses she now wore gave her a studious look.

More than five months had passed. Her life had settled into a comfortable routine, not exciting perhaps, but one she could live with.

She smiled at the man behind the newsstand counter. "*The Times*, please."

As he grabbed a copy from the stack behind him, she glanced at her watch. If she hurried she could get an earlier bus and put in an extra hour of work.

" 'Ere you are, miss."

"Thank you." She dropped change on the counter.

She turned away, feeling lighthearted, as she hadn't for months. The day was fine, a welcome respite from the rainy weather Londoners had been enduring. Her present translating job was interesting. All was right with her world.

Until she glanced at the closing lift door and met the eyes of a man she thought had died.

ANTHONY THEOPOULOS HAD it all. Even his names, both of them, had positive connotations. A woman he'd had a relationship with the previous year was a linguist. She had looked up his names and informed him that Anthony meant "of inestimable worth." He'd always known that Theopoulos meant "child of God."

So why wasn't he happy? For him life had settled into a rut. He swiveled his chair so that he faced his office window. Serenely blue skies accented by a couple of snowy clouds bathed the city of London in a benign warmth, making up for the chill rain that had spoiled the summer. In the distance Hyde Park spread out like a green oasis amid tall buildings. If he looked carefully, he could just glimpse the Serpentine, a curving crescent of blue. The trees lining its shores displayed the lush green foliage of late August.

Why wasn't he happy? He was exactly where he wanted to be in his professional life. A year ago he'd been promoted to his present position as manager of Worldwide Hotel Corporation's Northern European Division. At thirty-four he was the youngest executive ever to hold this position, a career dream come true.

His personal life? He frowned. Empty. It was the only term that came to mind, in spite of his busy social life and stack of invitations to this concert or that art opening lying on his desk.

Perhaps he needed a holiday. He glanced at the folder in his hand, the Top Security designation stamped in scarlet on the cover. After the trade conference...

He scanned the first of several lists detailing caterers, security staff and protocol. Usually he didn't get involved in the day-to-day routine of the hotel, but this trade conference was vital to the continued economic cooperation between several countries. Nothing could go wrong with the arrangements this time.

He had personally guaranteed it.

"Mr. Theopoulos."

Tony swung the chair back toward his desk as his secretary's beautifully modulated voice came over the intercom. After a year she still addressed him formally. He smiled. Quite a change from the easygoing camaraderie in the Montreal and Vancouver offices of Worldwide Hotels.

He depressed the talk button. "Yes, Marcia?"

"Mr. Theopoulos—"

He could have sworn her voice shook. His smile fading, he sat up straighter. He'd never known anything to ruffle Miss Marcia Johnson.

"There is a problem downstairs. In the lobby. Mr. Parker asks that you come and see to it personally."

Her flustered air was incredible. She was a woman who organized meetings and calmed the occasional unhappy guest with aplomb. Curiosity kindled inside him. "All right, Marcia. Tell him I'll be right there."

He rode down in the elevator, emerging into the hotel lobby, whose magnificence still had the power to awe him. The spacious area with its moldings and Wedgwood-blue accents could have graced the most elegant, stately home. Visitors hushed their voices as they came in from the street. It was as if they'd entered a cathedral.

Today the scene was in chaos. For the first time no clerk held court behind the solid-oak registration counter. No blue uniformed bellman stood next to the elevator. Even the doorman had abandoned his post, the braid on his shoulder distinctly askew as he leaned over Mr. Parker's pin-striped back. Tony hurried across the red-and-gold carpet to the Lobby newsstand. At least a dozen of his staff crowded around someone sprawled on the floor.

"Excuse me, please."

He pushed past Parker, who was crouching over the body of a young woman.

Parker looked up, his face creased with worry and disapproval. "This young woman, sir," he said, moving aside. "She seems to have fainted."

Kneeling, Tony grasped her wrist. The pale skin was cool under his fingers, the bones delicate, fragile. Deceptive, no doubt, Tony realized at once. She wasn't in danger of dying. Her pulse beat strongly under his fingers, rather more quickly than normal, but within acceptable bounds.

Above him Parker wrung his hands, agitated by the unprecedented desecration of the hotel's usual calm. "She just walked in and fell down," he said plaintively. "No reason at all. Her things were all over the floor. I put them together by her handbag. I hope that's all right, sir. She looks—"

"Parker, bring me a wet cloth." Tony's voice cut decisively through the man's rambling. "And get hold of yourself." He swung his head around. "The rest of you can go back to your stations."

He was only dimly aware of their departure and curious backward glances. Turning to the woman on the floor, he noted her neat attractive appearance. She wore a tweed skirt and light sweater over a pink oxford-cloth shirt. The clothes were of good quality, yet undistinguished as if she put little store in fashion.

One shoe, he noticed, had fallen off her foot and lay next to her calf. The toenails on the shoeless foot were painted a vibrant fuchsia only slightly muted by the weave of the stocking.

She moaned, and stirred under his hand. His surprise at the nail polish, which glared when compared to her conservative appearance, died a quick death. He turned his attention to her face.

Thick, barley-colored hair cascaded in glossy waves around an oval face, marked by a smooth, faintly tanned complexion. She had well-defined, regular features. Her straight nose and generous mouth gave her an individual, striking loveliness. Color began to return to her cheeks.

His senses came fully alert. Who was she?

Parker thrust a cold wet cloth into his hand. Curbing his curiosity, Tony took it and gently wiped her face. "Thanks, Parker. You can go back to the desk."

Parker hesitated. "Sir, you're in the middle of the lobby. Could I help you move her to a—uh—less prominent place?"

Tony glanced around. They were near the newsstand, hardly the middle of the lobby. Parker was a fussbudget. "It's my lobby, so to speak," he said crisply. "I'd like to know what caused her to faint before I move her."

Parker drew himself up to his full height, his wide full nose twitching. "Very well, sir. Shall I call a doctor, sir?"

"No, don't bother for the moment. She's getting some color back. It's probably nothing serious."

He pressed the cloth to her forehead, brushing back her hair. It flowed through his fingers like smooth satin, and gave off a scent of orange blossoms.

"He was dead. I know he was," she muttered.

Startled, Tony turned his attention back to her face.

"He was dead!" She lifted her head, her voice rising, but hardly above a whisper.

Tony glanced around. Those of the staff who were visible went about their business with their usual efficiency. A midafternoon quiet enveloped the hotel. "Who was dead?" he asked, turning back to the woman.

Her eyelids fluttered, then lifted. Tony found himself gazing into gray eyes so pale and clear they reminded him of rain. They widened fractionally as if in surprise before she blinked several times.

"Who was dead?" he repeated.

For a moment she looked puzzled, then an emotion flickered through her eyes that he could have sworn was fear. But instantly it was gone, replaced by bewilderment.

"Dead? No one was dead."

The back of his neck prickled. Something wasn't right here, and he didn't know what. Her voice. Somehow it had changed from when she had uttered the first low but vehement statement. He had no doubt that she was completely conscious, even when she lay back, breathing a little too quickly.

Her lids fell closed. They snapped open again. "My glasses?"

"Oh, you had a pair?" he asked, looking around. Beside the spilled contents of her purse he found them. He handed her the sensible, plastic-framed glasses and she put them on, blinking as she focused through the lenses.

"Can you stand?" he asked.

The clear gray of her eyes was blurred by the glasses, giving her an ethereal look. "What? Oh, yes, I think so." She moved her head, as if testing its condition and balance. Then, pulling her feet under her, she sat up.

With a deft movement of her hands, she gathered her hair into a coil and fastened it at the back of her neck with the pins. Little tendrils dangled free, charmingly, Tony thought. She strove for dignity, he knew; making a scene was not a normal occurrence in this woman's life. But the pulled-back hair only emphasized the pale vulnerability of her face.

"Yes, I'm all right." Taking a firm grip on his hand, she stood up, letting go as soon as she gained her feet. She groped with her foot. "I seem to have lost my shoe." A little tinkling laugh tumbled from her lips.

Tony knelt and retrieved it, holding it as she slid her foot inside. The cool fragility of her hand telegraphed itself through the fabric of his shirt. He realized all at once that he had forgotten his jacket in his office, and hid a smile as he cast a sidelong look at the main desk. No wonder Parker had almost frozen in disapproval. Shirt sleeves and an open collar with loosened tie were not appropriate dress for the lobby of the Regal Arms.

Shoe in place, the woman let go of his shoulder, extending her hand in a courteous gesture. Tony got up slowly, noting she was only two or three inches shorter than his six feet. She looked older now, probably around thirty.

"Wouldn't you like to sit down and rest for a moment?" he asked, reluctant to let her go. "Perhaps a cup of tea? Although personally, I think coffee would be just as effective."

Her brief smile dimpled her right cheek. "So would I, but I really must be on my way."

He had the feeling that if he hadn't been holding her hand she would have slipped away like a minnow underwater. "But you fainted. You can't go out just like that. It might happen again."

She pulled at her hand, a faint desperation coming into her eyes. Her mouth compressed. "Could I have my hand back, please?"

"Only if you'll tell me your name and let me make sure you get home all right."

But she didn't warm to his offer and jerked back her hand. Stooping to cram her things into her purse, she stood and faced him. "I wouldn't do that. You've been too kind, already."

His eyes narrowed. "Then what happened?"

She swallowed, floundering for words. Tony felt it again, the tickling at his nape that told him everything wasn't as it appeared, as she wanted him to see it. Her smile flashed, forced past lips that trembled despite her best efforts.

"Would you believe a female weakness?"

"No, I wouldn't," he said bluntly. "That went out with Queen Victoria." He couldn't keep the frustration out of his voice. Sensing her distress and wanting to help, he reached into his back pocket for his wallet and withdrew a business card. "Look, I'm Tony Theopoulos. Take this. In case you change your mind."

Her eyes, transparent as spring rain, held his. The flippancy had faded, leaving her face open and defenseless.

"I'm sorry." She looked about to cry. "I'm sorry to have involved you." Without a backward glance she turned and walked across the lobby toward the door.

For a moment Tony stared after her. Then he shrugged. That was that—an intriguing woman, but not for him.

He turned back toward the elevators, stopping abruptly as his gaze fixed on a white object on the carpet. The letter lay under a shelf of paperbacks. Bending, he picked it up, with renewed excitement.

"Wait!" He spun around. Too late. The revolving door swung gently. She was gone.

He brought his attention back to the envelope in his hand. It had been neatly slit, the utility bill inside paid well in advance of the due date.

Samantha Clark.

Her name? More than likely.

Back in his office he sat down behind his desk, his work momentarily forgotten. Samantha Clark. Who was she? And what had caused her to faint and the fear to flicker through her eyes?

He hadn't imagined it. She was afraid. Of what or whom, he couldn't begin to guess.

SAMANTHA HUDDLED in the corner of her seat as the bus rumbled through the narrow streets. Rush hour hadn't begun and she was almost alone on the upper deck. The pronounced sway made her stomach feel queasy, but the near privacy would help her regain her equilibrium.

A shudder ran through her body. It had been Dubray, a prominent government official, in the lift. She was sure of it. Yet she couldn't believe it. If by any remote chance he hadn't been dead, as she'd assumed in her panic six months ago, he should have been in prison.

The last time she'd seen him he'd been lying motionless on the white marble floor of her father's entrance hallway. She hadn't fainted then, only stared in horror as the other men around him had casually taken a tablecloth from the dining room cabinet and wrapped him up in it. Two of them had carried him out to a car, while the third, her erstwhile fiancé, Bennett Price, had mopped up the blood stains on the floor.

They hadn't known she was there.

Or had they? The question still haunted her.

She had gone to the house to sort through some of her father's personal things the day after his funeral. Although they had never been emotionally close, she was the only one who could handle certain details. A number of people knew she'd planned to go to the house that afternoon—James Michaels, several of her friends, her Aunt Olivia, whom she'd met on the doorstep on arrival. After a brief warm greeting Olivia had departed the grounds in her chauffeured car.

Bennett hadn't known she was there at the time of the incident. He had glanced up the stairs once before heading back to the kitchen, but she was sure she'd been out of sight. However, if he investigated, he would discover she had been there at the crucial time.

Now Bennett seemed dangerous. She had been ready to call off their imminent wedding a number of times in the weeks before the incident. But Bennett had been difficult and elusive, giving her no opportunity for privacy. Then her father's sudden death had clouded the issue further. In her grief she realized she needed time and space to rethink her future.

A future in which she no longer saw Bennett Price.

She had fled Montreal, canceling the wedding outright, and leaving word for Bennett: she was going away for a while to recuperate from her father's death. She had told James Michaels, the acting head of Smith Industries, the same thing, apologizing effusively. Not that it had affected the business, since she was no more than a rubber-stamping board member.

She could see the gossip—not that she cared. "Poor Samantha. She's done it again. Picked the wrong man."

The story of her life, but one she didn't intend to repeat.

Stupid to have fainted. She'd never fainted before, never even come close, not even when the sordid truth about Bennett had struck in such a brutal fashion.

As the bus continued its journey through the streets, she forced herself to close her eyes and relax.

Anthony Theopoulos. His image swam into her consciousness. His dark brown eyes, warm and compassionate, were full of questions he was dying to ask. He was a Canadian, his accent unique among the clipped tones of the British.

She'd almost given herself away. She couldn't be positive, but she feared she'd spoken at first in her normal voice, not the finishing-school British accent she'd carefully cultivated in the past six months.

She'd thought she was safe living under a false name, out of reach of Bennett or any of his reprehensible friends. Obviously an illusion, if Dubray was in London, and in apparent good health.

Bennett wasn't an accomplice to murder if Dubray had survived. She still didn't find much comfort in that. If Bennett kept close communications with men like Claude Germain, murder would be the least of his crimes.

One thing was certain—she wouldn't be buying a newspaper in the Regal Arms again. Not that Dubray knew her, but if he was in London, Bennett and his associates couldn't be far away.

The bus lurched to a stop. Samantha started. She'd passed her transfer point. She was going to be late reaching Professor Eldridge's house.

Making a sudden decision, she jumped up and scampered down the stairs, reaching the doors just as the conductor signaled the driver to proceed. The street teemed with people, shoppers with their bright bags, a number of tourists lifting their faces disbelievingly to bask in the sun after days of rain. A pair of punks in unrelieved black except for their fluorescent green hair gelled into lethal spikes sauntered past her. She smiled involuntarily. London in the past twenty years had shed its image of a dull, conservative city filled with correct and formal residents.

She liked the city; she liked her work, the people she met. Only late at night, during a rare spell of sleeplessness, did she allow herself to regret the job offer she'd given up to flee Montreal. She'd have been chief translator in the French ambassador's office, a prestigious position.

Slipping into a phone booth, Samantha slammed the door shut. The cacophony of traffic was dampened. She dialed a number, listening for the blips before inserting the coins she had ready.

"I'm terribly sorry, Professor, but something's come up," she said when her client answered. She knew Professor Eldridge as well as she knew anyone in London. He'd known she would be late today; he wouldn't mind if she took the rest of the day off.

"Eh?"

The professor was nearing ninety, and his hearing hadn't kept pace with his keen interest in life.

"You're not coming, dear?"

"I can't, after all." Sam had to shout into the phone as a city sanitation truck stopped next to the booth, its engine throbbing like a tank before battle. "What about tomorrow?"

"At ten?"

"Yes, that will be fine." Sam hung up the phone.

Dusk had fallen by the time she returned to her little flat near the Regal Arms. Mist shrouded the glow from streetlamps, a sure sign of autumn's approach. She was looking forward to it because, despite her extensive travels, she'd never been in this city during fall.

Idly she switched on the television news, debating whether to cook or to fetch some fish-and-chips from the corner shop.

A faint scraping sound drew her to the door at the back of her tiny kitchen. She opened it, smiling as Bagheera, her cat, wound his sinuous body around her legs.

"Hi, cat." She wrinkled her nose. "Been in the garbage cans again, haven't you?"

Damn. She'd done it again. Slipped. In England garbage cans were dustbins. What she'd thought had become second nature had regressed after one incident involving a familiar accent. Tony Theopoulos's.

Fish-and-chips it was, she decided. Her eyes rested on Bagheera as he plopped onto the middle of the floor and assiduously began to groom his sleek black fur. She would toss him some fish for a treat later. She realized suddenly how attached she'd become to the lean mysterious cat who'd shown up on her fire escape just three short months ago.

The doorbell buzzed its two-note summons, making her jump. For an instant the fright she'd had today and the hunted feeling she'd carried around for six months sparked to life. Her mouth went dry. No, it would be too much of a coincidence for Bennett to have tracked her down the very day she'd seen Dubray. No, they couldn't have found her.

Bagheera didn't seem too alarmed. After a glance at the door, he'd gone back to licking his paw and wiping it complacently over his pointed face.

The doorbell chimed again. Sam laughed in relief. It was the door to her flat, not the outside one. Probably just her elderly neighbor.

She threw open the door, bracing herself for the usual complaints about the price of bread and the austerity measures instituted by the present government. Her mouth fell open in a silent gasp. The man who stood in the hall with a bunch of daisies was the last person in the world she expected to see.

Chapter Two

"They really should have better security in these buildings," Tony Theopoulos said with a cocky grin. "An old lady just let me in. All I had to do was smile at her."

Samantha could only gape at him. His dazzling smile numbed her vocal cords. Pressing her lips shut, she swallowed, wishing she'd left the door closed, wishing she'd never gone into the Regal Arms, wishing she could miraculously rematerialize on another planet.

Groping for words, she tried to push the door shut. Much as she'd appreciated his concern this afternoon, she didn't want him here.

Claude Germain killed people as easily as anyone else swatted a bothersome fly. He made his living from the misery of runaways and other unfortunates, preying on their poverty to carry out his crimes. And she had every reason to believe that Bennett, whether or not he was directly involved, knew Germain and prospered from him.

She couldn't drag Tony into this mess.

As she fixed her gaze on his face, her dismay blossomed. He would not be easily discouraged. His chin thrust out, he'd wedged his foot into the doorway.

Bagheera abandoned his bathing and strolled over to inspect Tony's pant leg. Then, traitor that he was, he began to purr, winding himself in a figure eight between Tony's sneaker-clad feet.

Tony leaned down and ruffled the animal's ears. "Your cat likes me. Must mean something." He looked up at Samantha, his eyes glinting. "I don't want to intrude, but I do have something of yours you might want back."

"What's that?" she asked in a whisper.

"This."

He pulled out an envelope from his jacket, which she immediately recognized. With a sinking feeling, she opened the door wider and allowed him to step past her. She closed it, leaning back against the oak panels.

"So that's how you found me," she said, her voice low and hoarse. She cleared her throat, thinking. Her best defense lay in acting as normal as possible. No more fainting, no more palpitations. If she wished to maintain her cover, she'd better pull herself together and start behaving like an impoverished aristocrat. Her mask up, she asked, "How did you know it was mine?"

"Lucky guess, I'd say. And Parker's nitpicking habits. He never leaves papers lying about." He gestured with the flowers. "Have you got a vase for these? They're already starting to wilt. I've walked around the neighborhood three times waiting for you to get home. They're tired."

She didn't smile, but turned to go to the cupboard in the kitchen. There she fetched a vase and handed it to him. As if he'd been there many times, he filled it at the sink and stuck the daisies haphazardly into the water. He set it on the small round table, stepping back and smiling at his artistry. "Just what the place needs, a touch of color."

She suppressed a smile as she turned to face him. "Mr. Theopoulos, I think you'd better go." This time her voice was steady, tinged with indignation.

"I'm 'Tony.'" The brown eyes didn't waver as they studied her. "Why should I leave? We've only just met."

"You've no right to come barging into my life." Inwardly she was weakening. The temptation to let him stay tugged at her. If only things were different. If only she didn't have to hide.

"Perhaps not." He walked over to one of the over-stuffed chairs that had furnished the apartment when she'd bought it and sat down with easy, loose-limbed grace. "But then again, maybe I have. After you left, I thought of a lot of things that didn't add up about you."

"Add up?" she said, injecting scorn into her voice, while her heart beat so rapidly it threatened to choke her. "What do you mean, add up?"

He linked his fingers behind his head and sat back. For the first time she noticed that he'd switched clothes. He now wore a sweatshirt with an indistinguishable logo stretched across it and worn jeans that molded themselves to his long legs. The successful hotel executive? If she'd met him like this she would have mistaken him for a student despite the lines of maturity in his face.

Bagheera crouched in front of the chair, his green eyes avidly fixed on the stranger. Tony stared back at him, grinning at the cat's ragged scar that replaced the tip of one ear. When the cat tilted his head, the whimsical, lopsided look didn't go with the dignity of his demeanor.

Tony extended one hand. "Come on, cat."

Bagheera jumped up into Tony's lap and, after a moment, settled himself there. He purred in ecstasy as Tony sank his fingers into the sleek fur and began to massage the underlying muscle.

"Bagheera, don't be a nuisance," Sam said sharply.

Bagheera raised his head and regarded her with a brief, no-nonsense look before settling back down.

"He's not," Tony said. "I like cats. I like their independence, the way they know their own minds."

Regret tinged her anxiety. Tony was an attractive man, his manner and actions showing sensitivity and character. A good man to have on her side. Then again, her instincts had never been a reliable barometer where men were concerned. She couldn't rely on them.

Tony's cool, speculative glance rested on her face. "You don't add up," he said, picking up the dropped thread of conversation. "Drab clothes, but bright nail enamel where nobody will see it. Your shoes are Guccis, but they've seen better days." He paused, giving her a chance to comment. When she didn't, he added, "But it was the least obvious that raised the most questions."

She lifted her brows. "What was that?"

"The way you talk. The first words you said were in a different accent from the one you used afterward. And even then you don't sound exactly like anyone

I've heard here. Don't kid yourself, I've heard almost every accent in the British Isles by now, and I've got a good ear. Yours doesn't quite fit.''

"I've spent a lot of time abroad." She knew the game was up, but made a desperate bluff.

"Where abroad? Canada, perhaps?" She shook her head, but he went on relentlessly. "Eastern Canada, to be exact. The English-speaking part of Montreal. You can't fool me. I grew up there, too."

It was worse than she'd feared. They might even have crossed paths once. Realizing that her knees were about to collapse, Samantha sank down on the sofa.

She picked up the mug of coffee she'd made earlier, grimacing at the cold bitterness of the brew. Setting it down, almost spilling it as her fingers caught in the handle, she stalled. "Do you think anyone else noticed?"

"I doubt it. Parker was too busy wringing his hands, and the others had wandered away." Tony stroked the cat, his hands as relaxed as Sam's were tense. "So what's the story, Samantha? Are you an escaped fugitive or what?"

She eyed him warily, her eyes round and dark behind the owlish glasses. She would have to come up with a good story, one that sounded plausible. The questions he put to her were blunt, uncompromising, but implied a readiness to accept whatever explanation she was willing to give. But it had to approximate the truth. He would see through a lie immediately.

Yet the truth would endanger them both.

She gazed at him, the dark hair tumbling over his brow, the expectant look on his handsome face. She had to say something. "No, I'm not a fugitive, at least not the usual. I came here of my own free will." Her voice was cool, remote, her eyes carefully shuttered behind lowered lashes. "My father died. I needed time to myself."

"I'm sorry," he said with ready sympathy. "Were you close?"

"No, not really." As always when she thought of her father, vague uneasiness stirred in her. She should have cried when he died, but she hadn't. That lack heightened her guilt.

"Was that what you meant by the remark you made?"

"What?" Lost in her thoughts, she only half heard the question.

"Something made you faint," Tony said patiently. "You looked as if you'd seen a ghost, and muttered something about a dead man."

Dubray. Her breath hitched in her throat with an audible click. No, she couldn't tell him. The less he knew, the safer he'd be.

She gave a soft laugh to inject humor into the moment. "You might say that. I saw someone I thought I knew. I'd heard he'd died. His name's Dubray. It was a shock." She recited this without once meeting his eyes, her fingers plucking at a loose thread in the cushion next to her. "However, since I've thought about it, I realize I only glimpsed him. So I might have been mistaken."

"He was in the hotel?" Tony asked.

"Yes, going up in the lift." Her mouth was so dry she could barely continue the half lie. "But it closed before I had a good look."

"Do you know the man's name? I could look him up in the register. Of course, he'll only be there if he's a guest."

"I don't know if it's the same man." An outright lie she hoped didn't show on her face.

"Let's try another tack. How would you know if this Dubray was dead?"

She looked at Tony, her jaw clenching as she fought panic. She had truly painted herself into a corner. "I can't—I don't know." Her gaze dropped. "I was probably mistaken."

Evasions. Tony knew she was lying. Her body language betrayed her discomfort. And yet the precise, pseudo-British accent hadn't slipped once, and would have fooled anyone but a man like him.

He tightened his hand in the cat's dense fur, causing the animal to flinch and bolt off his lap. Bagheera stalked to the kitchen, tail high, the picture of affronted dignity. Tony barely noticed.

Who was Samantha Clark? he asked himself. He was fascinated despite the dangers that seemed to lurk there, behind that attractive facade.

Where had she come from? She had neither confirmed nor denied his guess at her origins.

She was afraid of something, something that had driven her from home. Despite her words, he was willing to bet that free will had little to do with her present circumstances. There was a dangerous secret in her past, involving a man she thought should've been dead.

A dead man who wasn't dead.

If he had any sense, Tony thought, he would get out of here before he was ensnared in a life-and-death situation. But something about her touched him, ever since he'd looked into those rain-clear gray eyes and seen the shadows lurking there. He'd tried to tell himself he'd imagined the fear, but he'd seen it glint there again.

"Samantha, if you're in trouble, you should tell someone. Why not me?"

She jerked her head up. "I don't know you, do I? How can I trust you?"

"Faith?" His brief smile was whimsical. "Or my honest face?" He stood up, stretching his arms above his head, his hand nearly touching the brass lamp fixture that hung from the plastered ceiling. "I guess the only thing to do is to take you out for dinner. Once you know me better I'm sure I can convince you to trust me."

She couldn't. It would be crazy to become involved with this man. But his warmth and whimsical charm drew her. She'd been alone for months; only through work and determination had she eluded loneliness. It always lingered there, threatening to engulf her.

"Trust me," Tony had said. But it was herself she couldn't trust.

Still, it was only dinner, and she realized she was hungry. He'd been kind to her; perhaps she owed him this courtesy.

"All right," she said, her worried frown fading. "But somewhere simple."

Grinning broadly, he pulled his sweatshirt. "Dressed like this? It'll have to be simple. How about the fish shop on the corner? Is it any good?"

"Sure, it's fine." She smiled tenuously, but inside she shrank like a young girl on an unexpected date with a boy she'd secretly fancied. "I've become one of their best customers."

Hearing a low meow, she went to the kitchen and stroked the cat's head, shivering a little as she recalled how Tony's lean fingers had caressed the same fur. Odd how, in spite of her consuming anxiety, she'd noticed such a thing. Quickly banishing the thought, she let Bagheera out for his nightly prowl of the neighborhood, locking the fire escape door securely after him.

OUTSIDE, THE MIST had thickened, and the evening was cool, especially after the unusual warmth of the day.

Tony pushed open the door of the fish shop, inhaling sharply at the steamy heat that clouded the windows. As they entered, the clamor of raised voices in several languages and the aroma of hot oil from the fryers swirled around them. Sam welcomed the noise and the activity, the tangy scent of vinegar and brown sauce.

Wiping her glasses on her sleeve, she grinned at the boy who manned the cash register, and ordered for both Tony and herself.

"In or out, miss?" he asked.

"In, please."

"Right." He yelled the order at his father, who sweated over the fryer at the far end of the high counter.

Sam groped in her purse for her wallet, but Tony placed his hand over hers. "I invited you. I pay," he said firmly.

The boy looked from one to the other, his black eyes bright with humor. Deftly ringing up the sale, he handed Tony his change, along with a receipt and number. "Ten minutes. The girl'll bring it to your table. If you can find one."

"I'm sorry," Samantha said over her shoulder as Tony pushed her ahead of him down the narrow aisle between the tables. "I should have asked what you wanted. But I'm in the habit of coming by myself."

Why that confession warmed him he couldn't have said. "It's all right."

A couple got up from a small booth, and Tony and Sam slid into it, grinning at each other like fellow conspirators as they saw the chagrin on the faces of two young men. They'd reached the table seconds too late.

As she and Tony dug in, Sam made a face. "I hate milk in tea. The waitress is new. The old one never put it in."

Tony looked at Sam quizzically. "I thought all Brits took milk in their tea."

"I'm—" She skidded to a stop. "We didn't in our family," she said firmly, making a gallant recovery.

"You mean you didn't sit on the terrace in the summer and pour tea from a silver pot into thin china cups?"

His tone was gentle, but she thought she heard an underlying sarcasm. Lifting her chin, she said grandly, "Of course we did, but we poured our own."

"It looks as if you've come down in the world." With a smile that didn't seem quite real he lifted his tea mug in a salute. "Welcome to the real world, Samantha Clark. Now how about telling me your real name and what exactly you're up to."

She knew he'd come back to this. Despite the humid heat of the room, a chill seeped into her. She crossed her arms over her chest defensively. "I can't. Believe me, I can't."

"Can't? Or won't?" He reached across the table and placed his hand over hers. "What is it, Samantha? What are you afraid of?"

His quiet concern tempted her. Only the fear kept her from spilling everything. "Nothing."

A muscle tightened next to his mouth. "Okay, we'll try a different approach. What were you doing in the Regal Arms this afternoon when you saw the 'dead man'?"

"I was buying a newspaper. Whenever I'm in the neighborhood, I buy a newspaper there."

"Why there, Samantha? There's a newsstand on the street corner."

She flushed. "Because I like the grandeur of the lobby. It reminds me—" But again she broke off, biting her lip as she refused to elaborate.

Tony nodded as if he understood. "So we have something in common. We're impressed by the lobby of the Regal Arms. What does it remind you of?"

Would it hurt, after all? "My grandmother's house. I used to spend a lot of time there when I was a child. The place was enchanting." Sadness crept into her low voice. "When she died, the house was sold."

"I'm sorry." Letting go of her hand, he lifted his cup, setting it down again when he realized it was empty. "Sam, let me help you."

"I don't need any help." She rose from her seat, abandoning her own mug of cold tea. "Shall we go? I have work tomorrow."

"Work?" he echoed as he followed her out the door into the cool misty night. "What do you do?"

She shivered as the dampness seeped through her jacket. "Translations. I'm fluent in German and French and I can work my way around Italian and Spanish. Right now I'm doing a literature text for a retired professor. French to English. It's an easy one."

They entered her building, climbed the stairs to the third floor. At the door to her flat, Sam fumbled in her purse for her key. She put it in the lock, eyeing Tony uncertainly.

"Uh, I'm really tired—"

"Miss Clark. Oh, Miss Clark."

The singsong voice interrupted them. Sam turned toward her neighbor. Miss Hunnicott was hurrying down the hall, her sensible shoes clumping on the worn Oriental runner. In her hand she held a large manila envelope.

"Miss Clark—" For the first time she seemed to notice Tony and stopped in midsentence. She surveyed him, disapproval flaring her thin nostrils. Until he smiled, and the censure turned to a coyness. She fluttered her sparse eyelashes. "It's nice to see Miss Clark with a friend," she said with a simpering smile.

"Thank you," Tony said, giving her the benefit of his most sincere, heart-breaker's grin.

"Miss Clark, this came for you today while you were out." She handed Sam the envelope. "I hope you don't mind that I signed for it."

"Not at all," Samantha said. "I appreciate it. Thank you." She weighed the package in her hand. Thin. No return address. Probably junk mail. Not that she'd occupied the flat long enough to receive much of that.

But who sent junk mail registered, special delivery?

Miss Hunnicott still lingered. "I knew it must be important. That's why I kept an eye out for you, Miss Clark."

"Yes. Thank you," Sam said again, aware of Tony's curiosity.

"Perhaps we could have tea tomorrow," Miss Hunnicott said in a wheedling tone when she saw she had less than all of Sam's attention.

"Perhaps," Sam said vaguely. "I'll see if I come in early enough in the afternoon."

Miss Hunnicott laid a soft, pudgy hand on Samantha's sleeve. "Please do, my dear. I'm always glad to have you."

"I'll try. Good night, Miss Hunnicott."

"Good night, dear." She started down the hall, then turned. "I wonder who will move into the empty flat on the second floor. I hope it's somebody interesting."

Sam paused. "Empty flat?"

"Didn't you see the sign outside?"

"Oh. Oh, yes." It must have gone up only that day; she hadn't paid any attention. "Good night, Miss Hunnicott," she said again.

The woman flashed Tony a grin and waited.

Samantha entered her flat quickly, without attempting to stop Tony who followed right behind her. She would sort him out later, after she escaped the velvet clutches of Miss Hunnicott.

Samantha moved to the kitchen to find a letter opener, and slit the envelope. She looked at Tony standing in the doorway, his hand braced on the frame. "I really am tired, Tony."

He gestured at the envelope. "I'll go in a minute. But look at your mail. It must be important."

His behavior was worse than her neighbor's, Samantha thought. She upended the envelope to remove the contents, noting the central London postmark. Out dropped a second, smaller envelope and a folded note. Picking up the note, she read the brief message.

"It's from my solicitor's office," she muttered. "Strange he didn't mention it when we lunched today. He could have just handed it to me instead of mailing it."

The note merely said that the enclosed envelope had come for her with a request that it be forwarded to the present address of Samantha Smith.

"Smith?" Tony said in an odd voice.

Damn. Samantha crushed the note in her fist, realizing too late that he'd read it over her shoulder.

"I thought your name was Clark."

"It's a mistake," she said hurriedly. "They've sent it to the wrong person." She turned, the paper burning her hand. "I think you'd better go."

Tony looked mutinous, then shrugged. "If that's the way you feel about it."

Without waiting to see if he went out the door, Sam smoothed out the note. The typed message read: "Mr. Collins is out, so I'm taking the liberty of sending this on to you since it appears urgent."

Collins's part-time secretary had signed it.

With a sense of foreboding, Samantha picked up the second envelope. In the bright kitchen light, the post-office stamp stood out clearly.

Montreal. The return address was that of Smith Industries. No wonder Mrs. Graham had thought it important.

Samantha's face went cold and still. Something was wrong. Smith Industries would not be sending her mail through Mr. Collins, since she had given them Amelia's Nice address. It had to be someone else, using the company stationery.

With trembling fingers she tore open the flap and pulled out the single sheet of paper, staring at the bright travel brochure advertising the amenities of Nice and the French Riviera. Scrawled across the photo of the golden beach were two words: "You lied."

"No." The word whispered past her stiffened lips. She closed her eyes, denying the truth. They had found her.

"Samantha?"

Through the roaring in her ears, she heard Tony's voice. Was he still here?

"Samantha, you look so strange. Are you all right?"

She was definitely not. Dazed, she turned to him. "I thought you'd gone."

Again he detected the inconsistency, a flatness in her vowels.

"Not yet," he said. "Good thing, too." He sank down beside her. "Samantha, what's going on? What scared you?"

Slowly, as if she feared it might turn into a snake, she unclenched her fist from the envelope. Like a condemned woman resigned to her fate, she unfolded the brochure. More red letters, crudely printed with a felt marker, leaped out at her. "You can't hide forever." Beside the words was a crude drawing of a gallows with a stick figure hanging from it, the neck twisted obscenely.

"Oh, no." Her eyes wide with horror, she dropped the paper on the table.

Gingerly Tony picked it up, staring at the message. "Who sent this, Samantha? What is going on?"

Samantha covered her face with her hands, as if by shutting out the light she could deny the horrible truth. Her hands slid down to her lap, where she clasped them tightly. "They've found me. They know where I am."

Chapter Three

"They? Who're they?" Tony dropped the brochure on a stack of magazines. Feeling totally out of his depth, he took her hand in his, rubbing it between his palms. "And what do you mean, they've found you? Who is it you're hiding from?"

She hid her face against his sweatshirt, breathing in the cool scent of the outdoors and the underlying warmth that emanated from his skin. "I can't tell you, Tony. It's better if you don't know." She lifted her head. "I'll probably have to move."

"How long have you been hiding?" Tony asked, without much hope of a straight answer.

But she surprised him, and her reply had a ring of truth he recognized. "Almost six months."

"And no one knows where you are."

"Only Mr. Collins, my solicitor. And he would never betray me." She stood up suddenly, urgent words tumbling from her mouth. "Tony, you can't stay here. I may be in danger. And you might be, too."

He remained where he was, staring at her. "Really? What kind of danger?"

A muscle jumped in her jaw as she tightened her lips. "I can't tell you."

Tony stood up abruptly, his knee knocking the table. The mug Sam had forgotten from hours ago fell over, spilling the dregs of cold coffee. "Damn. Where's a cloth?"

"In the bathroom. Under the sink."

Tony mopped up the coffee, which fortunately hadn't soaked through anything. Taking the cloth back to the bathroom to rinse it out, he paused on the way. "Sooner or later you'll have to tell me. I want to help you."

"I don't need any help."

"I think you do," Tony said calmly. "I'm not leaving until I get some answers."

"It's not your affair." But her protest was lost as the bathroom door slammed shut.

Samantha sank back into the sofa. What could she do now? Run again, somewhere else? She massaged the spot between her eyes where an ache began to throb. She had taken such pains to lay down a false trail, winding through Europe in a car rented under Amelia's name. She had been so careful, never making close friends, never letting anyone suspect she wasn't what she seemed, a black sheep of the aristocracy exiled in the anonymous city.

And Tony Theopoulos had been pushed by some diabolical fate into her life. How was she going to protect him as well as herself? He already knew, or had guessed, too much.

She glanced at the bathroom door. What was keeping him? All she could hear was water running, followed by splashing sounds in the sink.

Her eye fell on yesterday's newspaper, which had fallen off the table. She gathered up the scattered sheets, stopping short as she saw a photo displayed on the society page. It was Tony, a drink in his hand and a cool smile on his face. He stared back at her in a dark suit and white shirt that made him stand out from the crowd behind him. "The prominent hotelier Anthony Theopoulos was one of the distinguished guests at Lady Thompson's charity ball last evening" gushed the caption.

All the more reason to get him out of her life, Sam thought with a sinking feeling in her stomach. He moved in the kind of society she'd avoided since coming to London. She knew Lady Thompson. In fact, their families had known each other for years.

She couldn't see Tony again, risk being recognized by someone who could tip off Bennett. It might already be too late.

"Well?"

Samantha jumped. "You took long enough."

"Why? Were you timing me?" Picking up the newspaper, he frowned at the photo and dropped it without comment. He'd already read the story, which made him sound like a playboy, an image he refuted.

He settled down in the chair opposite and glared at her. "Who's looking for you, Samantha? What are you so afraid of?"

She opened her mouth, but Tony stopped her reply. "I know. You can't tell me." He shifted restlessly in the chair. "Isn't it time you told somebody?"

She gave the idea serious consideration. He could see the wheels turning in her brain. But in the end she shook her head. "No, it's better this way."

He let his foot fall to the floor with a thump and stood up. "Then I can't help you, either, can I? Good night, Samantha. It's been, uh, interesting." Then he closed the door softly behind him.

Samantha sat for a long moment as the sound of Tony's footsteps receded down the stairs.

He wouldn't be back.

It was better that way, she reasoned. Safer for him. And for herself, as well.

Forget Tony, she told herself firmly. He was too much like the men she'd always dated, successful and restless, always looking for the next woman, the next business deal. Her mistake with Bennett clung too freshly in her mind.

She couldn't get involved with Tony, no matter how concerned he seemed about her situation.

Her eyes fell on the brochure. Nice, playground of Europe. Someone had found out she was not in Nice and used her connections to Smith Industries to trace her. But why pick London? Smith Industries also had offices in Geneva and Milan.

Of course, they might have tried there. She had no way of knowing. Her spirits lifted slowly. The sender of the brochure with its threat would only know she had received it if she panicked.

It had to be a shot in the dark, impotent as long as she kept to her routine. She would just have to be careful, make sure she guarded her disguise scrupulously.

Her more immediate problem was Dubray. She was sure it had been Dubray in the lift. Or someone who looked enough like him to be his double.

There was one way to prove it. Pulling out the phone book, she looked up the number of the Regal Arms, dialing it swiftly. "Mr. Dubray's room, please."

"One moment, please. I'll look it up."

A short pause, then the pleasant voice was back.

"I'm sorry, madam, you did say Dubray?"

"Yes," Sam said impatiently. "Robert Dubray." Not that she had any idea what she would say if he came on the line. But confirming his presence in London might satisfy her need to prove she hadn't been hallucinating.

"We have no one registered by that name, madam. I'm sorry."

Sam bit her lip. Had she been mistaken then? "All right," she said into the phone. "Thank you."

She had seen him. She knew she had. But as she tidied up the flat and prepared for bed, doubts kept creeping in. Along with random thoughts of Tony, and his kind, dark eyes.

Samantha had never before noticed the patterns of light that crossed her bedroom ceiling when the nearby traffic light changed, but she learned them in minute detail throughout that sleepless night.

By MORNING, under vibrant sunshine, Samantha admitted she might have overreacted. It was premature to assume she had been found. Unless someone was already watching her, whoever had sent the note would have no way of knowing whether she'd received it. It would have been impossible to trace every piece of mail sent out from Mr. Collins's office.

Frowning, she poured herself a bowl of cold cereal, barely tasting it as she ate. For a moment she considered phoning her aunt. No, she couldn't. She trusted Aunt Olivia, but she knew her aunt was too fond of Bennett not to tell him about the call.

No, better to wait and see if anything else happened.

Putting her bowl into the sink, she went into the bedroom to dress for work. This time she wasn't going to be late.

She walked to the bus stop, pausing to buy a newspaper at a tobacconist's shop. The Regal Arms was going to be off-limits for some time, and Dubray was the least of the problem. She couldn't risk seeing Tony again.

She felt a momentary twinge of regret. He was an attractive man, with a quality of integrity that went deep. His gift of daisies still brightened her kitchen.

Professor Eldridge lived in Richmond. The underground would have been a more efficient means of transportation, but Sam hadn't lived in London so long that she didn't enjoy the vistas from the top of a double-decker bus. She willingly put up with the inconvenience of the ponderous vehicle's slow progress through the traffic.

The sun shone down on her head as she walked up the narrow street toward the professor's house. She wished she could pull out the bobby pins and let her hair wave loose in the free and easy way she'd once worn it. And at times she missed the distinctive clothes and makeup that had set her apart in any crowd. But safety lay in the unobtrusive guise that had become second nature.

The street, rough with cobblestones and worn asphalt, had seen better days. The drab rows of brick town houses were bleached of their former gentility.

Samantha pressed the buzzer next to the yellow-painted door, listening to the harsh peal of the bell inside. As she waited she idly surveyed the street. A long black Rover with black-tinted glass cruised by, then sped up, and turned with a squeal of tires into the next road.

She stared after it, wondering at the incongruity of such a luxurious car on this street. The thought fled as the professor's housekeeper opened the door.

"Oh, good morning, miss. Won't you come in?"

"Thank you." Samantha stepped into the dim hall, inhaling the homey scents of lemon polish and freshly brewed coffee.

"He's in the library, miss. Just go right through."

The library was a tiny room overlooking the patch of garden at the back of the house. It was crowded with books and mementos of a long and varied lifetime and there was hardly room for the desk that sat squarely in the center.

"Good morning, Miss Clark."

Professor Eldridge lifted his head and regarded her with eyes only slightly dimmed by age. He pushed his old-fashioned glasses up his nose and ran his fingers through the lock of hair that persisted in flopping over his forehead. The crown of his head was bald, gleaming in the light from the study lamp on the desk.

He stood up, extending his hand, a slight man of about Samantha's height. "I'm so glad you could make it this morning. At my age, one can't afford too many postponements."

"I had a bit of difficulty yesterday," Samantha explained.

The professor lifted one shaggy brow. "Oh? Not too serious, I hope."

"No, it's all right. But I may have to leave town."

Eldridge's affable face creased into lines of concern. "Not before you finish this work, I trust."

For a moment panic welled up in her. No attachments, she'd promised herself. Yet here she was again, trapped. She was proof that no one lived on an island. "No, we'll finish the book." She sat down and began to sort through her papers and dictionaries. "Shall we get to work?"

THE FRONT OF THE BUS, where she liked to sit, was occupied when she headed back to the city that afternoon. She moved toward the back, oblivious to the press of people around her.

She'd taken a moment this morning to call Mr. Collins. As she had suspected, he knew nothing of the envelope, citing the efficiency of his secretary. Samantha had been slightly relieved to learn no one had contacted him requesting her address, and he assured her that neither he nor Mrs. Graham would give it out.

She shifted the bag of groceries she'd stopped to purchase at a supermarket near Professor Eldridge's house, her mind straying to Tony Theopoulos.

Would she ever hear from him again? Not likely. She couldn't suppress the faint regret that rose up in her.

The bus lurched to a stop. She glanced out the window at the sea of cars hemming them in. They were on a winding street, clogged with traffic. Rush hour. She smiled ironically. Rush hour was when nobody was able to rush.

The traffic began to move again, sluggishly, and a horn honked on the street. The bus driver answered it with a hoot of his own. Sam looked down to see a large black car inch past the bus and force itself ahead. A niggling worry rose in her, but she set it aside.

Feeling frazzled and out of sorts, she finally reached her flat, hoping that Miss Hunnicott would not make an appearance. No such luck.

"Good evening, Miss Clark. Your telephone has been ringing all day. Most annoying. I couldn't even take my nap."

"I'm sorry," Samantha apologized, although what she could have done, she didn't know. But again alarm rent her. Who would be phoning her during working hours, when it was obvious she was out?

"It hasn't rung for the past hour," Miss Hunnicott continued.

"They must have given up. But I'm home now. If they try again, I'll pick up." She set down the bag of groceries and took out her key. "I'd better put my things inside."

"Your letter yesterday—" The faded blue eyes sparked with curiosity. "It was important?"

Sam nodded. "Yes. Thank you again. Goodbye, Miss Hunnicott." She hurried inside and closed the door. The woman's probing manner was typical.

The phone rang twice during the evening. The first time a man tried to sell her insurance. Annoyed, Sam hung up. Her number was in the phone book, making it available to anyone, but it was listed only as S. Clark, one of ten other S. Clarks.

The second time, Samantha was brushing her teeth. Her mouth was filled with foam as she picked up the receiver. But a humming silence was followed almost immediately by the dial tone.

Wrong number. Perhaps her persistent phone caller only called during the day. She wouldn't know, because she planned to work with the professor the next day, even though it was a Saturday.

She'd sensed the professor's urgency about completing the project, and had agreed to work then, a day she normally kept free.

LATE SATURDAY AFTERNOON, when Samantha arrived home, a policeman stood outside her door, deep in conversation with Miss Hunnicott.

"Miss Clark?" The old woman's high-pitched voice carried down the short hall. "Oh, she's an excellent neighbor, not like so many young people nowadays, with their loud music, purple hair and strange manners."

"Good evening, Miss Hunnicott," Samantha said rather more loudly than necessary.

"Oh, Miss Clark, this officer was just asking about you."

The policeman consulted a small notepad. "Are you Miss Samantha Clark?"

"Yes, I am," Samantha said in a clipped tone that hid her inward shaking. This was the very thing every fugitive feared, the attention of the police. "Is there a problem?"

"I hope not." He glanced at Miss Hunnicott. "Thank you for your help, madam."

"Not at all," she said, looking disappointed when the officer turned back to Samantha.

"Could we talk inside, Miss Clark? Shouldn't take but a moment."

He remained standing just inside the door, looking around the flat with a cool air that didn't fool Sam for a moment. She was sure he saw everything, took in every nuance of worn furniture and plain curtains. And the lack of anything uniquely personal on public display.

"You've lived here how long?" he asked, even though he must have extracted this piece of information from Miss Hunnicott.

"About five months."

"And you own the flat?"

"Yes."

"Flats like this don't come cheap." He was definitely probing.

"I have a trust fund from my grandmother." Did he know that she was Canadian? He hadn't asked to see any ID, which would show her real name. She couldn't help but wonder why. Perhaps she wasn't under suspicion as she feared.

"And you work as a free-lance translator?" he continued.

"Yes." She hesitated, then plunged ahead. "What is this about, Officer?"

Instead of answering, he fixed his eyes on the bright plastic bag she had hung on a hook on the kitchen wall. "You shop in the Lily Maid Market in Richmond? It's a long way from here."

"I'm translating a book there," Samantha said almost too crisply. She straightened and squared her shoulders. "It's convenient for me to shop before I come home."

"Did you today?"

She shook her head. "No, I worked longer than usual and came straight home."

"So you didn't pass the market at three o'clock, or see anything unusual?"

"No. At three o'clock I was still at Professor Eldridge's."

"And you left when?"

"About half past four."

The officer cleared his throat, scribbling in the notebook. "Professor Eldridge has a housekeeper, a Mrs. Howard?"

"Yes."

"Did you see her before you left the house?"

What was he getting at? "No, she'd gone to do some shopping for supper." Lifting her eyes to meet the policeman's, she felt her stomach suddenly flutter. "She might have been at the Lily Maid Market around three. She went out shortly before."

"We know. She was there."

"Then you knew I wasn't," Samantha said with a flash of temper. "Officer, would you mind telling me what you're after?"

He looked at her with maddening calm.

"After? Nothing, Miss Clark. If you have nothing to hide." He paused fractionally, then asked in the same even tone, "Do you have any enemies, Miss Clark?"

Her palms were wet and she surreptitiously wiped them on her skirt. Fighting down her panic, she managed to keep her voice steady. "Enemies? Why would I have enemies? I've nothing to hide."

"I'm sure you haven't, Miss Clark," he said, unperturbed.

She was completely unprepared for his next question.

"Could I see some identification, please? Just for our records."

Identification. What could she show him that wouldn't give her away? Sweat trickled coldly down her sides, dampening the shirt she wore under a pullover. Thinking quickly, she rummaged in her purse.

and came up with one of her business cards, showing her new name.

The officer pursed his lips as he studied the card. Samantha waited, her heart pounding. If he asked to see her passport, the gig was up. He'd spew all kinds of questions, such as had she changed her name? Not that name changing was illegal, but they'd wonder if it had been done with intention to commit fraud. Her situation could get sticky.

"May I keep this?"

She let out her breath. "Yes, of course. Could you tell me what this is all about?" The officer might be unaware of the trauma he had put her through, but she felt she had a right to know why she'd been quizzed the past fifteen minutes.

He snapped his notepad shut and tucked it with his pen into his pocket. "I was hoping you could, Miss Clark. But since you weren't at the market today—I'd be careful if I were you. There was an apparent kidnapping attempt at the Lily Maid about three-fifteen today. The manager called the police after witnesses said a woman was forced into a car. Someone saw a gun. Of course, reports vary a great deal in these cases. Eyewitnesses often make mistakes."

"Was anyone hurt?"

"No, that's what was odd about the incident. The victim was released less than a block away. It appears to have been simple robbery, after all. Only a purse was taken."

"I don't understand what this has to do with me."

"We questioned people who were in the store at the time, among them your professor's housekeeper, Mrs. Howard. In fact, she agreed to come down to the police station with us."

That's why she hadn't returned by the time I left, Samantha thought. "But she must have told you where I was."

"Yes, afterward. When the victim was brought to the station. You see, Miss Clark, Mrs. Howard caught a glimpse of the woman as she was being pushed into the car and thought it was you."

Sam's mouth dropped open. "Me? But she knew I was still at the house."

The policeman nodded. "That's what she said. She thought you might have left early. She caught only a glimpse of the car before it drove off. It was a black Rover."

"A Rover? I saw a black Rover a couple of times in the neighborhood the past few days. I wonder if it was the same one."

"You didn't get the license number?"

Sam shook her head. "No, I didn't. What happened with the woman?"

"She was set free and called the police. We brought her in to the station. Mrs. Howard saw at once that she was mistaken. But the woman did have blond hair the color of yours, and a similar build."

"You haven't recovered her purse?"

"Not so far. Probably in a dustbin somewhere by now." He touched the brim of his helmet. "Goodbye, Miss Clark. Thank you for your help."

What help? Samantha thought as she closed the door and walked back into the living room. She hadn't been any help at all, and she could have been if she'd only been more observant. The black Rover sounded too similar to the one she'd noticed on Friday for comfort. Was the car tailing her, after all? Was she the intended victim? Someone with her build and color—

ing had been mistaken for her. Had they snatched the wrong purse?

And if they were only interested in the purse, that meant they wanted IDs. Proof that Samantha Smith was Samantha Clark.

Someone was on to her. And that someone had to be Bennett. A shiver went down her spine. She had to be prepared, prepared for the worst.

Chapter Four

Tony gave Samantha a couple of days, but she was never far from his mind, that pale beautiful face with those haunted eyes like silver rain.

She intrigued him. The intangibles had hooked him, the change in accent, her evasiveness when he'd confronted her with it. He also sensed she was in trouble and his protective instincts shifted into high gear.

But even more so, a niggling worry tugged at the back of his mind. She might be linked to the conspiracy theories floating around London and Montreal the past six months.

If she came from Montreal and did translations, chances were she had a better-than-average knowledge of international trade. Had her presence in the Regal Arms been a coincidence? Or part of a plan? The upcoming trade conference between France and Canada had been postponed once due to security leaks. That was why London had been chosen for the meetings, rather than the more volatile Montreal.

Tony couldn't afford to overlook any possible threat to the conference's smooth execution. Not even the seemingly innocent Samantha Clark. While the dates had been obscured by tight security for weeks, speculations were beginning to appear in the press. The event would soon be announced in public, and then the dangers of its disruption would increase.

Samantha was hiding something. He knew it as surely as he knew she'd been dismayed to find him at her door the other night. And he couldn't ignore the dichotomy between her appearance and her demeanor. A self-effacing image might enhance her ability to find free-lance work, but it might also hide a more sinister purpose.

She was far better off than her simple clothing indicated. The flat was the first indication. It was an expensive piece of real estate, and even if she was subletting, the rent would have been beyond the reach of a free-lance translator.

In the bathroom he had found the most conclusive evidence. The cosmetics were of the highest quality, the most expensive brands. Crystal flagons contained French perfume. A large box of dusting powder might have been spun gold if one considered what it cost.

And the underwear drying on a little rack over the bathtub was made of pure silk and lace. Only her outer garments were plain and utilitarian. He would have given anything for a look in her closet, but since he'd already spent a few minutes in the bathroom, it would have been pushing his luck to snoop further.

The morning after he'd left her apartment, he'd awoken with a start from the fitful sleep he'd fallen into after spending nearly the whole night puzzling over the problem.

His photo in the newspaper. Had she hatched the idea of meeting him that morning when she'd seen the paper? The story had indicated he was from Montreal. What better cover than to strike up an acquaintance with him—expatriate Canadians meeting in London.

Yet that didn't add up, either. Her faint had been real. He would have sworn to it. And she hadn't encouraged him. On the contrary, she'd done everything she could to keep him at arm's length.

He couldn't figure her out. Even if she knew nothing about the trade conference, she was still a mystery.

He mulled it over all day Friday and most of Saturday, as he completed mountains of paperwork in preparation for the conference. He called room service for a sandwich at ten, laughing ruefully as he realized how odd his friends would have found it to see him in the office on a Saturday evening. He'd declined an invitation to a party at a duchess's mansion, and several offers of a more personal nature from women he knew. He'd been glad to use the excuse of work.

Samantha's image floated into his consciousness as he took a break. She wouldn't leave him alone. He frowned heavily. There was only one way to get rid of her once and for all.

He had to see her again, satisfy his curiosity, and then she would stop haunting him.

Making up his mind, he turned back to his desk and dialed the number he'd subconsciously memorized.

His heart jumped when he heard her low voice. "Samantha, this is Tony. How would you like to go for a drive with me tomorrow?"

DAMN, it *would* rain, Samantha thought as she got up on Sunday morning. The sun had held up the entire week, only to disappear at the weekend.

She let Bagheera in, gave him his food. While he ate, she showered and dressed in jeans and a sweater, her movements distracted. Had she made a mistake in accepting Tony's invitation, after all her fine earlier resolutions regarding him? But when he'd called last night, the warmth and charm in his voice had moved her to accept. A drive seemed innocuous enough, and a welcome break.

Her biggest danger of exposure lay in his curiosity. If she could disarm him with simple friendship, she'd be safe.

She had called Amelia in Nice late the night before, but the artist had assured her no one had contacted her about Samantha. In fact, Amelia had been working to complete a series for an exhibit. She hadn't seen anyone in two weeks except for a lost tourist who'd stopped by her isolated villa to ask for directions.

The incident at the supermarket frightened Samantha. In itself it might have been nothing but a weird coincidence. But when combined with the threat she'd received, it took on a sinister air. It'd be wise not to ignore it. On the other hand, hiding in her flat wouldn't keep her safe for long if someone was determined to find her.

Changing some of her habits might throw them off the track for a time. In the meantime, going out with Tony would take her mind off her problems, give her the illusion of normalcy.

She glanced at her watch—9:25. He said he'd be by at half past. Bagheera had settled himself in the living room chair to sleep off his nightly carousing. He opened one eye and blinked as she patted his head, then tucked his nose under his folded paws. Satisfied, she left him, knowing he'd be fine until she returned.

Half past nine. Taking up her purse and a jacket, she went out the door.

"GOOD MORNING."

Startled, Sam looked around as she descended the last flight of stairs. "Oh, good morning."

The man was about her own height and age, with curly brown hair and a friendly, engaging smile.

"I'm new here, haven't met many of the other residents." With a backward toss of his head, he indicated the floor above them. "My name's Jason Wheeler. I'm on the second floor. You are—?"

He was handsome in a boyish way. Harmless. She opened her mouth to answer. "I'm—excuse me, I'll be late. Goodbye."

Quickly she scurried down the rest of the stairs, stopping to catch her breath as she reached the street door. The man bothered her. He looked innocent enough, but when he'd asked her name, she had noticed his eyes. They were brown, but not warm like Tony's. There had been something hard, calculating, in them as he'd scrutinized her.

She shivered, remembering. But why should she trust Tony? Well, she would suspend judgment for the moment. She was only planning to spend a couple of hours with him, and as long as she reminded herself there was no room in her disjointed life for a man now, she wouldn't get trapped by falling for the wrong man again.

He stood outside, next to a white car. He was smiling, his eyes on the glass-paneled door through which she would come. She pushed it open. It was too late to back out now, even if she wanted to.

Tony felt his heart lurch as she stepped lightly down and headed toward him. Her movements were alluring, so quick and free, yet strangely at odds with the prim hairstyle and the spectacles that hid those beautiful silver eyes. "Hi. You're late." Inane. He hadn't been this awkward on his first date at fifteen.

"Only a minute or two."

Her laughter had a musical lilt that made the gray day light up.

"Cute car," she added, still a little off-balance from the encounter with her new neighbor. "But I thought all big shots drove a Rolls or a Daimler." As soon as the words were out, she could have cursed her errant tongue. Another slip.

Big shot? The phrase jangled in his brain. Did the British use "big shot"? He bent to open the passenger door, hiding his reaction as he made up his mind to listen closely, and question her again if he found an opportunity to do so without arousing her suspicions.

"I like this car," he said. "And it's mine. There's a Jag that comes with the job, but I only use it for what you might call state occasions."

Sam exhaled as he closed the door with a solid thunk. He hadn't noticed. She'd have to be more careful in the future. "Where are we going?" she asked as he threaded the Citroën BX onto one of the main arteries that carried commuters in and out of the city.

The single wiper swished monotonously, clearing the glass as the rain fell more heavily. "First to a small town in Surrey. I have to look at a hotel that's just come on the market. It might be suitable for our chain." He smiled at her, his face unclouded, honest, making Sam feel guilty at the duplicity of her behavior. "After that I'll be free, at your disposal."

"It's too bad about the rain," Sam murmured. "A picnic would have been nice."

"Just like Vancouver, where I lived for five years before coming here. Good weather all week and then rain on the weekend."

The hotel was a disappointment, a shabby little hole-in-the-wall with a bar that smelled of centuries of stale beer and sweaty bodies. The owners must have been desperate for a sale. The real estate agent practically twisted Tony's arm as they were leaving. "But the location, Mr. Theopoulos," he said. "You won't find another like it."

"I'm sorry," Tony replied.

The courteous regret in his tone made him rise another notch in Sam's estimation.

"It's not what I'm looking for," he explained.

He shook his head as they drove away, leaving the agent gazing after them from under a dripping black umbrella. "The owners are old. They want to retire to the coast, or to Spain if they make enough on the sale. But the place is too small and out of the way, even if the building's condition were better. I can't use it."

Rolling hills stretched around them, the expanse of green dotted with grazing sheep and the occasional stone cottage. The headlights Tony had turned on cut a glistening path on the wet asphalt road.

"Is he right about the location being a good one?" Sam asked.

Tony shrugged, slowing as they entered another village, a single street lined with thatched stone houses. "It's picturesque, but probably a little too far off the beaten track. It looks as if the owner didn't have much money for improvements the past few years." He downshifted as he pulled into the narrow parking lot of a pub. "This should do for lunch. Are you hungry?"

She'd skipped breakfast that morning, her stomach too tied in nervous knots as she debated the wisdom of seeing Tony. Now it rumbled, prodding her on. She laughed. "I might as well admit it. I'm starved."

Tony frowned at the blue Mini parked just beyond the corner of the pub. "I'm sure I saw that car in Swivington, by the hotel."

An uneasy fluttering began in Samantha's chest. "The estate agent's, perhaps?"

"No, I don't think so. It was gone when we came out. Well, no matter. It's probably somebody like us who didn't fancy the looks of the bar. They wisely decided to go to the next place up the road for lunch."

Still, Samantha entered the door in a prickly state. The few patrons inside were strangers, none of them resembling anyone she'd encountered in the past week, when her life had been turned upside down.

The interior of the pub was shadowy except for the warm cheer of a fire blazing in a cavernous fireplace. She supposed it could have roasted an ox, if the need arose. Old, stained-glass windows admitted a frail light through a veil of rain.

Tony placed their orders at the bar, then led Sam to a table in the corner near the fire.

She sat staring at the flames, wondering what to talk about. When a person hid significant events in her past, it was difficult to think of a subject unrelated to it.

Tony, too, was silent, his fingertips drumming lightly on the scarred wooden table. Samantha sighed, and he stirred. "Sam, what are you thinking?"

She shook her head. "Nothing." She threw him a quick smile. "I'm sorry I'm such poor company."

"It's the weather. It's easy to feel down on a day like this."

The barman brought their food, hot vegetable soup and thick cheese sandwiches made with homemade bread. They ate quickly, as if they both thought this outing was a mistake and wanted to end it as soon as possible.

A fresh gust of rain came in as the door opened, sending the flames in the fireplace crackling and snapping up the chimney. A burly truck driver, his felt cap angled over one ear, staggered in, burdened by a large carton that showed dark water stains at the corners. He set the box at the end of the bar, pulling an invoice from the inside pocket of a suede jacket that showed little of its original nap. The barman scrawled a signature, then reached under the bar and handed the trucker a white envelope, which he tucked into his pocket.

He touched the brim of his cap. "Thanks, mate."

With an unhurried rolling gait he walked out the door. A moment later a diesel engine roared.

The rain was falling with relentless persistence from a leaden sky when Tony and Sam returned to the car. The street lay deserted, its cobblestones shining darkly in the dull light.

The blue Mini was gone. "Guess he wasn't in the pub, after all," Tony remarked. "I didn't see anyone leave."

More coincidence? They'd seen the Mini twice in a space of hours. She'd seen a black Rover a number of times over the past week, although she still hadn't managed to get a license number. Was somebody shadowing her? Or was it really just one of those happenstances that occur every so often?

"Maybe they had business elsewhere," she said.

"Probably." He started the car. "Do you want the motorway, or shall we take the scenic route?"

"The scenic route, I think," she said, hoping to salvage the day.

The road, bordered by hedges on either side, was narrow and twisting. Tony drove with skill and confidence on what Samantha felt was the wrong side of the road. When he asked her if she'd like to try the car she barely restrained herself from reacting with horror.

"No, you drive. I'm enjoying the ride." Her lips were stiff and she wondered if he noticed.

"You have a license, don't you?" he asked.

"Of course I do." A Canadian one. "But since I don't have a car at the moment, I'm out of practice," she lied.

"Out of practice, or just not used to these roads?" he asked, more curtly than he'd intended. Frustration welled up in him. He'd learned nothing. All his questions and gentle probes had been met by silence or evasions.

She'd taken the risk. She would bluff again and hope to get away with it. But after today she would make sure she didn't see him again. Lifting her chin, she cast him an imperious look before returning her glance to the rain-streaked windshield. "I'll have you know I've been driving since I was sixteen—Tony, look out!''

From a narrow driveway, a truck, gray as the weather, lurched toward them. Tony wrenched the steering wheel to the right. The tires skidded on the rain-slicked pavement, sending the car toward a ditch on the opposite side of the road. At the last second Tony regained control, swerving the car inches from the truck's heavy steel bumper.

Samantha covered her face as metal scraped metal with a sickening sound. The car spun on the asphalt, once, twice, then shuddered to a stop in the shallow ravine at the side of the road.

All was still except for the patter of rain on the roof and the low throb of the engine. Incredibly she felt no pain, only a creeping numbness as the overdose of adrenaline drained away. Prying her hands off her face, one finger at a time, she opened her eyes, swiveling her gaze sideways to Tony.

He blinked once or twice, then shifted his legs as if they, too, had gone numb. As his foot slipped off the clutch, the engine died with a rough cough.

The car appeared intact, standing at a crazy angle to the road, its nose pointed skyward. Its rear wheels lay in the ravine; its front still clung to the road. The wiper completed a final sweep across the cascade of rain as the warning lights went on. The truck was gone, the landscape hazy and dismal as mist closed in around them.

Tony sat with his hands on the steering wheel. His face was white, his lips pressed into a grim line. ''Are you all right?'' he asked tightly, without looking at her.

She stretched her legs; feeling was returning to them, a fine trembling that made every muscle weak. Taking a deep breath, she laughed shakily. "Yes, I'm all right. Good thing we've got seat belts."

"Yeah." A single, abrupt syllable.

He restarted the car, putting it into gear, and gently fed it with gas. The front wheels spun helplessly on the slippery pavement.

With an angry twist he turned the key and jerked it out of the ignition. "It's not working. We'll have to get help."

Secondary reaction set in as Sam got out of the car. Her knees buckled and she grabbed the edge of the door to steady herself. For a moment the earth spun around her, but the cold rain soaking her hair and running down her neck jolted her to action.

"Here's an umbrella." Tony thrust it into her hands as he slammed the door and locked it.

Sam opened the umbrella, finding that two of the ribs were bent. She twisted at them and got them into acceptable shape.

Tony came around to her side, locking that door, as well. He spent a moment examining the ugly black dent in the rear fender. "Damn."

"It could have been worse," Sam said faintly. Actually, she was surprised the fender was still attached. Judging by the noise of the crash, she'd expected half the car to be bent in.

"Yeah. We could have been killed." Taking the umbrella from her hand, Tony held it high to protect them both.

Resentment blazed within her at his tone. "It's not my fault," she snapped. "I wasn't driving that bloody truck."

"I didn't say it was your fault. Damn umbrella." He glared at the tear in the fabric that allowed the rain to leak on their heads, then fixed his eyes on her. "You slipped again. You're supposed to say 'lorry.'"

"Truck, lorry. What does it matter?"

"What matters is that I'd like to know what the hell's going on." Tony bit off the words, not sure why he was angry but wanting to strike out at something. "Samantha, when are you going to tell me who's after you?"

Her heartbeat accelerated, and sweat broke out on her brow despite the chill that seeped into her bones from the rain. "What makes you think somebody's after me? I had nothing to do with the accident."

"No? Well, something's not right. That blue Mini was following us almost all the way from London. You're the one who won't talk about her past. It sure as hell wasn't following me."

She stopped in her tracks, then skipped to catch up as the rain pelted her. "So that's why you were interested in the Mini." She was proud of her steady voice even as her limbs began to tremble again.

"Yes. Now will you tell me the truth, Samantha?"

The truth? What was the truth? Threats and speculations? "I can't, Tony. Believe me. It could be dangerous."

"It's dangerous now." He stopped and faced her, tucking the handle of the umbrella under his arm as he grasped her shoulders. To her amazement, she realized his hands were shaking.

"Samantha," he said, his voice husky. "Somebody tried to kill you. That truck was headed straight for your side of the car."

Panic rose in her throat, but she shook her head, as if denial would alter her situation. "No. No."

"Yes, Sam. Yes." His eyes probed her pale face; his hands were gentle on her shoulders in a gesture that was not quite an embrace. "Samantha, when will you tell me everything? I want to help you."

Numbly she shook her head again. "Tony, please—"

His mouth tightened, but he knew he couldn't push her. "Never mind." He held her gaze a moment longer, then turned, keeping the umbrella over her head. "Later. We'll talk later."

Their breath plumed out in front of them as they walked on. They hadn't gotten far, when the sound of an engine sent them both spinning around, half expecting a new enemy to materialize out of the rain. The small rusty Toyota truck seemed innocuous enough, despite the loud crate of pigs in the back. Pulling past them, the farmer braked, waiting until they ran up.

"Need a lift? Saw your car back there. Roads can be treacherous in the rain."

"What we need is a tow," Tony said, pulling out a handkerchief and blowing his nose.

They climbed into the truck, crowding close together. Sam winced as the gears ground out, and the truck lurched forward. Tony's thigh next to hers, seemed to burn through their wet clothes. She almost expected to see steam rising.

Fortunately they reached the farmer's home, and watched as he retrieved his tractor. In no time they were back at the accident site.

When the tractor pulled the car free, they were on their way with a wave and a smile, all thoughts of scenic drives gone. Tony headed for the motorway.

He dropped Samantha off in front of her building, briefly touching her cold cheek with his hand before leaning over to open her door. "Samantha, we have to talk. I'll be back in half an hour, after I go home and change."

"Tony—" She faltered, knowing there was no escape. While she might have fought him had he demanded answers, she had no resistance to his honest concern.

Gently he ran his thumb over her bottom lip, his smile an odd mixture of solicitude and determination. "Don't look so worried, Sam. I only want to help."

She pushed herself out of the car, away from the seductive scent of his shaving lotion and the warmth in his eyes. "Tony, it's better—"

Her protest was lost in the roar of the engine as he drove off into the wet twilight.

Samantha entered the building, praying she wouldn't meet anyone. Her shoes squelched around her icy feet as she trudged up the stairs. Mud dripped from her jacket and her hair. She could only imagine what she looked like.

A hot shower restored her. Putting on a woolen sweater and soft sweatpants, she plugged in the kettle. If she kept her hands busy, she wouldn't have time to think. In the corner of the kitchen the washing machine moaned as it washed the mud out of her clothes.

The telephone rang and she ran to it, thinking Tony

had changed his mind and she'd been granted a reprieve.

Lifting the receiver, she never got a chance to speak before the voice paralyzed her vocal cords.

"Next time I won't fail."

Chapter Five

Next time I won't fail.

The strange, sexless voice rang in Sam's head as she crouched, shivering, in her chair. Bagheera was out prowling as usual and she was denied even the comfort of his presence.

When the door buzzer sounded, she leaped up as if she'd touched a live wire. Teeth chattering, she hugged her arms around her chest and pressed the intercom button. "Yes?"

"Sam? It's Tony."

Tony? She shook her head, still shell-shocked. Yes, Tony, of the gentle hands and warm smile.

To refuse him entry was a bigger decision than her mind could handle at the moment. She pushed the button, releasing the door.

She counted the minutes it would take him to climb the stairs. Even so, when the doorbell rang, she began shaking again. She opened the door, and as he entered, she glanced up and down the hall before slamming the door closed.

"Samantha." Tony grasped her by the shoulders and looked into her face, his own skin paling. "Samantha, what's wrong? Are you ill?"

All kinds of disasters percolated through his mind. She'd caught flu or pneumonia from their walk in the rain. She'd been mugged in the hallway. Her apartment had been burglarized. He discarded that instantly when he regarded the room's impersonal neatness.

He shook her a little as she stood in front of him, her body lax from some emotion he couldn't name. "Samantha, say something. What is it?"

Her mouth twitched as she fought the need to cry, to fling herself on his chest and hold him—hold him. Tears spilled over her cheeks, and she gulped, still fighting, but finally giving in.

She buried her face against his coat, her tears soaking the fabric already wet from rain. "Oh, Tony, I'm so scared. First the note, then the thing at the supermarket, now this."

He led her to the sofa, sat down with her, rocking her until the sobs eased. Awkwardly he patted her back. "It's all right, Samantha, I'm here. It's all right."

She burrowed closer and wrapped her arms tightly around him, inhaling the delicate fragrance of his hair.

Gently he kneaded the stiff muscles at the base of her skull, then he tilted her face up to his. "Samantha, I'm sorry I was short with you this afternoon. But I was upset. We'd almost been killed and I didn't even know why." He stopped short. "What thing at the supermarket? Has there been something else?"

She realized all at once that he didn't know. Yet how could he, when she hadn't told him. "Someone took a purse from a woman who looked like me. The police questioned me about it."

"Not as a suspect."

"No, of course not. As the possible victim. My boss's housekeeper saw the incident, mentioned me by name. The police traced me to here."

"Someone's trying to confirm your address," Tony said. "Why?"

She ignored the question. "That's what I thought."

"Who, Sam?" His hands tightened as tension filled him. "And why didn't you tell me this before? I might have been prepared for what happened this afternoon."

She opened her eyes. They were as cloudy as the mists that enshrouded a dreary day. "It wasn't an accident."

"No, it wasn't." He felt faint triumph that she knew better. "Samantha, what happened just now? Something else scared you."

Her lips trembled. "The—the—phone—" She shook her head, unable to go on.

"The phone? Did someone threaten you on the phone?"

She gathered the tattered ends of her control, pulling away from him. She jerked a tissue from a box on the lamp table and mopped her face. Crying wouldn't help, she told herself sternly. She should be calling the police.

Memories flooded back of Dubray lying in her father's hall, the cold ruthlessness she'd glimpsed in Bennett Price's face as he'd wiped the floor. No, she couldn't involve the police and give herself away. Not when she didn't know for sure whether she'd been found.

But she had to tell somebody. The pressure was building inside her, pounding her skull, hammering for release.

"All right, I'll tell you." Except for the slight catch in her voice, she sounded like her normal self.

"Yes, it's time." Tony leaned back, folding his arms across his chest.

"You were right, you know. I'm not British. I'm from Montreal. And my name is Smith, not Clark."

Only the merest traces of a British accent remained in her voice. For an instant Tony had the eerie feeling she was two people, her demeanor had changed so much. But at once she regained the almost imperious dignity she'd displayed in the hotel lobby the afternoon they'd met.

"I broke off my engagement."

Tony's brows rose. "That doesn't seem a very compelling reason to run away from home. Who was the lucky man?"

"Bennett Price."

"Of Price Enterprises?"

The fear she'd had about Tony communicating with Bennett resurfaced. "Do you know him?"

"Not personally. His business is well-known. We've never met. Different lines of work." Bennett Price. The name rolled around his mind, giving him a jolt, but he needed more. "What happened, Samantha? Did Price take it badly?"

"No. I don't know." The words rushed over themselves. "I didn't see him again, so I don't know how he took it." She licked her dry lips. "It was something else." In a flat voice she told him about her father's death and the incident at the house that day after the funeral.

Tony didn't say anything for several moments after she finished. When he spoke, his voice was quiet, almost contemplative. "He's the one you saw in the elevator, isn't he? Dubray didn't die—he must have recovered.''

Didn't he believe her? "He looked dead. And there was an awful mess." She shuddered, a violent convulsion that racked her body. "Bennett and the others were so cold-blooded about it, as if nothing had happened."

Her voice shook and she couldn't go on as she remembered the horror she had witnessed.

"Samantha." As if from a long way she heard Tony's voice, and realized he'd called her several times. "Samantha."

He shifted nearer and pulled her against him, wrapping his arms tightly around her to stop her trembling. "Please, Samantha, it's all right now."

She shuddered again and sat up, resisting the urge to lay her head on his broad chest. "It's not all right, Tony. Someone's after me."

"You've got me now, Sam. I'll help you. Can you tell me the rest? Were the men arguing?"

She pleated her brow, trying to remember. She could vividly see what had happened, but anything the men had said remained in a fog. She'd spent a hundred sleepless nights trying to recollect words, but nothing had so far emerged. Now she tried again.

"I heard the door open and close, then several voices. I recognized Bennett's and wondered why he was there. He was supposed to be out of town. I was about to go down, when another man shouted something I didn't understand. I couldn't see clearly because of the angle of the stairs, but I heard an odd sharp sound, then a thud, as if someone had dropped a heavy box or something." Her eyes grew round, the fear in them palpable. "I suppose that was the man falling. Oh, Tony, what if they find me?"

"I'm here," he said. His embrace tightened a moment, then he pulled back. "Sam, would they even have known you were there?"

"They could have found out. My Aunt Olivia knew where I was. Bennett might have asked her."

Tony frowned. "So he could have known what you'd seen, and might have wanted you shut up."

She sniffed, and nodded. "I'm sure of it."

Tony propped his elbow on the arm of the sofa and pressed his fingers into his forehead. "So you just took off. Didn't it occur to you there might have been an innocent explanation for what you saw?"

There might have been, except for the incriminating presence of Claude Germain. From him came the real danger. To a man like Claude Germain, anyone who got in his way, however innocent, was expendable. "If the man was merely hurt," she said carefully, "why didn't they just call an ambulance? Wouldn't that be the normal thing to do?"

"Maybe they didn't want to waste time. Maybe they took him straight to a hospital."

"I suppose it's possible. But you have to understand Bennett was supposed to be out of town until the end of the week. I wasn't supposed to see him until the day of the wedding. And the way he looked when he glanced up the stairs—it frightened me. I thought I knew Bennett. But in that moment I suddenly realized he was a total stranger."

"Did you talk to him before you left?"

"No, I was too frightened. I did call his office to see if I'd just had a horrible nightmare. But his secretary said Bennett was still out of town. Needless to say I realized the situation was dangerous. I wrote him a letter, mailing it to his office. Then I left a letter for my Aunt Olivia, telling her I needed a holiday. The same message went to James Michaels, Smith Industries' CEO. James has always been like an uncle to me, and oddly enough, he never liked Bennett. He must have been glad to hear I broke off the engagement. Don't worry, I didn't take any chances." Briefly she sketched her convoluted journey through Europe, and the arrangements she'd made with Amelia and Mr. Collins. "I changed my hair color in Toronto."

"What about from Nice to London? It's obvious they traced you there, although it took long enough."

"Amelia frequently travels to Paris or London by rental car. She made an arrangement for me to take one, in her name. The trail would have ended in Nice. As far as anyone is concerned I could be anywhere."

"But you got that note on the brochure."

"That might have been a lucky shot in the dark. They might have tried sending mail through our other European offices, as well. No one else knows where I am."

Tony frowned thoughtfully. "These threats and the accident. Is Bennett the vindictive type?"

Bennett? Bennett with Germain seemed triply lethal to her. But she knew he was trying to get at a particular motive. "You mean is he the jealous type who'd come gunning me for jilting him?"

Tony nodded. She twisted her fingers together in her lap. "I don't know. Once I would have said no. When he wanted to be, he was charming. He had great success in business because he knew how to mesmerize people, how to get them to agree with him. But with me or with his closest friends, he was often moody, intense. He got angry very quickly. Once he rammed a car door because someone opened it on the street when he was passing. But more often it was in his attitude. He had very little tolerance, especially for those he called bums—the unemployed, the homeless. He'd make donations to animal activists, saying animals couldn't help their situation but humans could."

Tony's brows shot up. "And you were marrying this guy?"

"He's a much-respected businessman, and our marriage was considered a good match."

Tony snorted. "Was it going to be a marriage or a business merger?"

From her present perspective she could understand his viewpoint. At first Bennett had seemed an ideal partner. After she'd experienced a disastrous relationship with an impoverished Italian prince during her last year at a Swiss finishing school, she'd been wary of fortune hunters. Bennett was rich, successful and charismatic. But as the wedding date drew nearer, she'd felt as if a noose were tightening around her neck.

"A marriage, of course," she shot back so heatedly the reply sounded defensive even to her ears. "At least we both had our eyes open."

"And your family approved, no doubt." Tony's mouth turned down at the corners. "I know what those Westmount families are like. The right schools, the right colleges, the right careers and finally the right marriages."

"We didn't live in Westmount during my teens," Samantha said. "We'd moved to the suburbs. Besides, I haven't lived at home for years."

"But you kept up the communication."

"They were my family. It meant a lot to my aunt, who was like a mother to me since my own died when I was an infant. She and my grandmother. Aunt Olivia approved of Bennett." She lifted her eyes, noting the frown that creased his brow. "Tony, it's silly to argue about this. I wasn't going to marry Bennett. I was planning to break off the engagement when my father died. With the funeral and everything I hardly saw Bennett. Then he went on his supposed business trip." She spread her hands. "Please understand, it wasn't a simple matter. This was the third engagement I broke off. It's not easy to admit failure again."

Under other circumstances, his look of surprise would have been comical. "You were engaged three times? Samantha, you hardly seem the type."

"I know. I've changed. I'll never be that person again." Her breath caught in her throat and she bit down on her bottom lip. "I could have been a princess. I was engaged to an Italian prince, but I broke it off. He had a penchant for skiing in Saint Moritz, sailing in Antibes and an aversion to work. He'd gone through the family fortune, then the money left him by an elderly widow he'd married before he met me. She'd conveniently died soon after—worn out, no doubt. Of course he didn't tell me any of this, but I found out later." She broke off, hugging her arms to her chest.

Tony felt relief. Contrary to what he might have thought, given her background, she wasn't a playgirl, blithely cutting a swathe through hordes of men, leading them on, then dropping them when she got bored.

"That's once," he said gently when she didn't speak.

"Yeah. It seems I couldn't stop there. Right away I started seeing a boy I'd known since kindergarten. I was on the rebound from the prince. Luckily I came to my senses in time. Such a gentle boy. I hated to hurt him, but I'm sure he now realizes it was for the best."

She lifted her hands and rubbed her temples, her mouth turning down in self-disgust. "Oh, forget it. I was a fool."

"We're all fools sometimes," Tony said. Far from undermining the attraction he felt toward her, her story only increased his fondness. She was human; she'd made mistakes and been hurt, and yet showed compassion for others who had also been hurt.

The knowledge warmed him. He'd been afraid her aloofness might be her whole personality.

But none of this solved the immediate problem of who was harassing her.

"Do you think Bennett's found you?"

She gave a harsh laugh. "I'd say we can assume that. Or one of the other men."

Tony looked at her, his eyes narrowing. "Did you know any of them?"

"Yes, Robert Dubray, the man I thought was dead. But he's hardly likely to be after me. He would have been too busy looking after his own skin."

"What do you mean?"

"Oh, there was some sort of scandal in city hall. I don't remember the details. I never thought I'd ever see him, so I didn't pay much attention to the stories."

Tony's thoughts raced. "Anything else?"

"No. Yes." She closed her eyes, again feeling the gut-wrenching fear that had left her waking in a cold sweat ever since she'd run away from Montreal. The terror was beginning all over again. And since Tony was now involved, it was better that he knew the worst. "Yes, I saw Claude Germain."

Tony stared at her, an icy chill creeping over his skin. "Claude Germain the mobster?"

"Yes."

He gulped. "No wonder you ran." For a long moment he was silent. Claude Germain. Here was the first concrete evidence that Samantha's problems might be linked to the upcoming trade conference. If rumors were to be believed, Claude Germain had been behind the threat of assassination that had aborted the trade conference last April. Because of the continued uneasy relations between French- and English-speaking factions in Quebec province, the conference had been rescheduled to take place in London. Was it possible someone would boldly make a move at this new site?

And what role did Robert Dubray play? If Dubray was connected with Germain, his presence in the hotel might have significance far beyond what Samantha had imagined.

"We'd better check if Dubray is really at the Regal Arms," Tony said, moving toward the phone.

"I've already done that, Tony. He wasn't registered."

"He wasn't? Well, that doesn't prove it wasn't him. He might have been in the hotel to see somebody, or for a meeting." He sat up straighter. "You know, Sam, we should be able to find out if Dubray was killed. A body is not so easy to get rid of. Of course, there is dumping in a wooded isolated area, but when the dead man's prominent, he'd at least be reported missing."

"Newspapers," Sam exclaimed. "It would have been in the newspapers." She turned toward him, her face suffused in color. "Tony, where can we get hold of back issues of the Montreal papers?"

All Tony's earlier suspicions about Samantha evaporated. Her fear and willingness to help were genuine. They both needed to get to the bottom of this odd mystery. An assassination might unfold at his hotel. And if so, he needed to thwart it. Also, this attractive woman seemed to be at the center. Resolving her dilemma might resolve his own. Besides, he was growing to care for her. . . his earlier attraction deepening. Turning back to her, he smiled. "The Montreal papers are part of a major newspaper consortium, aren't they? Either a library or one of the offices on Fleet Street should have copies in their archives. If we can get a look at them, we should find out something."

"When?"

"Tomorrow, first thing. The libraries are closed now. Can you take a day off?"

"I suppose. I'll work some evenings to make it up if I have to."

WHEN THEY CAME BACK from dinner an hour later they met Jason Wheeler on the second floor landing.

"Good evening, Miss Clark," he said, shifting the basket of laundry in his arms. "Did you enjoy your day out?" He didn't address Tony, merely nodding in his direction.

"Yes, I did," Samantha lied. "Except for the rain." She studied him suspiciously a moment.

Wheeler caught on. "How did I know your name? That was easy." Propping the basket against his hip, he gestured airily. "I asked Miss Hunnicott. Translations? That's what you do, isn't it? How are you at French?"

"Fluent, Mr. Wheeler," Samantha said crisply, wishing he'd move aside so they could get by.

"Then I might bring some work your way," Wheeler said. "I do business with a company in France. Just started, as a matter of fact. My French is rusty, so I wouldn't mind getting some letters translated."

"I am rather busy now—"

"Oh, I'm not in a hurry."

"Well, we are," Tony cut in. "Excuse us, please."

The man's expression didn't alter from its somewhat vacuous affability. "Sorry. I won't keep you." He walked down the hall and disappeared into his flat.

"That guy gives me the creeps," Samantha muttered as they climbed the last flight and headed for her door.

Tony scowled. "Keep clear of him. Might be hard, though. He's interested in you. I know that look."

Something possessive in his tone annoyed her. "I can handle it."

Eyes narrowed, he looked at her. "I'm sure you can. But be careful."

"Be careful," Samantha said irritably. "That's getting to be the story of my life."

"You could go to the police," Tony said quietly as they entered the flat.

Samantha shut the door. Her heart lurched as she saw the soft warmth in his face. His black hair had dried in little ringlets. She wanted to reach out and smooth them back where they tumbled over his forehead. Clenching her hand, she restrained the urge.

While it had been a comfort to talk to Tony, she couldn't allow herself to rely on him. She had to solve this mess she'd made of her life. Then she might be free— Free for what?

Bemused, she shook her head. Love was not in the near future. Not until she was very sure.

"You should have gone to the police in Montreal," Tony said. "All this hiding might not have been necessary."

The fragile bubble of intimacy burst. "I was scared. And now, what do we have to tell them? Nothing but guesses."

"Maybe tomorrow we'll find something." Tony reached for her hand, but she stepped back. Frowning slightly, he said, "Samantha, will you be all right tonight?"

"Sure I will." Her laugh was brittle. "I was all right before."

He still hesitated, reluctant to leave her. He couldn't have explained why, but he wanted to stay close.

"It's all right, Tony. I'll be fine. I'm just tired, that's all. It's been quite a day. Bennett's hardly likely to find me tonight."

"Not unless he's narrowed down your location. Sam, where's that brochure? Maybe you'd recognize the writing."

"It was printing, Tony. It looked like a child's scrawl. No one would recognize it." Nevertheless she began to shift the day's newspaper on the coffee table, folding it neatly before riffling through the stack of magazines. "Damn, where'd it go?"

She took up each magazine, shaking it in case the brochure had gotten tucked between the pages. Nothing fluttered free.

"Are you sure you left it there? You didn't put it in a drawer or anything?"

"Positive. It was here, I'm sure." She straightened the items on the table, the familiar panic tightening her chest. Lifting fearful eyes to Tony, she whispered, "Someone's broken in here. The brochure's gone, and so is the envelope."

Chapter Six

The phone rang. Sam whirled around to face it, her heart pounding. Finally on the fourth ring she picked it up. "Yes?"

"Miss Smith, are you there?" The agitated voice sounded harsh in her ear and it took her a second to realize who the caller was.

"Yes, I'm here." Samantha gripped the receiver. Mr. Collins rarely phoned her, leaving most communications to Mrs. Graham, his part-time secretary. "Has something happened?"

"My office was broken into. The police are here now, checking for fingerprints."

Samantha sank down on the carpet, her head rolling back against the sofa. She felt cold all over. "Was anything taken?"

"I haven't done a thorough check, but it seems a file with my monthly statements to you regarding Smith Industries is gone. Hardly state secrets, but they did contain your address and you'd asked me to keep it confidential. I'm sorry, Miss Smith. Terribly sorry."

Too late. Her heartbeat stepped up in rhythm. "Don't think twice about it, Mr. Collins. Send me a bill for the damages."

"I'm sorry to bring you distressing news, Miss Smith. If there is a problem, perhaps you should go to the police. They can help."

Could they? Sam hung up. She had nothing concrete to tell the police. Or show them, not even the brochure.

"What is it?" Tony asked tensely. He'd been going crazy watching the play of emotions over Sam's face. The fear notched up another degree in her rain-silver eyes. "What's happened?"

"They know where I am." Her voice was flat. "Even if they were just guessing before, they know now. My solicitor's office was broken into, my file with my address stolen. It can't be a coincidence. After they grabbed the wrong woman's purse, they must have gotten desperate."

A muscle quivered in Tony's jaw. "That does it. You're staying at my place for the night."

Sam raked her fingers through her loose hair, pushing her glasses up onto her forehead as if their weight was suddenly too much to bear. "Tony, you'll be taking a risk, too. Don't worry, I'll lock the doors."

"You lock them every time you go out, don't you? That didn't stop someone from getting in and taking the brochure."

The thick suffocating nightmare of her situation lowered over her, threatening her sanity. "Damn it, I never thought it would end up like this. I should have handled it differently from the first moment in Montreal. I can't let you get involved."

"I'm already involved." And perhaps more than she suspected. Placing his finger under her chin, Tony tipped her face up. "Look at me, Samantha. See, my eyes are open. I know what I'm getting into. I'm willing to take the chance." *For you,* he added under his breath, shocked at his thought. Where had it come from? "If you want, I'll sign an affidavit swearing you're not responsible for anything that happens to me."

Laughter twitched on her lips and he knew he'd won his point. "You need me, Sam. You need somebody, and I don't think we have enough to go to the police at this moment."

She admitted he was right. He could help her. Independence had become such a habit she'd almost forgotten what it was to have someone care what happened to her. She looked at Tony. His eyes were soft, his smile tender and open. No, he hadn't made the offer because he thought she couldn't take care of herself. He'd made it because he was honestly concerned about her safety.

"Yes, I'll come," she said, and discovered her words soothed her.

His smile broadened. "I'm glad, Sam." He walked over to her, his steps sure, unhurried. Setting his palm on her cheek, he stroked her lips with his thumb.

Her lips parted, as an unfamiliar sensation came to life within her. With surprise she recognized it as desire, an emotion she hadn't allowed herself to experience in so long she'd almost forgotten what it felt like. She pulled away.

Her movement was electric. Tony stood back. "I'm sorry, Samantha. I shouldn't have touched you."

But I wanted you to. The thought slammed through Sam's mind, almost shocking her with its intensity. "It's all right, Tony. Forget it."

As she began to pack, he stood by the bedroom window, cursing his impulse. If it wasn't for the trade conference and her possible connection to it, he would have followed through on his desire to kiss her. As it was, he was the one hiding something now. He'd had enough of games with women like Sheilah and Rebecca, who'd wanted the high life-style his income would provide, and little true intimacy. Only total honesty would do here now. Personal involvement would have to be limited.

"We should learn something tomorrow," he said in an effort to restore his equilibrium. "Then we'll decide what to do next."

Yes, the newspapers would be their first step.

Worldwide's reputation was on the line. Tony knew it, and was prepared to go to any lengths to ensure that the conference went according to plan. No hitches. Not even a hint of them.

Tony lived in a mews townhouse only seven blocks from Samantha's flat.

"So close," she said as he pulled into the open garage at one end of the compound. "It's surprising we never ran into each other shopping."

"I guess it wasn't the right time." Tony helped her out of the car, frowning as he saw her looking at the disfiguring dent in the fender. "Don't sweat it, Sam. That's why I carry insurance." He lifted her bag out of the trunk. "You're not going to believe this, but the day you fainted in the lobby of the Regal Arms I was sitting in my office thinking my life was boring. You certainly shook me out of that."

The dimple came and went in her right cheek as her lips relaxed in a glimmer of a smile. "Are you sure you aren't wishing you were still bored?"

He shook his head vigorously, and gave a mock scowl. "Not at all."

And the truth had hit him suddenly that even without the mystery in her past, he would have felt the same way. She was the most fascinating woman he'd ever met.

THE HARSH CLAMOR of the phone jolted him out of a pleasant dream in which Samantha lay beside him in his bed. Her skin was warm silk, bare—

"Yeah?" Blearily focusing one eye, he saw that it was 3:35. The room was dark except for the red figures on the clock radio.

"Yeah?" he repeated when no one spoke. "Who's this?"

"Could I speak to Samantha Smith please?" The sexless voice pronounced the words with an odd precision, as if the speaker were used to another language.

A deluge of ice water couldn't have woken Tony more abruptly. "I think you have the wrong number."

Apparently his quick thinking wasn't enough. After only a slight hesitation, the voice said, "Anthony Theopoulos, you will regret you ever met Samantha Smith. Get her out of your life before it's too late."

"Before what's too late? Oh, hell!" The buzz of a vacant line hummed in his ears.

He cradled the receiver and lay back, willing his heart to stop pounding. Adrenaline surged through him, arousing unfamiliar thoughts of violence. He wanted to get his hands on the person who was making the calls. He wanted to fight flesh and blood, not a ghostly voice on the phone. Knowing Sam was in danger awakened all his protective instincts.

Still, she was safe here. The compound that contained his house along with five others was closed off from the street by a tall iron gate. Only the residents had a key. The solid brick wall of a warehouse protected the tiny gardens behind the houses. Unless the caller could fly, he couldn't touch Samantha.

SAMANTHA'S GRIMY HAND left a dark smear across her forehead as she brushed back a strand of hair. "What a job this is. I never thought we'd have to sort through the actual papers. I assumed they'd have them on microfiche or something."

The subbasement of the library where back issues to international newspapers were kept, was dark and gloomy, most of the available space was piled high with boxes. A naked bulb that barely lit the work area swung over their heads.

"Have you found anything on Dubray?" Tony asked.

"Not, yet, but I'm still working on the earlier months." She reached from another bundle from the large file box, unfolding the top sheet and scanning the headlines. "I didn't know they could print so much about so little. And you're wasting your day. Won't they miss you at your office?"

Tony gave a noncommittal grunt. "Not likely. Probably glad I'm out for once."

Samantha slapped shut the newspaper she was looking over, folding it and replacing it in the box. She picked up the next one. Her heart accelerated. "Tony, here's the story about Dubray."

The account was accompanied by a grainy photo of Dubray surrounded by lawyers and police, his face hidden behind his raised briefcase.

"'Robert Dubray of Planning and Development has resigned from city hall amid rumors of scandal. Officials declined to comment, but a reliable source informed this reporter that charges are involved,'" Tony read over Sam's shoulder. He glanced at the date. "March 7. That was just before you left, wasn't it?"

"Yes." She bent to the boxes, sorting the papers by date. "Let's see now. We have to find the one for the day I left." Quickly she leafed through it, then picked up the next day's edition. "Um—hmm. City News. Dubray's scheduled court appearance was postponed when he failed to appear. Seems he was kept overnight in hospital for observation after a minor car accident. He was released the next day."

"There you have it, Sam. They took him to a hospital and made up a story to explain the injuries."

"Of course." She looked up at Tony, her eyes dancing with excitement. "Do you realize what this means? Dubray was alive after I saw him. There was no murder."

"You're off the hook." The words seemed to stick in Tony's throat.

Sam's euphoria died. "No, I'm not. There's Germain. Being seen with him would incriminate Bennett. And Dubray." She sat back on her heels. "Maybe Dubray is behind what's happening to me. Maybe he saw me that day and recognized me. He could easily have seen my picture in Bennett's office or someplace. He might be trying to hide his association with Germain—not that it appeared too amiable."

"Yeah." Tony nodded, his mouth grim. "Okay, let's both concentrate on March, see if we can find out what Dubray was charged with."

They plodded on, becoming dirtier and more disgruntled. Then Sam found something. "Dubray is mentioned again, later in March. The charges against him were dropped. No one seems to know why, or even what they were. Somebody must have had a lot of pull to keep that out of the press. The reporter says there were hints that embezzlement of city funds was involved."

"That would get a man fired all right," Tony agreed. "But I wonder what's the real story. Does it say what Dubray went into afterward?"

"Only that he has plans to enter private business." She frowned, her silver eyes contemplative. "I wonder if he was looking for work with Bennett's company. He must have been a good engineer to have the job he did at city hall. But that still doesn't explain what I witnessed in my father's house."

"Sam." Tony's voice, sharp with a questioning note, cut into her ramblings. "Here's something on Germain. I guess you won't have to worry about him anymore."

A chill enveloped her whole body as she focused on the picture of a man with small eyes and a hard, emotionless face above a thick neck. "Claude Germain." Her lips soundlessly formed the words. "He's dead."

For an instant the headlines above the story blurred, then she read them aloud slowly. " 'Suspected Mobster, Claude Germain found dead in his car.' "

She closed her eyes, letting Tony read the report.

"'Germain died of a single bullet wound to the head. While there are no leads, the slaying has all the earmarks of a professional hit.'"

"When did this happen?" she asked, her eyes flying open.

Tony turned the paper over. "About a month ago. At least that eliminates Germain as the one who's been harassing you."

Samantha waited for a rush of relief, but it didn't come. "Yes. And leaves Bennett as the likeliest suspect." She felt chilled. Somehow Bennett, who knew her, seemed more dangerous than anyone else.

They searched through the remainder of the papers, but found nothing more of interest. Tony, without bringing it to Sam's attention, carefully scrutinized the reports covering the canceled trade conference back in April. No reason was given, only that the French delegates were angry because security precautions were not up to standards. The news stories contained nothing he didn't already know, and no mention of Dubray.

Tucked away at the bottom of a page, in an edition a few days later, was a one-sentence item saying that the premier of Quebec had survived a nonconfidence vote in the provincial legislature. It didn't give details, and Tony had no way of knowing whether there was a connection between the two events.

Packing the last of the papers into a storage box, Tony glanced at his watch. "Parker has the afternoon shift today. We should be able to catch him before things get too busy."

"Parker?" Samantha got up and dusted her palms together. "Oh, you mean the English-butler type who was so affronted by my fainting in the Regal Arms."

"The very one." Tony grinned as she hitched up the waist of the jeans he'd lent her for their task. "He won't like the way we're dressed, either, but that's too bad." He took her arm and headed them for the freight elevator that was the only way out. "Seems to me we've found a lot more questions than answers. But Parker might be able to tell us something." He grimaced as he glanced back at the piles of dusty storage cartons. "At the moment I don't care if I never see another newspaper again."

In the taxi to the hotel, Tony turned to her. "What are you thinking?"

"That I'd better make a call to Montreal to check a few things, like what Bennett is up to these days. James won't give me away. In fact, he'll probably be happy to hear from me, although he must have received a post card or two sent through Amelia."

"Good idea, Sam. I might make a call or two myself. I want to contact Jacques, an old friend of mine who might be able to tell us more about Dubray and the mysteriously dropped charges."

The lobby of the Regal Arms was as stunning as Samantha remembered. Parker presided behind his counter with a dignity and devotion that would've been suitable for Buckingham Palace. At least he appeared to; Tony had to suppress a smile when he saw the man slip a copy of a racing form under the old-fashioned ledger on the desk.

"You remember this lady, don't you, Parker?"

Parker lifted his chin to an even loftier elevation, his nostrils flaring as he noted the way they were dressed. "Yes, I do, sir."

Tony leaned his elbows on the counter, setting his foot on the brass rail that ran around its base. "Do you remember what happened just before she fainted? A group of men were getting into the lift. Were they registered here?''

Parker's high cheekbones flushed with color. ''Sir, no one would get in the lift without checking at the desk first.''

''That's fine,'' Tony said hastily. ''I wasn't finding fault with your work. One of them was called Robert Dubray. He wasn't registered on that day. Sam, what does he look like?''

A vivid image flashed into her mind. Fighting for precise words, she said, ''He's average height, a little stout, bald on top with a rim of dark hair.''

''Glasses?'' Tony asked.

She bit her lip in concentration. ''Yes, I think so. And his suit was light brown, almost tan. Not a color you see much in London, even in summer.''

Parker grimaced. ''Yes, there is a Mr. Dubray.'' He riffled through the little box of registration cards.

''He's staying here?'' Tony asked. ''But you checked, didn't you, Sam?''

''Yes, I did.''

Parker pulled out a file card. ''He used his company name, Sunset Consulting Engineers. He's in a suite on the fifth floor.''

''Where does this company have its office?'' Tony asked.

''Montreal, Canada. I believe Mr. Dubray is here for an architects' convention.''

''Okay,'' Tony said. ''Thanks.'' He turned toward Sam. ''It seems that our Mr. Dubray landed feetfirst after he left city hall.''

''So he wasn't seeing Bennett about a job,'' Sam said as they waited for the elevator. ''I wonder what he was seeing Bennett about, and what caused the apparent falling out with Germain. Tony, I certainly hope either James or your friend Jacques can give us some facts.''

THE MAN BESIDE THE NEWSSTAND waited out of sight until the elevator door pinched closed. Good thing his associate had been able to catch Theopoulos's order to the taxi driver. He'd phoned at once with the information.

The man put down the book he was examining and sauntered over to the house phones. ''It's time for the next stage of the scheme. A connection had been made sooner than expected. Worrisome, really. It spells lots of trouble.''

Chapter Seven

"Do you want to make your call first?" Tony asked
when they reached his office. "It'll take me a minute
to look over my messages." He waved the bundle of
pink slips in his hand.

"Thanks." Mindful of her dusty clothes, she
perched on the edge of a leather chair while she dialed
the long series of numbers for the overseas call. A
moment later she put down the receiver. "Tony, you'd
better try yours. James's line is busy."

Tony had better luck, getting through almost at
once. "Jacques? Tony, here. How's it going?"

Samantha moved to sit on another chair until the
conversation was through.

Tony hung up the phone, a strange expression on his
face. Samantha stared at him, her stomach beginning
to churn. "What is it?"

Saying nothing, Tony passed a pencil slowly from
one hand to the other. Samantha's stomach increased
its gyrations. "What is it, Tony?" Her voice rose.
"What's wrong? Has something happened to—" she
swallowed down her nausea "—my aunt? Damn it, I
knew I should have left my whereabouts with somebody."

"No, nothing's happened to anybody, as far as I know." He stirred restlessly, tilting his chair back and sliding the pencil along his jaw in a gesture that was almost hypnotic. How much could he tell her? He was under orders to say nothing about the upcoming trade conference, yet it was increasingly apparent that Samantha was connected in some way.

"Sam, did you know that Bennett's involved in politics?" The tiny item he'd seen in the paper jumped back into his mind. "He's rumored to be financially supporting a Paul Messier, who was recently elected opposition leader in Quebec. With the Quebec premier's position shaky, he could be the next premier."

Samantha swallowed, forcing herself to calm. She'd overreacted. But Tony's face had carried the strangest expression. "There's nothing sinister about that, is there?"

"Not in itself, no. But in view of what you've told me about Bennett, I wonder what kind of candidate Messier is. I've never heard of him."

"Neither have I," Samantha said firmly.

Tony got up and strolled to the window. Standing there he pushed his hands into his back pockets. The faded jeans and old chambray shirt he wore made an incongruous picture against the luxury of the office. "I've asked Jacques to check up on Germain—how well he knew Bennett, that sort of thing. Jacques is a lawyer. He'll keep it quiet. Bennett won't know."

"That's probably wise, since Bennett might not be too happy if he finds out he's being investigated." She got up from the chair. "I'm going to try James again."

"Wait a minute, Sam."

He turned to face her. His body was a dark silhouette against the bright window and she couldn't make out his expression.

"Was your father in business with Price?"

"Not as far as I know. But my Aunt Olivia mentioned that she'd invested money in Bennett's company. She seemed quite keen on me doing the same."

"And did you?"

Samantha nodded slowly. "In a manner of speaking. But it wasn't strictly an investment. I made Bennett a loan. A handshake would have bound it, especially since at that time we were still planning to get married, but Bennett insisted on having a lawyer draw up a contract. The loan is to be repaid by September 15."

"How, if Bennett doesn't know where you are?"

"It's to be paid directly to my Montreal bank."

Tony moved back to his desk, perching on the edge of it. "I take it the amount was substantial. If something happened to you, Bennett wouldn't have to repay it."

"I suppose not." She sat in the leather chair, folding her hands in her lap so that Tony couldn't see their trembling. "But a lot of people borrow money. They don't bump off the lender to avoid paying it."

Tony rubbed his palms down his thighs. "Samantha, there's something weird about this whole situation. It doesn't make sense."

Exactly what she'd concluded. She hunched down in the chair, forgetting the state of her clothes. "If I hadn't fainted that day, you wouldn't have met me. You wouldn't be involved in this."

The grin he flashed her was quick and spontaneous. "Sam, I wouldn't have wanted to miss this experience for anything. And don't apologize for fainting. You'd had a shock.''

"I really thought Dubray was dead. He looked dead.''

"Nobody's dead unless you take his pulse and can't find it. And maybe not even then." He flipped the pencil in his hand idly back and forth. "Sam, if you had married Bennett, what would he have stood to gain?''

"Gain?" She sat upright. "Not much. After my experience with the prince, I made sure of that. About the only thing I learned at that finishing school was to beware of fortune hunters.''

"Oh, I wouldn't say that was all you learned. You pulled off the British aristocrat act perfectly." He eyed her present appearance. "Of course, today that would hardly work. Just how wealthy in your own right are you?''

Her eyes narrowed. "Why do you want to know?''

"Just keeping things in perspective. *Did* Bennett stand to gain by your marriage? Would he have had more clout in business, getting loans or contracts, making lucrative connections?''

Sam had never talked about finances with anyone outside of her family. Indeed, she had been brought up to believe such discussions were in the worst of taste. But with Tony, the rules didn't seem to apply.

"Since my father's death," she said, "I hold the controlling number of shares in the company. Of course, Bennett didn't know my father would die when he did. Bennett might have thought he could influence me to let him into the business. But he didn't seem to need that. He was a success." She chewed on her bottom lip, drawing Tony's attention to its luscious curve. He'd almost kissed her that time . . .

Resolutely he squelched his distracting thoughts. "Was there any kind of a prenuptial agreement?"

Her level gaze didn't waver. "There was, but since the marriage didn't go through, it's not valid."

"You didn't sign it, did you?"

"Why, yes, I did. It's common procedure among the people we associated with. Simplifies all the legalities concerned with setting up housekeeping."

Tony shivered, an icy dread cascading through his blood. "What were the terms? Half your father's corporation if you died?"

Samantha stared at him, wondering if he was joking. "Of course not. There was nothing in it about my father's corporation. There was only my grandmother's trust fund, which was mine outright. The loan came out of it. But even then Bennett wouldn't benefit unless we stayed married at least six months."

"And if you divorced after that time?"

"If we divorced after six months and before a year of marriage, Bennett's claim was limited to two hundred thousand dollars. If either of us died, the survivor was entitled to half the joint estate."

Would a man murder someone for that? Tony asked himself. Maybe, if the estate was substantial, something he didn't know and hadn't quite the nerve to ask. "What about insurance? Did you have a life insurance policy?"

"Yes."

"Who's the beneficiary?"

"Bennett is, but—"

"How much?" The words snapped across her like a released rubber band.

"One million."

"Any conditions?"

"Not that I know of."

"So if you die, he gets one million dollars. And," he added musingly, "if there's a double indemnity clause, such as for accidental death, it could be two million. Plus half your estate."

"But if he dies, I'd benefit. So I have as much a motive as he does."

"You don't, because you don't need the money. You have your grandmother's trust fund."

"I suppose so. But it still doesn't wash. The policies wouldn't activate until we married. So your little theories don't hold water."

"Um-hmm." Tony leaned back, closing his eyes. "Some of them might."

"But we never married."

Tony's eyes popped open, their gaze hard and probing. "Are you sure?"

"What do you mean?"

"Well, you'd done all the legal stuff, purchased the license and so forth. What would stop dear Bennett from forging a certificate? He could have told all your friends he was meeting you in Reno or someplace, then come back with a marriage certificate. No one ever asks to look at those things, anyway."

She glared at him. "You've got a sick mind. How would he explain the fact I'm not living with him?"

"Easy. You used to travel a lot. He could say you had a job somewhere. Samantha, you have to face facts. There's something going on and you're in danger. Since I don't think you've made enemies here, it's logical to assume Bennett's behind it, especially in view of what you saw before you left. He must have gone crazy trying to figure out why you'd walked out without leaving a forwarding address.''

Samantha clenched her fists, anger burgeoning inside her. Murder. Bennett wasn't a murderer. An accomplice at worst, but if there was no murder, he wasn't even that.

"I was engaged to the man. He wouldn't try to kill me."

"Greed and desperation make people act strangely."

"Not that much." She got up from the chair and marched across the carpet to his desk. "And just to prove it I'll phone Aunt Olivia before I try James again."

"Be my guest," Tony muttered.

She took the telephone receiver he held out, making sure she didn't touch his hand in the process, and dialed. Tony sighed. "I didn't do anything. I'm just trying to help you figure it out."

She grimaced at him, and waited while the various beeps and buzzes played themselves out. The phone rang at the other end.

On the twelfth ring a female voice answered. "Olivia Smith's residence."

"Oh." Sam was momentarily taken aback. Her aunt rarely allowed her housekeeper to answer the phone. "Is Olivia there, please?"

"I'm sorry. Miss Smith is in London on vacation."

London. Sam managed to stammer a thank-you and hung up. Hiding her consternation from Tony, she smiled shakily. "She's not there. I'll try James now."

"Michaels here."

His voice was low, stern, as if he resented being disturbed Samantha thought. "Hello, James. How are you?"

"Samantha! Where have you been? All these months. I can understand your wanting a holiday, but you've been gone so long and we haven't heard anything, I was about to hire a private detective."

Alarmed, she frowned. The company had always gotten along without her. And the statements from Mr. Collins each month had assured her that the quarterly dividends were being credited to her account. "Why? Is something wrong?"

"No, nothing, except that Bennett's been going crazy. He was frantic when you left. We were quite concerned."

"I'm sorry. Tell Bennett I'm sorry, too."

"It'll have to wait. He's gone on a business trip, to Europe."

A chill slithered up her spine and the sickness rose like acid in her throat. She could hardly force the words past her chattering teeth. "Where in Europe?"

"London. Samantha, are you all right? You sound strange."

"Yes, I'm all right." She shut out the horrifying thoughts that thundered through her head.

"Will you be coming home, Samantha?" James asked with sincere concern.

"I'm not sure what my plans are yet. Good night, James."

"Good night, Samantha."

"Well?" Tony asked when she sat down, her eyes blank as she stared into space. He clenched the sides of the chair in order to restrain his impulse to go to her, to take her into his arms. But he knew that whatever it was, she would tell him in her own time.

"Bennett's here."

"Here?"

"Here in London. Tony, that means he could have done all those things if he knew I was here."

"How long has he been in town?"

"I don't know."

"What about Robert Dubray? If they had dealings in the past—" Setting his jaw, Tony got up from the chair.

At the mention of Dubray's name, a new and unwelcome thought struck Sam. "I wonder if Bennett is staying here, too." She shivered. Could he have been that close without her knowledge? Perhaps he'd seen her in the lobby and traced her to her apartment.

Standing by the desk, Tony dialed the single digit that would connect him to the front desk. "Parker, get me the number of Robert Dubray's room. And find out if a Bennett Price is a guest in the hotel." Brief pause. "Yes, I'll hold."

A moment later he hung up. "Price isn't registered. Dubray is in 517. He's had quite a few meetings, Parker tells me, even a party one night that had the people in the surrounding rooms complaining about the noise." He took her hand, pulling her to her feet. "Come on, let's see if Mr. Dubray is in."

"Shouldn't you check first?" Bennett wasn't there. Relief made her light-headed.

"No, I'd rather surprise him."

They rode down to the fifth floor. The paneled corridor was quiet during the early evening hour as people dressed for dinner or a night out on the town.

Halfway to 517 Tony stopped, laying his hand on Sam's arm. "Would Dubray know you?"

Sam shook her head. "No, I don't think so. Even if he'd seen a picture of me, my hair is different now. And we've never met."

"Then how did you know who he was?"

"He ran for mayor once. His picture was all over the city."

Tony looked interested. "Oh, really? Before or after he got into City Planning?"

"During. Planning isn't a political position. If he'd won, he would have resigned. He ran as an independent."

"Oh," Tony said, chewing this over as they continued down the hall.

Dubray answered the door on the first knock. He must have been getting ready to go out, for he wore dress pants with suspenders over a white shirt. A red tie hung loosely from his starched collar. He gave no sign of recognition as he ran his eyes over first Samantha and then Tony.

"Yes?" His French-Canadian accent was barely perceptible. "May I help you?"

"I'm Anthony Theopoulos. I guess you might say I'm in charge of this place. May we come in?"

Dubray opened the door wider. "Of course. If it's about the party the other night, please accept my further apologies. I hadn't realized we were so loud."

"No problem," Tony said.

Samantha looked around the room, furnished with comfortable chairs, a sofa and various tables, including a large one that could be used for dining or for conferences. The room was tidy, no clothes strewn about. But, then, Dubray had the adjoining bedroom to relax in, out of sight of clients or colleagues.

"Can I get you a drink?" Dubray asked, moving over to the small refrigerator in the corner.

Tony settled himself on one of the upholstered chairs, motioning Samantha to do the same. "A club soda, if you don't mind." He lifted his brow toward Samantha. "Agatha, how about you?"

Agatha? Sam nearly choked. "Nothing, thanks." Out of sight of their host she scowled at Tony.

"So what can I do for you?" Dubray asked as he approached Tony with the glass in his hand.

Tony had worked out various scenarios in his mind as they'd ridden down in the elevator but finally decided something close to the truth would be easiest. Elaborate lying required prodigious mental gymnastics and a phenomenal memory and he doubted he was up to it. "Have you talked to Bennett Price lately?"

If they hadn't been watching him closely, they wouldn't have noticed the startled jerk of Dubray's hand. He recovered at once, and extended the glass to Tony. Tony ignored the wet track of the soda that had dripped over the edge.

"I haven't seen Price in months. We were mere social acquaintances. Why do you ask?"

Tony decided to follow a conservative tack. "A representative of Price Enterprises has approached Worldwide Hotels with the idea of building a hotel with extensive shopping facilities near Heathrow. He suggested you as a person who could vouch for their financial integrity."

Dubray shook his head. "I can't imagine why he would. I've never had anything to do with Price or his company."

Tony coolly drained his glass. "He must have been misinformed then." Standing up, he set the glass on the table. "Thanks for the drink. I'm sorry to have taken up your time. Agatha?"

Gritting her teeth, Sam followed him toward the door. They had only taken a step in its direction, when a knock sounded. "Excuse me," Dubray muttered. "That must be the man I've been expecting."

He opened the door, greeting his visitor enthusiastically. "Come in. Come in. I'm so please you could make it."

"What the hell . . ." Tony mumbled.

Beside her Samantha felt Tony stiffen momentarily, then he strode forward decisively.

"Maurice St. Clair," he exclaimed. "Fancy meeting you here." Taking the man's hand he shook it vigorously.

Dubray frowned, his expression perplexed. "You know each other?"

"Of course we do."

Tony's reply was so effusive Samantha couldn't believe her ears.

"Why, Maury and I were at university together. How's it going, old man?" He tugged at the man's lapels. "Nice suit you've got there. But, then, you always knew how to dress."

Maurice St. Clair didn't look pleased, although he covered it well. Samantha stared at the men, perplexed by Tony's odd behavior and St. Clair's and Dubray's discomfort. What was going on?

St. Clair forced a smile. "Tony, what brings you to London? Pretty lady you've got there. You haven't lost your touch."

"Mr. Theopoulos runs this hotel," Dubray said with an edge to his voice. "He and uh, Agatha, were just leaving."

"Yes," said Tony. "Well, good to see you again, Maury. Give my love to—Betsy, wasn't it?"

"She's history," St. Clair said flatly. "I'm playing the field these days. Less hassle."

"Well, good luck with your business."

"Agatha?" Samantha cried, indignantly, as they stepped into the elevator, which clamped shut.

"You said you'd never met, but I didn't want to take the chance he might have heard your name."

"And who is Maurice? Did you really know him?"

Tony turned innocent eyes on her. "Would I have faked that? Yeah, I knew Maurice. He was quite a rebel at university. Nearly got himself kicked out once. Grew up poor, but he looks like he did all right for himself."

"Sounds like old home week," Sam said sardonically. "Bennett here. Dubray here. And now Maurice."

Tony regarded her closely. "I think you need some food in you, Sam. You're looking downright disagreeable."

He'd made such a fool of himself in there, Sam mused. Tony had practically fawned over the man. Was it an act? Or was there some reason behind it?

"How well did you know this Maurice?" she asked.

"Not all that well. Why do you think I put on that old buddy act? With his background, dear Maury might be useful for casting light on the inner workings of Quebec politics. We may need it yet, since the subject keeps cropping up everywhere we turn."

"Oh, I see." She wasn't sure she did. "What do you suppose his business with Dubray is?"

Tony shrugged. "Your guess is as good as mine."

They began to walk the short distance to Samantha's flat, stopping on the way at a pub for a bite to eat.

"How soon do you think you'll hear from your friend Jacques?" Sam asked as they emerged later into the bustling city night.

"Not long. A day or two, I should think. Sam, will I see you tomorrow?"

She shook her head. "I have to work. I really do," she insisted as he frowned. "The professor is counting on me."

"Okay, but remember what I said."

"Don't stand near the tube platforms." Samantha gave a humorless laugh. "Oh, Tony, it's probably all been coincidences, blown out of proportion by our imaginations. Hello, what's that?"

Up the street, the red-and-blue lights of emergency vehicles strafed the night sky.

"It looks as if it's your building," Tony exclaimed.

They ran the remaining half block, coming up to find several of the residents and the building manager standing on the sidewalk. The ambulance attendants were lifting a stretcher on which lay a white shrouded figure. They rolled it into the back of the vehicle.

"What happened?" Sam asked the building manager, a thin woman in her fifties, who was wringing her hands in agitation.

"It's Miss Hunnicott. She fell down the stairs." The woman's voice broke. "She's dead."

Chapter Eight

An accident? The question resounded in Samantha's mind as she accompanied a silent Tony up the stairs, the very stairs that had killed Miss Hunnicott.

"I should have been nicer to her," Samantha muttered with the unfounded guilt that survivors frequently feel.

"You were nice to her," Tony said firmly. Taking the key from her hand as she fumbled with it, he deftly unlocked the door.

In the flat they found another surprise.

On the table propped against a vase of wilted flowers, neglected during Sam's busy weekend, was a note.

"No, not another one," she moaned. The room spun around her as bitterness rose in her throat.

"Don't touch it." Tony's voice was sharp as he steadied her. "There may be fingerprints."

She lifted despairing eyes to his. "You don't really think that, do you? He wouldn't be so stupid."

You could be next. Without touching the note, Tony read the lurid red letters, made with a felt marker, the printing as crude as a child's. "Same as the other one," he muttered. "Too bad we don't have it."

"What good would it do?" Samantha pulled away and stood in the middle of the room, hugging her arms around her waist. "Poor Miss Hunnicott, I should have warned her."

"About what?" Tony dropped the note on the table. "You don't even know if her death had anything to do with you. Your tormentor may have just taken advantage of the accident."

With an effort of will, she pulled herself together, her eyes falling on the note. "At least this time we have something to show the police."

She went to the window, noting the police car's dome light swirling lazily below. "They're still here. Tony, I have to talk to them."

But her joints felt frozen; she wasn't sure she could negotiate the stairs. She turned and dizziness swam through her head. Her steps were as stiff and jerky as a puppet's, yet she managed to inch toward the door.

"Tony, I—"

He reached her just in time to help her take a seat on the sofa. "Samantha, just sit tight. I'll bring the cops up here."

By the time she heard his returning footsteps, along with a heavier tread, she had managed to drink a glass of water and was feeling marginally better.

"Samantha," Tony said as they came into the flat. "This is Detective Inspector Allen."

Allen was a muscular man of about forty whose jowly features appeared phlegmatic until one saw the keen intelligence in his eyes. "Good evening, miss," he said, nodding politely. "I've radioed for a fingerprint expert. In the meantime perhaps you could tell me what's been going on."

Samantha related the events of the past week, as well as those that had driven her from Montreal. Allen wrote everything down in a small notebook, interrupting only occasionally with a question to clarify a point. "And you say this Bennett Price is in London at the moment?"

"Yes, as far as I know." She shifted restlessly on her chair at the kitchen table, where they had gone in order to leave the living room free for the fingerprinter to do his job. "But I can't believe Bennett would go to this length to cause trouble for me. And there's no reason, since Dubray is very much alive."

The detective permitted himself a small smile as he closed his notebook. "It's not only scorned women who go after revenge."

"Bennett wasn't a passionate man," Samantha declared, pretending she didn't notice Tony's reaction. His brows shot up, quizzically.

"Do you have any idea where he might be staying, Miss Smith?" the inspector asked.

Samantha shook her head. "No. It's even possible that he had a flat of his own here, since his company had a number of business interests in England."

Inspector Allen rose from his chair. "That will be all for now then." He patted her shoulder. "We'll contact you if anything develops. And I'll ask the man on the beat to keep an eye out for anything unusual in the neighborhood. Good night."

"BENNETT WASN'T a passionate man?" Tony said as soon as the policemen had left. "Samantha, was that what you wanted in a husband, a man who wasn't passionate?"

The inspector's competent pragmatism and the assurance that the police were prepared to take her seriously had done much to restore Sam's equilibrium. "I might have guessed you wouldn't let that pass," she said tartly. "I had passion once, but it ended disastrously. I made up my mind then that I wasn't getting involved in another relationship without keeping my eyes open."

"Oh, really, Samantha. You're an intelligent, attractive woman. You're not likely to spend your lifetime alone." He placed his hands on her shoulders, his head bending toward her. "You just haven't met the right man yet."

Maybe she had, and she didn't know it yet. Tony was different from the men she'd known, despite the tone of the news story she'd seen. Yet for now she wasn't ready for the deeper intimacy that his presence promised. She pulled back, giving him a level gaze. To her surprise, he seemed just as surprised by the unguarded moment.

Clearing his throat, he said, "Sam, it's time I went."

While he was still able to. He couldn't afford to get involved. Yet. That conference, and the people she'd known, must have goaded him into rash behavior. He had to get better control over his impulses.

Raking his hand through his hair, he looked at her downcast head. "Will you be all right alone?"

Numbly she nodded. "With the police keeping an eye on the building on their regular patrols, I should be okay. And all the residents have been cautioned about keeping the outer door closed and locked." She licked her lip, feeling his closeness. "Tony—"

His eyes rested on her flushed face, intent, yet with a curious detachment. "Yes?"

"What about my things at your place?"

"Don't worry about them. I'll bring them by in the morning. What time do you leave?"

"Early. About seven-thirty."

He laughed. "That's not early. I'm usually in my office by then. You're up at seven? Good. I'll drop them by then. Good night, Sam."

Without touching her again, he walked out the door.

TRUE TO HIS WORD, he stopped by early the next morning. Sam had just gotten up, when the downstairs buzzer sounded.

She let him in, still dressed in her robe, a satin garment he eyed with appreciation. She had a tousled sleepy look that made him regret yet again his restraint the night before. Even seeing her now, her face pink, faintly creased with sleep along one cheek, made him want to touch her, find out if her skin was as warm and silky as it looked.

"I slept in." Her voice was husky, her hand unsteady as she dragged her tangled hair back from her face. "I'm sorry."

"Don't be. You look beautiful."

There was no doubting the sincerity in his quiet tone, and she smiled. "Do you have time for coffee? It'll take only a minute to make some."

He shook his head. "No, I've got a meeting. I have to get going."

"You mean other people work this early, too?" Her smile broadened.

"Some." He sobered. "Sam, any disturbances during the night?"

"No, not even the phone."

His brows drew together. "I tried you last night, about eleven, just to make sure you were okay, but your line was busy."

"Busy? It couldn't have been. I didn't call any-one."

He strode across the room to the phone and put the receiver to his ear. "Seems to be okay."

"Didn't you try again?"

"Yes, but it was still busy. Then I had a business call from Vancouver, and by that time it was late. I didn't try any more."

Samantha shrugged. "Probably just a glitch in the system."

"Yeah, probably." He touched a fingertip to her cheek. "Take care, Sam. And be careful."

"I will, Tony. Thank you."

"DID YOU HAVE TO kill her?"

The man in the phone booth hid his trepidation under a facade of righteousness. "Nosy old bitch. She saw me coming out of Smith's flat. She blabs everything she sees. The game would have been up."

"Well, I don't like the publicity. It's in the morning paper. We don't need that kind of exposure at all."

"Won't happen again, boss."

His employer was silent for a long moment. "Not without my orders."

The edge in his voice cut deep. The man heard the power in it, and the threat. "Sorry, boss," he blus-tered. "I thought—"

"I don't pay you to think. I pay you to keep an eye on things and report to me. What about Theopou-los?"

"He didn't stay the night, but he came by this morning. Only stayed a minute, though." He sniggered nastily. "Wish I'd wired up a video camera instead of just the bug."

"Keep your dirty mind on business," the boss snapped. "And no more free-lancing. I'll do the thinking for both of us.

THE BUILDING MANAGER was dusting the front hallway when Sam returned that afternoon. "You wouldn't know anything about Miss Hunnicott's funeral, would you?"

The woman pursed her lips. "She had distant relatives in Scotland. I believe the body's been shipped there. Such goings-on."

"Do you have the address? It might be nice to send flowers." A niggle of guilt still tugged at Samantha's conscience, although, as Tony had pointed out, there was nothing she could have done about the old lady's death. Even the police didn't seem to think it was anything more than a simple accident.

To her disappointment, Tony called and said he had to work late. "I've got meetings that'll probably last to midnight. Sorry, Sam. Rain check until tomorrow night?"

"Of course, Tony. See you then."

Bagheera meowed plaintively as she hung up the phone. "Yes, cat, I'll let you out."

Alone, she prowled around the flat, occasionally going to the window to look out. The weather had become warm again, but the trees in the little park down the street were showing signs of encroaching autumn. Some of the leaves had turned yellow. Under the trees ripened seed pods lay among the chrysanthemums on the verge of bloom.

Samantha made a sound of frustration. As little ago as a week she hadn't minded her own company. But Tony had changed all that.

Picking up a sweater, she decided she needed noise and activity. She'd go to the fish-and-chip shop for supper.

Once there, Sam put in her order, then took a seat at a corner table.

Sam sipped the tea the waitress brought and let her mind wander. But when a shadow fell across the table she raised her head. "Thank you—"

She froze. It wasn't the waitress with her meal, but Jason Wheeler. He stood next to the table, a smile fixed on his narrow face.

"Good evening, Miss Clark. Mind if I join you?"

Yes, I do mind. Before she could voice her objection, he sat down.

"Terrible thing about the old lady," he went on conversationally, as if they were old friends.

"Yes, terrible," Sam murmured, glancing up to see the waitress approaching with her fish-and-chips.

"Good-looking bloke you're seeing," Wheeler said as Sam began to eat. "Serious?"

She paused, the fork halfway to her mouth. "I didn't see you in the crowd outside the building." Actually, she hadn't given it any thought until now, but most of the building's twenty or so residents had been there.

He waved his hand airily. "Oh, I was around."

His attitude irked her. "Do you think it was an accident?" she asked, adopting a casual tone.

Wheeler's eyes narrowed. "Sure it was an accident." He turned his head as the woman brought his food. "Thanks, love." Picking up his knife and fork, he cut into a sausage, releasing the spicy aroma of the meat. "Of course," he said after a moment, "the story goes that the old lady had money that her relatives wanted to get their hands on."

Samantha glanced at him sharply. "Where did you hear this?"

"Why, from dear Miss Hunnicott herself." He put a piece of sausage into his mouth, chewing and swallowing it. "I had tea with the old thing the other day."

Possibly one of the occasions Sam herself had declined, she thought with a sick feeling. From under downswept lashes she studied Wheeler. His speech was peppered with colloquialisms, but that didn't mean he wasn't educated. He wore good clothes, his hair was clean and well groomed. He looked innocuous enough.

Sam shook her head. Soon she would be suspecting everyone she met of mayhem and murder.

Rational thought didn't change her initial impression. She didn't like him. There was something—some quality of evasiveness that his bluff exterior couldn't quite disguise.

Forcing a smile to her lips, she asked, "Did you enjoy yourself?"

"Oh, immensely. Such an interesting lady. But she did mention her relatives." He lowered his voice, inclining his head so that the heat of his breath fanned her face. "Said they were waiting for her to kick off. 'I wouldn't put it past some of them to speed the process along.' That was how she put it."

Sam pushed her half-full plate away. Her appetite had fled, the food she'd eaten sitting in her stomach like lead.

"But the police questioned everyone. No one seems to have seen any strangers around."

"The police don't spill everything they know or think," Wheeler said darkly. "Otherwise how could they operate?"

"I suppose you're right."

She accepted a refill on her tea, pretending she didn't see the waitress's frown as the woman took away her plate. Wheeler ate his sausages and chips, mopping up the last of his ketchup with a slice of bread. He leaned back in the seat, fumbling in his pockets for a cigarette. "You don't mind, do you, love?"

The smoke from the fryers was dense enough that it hardly mattered. "Go ahead."

He lit the cigarette, blowing out smoke rings that drifted lazily toward the ceiling before dissipating into formless wisps. "Your work, translating, must pay well."

Was he fishing for something? "It's all right," she said coolly. "What do you do?"

He tapped the cigarette over the ceramic ashtray, his fingers curling around the filter. "I'm a consultant." When she looked blank, he amplified. "You know, telling people what investments will make them money and so forth. If you'd like some advice, first time's free. Might save you some taxes."

"I'll think about it," she said carefully.

He insisted on accompanying her to her floor, one flight above his. "Can't have you taking a nasty fall on the stairs, can we?"

She didn't like his unctuous tone, or the way he crowded her.

At her door, he waited until she had her key out. "You wouldn't invite a lonely man in for coffee, would you, Miss Clark?"

Whether it was the hangdog look or his continued polite formality, or her faintly guilty consciousness at feeling dislike for him, she couldn't analyze.

"All right, but only for a moment. I've an early day tomorrow."

"Important job?"

"Not critical, but it's important to my client. And it's almost finished, so I'd like to wrap it up. Go in and sit down. I'll get the coffee."

When she brought the tray in, Wheeler had made himself at home. He sat on the sofa, leafing through a magazine from the stack on the coffee table. "Thank you. That looks very nice."

He added milk and sugar to his coffee, sipping it with obvious appreciation. "Where'd you learn to make good coffee? What passes for coffee in the fish-and-chip shop wouldn't make it anywhere else as mop water."

Sam laughed, her misgivings temporarily consigned to the nether regions of her mind. "From my grandmother."

"Grandmother, eh? And where would she be?"

"In heaven, I presume. She died."

"Oh, I am sorry. Was it recent?"

Sam shook her head. "No, it's been several years."

A little silence fell. Then Wheeler said, "Where's the boyfriend tonight?"

He's not my boyfriend. The words were on the tip of her tongue, but she held them back. Wheeler didn't seem the aggressive sort, but just in case, it was probably prudent if she let him think it was serious between her and Tony.

"Work," she said, without bothering to elaborate.

"In business, is he?"

"Yes."

It was late by the time Wheeler left. Samantha pushed the door shut behind him and threw the bolt, her breath gusting out in relief. She tidied the living room, washing the coffee cups and putting them away. In her bedroom she took out clothes for the next day, laying them over a chair. She looked out of the window, reassured when she saw the street was deserted except for the lines of parked cars. The blue Mini, which she still wondered about, was parked directly across from her building. Most of the lights in the flats across the way were out.

She opened her window a crack, letting in fresh air. Tomorrow would be fine, she thought, pausing when she heard the crisp tread of feet on the sidewalk. Holding her breath she waited, not that anyone could reach her up here.

A moment later she exhaled. A bobby, his arms swinging at his side and his round hat set at a jaunty angle, was on his beat. As she watched, he paused in front of the building, going up the short walk. Reassured, she turned away. Obviously Inspector Allen's order to keep an eye on the building was being carried out.

She showered and changed into a night dress, going back to the bathroom to brush her teeth. She rinsed her mouth, then pressed the soap dispenser to wash her hands.

Under her horrified gaze sticky crimson oozed over her fingers and dripped into the sink.

Chapter Nine

Her stomach churned and Samantha bit back a scream. She swallowed hard, then her fright turned to anger.

Ketchup.

In her mind she saw Jason Wheeler mopping up his plate with a triangle of bread. Bringing her fingers close to her nose, she sniffed. Yes, it was definitely ketchup.

With a savage twist she turned on the tap, rinsing her hands clean. The last of the ketchup vanished down the drain in a pink swirl. Only a sticky drop still hung from the nozzle of the soap dispenser.

Damn. Damn. Sam jerked the towel from the rack and dried her hands. Her face stared back at her from the mirror, pale and scared. For just a second she gave in, resting her forehead against the cold glass. She gripped the edge of the sink, her hands shaking as tears seeped from under her tightly closed eyelids.

Was Jason Wheeler the culprit? He could have gone into the bathroom while she was in the kitchen making the coffee. No, that wasn't likely. She would have noticed if he'd been gone that long.

On the other hand, anyone could have come into the flat during the day. Locked doors didn't seem to present any barriers to her tormentor.

But it was all so stupid. None of the things that had happened would have proved fatal, except perhaps the incident with the truck, and there she had been saved by Tony's hair-trigger reaction and the absolute responsiveness of the car.

She slapped down the towel and went to the phone to dial the police. As she might have expected at this hour, Inspector Allen wasn't in, but when she gave her name, the polite voice asked her to hold.

"Could I have him call you?" the duty officer asked a moment later.

"Yes, all right," she said, gripping the phone so hard her fingers hurt.

Less than five minutes elapsed before the phone rang. She snatched it up.

"Inspector Allen here. What can I do for you, Miss Smith?"

"Someone's either playing a bad joke or they're trying to make me crazy," she said starkly. "There is ketchup in my soap dispenser. You've no idea how much that looks like blood when you've got it all over your hands."

"I can imagine," the inspector said dryly. "Is there anything else amiss?"

"I haven't looked," Sam said. "I called you right away."

"Good, good. It may be just a prank, but I'll come and check it out. By the way, we've found nothing on fingerprints. The note was clean."

She'd expected nothing else. "How soon will you get here?"

"About fifteen minutes."

"I'll be waiting."

She hung up, then on impulse dialed Tony's house. No answer.

She didn't have his office number, but since it was in the Regal Arms, the front desk would connect her.

"Anthony Theopoulos's office, please."

"I'm afraid he's not there. He's in Mr. St. Clair's room. Hold on and I'll connect you."

Mr. St. Clair? Sam stared at the receiver in shock. Maurice St. Clair might have been an old acquaintance of Tony's, but she'd hardly gotten the impression either of them was interested in reminiscing about their university days.

"St. Clair." The voice startled her so she almost dropped the phone.

"Uh, yes. Is Tony there?"

St. Clair said nothing for a long moment. Then with unmistakable caution he asked, "May I ask who's calling, please?"

Curiouser and curiouser. "Samantha Smith." Not for anyone was she going to call herself "Agatha" again. Besides, it was unlikely that St. Clair would recognize her name.

She heard mumbling in the background, a buzz of static as the phone was taken up. "Yes, Sam?" Tony sounded brusque, even annoyed.

"I'm sorry to disturb you, but there's been another incident."

That seemed to shake him. "Are you all right?"

"Yes. I've called Inspector Allen. He's on the way."

"Good. So it's well in hand then?"

She could hear voices behind him, more than one. Who was with him? And what was Tony's business with St. Clair, a man he professed not to have seen in at least ten or twelve years?

"Sam, do you want me there?"

To her ears he sounded distracted, not as if he were about to rush to her rescue. "No, it's okay. The inspector will check it out."

"I'm sorry, Sam, but I have to go. I'll talk to you tomorrow."

Without giving her a chance to say goodbye, he hung up.

Sam stared at the phone in disbelief, then slowly put down the receiver. Maurice St. Clair. She'd thought Tony's behavior was odd in the hotel room with Dubray. And now this, after his vehement declarations that he would help her, protect her.

How much did she really know about Tony? She'd stumbled accidentally into his life, but perhaps his interest in her was more than a coincidence.

Well, from now on she wouldn't count on his help. Ultimately she could only trust herself.

The first thing Inspector Allen did upon his arrival was check the flat thoroughly. Sam had spent the interval huddled on the sofa, feeling colder than she'd ever been in her life. Was there nobody she could depend on, nobody she could trust? Even Tony, who'd so quickly entered her life had seemingly let her down.

She followed Allen's leisurely progress around the flat, watching as he opened closets and swept aside the neatly hung garments to check behind them. He looked in the cupboards, in the musty space under the kitchen sink, even stood on the toilet seat to check inside the old-fashioned tank high on the wall.

"Looks clean," he pronounced at last. He picked up the soap dispenser. "I'll take that with me. Not that

I expect to find anything.'' He cracked a smile that was obviously intended to cheer her up. ''Maybe he used a rare brand of sauce and we'll be able to trace it.''

Sitting down on the sofa, he pulled out his notebook. ''Now can you tell me who had access to this flat? Not that we can rule out the person who left the note yesterday. Someone seems able to defy locks. But for the moment, we'll stick to the known.''

''Well, there's Jason Wheeler. He was in here tonight. I suppose he could have done it, but I can't imagine why. I hardly know the man.''

The inspector's brows rose. ''Oh? A recent acquaintance then?''

''You must have spoken to him. He lives one floor down. Just moved in last week.''

''Mmm.'' Allen flipped back several pages, running his fingertip down a row of names. ''No, doesn't seem to be here.''

''Wheeler said he was around after Miss Hunnicott's death.''

''Did he? I don't have him down. There're two flats on each floor, except for the ground floor, which has the equipment room and the manager's flat. I've talked to all the occupants except for the couple in one of the fourth-floor flats, who're away on holidays. But I don't have Jason Wheeler. Two A? Is that his flat number?''

''I think so.''

''Well, I tried the door yesterday, but no one was there. I suppose I'll have to try again.''

''Tonight?''

''No, not tonight. We have no evidence to connect him with the ketchup. We can't accuse a man for no reason. What about your friend of last evening? Have you known him long?''

''Not long. But he's a respected businessman. He wouldn't do anything to harm me.'' But did she really know that? He had been in Maurice St. Clair's room this evening and he hadn't sounded too pleased to find her on the phone.

''Did he have an opportunity?'' Allen went on doggedly.

''I suppose so. He was here last night for a while.'' But he had been so sweet. Surely a guilty man wouldn't have shown such caring and tenderness.

''Anyone else?''

''No one else that I know of. It looks like someone's trying to rattle me, make sure I know he can come and go as he pleases.''

The inspector closed his notebook. ''Nothing else appears to be touched. I'm sure you'll be all right if you chain the door.''

''Tell me,'' Sam said in a pleasant voice as the inspector put on his coat at the door. ''Was Miss Hunnicott's death an accident, or did somebody push her?''

The detective regarded her through narrowed eyes. ''It's a police matter, but I can say this much. The autopsy results were inconclusive. We're calling it an accident for the moment.''

A diplomatic answer if she'd ever heard one. Sam ground her teeth but wished the man a polite goodnight.

Tense and dispirited, Sam padded around the flat. The walls around were beginning to feel more like a prison than a shelter. In the kitchen she picked up the day's mail, which she hadn't gotten to. She riffled idly through the envelopes, mostly junk. The last one caught her attention. The return address was that of Mr. Collins's office.

Another threat?

Postmarked London, it had been sent from the Grosvenor Hotel. She tore it open, scanning to the bottom of the short note inside.

Aunt Olivia.

"Dear Samantha," her aunt had written. "I'll be in London for several weeks. I'm giving this to Mr. Collins to forward to you, wherever you are. If you receive it, please get in touch. Perhaps we can get together."

New energy pulsed through Samantha's veins. Aunt Olivia knew Bennett, was familiar with many of his business dealings and social acquaintances. Just the person to quiz to find out what Bennett was up to.

She looked at the clock. It was after midnight. Going to the living room, she picked up the phone, dialing the Grosvenor's number, which was displayed on the letterhead. Olivia was a night person who often read for hours in bed.

She was right. Olivia answered the phone at once.

"Aunt Olivia, this is Samantha."

"Samantha. Already? How nice to hear from you. Where are you?"

Until that instant Sam hadn't realized she must make a decision. Was she going to go on hiding? Or was she going to face the past, dangerous or not?

"I'm here in London." It hardly mattered, she realized. The police knew her story; they'd offered protection. And her mysterious enemy had probably known who she was for days. "Practically around the corner."

"Isn't that wonderful?" Aunt Olivia said. Her tone changed into one of mock severity. "What have you been up to, Samantha? It wasn't very nice of you to run off like that and not tell anyone where you were going.'

"I needed some time to myself. I'm sorry you worried."

"Of course not, child. I didn't worry. You're an adult. Do what you want. I only wondered."

"I'd like to see you, Aunt Olivia. Could we have lunch?"

"I'm afraid I have tomorrow and Thursday scheduled-up, but after that I'm free."

Sam bit her lip in frustration. "You wouldn't be able to see me sooner, would you?"

"I'm afraid not, Samantha. I've promised these people. But I've got an idea. How about if we go to Paris for the weekend? It'll be like old times."

Old times. That might work in her favor. They would have more time to broach the topic of Bennett, and in casual circumstances.

"Yes, that sounds like fun," she said. "I've got a job, but it'll be finished Thursday."

They discussed details, then hung up. Sam stared at the phone for a long moment. Aunt Olivia hadn't asked her any questions, nor had she seemed particularly surprised to hear from Samantha.

Was it possible she'd known Sam was in London?

TONY FINALLY CONTACTED Sam at 6:45 on Thursday morning, waking her from a sound sleep.

"Where have you been?" Even through her early-morning grogginess she could hear the impatience in his voice. And the anger. "Your line is either busy or you're not there. I've been going crazy thinking about you. Fortunately Allen told me you were okay, at least when he left you Tuesday night."

"I was at Professor Eldridge's until late last night. I went straight to bed. The line couldn't have been busy."

"It was, for half the evening," he insisted. She heard the deep inhalation of his breath. When he spoke next, he sounded calmer, as if he'd reined himself in. "What did Allen say about the latest incident? Damn, I don't even know what it was."

She was truly awake by now. Sitting up in the bed, she raked back her tangled hair. "Ketchup in the soap dispenser. Just your ordinary Friday the thirteenth kind of joke. Nothing life threatening."

"And since?"

"Nothing's happened. But as you pointed out, I haven't been here."

"Well, I may have something. Do you know anything about Quebec separatists?"

"What? I thought that sort of thing died out years ago. Wasn't it in the early seventies that there was such a fuss? I think I was in junior high, or maybe it was before then. What does that have to do with Bennett or what's going on now?"

"I'm not sure," Tony said. "So Bennett never mentioned where his sympathies might lie?"

"Never." Sam was positive. They'd never discussed politics.

"I have to talk to you, Sam," Tony said. "It's too complicated to go into on the phone. When can I see you?"

"Monday." She thought for a moment. "Yes, I should be back sometime Monday."

"Monday!"

Tony's bellow could have reached her without the electronic benefit of the telephone.

"It can't wait until Monday."

"Well, it will have to. I'm going to Paris with Aunt Olivia for the weekend."

"Aunt Olivia? *Your* Aunt Olivia?"

"My Aunt Olivia. Who else would it be? I told you she was in London. She's at the Grosvenor. I got a note from her through Mr. Collins and phoned her. She's the perfect person to tell me what's been going on with Bennett."

"I guess that means you're out of hiding for good." He sounded oddly subdued.

"There wasn't much point any more, was there? Look, Tony, I have to get to work if I'm going to finish up today. That's why I stayed so late last night."

"It's dangerous at night on the buses or the tube."

"Tony." Her voice rose in exasperation. "I took a taxi home. The professor insisted. And you weren't available the other night. I can manage my own life. I always have."

"So that's what this is about. I should have come over Tuesday night." The statement was rich with meaning.

"As it turned out, I handled it without you. Goodbye, Tony. Call me Monday."

Gently she hung up, cutting off his shout of protest. The phone immediately began to ring again, but she closed her ears and went into the shower, where she turned on the water. Tony had to learn she hadn't relinquished control of her life to him just because he'd offered a sympathetic shoulder once or twice.

She was strong. She could handle it herself. She was going to Paris.

Then why did she feel like crying?

IN SPITE OF the ninety-minute delay caused by flights stacked at Heathrow, Samantha and Aunt Olivia arrived in Paris in time for lunch on Friday. Checking into the hotel where Olivia had made reservations for two single rooms took only moments.

"This hotel?" Sam asked in dismay as Aunt Olivia signed the register with a flourish.

"Of course, my dear. Haven't I always stayed here? It may be under new management, but I understand the standards are as high as ever. I wouldn't dream of staying anywhere else."

Neither would Sam, under ordinary circumstances. She also had enjoyed the pleasant, refined atmosphere of the Paris Etoile on several occasions, the first time as a child of ten in the company of Aunt Olivia. But the Paris Etoile had become the Worldwide Etoile, part of the company Tony worked for. It made her feel strange to stay in one of Tony's hotels, especially after her abrupt dismissal of him.

"It's all right, isn't it?"

Aunt Olivia's firm voice told Sam she had no patience for arguments. And Sam acquiesced. Her objections were too nebulous to put into words, and in any case, she hadn't told her aunt about Tony.

"We'll go out for lunch now," Olivia continued. "The concierge will see that our cases are taken to our rooms."

"How is Bennett?" Sam asked when they were seated in the sunny courtyard of a restaurant. It was Olivia's favorite.

"He's held up surprisingly well considering his desolation at your departure."

Desolation? Sam almost laughed. Desolation was not an emotion she associated with Bennett Price. But if that was how he'd chosen to display his disappointment in public, then so be it. He must have wanted their marriage very badly. For the money? She shook her head behind the menu the waiter had placed in her hands. She couldn't figure it; Bennett had stood to gain very little from her in that area.

Aunt Olivia, usually a nonstop talker, showed no sign of elaborating as she perched her reading glasses on her nose and perused her menu.

Sam tried one more tack. "His business is going well, I take it?"

"Hmm?" Olivia peered over the tall menu at Samantha. "Oh. Oh, yes, his business is doing very well. I think I'll have the seafood salad."

"I'll have the same," Sam said, without having read a word.

"And a bottle of champagne," Olivia ordered as the waiter picked up the menus. "We have to celebrate."

"Celebrate what?"

"Why, our finding you, of course. We missed you, Samantha. We'll be glad to have you back."

Samantha stared at her. "I haven't said I'm going back."

"You must suit yourself, Samantha, but we love you. And Montreal is your home."

Samantha felt stunned. The uneasy feeling she'd had on the plane returned. Olivia, always lively and restless, seemed higher strung than usual, one moment chattering about people they both knew, the next falling into an introspective silence that was unlike her.

People didn't change that much in six months, or did they? Outwardly Olivia looked the same, her artfully coiffed blond hair gleaming, her smooth skin belying her fifty years even in the sunlight.

Olivia leaned forward. "We must do some shopping this afternoon, Samantha. Why did you leave all your good clothes behind?" She waved her hand. "No matter, you need some new things anyway." Her smile widened. "It'll be like old times, the two of us taking the shops by storm."

After the work she'd put in that week and the upheavals her life had undergone of late, shopping was the last thing on Sam's mind, but she smiled and graciously agreed. She didn't have the heart to disappoint her aunt.

The Champs Elysées was bathed in sunset by the time they returned to the hotel, laden with parcels and bags. Olivia wore the look of a woman who has taken on the world of merchandising and won. Sam's feet ached. She didn't need all the clothes her aunt had pressed on her, insisting she pay for them.

"What's the family fortune for if not to spend on nice things?" she'd said in answer to Sam's protests.

It was the old days all over again, and for a time Sam allowed herself to wallow in pleasant nostalgia. But as they rode up to their rooms, her earlier uneasiness flooded back.

Not once had Olivia asked for the story behind Sam's abrupt flight. Sam would have thought she'd be dying of curiosity. With no mother and a distant father, Olivia was the one Sam had always confided in as a teenager—not quite a parent, but more dependable than a friend. Sam knew her aunt. Olivia had a boundless curiosity about human relationships, especially those nearest and dearest to her.

The elevator door slid open. "Don't you want to know what happened with Bennett and me?" Sam blurted out.

Olivia eyed her with nothing more than mild interest. "You're an adult now, dear Samantha. I wouldn't dream of poking into your affairs. Do you have your key? Here are our rooms. Shall we meet in an hour or so? I've made reservations in the restaurant downstairs. They have a new chef, who is considered one of the best in Paris." She patted Sam's shoulder. "An hour then."

Sam closed the door of her room, puzzled. Was it possible her Aunt Olivia had been cloned and they'd left out some vital ingredient? Something didn't add up. And she wasn't learning anything about Bennett's present feelings toward her or whether he was behind the threats in London.

The large bouquet of red roses on the bureau caught her eye immediately. A heavy and sweet aroma clung to the air. Sam's skin suddenly quivered with an odd sense of foreboding.

She walked across the room, her feet dragging on the dense carpet. Nestled among the blossoms was a white envelope. Her fingers shook as she tore it open.

The words were typed in stark black letters: "Time is running out."

Chapter Ten

The room faded to a swirl that spun around her. Sam's nerveless fingers lost their grip on the card and it fluttered to the carpet.

Even here she'd been followed. She wanted to scream. She wanted to throw the flowers across the room.

Instead she gulped in air and backed slowly toward the door. Jerking the handle, she opened it and fled down the hall to her aunt's room.

"Aunt Olivia, let me in." She banged on the heavy oak panels. "Let me in."

The door opened so abruptly that Sam almost fell inside.

"What is it, child?" Olivia frowned as she reached for a robe.

"The roses," Sam gasped. The trembling started in her knees and traveled up her body, leaving a trail of clammy sweat.

"Roses?" To Sam's amazement Olivia smiled. "Wasn't that kind of the management to send us roses?"

Sam's eyes widened as she saw the vase on her aunt's bureau. White roses. "The management?" she stammered, forcing the words past the constriction in her throat. "But the note—"

"Note?" Olivia's brow creased as she fastened her robe over her slip. "There was no note."

"There was with mine."

Olivia pulled open the door. "Show me."

The door to Sam's room yawned open before them. Inside the room seemed undisturbed. Sam's purse lay on the bed where she'd dropped it. The fragrance of the red roses scented the air.

"Where is this note?" Olivia demanded as Sam came to a halt in the center of the room.

Frantically Sam searched every corner, her gaze skittering around the room. "It's gone. It's not here." Her shoulders slumped. Was she going crazy?

Aunt Olivia wrapped an arm around Sam's back and led her to the bed, sitting down beside her. "Samantha, you seem overwrought. Have you been working too hard?"

Working too hard? If only that were the problem. With an effort Sam gathered her composure. "There was a note, but it's gone now."

"What did the note say?" Olivia asked gently.

"'Time is running out.'"

"Sounds like something out of a fortune cookie." Aunt Olivia's laugh tinkled. "It's probably somebody's idea of a joke." She laughed again, and gave Sam an arch look. "I saw the young man at the desk staring at you. I think you've made a conquest."

Sam barely heard her, but revulsion welled up in her before she swallowed it down. Plastering a smile on her face, she moved away from her aunt. "Yes, it probably was a joke. I'm sorry I bothered you. I'll be ready shortly."

Olivia walked toward the door, looking back at Sam briefly with an indulgent smile. "Take your time. And then come to my room. I'm sure a good dinner will fix you up."

IN THE DINING ROOM the head waiter greeted Olivia like an old friend and led them to an excellent table by the windows. Samantha glanced around as they waited for their drinks. The room was half-empty, filled with the golden light of sunset.

"We missed you, Samantha." Olivia leaned back in her chair after sipping her gin and tonic. "Bennett was almost beside himself when he returned from his business trip and found you were gone."

What business trip? It was on the tip of Sam's tongue to ask, but instead she said, "I left him a letter."

"A short note saying you couldn't go through with the wedding is hardly an explanation."

Olivia's tone remained mild, but Sam heard the censure in her words.

"And then six months of nothing more than an odd postcard from Nice. Have you been in London the whole time?"

Sam took a fortifying swallow of her spritzer and wished she'd ordered something stronger. "Almost."

"And you didn't let us know."

"As you said, Aunt Olivia, I'm an adult. I needed to be on my own for a while." She paused, her eyes on the bubbles erupting from the surface of her drink, as she leaned back in her chair. "Aunt Olivia, is Bennett still in London?"

For an instant Olivia appeared startled, her hand remaining in midair as she lifted her glass. She drank from it, her eyes guarded as she peered at Sam over the rim. "How did you know Bennett was in Europe?"

"I talked to James Michaels a few days ago. He happened to mention it."

"Well, I may be having a vacation, but for Bennett it's strictly business. Samantha, you know you let him down. And made yourself look like a fool to boot."

Samantha stared at her aunt. Olivia had never spoken to her in this manner. "Isn't it better to look like a fool before the wedding than end up in a divorce court later on?" she asked tightly. "I'd think you'd be glad I realized it wouldn't work before we actually married."

"Why couldn't you go through with it? You broke off two previous engagements. I was sure this time you knew what you were doing."

Sam clenched the stem of her glass. Knowing her aunt's words conveyed truth, she muttered, "Maybe I'll never marry." An image of Tony flashed through her mind. She quickly banished it. She'd thought he might break her unfortunate cycle of attracting the wrong men, but even that hope seemed to have been dashed.

"It's not too late," Aunt Olivia said. "You can still marry Bennett. He would forgive and forget."

Would he? Sam thought cynically. But why her? She couldn't see him as sentimental. It had to be the money. "No, Aunt Olivia. I'm not marrying Bennett. Besides, if he wants to speak to me, why hasn't he contacted me?"

Olivia shrugged delicately. "He's been tied up with business."

The meal was served, each course presented with the grace and elegance French restaurants are known for.

Samantha welcomed the silence as she and Olivia applied themselves to the delicious duck garnished with peaches, mixed salad, and perfectly roasted new potatoes.

Samantha couldn't fathom the change in her aunt. Olivia had always been a charming companion, impulsive but generally unperturbed when things didn't go according to plan. This evening she seemed tense and at times defensive. On the telephone in London, as well as earlier today, she'd professed unconcern at Sam's flight, saying she was an adult. Yet now Sam felt like a scolded child.

Sam resented it. She and her aunt had been friends, more truly equals than anyone would have expected considering the twenty-year gap in their ages. But Olivia had this evening stretched the bonds of friendship to the breaking point.

However, by the time the pear tart was served along with their after-dinner coffee, Olivia appeared to regret her earlier remarks.

She reached across the table and squeezed Sam's hand. "I'm sorry, dear. Can we be friends again?"

Sam squeezed back, then on impulse leaned over and kissed her aunt's cheek. "Of course, Aunt Olivia. Haven't we always been?"

Olivia smiled, the tension at the table dissipating. "You know, Samantha, I've always loved you like a daughter. I only want what's best for you. Samantha, what's wrong? You look so strange."

And well she might, Sam thought. She could hardly believe her eyes. Tony was walking across the dining room toward them.

What was he doing here? Surely he couldn't have been so upset he'd followed her to Paris.

And what was she going to do now? She'd hoped the weekend with her aunt would take her out of the firing line. And reap answers to some pertinent questions.

Getting away from Tony for a spell had seemed a good idea, as well.

With an effort she pasted on a smile, hoping it didn't look as false as it felt.

"Hi, Sam." He grinned at her before turning to Olivia. "And you must be Sam's Aunt Olivia." He shook her hand enthusiastically. "Sam's told me all about you. I'm Tony Theopoulos." He glanced back at Sam. The rain-clear eyes were dark and troubled. Despite Sam's professed fondness for her aunt, he sensed tension at the table. "May I join you?"

"Of course," Sam said at once. It would have been churlish to refuse him, but a hundred questions collided into one another in her brain.

The waiter chose that moment to approach their table with the check. "It's my treat, Sam," Olivia insisted, signing the slip with a flourish.

While she was occupied, Sam took the opportunity to whisper into Tony's ear, "What are you doing here, Tony?"

His affable smile slid away, leaving behind a range of turbulent emotions. "There's something we have to discuss, Sam. It couldn't wait until Monday." He hesitated, then added, "I may need your help."

She stared at him. "My help? What—"

"Shh. Later."

He fixed the smile back on his face as Olivia asked him how he knew Sam. "London is like a small town. We Canadians usually manage to find one another."

Olivia frowned thoughtfully. "Theopoulos, you say? I believe I've met your father. Isn't his name Damian?"

"That's right," Tony said.

"Charming man. I'm surprised you and Samantha never met in Montreal."

"I haven't lived in Montreal for some years, and I'm in a different business from my father."

"Hotels, isn't it? It must be exciting."

Tony's eyes were on Sam, serious and very dark. "It has its moments."

"But don't you miss your family?" Olivia asked. "And Montreal? Samantha does, don't you, Samantha?"

"Only occasionally," Sam said. "How did you know where we were staying?" she asked. "Or did you just happen to drop by?"

"You mentioned that Olivia was staying at the Grosvenor. I phoned a friend there and he told me Olivia would be here for the weekend. No big mystery."

"I left word of my destination in case anyone called for me," Olivia said. "Did you know, Samantha, I've taken a part-time job—volunteer, of course—working in Paul Messier's office?"

Olivia often helped out with fund-raising projects, but this was the first Sam had heard of her getting interested in politics. "Oh, isn't he the one who's the new opposition leader in Quebec?"

"Yes, but if there's an election in Quebec, he's likely to become the next premier of the province," Olivia said. "And from there he hopes to gain support to run on the federal level. Of course, that may take several years. Paul's young, but he has all the earmarks of a great leader. It's time we had some new blood in government."

Tony had again lost his affable expression. He looked worried and, Sam thought suddenly, tired. "Is Bennett Price financing Messier's campaign?"

Olivia gave him a brilliant smile. "Not by himself, of course. There are laws limiting party contributions. But Bennett likes Paul. He thinks he'll be good for Quebec, make the federal government take us more seriously. We need a strong spokesman for our rights. Just look at the way they're handling that St. Lawrence fishing business and other trade agreements."

"Didn't they have a conference on that last spring?" Sam asked.

"It was postponed." Olivia's mouth turned down. "It seems there was a security leak."

"Involving Robert Dubray, I understand," Tony said with crisp emphasis.

Until this moment Sam had thought the conversation innocuous, but all at once Olivia's face turned pale. "What do you know about Robert Dubray?" Her voice was barely above a whisper.

"Nothing much. Only what I read in the papers. And what I heard from Maurice St. Clair. Do you happen to know either of them?"

Olivia gave a short laugh that sounded rather strained. Her face returned to its normal color. "I know Dubray, of course. He and Bennett—" She broke off. "Never mind. It's all in the past now."

"What did he and Bennett do?" Sam asked, holding her breath as she waited for the answer. "Did Dubray, when he was at city hall, help Bennett get contracts?"

Aunt Olivia turned her eyes toward Sam, her face wiped clean of any emotion. "Of course not, Samantha. Why would Bennett risk his reputation?"

"He seemed to need the loan I extended to him last spring. You wouldn't know why, would you?"

Olivia reared back in her chair, her eyes cold. "Samantha, I'm surprised at you. Every company has occasional cash-flow problems. Bennett is good for the money."

"How do you know, Aunt Olivia?"

"Your father had Bennett thoroughly investigated before he allowed you to get involved with him. His business is solid. So solid that I myself invested in the company. I've received an excellent return on my money. You should have followed my advice, Samantha. You should have married Bennett."

"Aunt Olivia," Sam said warningly. "You promised to leave the issue alone."

Olivia's apologetic smile appeared to be aimed more at Tony than at Sam. "So I did. Forgive me, Samantha. You, too, Tony, for airing the family linen in public."

"Not at all." Tony lifted the tall frosted glass the waiter had set in front of him. "Here's to health and success."

An odd toast, Sam thought, sipping from her own half-full wineglass. But after a moment Tony explained, "It's an old Greek saying. Without one, the other isn't much use."

Olivia laughed heartily. "There's wisdom in that. I must remember it." She drained her second gin and tonic. "You'll excuse me, won't you, Tony, for a moment. Coming, Samantha? Not that you need to powder your nose. How nice to be so young."

"I'll wait here, if you don't mind, Aunt Olivia. You go on."

As soon as Olivia was out of sight Sam leaned across the table. "Okay, Tony, what is going on? What did you have to tell me?"

"Maurice St. Clair wants to see you. I told him who you were. He wants to ask some questions about that day you left Montreal."

"Why?"

His eyes shifted away from hers. "I think I'll let him tell you. How soon can you leave here?"

"Aunt Olivia has arranged some excursion for tomorrow."

"Can you cancel it?" Tony asked.

"No, I can't. And I don't want to. Tony, I only came so I could talk to her about Bennett. I haven't found out anything about him yet. I need to stay."

"I guess it'll have to wait then." He drank deeply from his glass, savoring the bite of the mineral water and letting it soothe his frustration.

Sam looked at him, wondering at his morose contemplation of his glass. "What was Maurice's business with Dubray?"

"How should I know, Sam? I couldn't very well just ask him."

"No, I guess not." She toyed with her empty wineglass, feeling as if she were banging her head against a wall. "What do you think of Paul Messier?"

This seemed to reach him, for he sat up straighter.

"I think your aunt's an optimist to think he'll get into power quickly. Still, money and influence in the right places might pave his way. Bennett's money."

Sam was shocked. "But that would be illegal."

"Sure it would be, but do you think a few laws would stop a man like Bennett if he wanted something?"

She thought back over the past week and the frightening events that had befallen her. Bennett had to be at the bottom of things. She shivered. "An election is up to the people."

"And people can be manipulated. But yeah, I agree, to a point. For Messier to make it in federal politics, one of the present party leaders would have to resign, and none of them looks about to."

He poured himself another glass of water from the bottle on the table. "Your aunt seems very fond of Bennett."

Sam shrugged, more to ease the tension than anything. "She always has been. Tony, you tracked us down. Did you also manage to find out where Bennett's staying?"

"No, but I tried. He's not in any of the major hotels." Leaning forward, Tony took her hand in his, rubbing it gently. "Sam, have you told your aunt what's been happening?"

"No. I didn't want to worry her." She debated whether to tell him about the note with the roses.

"She doesn't look the fainting type."

"She's not." Sam shifted restlessly in her chair. "I guess I'm afraid she won't believe me. She didn't believe me about the note tonight."

Tony sat up, every sense on the alert. "Note? What note?"

"The management sent roses to each room. Mine had a note with it. 'Time is running out.'"

"Let me see it."

"That's just it, Tony. While I was in Aunt Olivia's room, the note disappeared."

Tony slumped back. "So there's no evidence. Sam, I don't suppose you could take me with you tomorrow."

"Take you with me?" Sam gave a short laugh. "Tony, I know what you're thinking, but I'll be perfectly safe with Aunt Olivia. You won't need to worry."

"You're right, of course." Tony swallowed his frustration. And his fear. There seemed to be enemies all around her. Even here she'd been threatened. He wasn't even sure her aunt could be trusted. But he couldn't fight phantoms.

Olivia returned to the table at that moment, forestalling any warnings he might have given Sam.

"Are you here on business, Tony?" she asked brightly.

Her chic hair and flawless attire suddenly irritated him. "Yes," he lied. Abruptly he got up from his chair. "And I'd better see to it. The hotel manager is expecting me. Good night, ladies. I hope you have a pleasant day tomorrow."

TONY WAS UP EARLY the next morning, loitering in the back of the hotel where he could keep an eye on the lobby. He planned to booby-trap Olivia.

The elevator door opened and Olivia stepped out. Alone. As soon as she entered the dining room, Tony sauntered toward her, as if he'd just come out of the manager's office. "Good morning, Olivia. Isn't Sam with you?"

"She'll be along shortly. She's eating in her room."

Bingo. Tony had guessed right.

"Won't you join me? Although I realize I'm hardly a substitute for Samantha."

"I'd be happy to join you." Tony smiled. Maybe he could get her talking. Sam's absence would work to his advantage.

"How well do you know Samantha?" Olivia asked after she'd ordered coffee and toast.

"We've been out a few times," he said carefully, wondering what was behind the question.

Olivia nodded. "I must warn you that Samantha hasn't shown very good judgment where men are concerned. Bennett had a stabilizing effect on her. But she apparently didn't see how good he was for her. Her running away was ill-conceived and impulsive. I do hope she'll come to her senses."

"Sam seems quite stable to me."

"She's nervous and jumpy," Olivia pronounced. "Anyone who knows her can see it."

Sure, Tony thought. She'd been fighting shadows. Samantha had shown remarkable courage considering her circumstances.

"I suppose she's attracted to you," Olivia went on. "But don't be fooled. Bennett is the man for her."

Tony didn't believe any such thing. Nothing about Sam indicated she felt anything except dislike for Bennett. He decided to risk a direct offensive. "How far would Bennett go to get Sam back?"

Olivia's mouth dropped open, spoiling her elegant facade. She snapped it shut, a guarded look deepening faint lines around her eyes.

"What do you mean by that?"

Having scored, Tony considered it prudent to back off. "Nothing particular. Just that for a man who wants a woman, he's not trying very hard to court her."

"He's busy." The words were clipped. Olivia glanced at her watch, then rose from the table, the toast lying uneaten on the plate in front of her. "The driver will be here soon. I must see if Samantha is ready."

"Give her my regards." Tony watched as Olivia walked to the elevator, her back stiff. End of round one. He shrugged slightly and reached for a slice of toast.

A short time later he saw Sam and her aunt get into a BMW sedan driven by a chauffeur. Was Sam in danger? Although he didn't completely trust Olivia, he couldn't see her harming Sam. The woman he was falling in love with would be safe enough for the day. In any case, short of following them, what could he do?

"WHO IS THIS FRIEND we're seeing?" Sam asked as the car left the city traffic and purred onto a broad country road lined with chestnut trees.

Aunt Olivia patted her knee. "It's a surprise. You used to like surprises, didn't you, Samantha?"

There had been too many surprises packed into the past few weeks. Sam suppressed a shiver. "I was a child then."

"You'll like it, Samantha." Olivia's smile was confident. "You'll see."

The driver turned off into a narrow lane. White Charolais cattle grazed in the grassy meadows on either side. The pastoral tranquillity was broken only by the sight of a power plant in the distance and the column of steam that drifted lazily into the blue sky.

"Here we are," Aunt Olivia announced as the car stopped before a sturdy wooden gate set in a high brick wall. The gate stood half-open, and the garden beyond was lush with roses, asters and bright yellow chrysanthemums. "It's just a simple country house."

Simple, perhaps, Sam thought as they stepped through the gate and started up the flagstone path. But it certainly looked substantial, a two-story building made of softly weathered bricks and topped with a tiled roof. Lace curtains billowed from several windows that stood open to the warm day.

They had almost reached the front door, when Olivia laid a hand on Sam's arm. She wore a worried frown, her brow pleated above her nose. "Now, Samantha, I want you to promise you won't be angry. I'm doing this for your own good."

Before Sam could formulate a reply, the door opened.

"Hi, Sam," said Bennett Price, a broad smile on his handsome face. He held the door open for both of them. "I'm so glad you could come."

Chapter Eleven

Bennett here? How could Aunt Olivia have done this to her? Anger mixed with fear inside her.

"Come in," Bennett said, pulling the door wider and gesturing with his hand. "I've got coffee waiting on the terrace."

Sam took a deep breath, slowing her racing heart. Bennett looked as she remembered him, suave, well dressed in corduroy trousers, tweed jacket and a knit shirt with a designer symbol on the pocket. Normal. A man spending the weekend at his country home. There was no danger, she tried to convince herself. She knew the man; she'd been engaged to him. And if he meant her harm, there was nothing he could do in front of Aunt Olivia.

Glancing sideways at her aunt, she took in the smiling face. Why, Olivia sincerely believed she was doing the right thing. In this instance Sam would have to make the best of the situation. She would stay for coffee. After that she would find some excuse to leave, with or without her aunt.

To Sam's surprise, Bennett's manner continued to be friendly as he led them through the house and onto a sunny terrace at the back. A table was set with china cups, a silver coffee service and plates of pastries. He held each of their chairs in turn, and poured out the coffee before seating himself. He took the iron-wrought chair next to Sam.

"Cream and sugar, Sam?" His eyes were very blue, free of guile or rancor as he passed her the tray.

"Thank you." She stirred her coffee, inhaling the rich aroma. "How have you been, Bennett?"

"Fine. Couldn't be better, in fact. Business is booming. Have an éclair. They're very good. What about you, Olivia?"

Olivia gave her charming laugh, the one she used mainly on men. "Not for me, thanks. Too many calories."

"You needn't worry," Bennett said graciously. "But if you feel you'd like some exercise, we could go riding later."

"We'll see."

He turned to Samantha. "How about it, Sam?"

"I don't have any riding clothes." The light breeze cooled her skin. "Some other time."

"Really, Sam, it's no problem. There are plenty of spare clothes in the cloakroom."

Sam gulped down some of her coffee, fighting against her urge to flee. "Okay, we'll go riding, if that's what you want." Better to agree than argue.

Olivia declined, saying she'd rather explore the gardens and adjacent orchard. Bennett chatted pleasantly as he showed Sam to the cloakroom at the back of the house.

"I'm sure you'll find something to fit you here." He turned, leaving Sam staring after him as he left to saddle the horses.

Could two people change this much in six months?
First her aunt. Now Bennett. Actually, Bennett hadn't
changed much. In fact, his affable good nature reminded her of how he'd been when they'd started
dating. He'd been thoughtful, bringing her flowers
and consulting her on what they would do, where they
would go. It had only been in the last weeks before the
wedding that he'd become uncommunicative and difficult.

She thought back to that day at her father's house.
But she was too weary to conjure up the unscrupu-
lous expression she'd glimpsed on Bennett's face.
Shaking her head, she dug jeans out of the closet,
holding them against her to judge the size. The incident was beginning to seem more like a half-
remembered nightmare than reality.

When she came out a few minutes later, she was still
on guard, but her outward composure indicated only
the anticipation of a pleasurable ride in the country.

Bennett was waiting at the end of the terrace. "I see
you even found boots," he said, leading forward a
chestnut gelding and a tall bay mare.

Sam lifted her foot and smiled. "A little snug, but
they'll be fine. It's not as if we're walking."

He laughed, and held the stirrup as she mounted the
gelding, adjusting the leathers to her leg. His touch
was impersonal, adding to Sam's perplexity. If he
wanted her back, as Aunt Olivia had implied,
wouldn't he show some passion?

The horses cantered down the path through the orchard, breaking into a gallop once they reached the
open meadows. Samantha's mount was skittish, but
she welcomed the struggle with the horse, an element

over which she had control, if not by physical power, then with the strength of her will.

A fence appeared ahead. Sam leaned forward, slackening the reins marginally. The chestnut inclined his head and cleared the wooden rails with room to spare. Tossing back her hair, Sam laughed in exhilaration.

She glanced at Bennett, whose mount had also cleared the barrier. "Thanks. I hadn't realized how much I missed riding."

They slowed to a trot, then a walk. The sun beat down on Sam's head and for the first time in days she felt free, happy. Even the presence of Bennett couldn't dampen her spirits.

Until he suggested they stop. "Sam, we need to talk."

She kept her eyes fixed on a point between the horse's ears. "I don't think we have much to talk about."

"We do." His voice was low, but a harsh note in it brought her head around. "Our marriage, for example." He nudged his mare close to her and took hold of the chestnut's bridle. "Let's stop here for a moment."

Samantha searched his face. Deep lines of tension bracketed his mouth. He looked strained, dark smudges from lack of sleep evident in the strong sunlight. "Okay, for a moment."

They dismounted in a copse of trees, tethering the horses to a fallen log. Sam sat down with her back against a tree trunk, stretching her legs in front of her. Bennett fussed with the horses, then, dusting his hands, came over and sank down on the grass next to Sam.

"You know, Sam, it wasn't easy tracking you down."

She hadn't expected him to volunteer the truth. Deciding she would learn more about his intentions by keeping cool, she lifted her brow, affecting nonchalance. "Oh? I don't know why you went to all that trouble anyway, Bennett. I left you a letter saying I was leaving. Our relationship was finished."

"Not as far as I was concerned." Bitterness crept into his voice. "Still, I was willing to give you a few months to sort yourself out. You were upset over your father's death. But I thought you'd come back on your own. And those postcards weren't too helpful. By the middle of July I was worried. I hired somebody to find you. You covered your tracks well, Sam."

"Not well enough, obviously," Sam said. "How did you find me?"

"Bank records. Your Montreal bank made a large transfer to London. That narrowed down the search."

Sam stared at him. When she had purchased her flat, half the price had been paid on signing. She'd had enough funds in the account she kept in London for vacations and shopping expeditions but had had the balance transferred through Mr. Collins. "I thought bank transactions were confidential."

"You have to know the right people. But even after that it wasn't easy, since the transaction was made under your changed name. Through real estate sales, which are on public record, we narrowed it down. There were two possibilities, you and another woman in St. John's Wood. She looked a lot like you." He smiled almost sadly. "I'm sorry if I frightened you with that note on the brochure, but we had to make sure it was you."

Hot rage spurted through her. She wanted to knock the complacent smile off his face. But she quelled her anger firmly. "So you had somebody watching my flat."

"I'm afraid so, but when you didn't react, we had to do something else to confirm where you lived. That bumbling idiot grabbed the wrong woman, but he redeemed himself by getting your address from Collins's office, along with some other information we needed."

"What about Miss Hunnicott?" Sam had regained an icy control.

"Who?"

"The old lady who lived in my building. She was killed."

Bennett spread his hands wide. "Not by me. I don't prey on old ladies." He plucked a blade of grass and chewed on the end of it. "Why did you go, Sam? The real reason." He spoke with deceptive quiet, but as he lifted his eyes to hers, they glittered dangerously.

Bracing her spine, she said coolly, "I realized you weren't the man I'd thought. I'd made a mistake."

He reached over and ran his fingertip softly down her cheek, smiling faintly as she pulled away. "Your mistake, Sam? Or mine? What did you hear that day?"

"What day?" By some miracle she kept her voice steady, hiding the trembling in her hands by clasping them around her knees. "I don't understand."

"I think you do," he said silkily. "Otherwise you wouldn't have changed your appearance and your name." He eyed her speculatively. "You want to know what I think? You were scared and you ran. But it's time you stopped. Our marriage would work. It's a whole different game now.''

Sam jumped to her feet, running to her horse and yanking free the tethered reins. ''It's not a game, Bennett. It's never been a game. I couldn't marry a man who had so little feeling.''

''Little feeling,'' he snarled. He rose and followed her, clamping his fingers around her arm. ''I wanted you, never mind that you were the ice princess. I knew, Sam. I knew about the Italian and that little wimp you led around by the nose.''

New anger kindled within her, giving her strength to pull loose from his hold. She leveled her gaze at him. ''That was in the past. I learned from that experience. I thought you were different, but I found out you weren't what I wanted in marriage, either. It's not a crime to make mistakes, not if you learn from them.''

''I wasn't good enough for you. Is that what you thought, Sam?'' His face was flushed, his tone ugly.

''That had nothing to do with it. Marriage should be based on love, and I don't love you.''

''Love.'' He spat the word as if it tasted bad. ''Only fools marry for love. Smart people marry for opportunity. You'd be wise to go along with me and make our marriage a real one.''

Sam paused with one foot in the stirrup. Had he taken leave of his senses? ''We're not married,'' she said tonelessly.

His smile was terrifying.

''Oh, but we could be, my dear Samantha. So easily.'' Reaching into the inner pocket of his jacket, he pulled out a stiff paper, which he calmly unfolded.

Sam set her foot on the ground and absently rubbed her mount's neck as she stared at the document in Bennett's hand.

"A marriage certificate, Samantha. All you have to do is sign it. We'll tell everybody I arranged to meet you in London and we got married. No one would know the difference."

"This isn't legal." Sam's lips felt stiff, as if her mouth had frozen.

"Isn't it, Sam?" he taunted with a mirthless laugh. "I've laid the groundwork well. Once it's signed, it will stand up."

Would it? She didn't know, not without consulting a lawyer. But she had no doubt that Bennett had plenty of tricks up his sleeve. If she died, and he could prove they'd been married...

The terms of the prenuptial agreement swam in her head. Six months were nearly up. Was she more valuable to him alive or dead? The wind sighed in the trees, shaking loose some dry leaves, which fluttered past her. Next to her the horse chomped noisily on a tuft of grass. Their isolation hit her. If Bennett wanted her dead, a riding accident would be the perfect cover.

"What do you want from me, Bennett?"

"Your cooperation."

She swung herself up into the saddle, gathering the reins. The horse, sensing the tension in her, danced nervously, teeth snapping on the bit. Before Bennett could react Samantha slapped the animal's neck with her open palm, sending him into a wild gallop down the hill.

"Hey!"

She heard Bennett's yell but made no attempt to stop her headlong race across a dried-up water hole.

She kept her balance as they leaped a rail fence. The horse stumbled once, but by sheer reflex she managed to keep him on his feet.

Fifteen minutes of hard riding brought her to the stable yard. She reined the animal in, noting that foam lined his mouth. The stall boy came out and took the reins. "Take care of him. See that he gets an extra measure of oats."

She tore through the back door of the house, nearly colliding with Aunt Olivia.

"Samantha, what's the matter?"

"We're leaving, Aunt Olivia," Sam said, adrenaline pumping in her blood. She held up her clothes, which she'd grabbed from the cloakroom. "Get the car ready. I'm just going to change."

The lock on the bathroom door, she knew, provided no more than an illusion of safety. She scrambled out of the borrowed clothes and into her own, stuffing her stockings in her pocket. She didn't want to take the time to pull them on.

But when she came out it was already too late. Bennett stood in the hall, with Aunt Olivia beside him. Whether Olivia was involved in every aspect of Bennett's shady affairs, Sam didn't know, but her comments about the wisdom of marriage to Bennett came rushing back. In that matter she was completely with Bennett. And against Sam.

"Samantha, can't you go along with it?" Olivia pleaded.

Sam could have sworn she saw tears in the woman's eyes. "Don't you see what he is, Aunt Olivia? He's deceiving all of us. He's been lying all along."

"You let him down," Olivia said. Her voice softened. "Sam, can't you just pretend for a little while?

It would be so much easier. Bennett has made a few mistakes in the past, but with you and the respectability of Smith Industries behind him, everyone will forget that. Please, Samantha, just for a year or two, until Paul gets into power in Ottawa.''

"A year or two," Sam said scornfully. "Do you really think you can get a virtual unknown into power in that time? What are you, Bennett, a magician that you can depose a solid political leader in that time. Voters have the final say, not you."

"The higher the position, the harder the fall." Bennett sounded unperturbed, almost bored. "We all know what a precarious perch it can be."

"Well, I don't want anything to do with it," Sam retorted. "And I refuse to lend my support to any candidate you might want in office."

Clenching his fists, he took a step toward her, his face red with rage. With a worried frown, Olivia laid her hand on his arm. "Please, Bennett, there's no need to get upset. I'm sure Samantha will change her mind once she's thought about it."

His anger vanished as he regained his composure. Only the glitter in his eyes betrayed his true feelings. "You're right, of course, Olivia."

His smile was more a snarl, but Samantha refused to flinch. "Come on, ladies. Shall we go to lunch?"

Lunch? The thought of eating at Bennett's table turned Sam's stomach. "I seem to have developed a headache," she said, not caring if either of them believed her. "Is there someplace I can rest?"

Instantly Aunt Olivia was the picture of concern. "Poor dear. I'll take you to a guest bedroom and bring you an aspirin."

Protecting the valuable commodity, no doubt, Sam thought with black irony. Upstairs she listened to the indistinguishable murmur of voices below. Somehow it was far from soothing. She had not taken the aspirin, fearing it would make her sleepy. She would want her wits about her when it was time to leave.

Downstairs the murmurs softened. No doubt Bennett and Olivia were discussing her aberrant behavior. A new flare of rage sped through her. Did he really think he could keep her a prisoner, or force her to cooperate with his devious plans?

She closed her eyes, clenching her hands in her hair. Once more she sought to understand Bennett's motives, and once again his motives eluded her.

An hour later, she heard footsteps on the tile floor, and voices coming closer, though still low. But suddenly she heard Olivia mention Tony. "He could be a problem. Sam—"

Bennett interrupted, his tone soothing. "Don't worry. I'll take care of it."

Sam rose and made her way to the hallway. On the top landing she stood. "Oh, there you are, Samantha," Aunt Olivia said calmly, looking up at her. "Shall we go?" She turned to an impassive Bennett. "Thank you, Bennett. You'll be in touch?"

"You can count on it." Bennett smiled as Sam stepped down the stairs. "Goodbye, Sam. You'll think about what we discussed, won't you?"

"I don't need to think," Samantha snapped. "You already know the answer. It's no—*n-o*—no."

Bennett shrugged in apparent unconcern. "Give it a day or two, Sam. You might change your mind."

Fat chance, Sam thought as she and Olivia walked down the path to the waiting car.

The drive back to the Etoile was uneventful. Sam stretched her stiff muscles as she got out of the car, working out the cramps that had developed from tension.

Going up in the elevator, Aunt Olivia made yet another attempt to calm Sam down. "Samantha, if you'd rather, we can go back to London tonight. I can change the tickets if there are seats available." She frowned. "That may be a problem, though."

"Let me know if there's anything," Sam said. "I think the weekend's been spoiled for me."

Olivia touched Sam's arm. "Samantha, please. Bennett means well. He needs you."

"For what?" Sam said more coldly than she'd ever spoken to her aunt before.

But Olivia didn't answer the question, merely saying, "Give him a chance, Sam. That's all I ask. And that's all Bennett asks."

"Later, Aunt Olivia." Sam exhaled gustily. "We'll discuss it later."

In her room she went straight to the telephone. She was under no illusion that leaving would be simple. Bennett would try again. She dialed the manager's office, expecting to find Tony there. The phone was picked up almost at once. Sam didn't wait for a greeting. "Tony, I need your help."

A man's voice, strongly accented, answered. "I'm sorry. Monsieur Theopoulos is not in, but we expect him momentarily. Is there a message?"

Sam thought quickly. By the time she packed Tony would probably be back. "Tell him Sam called. Ask him to meet me at the front door of the hotel. Oh, and please have my bill ready."

"Mademoiselle . . ."

The man sounded shocked.

"You're not leaving already?"

"I have to," Sam said. "I'll be down shortly."

Within five minutes she was back in the lobby, handing her Visa card to the desk clerk. Shifting from one foot to the other, she waited in agony while he clicked it through the processor. Then he handed her the slip to sign.

Where was Tony? she wondered as she scrawled her signature. Her eyes panned the entrance to the dining room, but his comforting figure didn't appear.

"Voilà, mademoiselle. Merci."

She tucked the card and her copy of the slip in her purse. Still no Tony. Picking up her bag, she headed for the door. She would just have to hail a taxi outside.

The door had barely closed behind her when she saw Bennett come running toward her. The fellow who'd chauffeured them into the countryside was close behind. Damn, Bennett must have guessed her next move.

Running to the curb, she dashed between the parked cars and put out her hand for a taxi, waving desperately. Out of the corner of her eye she could see Bennett coming nearer. She gambled and took a step into traffic. A Mercedes swerved, the driver leaning on his horn and throwing her a disgusted look.

Bennett had almost reached her, when a tiny gray Renault roared to a stop in front of her, nearly crushing her toes. Tony. Relief flooded her, but before she could move a pair of heavy hands grabbed her arm. "Samantha, you're coming with us."

"No." She struggled against Bennett's hold. "You said I'd have time to think things through."

"You're running away again."

"I'm only going out for a little while," she lied, but the overnight bag she carried gave her away.

She heard Tony shouting at her from the open passenger door of the little car. "Quick, Sam, get in."

The two men tightened their grip on her arms. Even when she swung the bag and kicked at their legs, she couldn't get free.

The traffic roared by, almost skinning the trio struggling in the street.

"Tony," she cried, amazed that no one would stop and help her. She was dragged closer and closer to the black car parked three cars ahead. Incredibly, with one final wrench she broke free.

"Sam, here," Tony yelled as he rushed up to her.

"I wouldn't." Bennett's voice dripped with menace.

Terrified, Sam glanced from Tony to the gun in Bennett's hand. She hesitated, her eyes wide with horror. Tony saw she'd lost her glasses.

"Sam, quick." It was a risk, but one he had to take.

He grabbed the bag she still held, and her hand. Together they raced back to his car. Tossing the case in the back seat, Tony helped Sam in, slamming the door. Leaping over the hood, he yanked open the driver's door as an approaching car screeched to a stop. Shifting into gear, he floored the accelerator. The force of the start banged his own door shut, and in the moment before the stopped car could get moving, Tony executed a wild U-turn. Behind them the man with the gun shook his fist, but he didn't shoot. Smiling grimly, Tony turned his attention from the rearview mirror to the road.

"I take it that was Bennett." He stopped for a traffic light, shifting gears and accelerating as it changed to green. "What the hell's he doing here?"

Samantha's breath rushed in and out of her lungs, a raw agony in her throat. "Don't know—for—sure. Following—me—I think."

"How'd he know where you were?"

She slumped down, pulling the seat belt across her chest and locking it in. "Aunt Olivia took me to see him."

"Uh-huh, so she's in on it, too."

Samantha's brow creased. "I'm not sure. She seemed to be doing only what she thought was best for me."

Tony released a burst of laughter. "Come on, Sam, you can't believe that. You're an adult."

"Well, she's always been like a mother to me," Sam said defensively. "She wants me to be settled. And she likes Bennett."

"Which doesn't say much for her taste."

Sam stared at the street, clogged with traffic. "To her Bennett is every woman's dream, good-looking, successful, rich."

"And if he married you, he'd be richer."

The implications of what Bennett had said suddenly hit her like a punch in the stomach. "Tony, he says he can make it look as if we are married."

"What?" Tony made a right turn that must have inconvenienced several drivers judging by the shrieking brakes and the blaring horns behind them. He slammed the little car to a halt on a quiet side street. "Tell me exactly what he told you."

Her voice shaking, Sam explained about the certificate.

Tony drummed his fingertips on the steering wheel. "It's possible, if he knew the right people. But I don't know if it would stand up in court. I wonder what he's after."

"He wants to make the marriage a real one, but I don't see why."

"Your money."

Sam banged her fist on the armrest next to her. "Damn it, Tony, can't you quit harping on that? He doesn't stand to gain that much."

"Still, it seems the only viable motive at this point. What does your aunt have to say about all this?"

"She wants the same as Bennett." Sam gnawed on her bottom lip. "In fact, she practically begged me to go along with Bennett, if only for a little while."

Tony turned toward Sam, drawn by the desolate note in her voice. He could understand what she was going through. The fright of the attempted abduction—or whatever Bennett had had in mind, the lack of support from her only living relative. She must feel betrayed on every side.

He took her hand in his. It felt cold, lifeless. "What did you tell her?"

"I told her I needed time." She looked at Tony, her eyes dark and stricken. "Both she and Bennett seemed to agree to that. But it's obvious Bennett must have changed his mind."

"Probably didn't want to act in front of your aunt. Which means she's probably not in as deep as we thought."

"No, I don't think she is. But she seems different, nervous somehow. Oh, Tony, what can I do? I don't know who to trust anymore."

He wrapped his arm around her shoulders, resting his cheek against her hair, breathing in the fragrance of it. "You can trust me, Sam."

"Can I, Tony?" she asked sadly.

His embrace tightened fiercely. "Yes. You can. Believe it, Sam."

She breathed in the clean woodsy scent of him, and it comforted her. Under her cheek, his heart beat steadily. He felt safe, an oasis of peace in the nightmare day. She clung to him as if he were the only buffer between her and hellish reality. "Trust me," he had said. There was no one she should trust, but for a moment she could pretend.

"Yes, Tony, I trust you."

Chapter Twelve

"Okay, Sam, here's what we'll do."

To Sam's surprise, Tony let her go and moved back to his side of the car, then he scanned the street.

"I'll go over to that phone booth and see if we can get a flight back to London." He briefly touched her cheek. "Wait here."

"I got lucky," he said when he came back. "There are several seats on a flight this afternoon. We have to get there, however, as quickly as possible."

"Bennett's bound to realize we'll head back to London. He wouldn't be on the same flight, would he?"

Humor flickered through his eyes. "Why? Scared he'll hijack the plane to get even with you?"

Sam didn't smile. From what she'd seen Bennett was capable of anything. "I wouldn't put it past him."

Tony restarted the car, letting it idle for a moment. "Don't worry, Sam. I checked it out with someone I know down at the booking office. Bennett's not on any flight in the next two days. And the seats they gave us are among some last-minute cancellations. So unless he booked under an assumed name, which wouldn't be very easy to pull off with visas and so forth, we're safe."

"Until he catches up with us again." Sam thought of the snatch of conversation she'd overheard. "Tony, why don't you let me go on my own? As long as you're with me, you're in danger. Aunt Olivia mentioned you to Bennett, and he said he'd take care of you."

"That's hardly a threat," Tony scoffed, putting the car in gear. "Did they know you heard them?"

Samantha wrinkled her brow. "They might have, although they didn't look too put out when they saw how close I was."

"That's just it, Sam. Has it occurred to you they're trying to intimidate you? Even to the extent of implying a threat to me."

"But they don't even know there's anything between us." Heat ran up Sam's face and she turned her head. "Not that there is anything," she said, backtracking quickly.

"Isn't there, Sam? Your aunt saw us together. She's not blind." Amusement laced his voice as he turned back into the traffic. "Sam," he added gently, "I'm not going to let you go this alone. Whether you like it or not, I'm going to help you."

"Even if it's dangerous?"

A reckless grin curved his mouth. "Especially if it's dangerous. You need someone to help you get to the bottom of this. Besides, I—" *love you?* He caught the words in time, the thought too startling to utter. "I care about you," he amended hastily.

It was rapidly becoming much more than that, he knew. Over the past week his admiration for her courage, his attraction to her beauty, even his sometimes frustrating impatience with her stubbornness, had quadrupled. Was he ready to love her? He turned over the idea in his mind, testing it. The idea was new, too new to assess this minute, he realized. Once the conference was over...

"Do you think Bennett is looking for us?" Sam asked, breaking Tony's introspection.

"Probably. How well does he know Paris?"

"I don't know. He's come here on business in the past. But there's always the chauffeur. He might recognize this car if he saw it again. That reminds me," Sam added. "I haven't thanked you for coming to the rescue."

Tony grinned at her. "No thanks necessary. I got your message that you were leaving, and I figured you must be in some kind of trouble."

They were cruising along one of the main boulevards that crossed the city. Tony's eyes lingered too long on the rearview mirror. "What color was the BMW?"

"Blue. Medium blue," Sam said. "Why?"

"Because I think it's behind us."

Sam craned her neck to look back. A white Peugeot followed them and behind it came a blue BMW.

"Well?" Tony said, braking for a light. "Is it the one?"

"I can't tell. Wait, he's catching up. Tony, it's him. I can tell by the gold-rimmed sunglasses." She frowned. "But he's alone. Where's Bennett?"

"Who cares? Hang on, Sam. We're going to lose this guy." His body tensed for action, but he had to rein in his eagerness. "As soon as the light changes."

"How did they find us? The car they were dragging me to was facing the other way."

"Must have been parked on the other side of the street and followed us. That turn we made caused confusion, but the driver could have run across the street and reached the other car."

Sam braced her hand on the dash as the light changed. The car screeched across the intersection. "We stopped in the side street—Tony, watch it, you just went through a red light."

"So did the BMW." The two-note cadence of a siren rose behind them. "Oh, oh, here come the cops."

Instead of slowing down, Tony sped up, nipping in front of a delivery truck slowing for a turn. He whipped the steering wheel around and set the Renault down a narrow lane, then made a quick left turn, followed by a right. The scream of the siren faded in the distance.

A short run the wrong way down a deserted one-way alley brought them into the parking lot of a large hospital. Tony downshifted and pulled sedately into a parking space. He turned off the engine, his breath coming in uneven spurts.

"Now what?"

Turning his head, he looked at Sam. Like him, she was breathing hard. Excitement and an excess of adrenaline stamped two bright spots on her cheeks. Instead of shivering with fear, she looked ready to take on Bennett, his thugs and the entire police force of Paris.

Tony felt as if a fist had clenched his heart and then let it go. "Sam, you're beautiful," he whispered, hardly aware of what he was saying.

Passion unfurled within her, sending her into Tony's warm embrace.

"Sam, you're so sweet."

His mouth came down on hers. She savored the scent of him, his softness, but then he pulled away.

"If only we had time."

Sam closed her eyes, swallowing her disappointment. She knew he was right, but she relished the lassitude that felt almost as profound as the aftermath of love.

Tony drove out of the parking lot, keeping to little-used alleys and side streets until they reached the *autoroute* that would carry them to Charles de Gaulle Airport. There was no sign of pursuit.

"I'll phone the hotel about the car," Tony said as he found a parking spot. "They'll get somebody to pick it up."

Their flight was already being called when they entered the busy terminal. A short time later they were taxiing down a runway.

LONDON GREETED Sam and Tony with stormy clouds and gusts of rain that beat on the windows of the double-decker bus they took into the city.

"As soon as we get home, we're going to have to see Maurice St. Clair," Tony said as the bus negotiated streets crowded with Saturday shoppers.

"I don't understand why he wants to see me," Samantha said. "Who is he, anyway?"

Tony hesitated, then said softly, "I'll tell you, but this is in the strictest confidence. He works for the Canadian government."

"The government?" Sam echoed. "I thought you told me he was a rebel in your university."

"He was, but it seems he left that behind a long time ago. He's a completely respectable civil servant now. He's investigating Dubray."

"But he met with him. Wouldn't Dubray have suspected anything?"

Tony laughed softly. "My dear innocent, that's the secret of expert investigation. You make business deals with the investigatee. Throws him off the scent. Skulking around, putting a tail on people, things like that make people suspicious."

"What's he investigating Dubray for? That business that got him fired from city hall?"

"Sam, I don't know. I certainly didn't expect Maurice to tell me. And he doesn't want anyone to know he's anything other than an ordinary businessman."

Sam nodded. "He's not investigating Bennett, as well, is he?"

Tony shrugged. "As far as I know, Bennett hasn't done anything that warrants investigation. At least, if he has, no one's found out about it. Nor about any association he had with Germain. The incident you witnessed might be the only time they met in person. That makes you dangerous to him."

Sam remembered with a chill Bennett's words about precarious positions. "He's up to something, Tony. I know it. And it's to do with politics and Paul Messier. I think he'd like him to become prime minister."

Tony scowled darkly. "High hopes."

After hearing the determined, almost fanatical tone of Bennett's words that afternoon, Sam couldn't quite laugh off the idea as completely preposterous. "That's what I thought. The present prime minister is young and vigorous, hardly likely to step down even if he were defeated in an election. And Messier would have to become federal party leader first."

"Money, a lot of money in the right places. Also having you on their side as Bennett's wife wouldn't hurt. Even political supporters increase their own and their candidates' credibility if they project the right image."

"Tony, you know it's not that simple. There are laws about political contributions. And none of the present party leaders look about to resign."

"Enough money could dig up something that could force a resignation. Nobody's past is completely clean. Or if they were to die—"

An icy chill ran up Samantha's spine. Was that what Bennett had in mind? To kill in order to open up Messier's opportunities?

Assassination. The word struck Tony's mind with the same velocity. The conference would present an almost irresistible temptation to would-be assassins. And that would certainly shake up the political hierarchy in Canada.

Since the new date had been determined, the organizers had received the usual veiled threats from anonymous sources. Although nothing was dismissed out of hand, the threats were treated as a familiar annoyance. They were investigated, but always proved to be hoaxes.

Maurice had hinted at deeper trouble, but again had produced nothing to back it up. This business with Bennett Price put the matter in an entirely different light.

Tony took Samantha by the shoulders, his grip hard and urgent. "Sam there's got to be something we're overlooking. Bennett's got a plan and we can't see it. And it's probably staring us right in our faces. The sooner we talk to Maurice, the better."

Her eyes widened at his sudden agitation. "Yes, but first I need to call James. Maybe he knows if Bennett's had anything to do with Dubray lately. My aunt's reaction when I mentioned his name was jarring, to say the least."

"I THINK it would be safer if you stayed with me for a few days," Tony said when they reached Victoria Station.

And, as Tony had pointed out earlier, Bennett knew where she lived. After the kidnapping attempt, who knew how far he would go to hush her up? She was safer away from there until they knew more and could formulate a plan of action.

She made only one condition. "We have to go over to my flat later and feed Bagheera. He must be missing me."

Once in Tony's house Sam put through a call to James Michaels.

"Sorry to bother you at home again, James," she said without preamble. "But there are a few things I need to know. Have you ever heard of a man named Maurice St. Clair?"

She could hear the humming of the transatlantic line as the silence lengthened. "Sorry, Sam," he said at last. "Doesn't ring a bell."

Sam looked across at Tony. "I guess it doesn't matter anyway. Now, do you remember the case of Robert Dubray, the man who resigned from city hall under a cloud? Do you happen to know what he did that caused him to lose his job?"

"I can't say that I do, Sam. But if you give me a little time, I can find it out for you. What's your number there?"

For an instant she hesitated. Hiding had become second nature to her. She shrugged. If Bennett knew where she was, it would be ridiculous to hide from James, a man she trusted impeccably. "It's in London. At the moment I'm staying with a friend." She recited the number.

"I'll call back as soon as I can."

"Well?" Tony said when she hung up.

"He's never heard of St. Clair, but he's going to check on Dubray."

Tony let out a long sigh. "Okay." He got up and walked to the phone. "I'll give Maurice a call, tell him we'll be by later."

"Yes, it shouldn't be long before James gets back to me."

Crossing her arms, Sam began to pace about the room. "I wonder what Bennett's up to," she mused aloud when Tony had finished his call.

Tony sat back in his chair next to a window overlooking the courtyard. "Politically? Or with you?"

"Both. Why did he try to kidnap me? He knows I'm not a pushover. At least he should by now."

"Obviously he thought he could put some kind of pressure on you. Sam, would he be able to gain control of Smith Industries through you?"

"I don't see how. I've got controlling interest."

Tony closed his eyes. "Okay, but is it possible that he could make your marriage look real, give people the idea everything was okay between you? Your aunt wants to believe that. Maybe others would, too. And is it also possible that he could make you look somehow incompetent so he could gain control over your shares?"

"Tony!" Sam wasn't sure whether to laugh or rage at his preposterous scenario. "That sort of thing only happens in Gothic novels and silent movies."

Tony shook his head. "Don't be too sure. Everything that's happened lately—they haven't hurt you, but they've certainly made you nervous. You've gone to the police, who insist there's not enough evidence. Much more and they're going to dismiss you as a crackpot. Sam, maybe that's what Bennett wants."

All levity fading, Sam stared at him. Was that possible?

The phone rang. Without thinking, she snatched it up.

"Samantha, I found out about Dubray."

"Good." She exhaled sharply. "Did he use his influence to get Bennett contracts?"

"No."

James sounded momentarily startled.

"No, nothing like that. He was embezzling money."

"Is that all?" Interesting though the information was, Sam didn't see how it connected to the present situation.

"No, it's not all. Apparently Dubray was also suspected of leaking security information to the wrong people."

"But Dubray didn't even go to jail. We checked the newspapers and they said the charges were dropped."

"Yes. He replaced the money he embezzled."

Replaced the money? An awful suspicion suddenly took form. Bennett and Dubray. "How much was it?" As if she didn't know the answer.

"One and a half million dollars."

Sam clutched the phone as if it would save her from the quicksand that had formed under her feet. Exactly the amount she had lent Bennett a week before the canceled wedding.

She took a deep breath, holding the anger at bay. "What about the security thing?"

"It appears he came up with some story about mixed-up documents. Without definitive proof, they couldn't make the charges stick."

And Dubray got off free and clear, perhaps solely thanks to Bennett.

James's mellow voice interrupted her troubling speculations. "Interesting that you should be in London and ask about Dubray. A conference he'd be attending has been rescheduled for London, this week. The news has just been released. The French reps were quite put out last time it was canceled, so it was considered politic to hold the conference on neutral ground. Originally it was to have taken place in Montreal."

"Is that all you have, James?"

"That's all. Oh, except for one thing. After your father died, his secretary found some items marked personal, in his office safe. I thought you'd like to have them, but you'd gone. Would you like me to mail them to you?"

Sam had long accepted the reality of her father's devotion to his work. He hadn't even kept a photo of her or her late mother on his desk. But perhaps there had been something, after all. "Sure, James," she said, surprised that her voice shook. "I'll give you the address." She recited the number and street.

"Good," James said. "I'll send it by the most expedient method. Samantha, any chance of you coming home?"

When this is all over, she thought, feeling suddenly depressed. *When we figure it out.* "Soon, James," she said. "Soon."

She hung up the phone and faced Tony. "Something's upset you," he said with the intuitive sensitivity she'd learned to expect from him. "Tell me."

He held out his arms, making her smile briefly. Even though there was room for her in the large chair, she forced herself to refuse the comfort he offered. She had to be strong.

Sitting down on the sofa, she related what James had told her, only revealing anger when she came to the part about the loan. "I wondered why he needed the cash when he could have borrowed against his business." She clenched her fists in her lap. "He makes me so mad. He must have known I'd never condone that underhanded business."

"Precisely why he needs you now. Your honest image."

Her mouth turned down at the corners. "Sure. Tony, that conference. It can't be a coincidence that Dubray is here just now, can it?"

"That's what's been worrying me all along." Looking distinctly uncomfortable, Tony shifted in his seat. "Of course, no one knew Dubray was here until you pointed it out. And Maurice was very close-mouthed about him. He didn't tell me why he was investigating the man. Dubray was supposed to be staying only for the architects' convention, but it ended several days ago and he's still in the hotel. That's when we began to wonder if he was staying for the trade conference."

Sam stared at him. "Then you knew about the conference, and you didn't mention it."

"I wasn't allowed to, especially since the Regal Arms is hosting it. And you weren't involved, even if you did spot Dubray. But as Maurice pointed out to me the other night, you might be useful to have on our side. We're going to have to rethink everything. Nothing can go wrong this time. The conference is important, perhaps even critical to Canadian-French relations."

"Oh? How important?"

Tony shifted in his chair, leaning forward and clasping his hands between his spread knees. "So important that the identities of some of those attending is still under wraps. Rumor has it that it may involve the top leaders of both countries. We've got rooms reserved for some of the delegates, and some suites left open for anonymous persons."

Sam's eyes widened. "Is it possible that Bennett is planning to do something to disrupt the conference?"

"I've been wondering about that, too, ever since you told me about Bennett. But with the security they're instituting, I don't see how. He wouldn't be allowed within a mile of the hotel."

Sam jumped up. "Tony, don't you see? A bomb or an assassination. Death or scandal, it wouldn't matter. Bennett referred to 'precarious heights.' That would certainly topple somebody from there." Half-defiantly, she fixed her eyes on him, but he didn't laugh.

"You know, Sam, maybe that's not as farfetched as it sounds." Getting up, he pulled her to her feet. "Let's go see Maurice."

Chapter Thirteen

Maurice St. Clair had a suite on the fourth floor of the Regal Arms. To Samantha's surprise, Inspector Allen sat on the leather chair in the sitting room.

"So nice to see you again, Miss Smith," he said with a warm smile. "It was kind of you to be willing to get involved in this desperate situation."

St. Clair walked in from the adjoining bedroom. "Oh, you're here, Tony. Sit down."

Tony introduced Samantha.

St. Clair smiled and held out his hand. "I'm so relieved. Your name really isn't Agatha." She smiled, noting his grip was firm, engulfing. "Tony's a lucky man."

"Thank you," Sam murmured, discreetly pulling at her hand. His smile didn't waver as he let go, but an odd, calculating expression seemed to pass through his eyes. It was gone so quickly Sam thought she must have imagined it. Not knowing what was expected of her, she felt jittery enough to imagine goblins hiding in the closet.

As soon as they were seated, St. Clair came straight to the point. "Samantha—first names are simpler, aren't they?—what do you know about Robert Dubray?''

"Only what I've read in the papers and what I heard today. He's an embezzler, and a traitor.''

St. Clair nodded. "I understand you saw Dubray last March under rather unusual circumstances. Could you tell me about it?''

Samantha looked at Inspector Allen. "I told the inspector the whole story. Didn't he tell you?''

"I'd like to hear it in your own words. Please.''

"Okay.'' In a quiet, emotionless voice she related everything she'd seen.

When she finished, St. Clair sat for a long moment lost in thought. "You don't have any idea what they were talking about?''

"No. I told you, it's a large house. They were only there a short time.''

He nodded. "Anything else?''

"Yes. The embezzled money. I think Bennett gave Dubray the funds to pay it back. The time factor seems to confirm it.''

St. Clair pursed his lips, making no comment on this. "And you have no idea why Germain was there.''

"None at all. I'm sorry I can't be more helpful, but maybe if you told me what you expected of me... What's this all about?''

St. Clair looked at Inspector Allen, who nodded faintly. He turned back to Samantha. "Dubray is considered a security risk. Aside from the leak that was traced to him last spring, we found out he used the money he stole to support a radical group that wants an independent Quebec. They've been involved in several demonstrations calling for a pure French Canada and no Canadian ties with France. Some of their confrontations with the law got quite ugly. We're afraid they might try to disrupt the conference here."

"But I really don't know anything, except that Bennett also favors an independent Quebec. He's supporting a politician named Paul Messier."

St. Clair frowned thoughtfully. "We'll check it out. It might take a while, though, especially if he did it anonymously. And we don't have much time. As for Paul Messier, he has achieved a certain popularity. But I wouldn't worry about him. He's innocuous enough."

"But will he remain that way, with Bennett behind him?" Sam persisted.

"It's not important. We have to see that this conference goes off according to plan. Then we'll worry about Price and Messier." He steepled his fingers and gazed into her face. "Samantha, I'm working with the police and the RCMP, who will be arriving in a day or two to coordinate security arrangements. I'd like you to be in on it. You know Price. You might recognize some of the people who work for him. Although we're checking out all employees concerned, it's still possible for somebody to infiltrate with false identification."

He paused and threw Tony a low-key smile. "I'm sure Tony will appreciate your help." Then he got to his feet, indicating the meeting was over. "Thank you all for coming. Tony, don't forget our meeting tomorrow."

"DOES HE REALLY WANT my help, or does he just want me where he can keep an eye on me?" Samantha said in a disgruntled tone as she and Tony walked home. She shivered, drawing her coat collar around her neck.

The rain had subsided, but the wind had the bite of autumn.

They had stopped at Sam's flat, where everything appeared as usual. Bagheera had met them on the fire escape and they'd put out a fresh supply of food for him.

"I don't think the information I gave him was anything new."

"Probably it wasn't," Tony agreed. He gave her hand a reassuring squeeze. "But he's right, you know. You do know Bennett and his people, and we need you on-site."

"What's to stop Bennett from hiring somebody new?"

"Nothing, I suppose." He stopped and pulled her close to put a shielding arm around her shoulder. "Look, Sam, it's all speculation. We've got no evidence that Bennett is even aware of the conference."

"I know," Sam said, her voice muffled against his coat. "That's what makes it frustrating. But the way he talked about government leaders gives me a bad feeling. Bennett can be ruthless."

Tony let her go and they resumed walking. "But there's no reason even to question him. As far as anybody knows he has nothing to do with the conference. He's certainly not on the guest lists. Bennett's never been in trouble with the law, at least nothing that can be proved. On the surface he's an exemplary citizen. And here he's a foreigner. The police have to be careful about making a false arrest. They don't want an international incident."

"That means," said Sam, "that the pressure is on us to keep our eyes open."

Tony took out his key and unlocked the mews gate. "And the security staff." He stepped aside, admitting Sam, then carefully relocked the gate.

"Some of the delegates are staying at the Regal Arms, aren't they?" Sam asked as they walked across the courtyard. "Which ones?"

"Some of the Canadians." They entered Tony's town house, and Sam breathed in the welcome warmth. "But they've also provided some of their own security. Several of the security staff have already arrived. Parker has been complaining. He sees their stringent checks as a comment on his meticulous management."

"They're already preparing?" Sam realized at once that the elaborate procedures confirmed the attendance of more than low-level diplomats. "Which reps are staying there?"

"The Quebec premier and his staff." Tony took her coat and hung it up. "The federal cabinet minister involved is staying at a different hotel as a precaution, as are some of the other delegates. After what happened with Mrs. Thatcher a few years ago when her hotel was bombed, they're not taking any chances."

Sam let out a long whistle. "But this isn't a volatile situation, is it?"

"It could be. There are people who feel very strongly about some of the issues." Tony gestured her to a seat. "Do you want coffee?"

When Sam shook her head, he sat down. "Sam, after the demonstrations last spring about fishing rights and the breach of security, which they traced to Dubray, they're being doubly careful."

A strange feeling that Tony had known more about the situation than she dawned on her. "You mean you suspected Dubray before we talked about him?"

Tony's brow lifted in surprise. "Actually, no. You drew our attention to Dubray. And to Bennett. Your conclusions led us to wonder if there was a connection, especially since Dubray's here. Of course, it may have no significance at all. He hasn't been in any position of any power since he was ousted. In any case he's scheduled to leave in a couple of days. He'll be gone before the delegates arrive."

"I don't like it." Sam couldn't shake off a feeling of dread. And the fact that her money had been used to get Dubray off the hook. "I wonder if Bennett's planning to pay me back."

"I'd say he's planning on paying you back for something," Tony said darkly. He leaned forward earnestly. "Sam, promise me you'll be careful, at least until the conference is over. By then the pressure should be off. If nothing happens, then we can see Bennett again, together, and find out what he wants."

Sam gave a nervous laugh. "Do you think he'll tell us?"

Tony's mouth tightened into a grim line. "We'll see."

"THIS REALLY IS a bore," Samantha muttered late Sunday afternoon after hours of checking lists of hotel and catering staff against references and security clearance files.

"I know," said Marcia, Tony's secretary, as she brought in another armful of files and dumped them on the desk.

Sam buried her face in her hands and groaned. She'd be there until midnight.

"Chin up," Marcia said with a smile. "We're all in the same boat. We're working on Sunday."

"Tony's still in his meeting, is he?"

"Yes, and it looks as if it's going to be a while yet. I heard they'd sent out for sandwiches."

Sam stood up and reached for her purse. "I think I'll take a break and go down for some coffee. Coming?"

"No. But thanks, anyway. I'd better hold the fort here."

Downstairs the lobby was quiet. The desk clerk who had the morning shift looked up as Sam passed by on her way to the coffee shop. "Oh, Miss Smith, there was a package for you. If you want to pick it up, security should be finished with it by now. It's in the manager's office."

A package? Samantha frowned. Who would be sending her a package? Who would know she was working here today?

As soon as she pushed open the door of the manager's office she knew something was wrong. Half a dozen men, Tony among them, looked at her, their faces set in grave lines. On the desk before them lay a brown paper package about the size of a shoe box.

Tony immediately walked over to her and took her in his arms. "Samantha, we're waiting on the bomb squad. It looks as if somebody sent you a present."

Maurice St. Clair and another stern-faced man, who was introduced as Bob Green, chief of security, began firing questions at her. "Miss Smith—" no more friendly "Samantha," obviously "—Miss Smith, who would want to harm you?"

Sam shivered violently. "I don't know," she cried, tears pressing against her closed eyelids. "It could be my ex-fiancé. My only proof is that he tried to kidnap me in Paris."

The men looked at one another. "Do you know where he's staying?"

"No, I don't."

Tony stroked her back, alarmed at the tremors coursing through her. "I checked with the major hotels in the city. He's not at any of them. He may have a flat of his own."

"Get somebody to check on it," Green barked to one of the other men.

"And I'm taking you home, Samantha. You'll be safer there. A cop's been assigned to guard the gate."

EXHAUSTED AND OVERWROUGHT, Samantha slept nearly around the clock. But in the morning, she walked into Tony's kitchen with a stiff spine and a determined look on her face.

He glanced up from the toast he was buttering, his concern evaporating with a broad smile. "I see you're ready to fight back."

"You bet," she declared, pouring herself a mug of coffee. "Did they find out what was in the package? Was it a bomb?"

"Yeah, but it wasn't much of a bomb. It was designed to make a lot of noise but not create much damage."

Sam scowled as she bit into the slice of toast Tony set before her. "Bennett's behind this."

"You don't know that, Sam."

"Don't you see, Tony? Everything that's happened has been scary, but none of it really dangerous. He wants something, but he doesn't want to hurt me."

"Not yet," said Tony soberly. "I've been thinking about those prenuptial arrangements you told me about."

"So have I. If he could validate our marriage, that would give him a certain legal interest in my business affairs. Then, if I looked to be incompetent, he could gain control of my family assets."

Tony nodded. "Maybe to the point of taking over Smith Industries." Walking around the table, he tilted her face up to his and kissed her. His mouth tasted of coffee and sweetness and incipient desire. "Sam, I think it's better if you don't come to the hotel today."

"Why not, Tony? You said yourself you needed the extra help."

"I don't know how safe it is. Sam—"

She stood, the abrupt movement upsetting her coffee mug. "Are you ordering me, Tony?"

Bewildered by the sudden chill that stabbed him, he stared at her and raised his hands. "I hope I won't have to, Sam."

"Then don't," she snapped, hating herself but unable to stop. The tension of the past few days had taken its toll. Her reactions were hair-trigger, forged by stress rather than logic. "Tony, I don't take orders from anyone. Is that perfectly clear?"

Tony looked taken aback, his face registering a mixture of embarrassment and perplexity. "Sam, I didn't . . ."

"Men never do," she informed him succinctly.

She whirled around, but before she could take a step, he grabbed her by the shoulders. "Let me go." She struggled free of his grip. "Tony—"

"Listen to me, Sam." The look in his eyes warned her not to argue, yet she could see fire beneath the anger. And traces of the tenderness he'd always shown her. Her indignation died. This was Tony. His hands had never given her pain; his gentleness helped mend her dreams.

She might even love him; the emotion that flooded her was too new, too powerful to name clearly. Still, she wouldn't cave in. "I'm coming with you, Tony."

He conceded with ill-grace, throwing up his hands. "Okay, but don't be long."

To SAMANTHA'S SURPRISE Aunt Olivia phoned shortly after lunch. She sounded her usual ebullient self. "When I didn't get an answer at your flat, I thought you might be with Tony. Samantha, I'd like to say I'm sorry the weekend was spoiled. I wouldn't want there to be hard feelings between us."

The special love she'd always felt for her aunt returned. "Neither would I, Aunt Olivia."

"I only did what seemed best, Samantha. I thought you'd be happy to see Bennett again. After all, you were friends before your engagement."

A slight stretching of the truth, Sam thought, but she let it pass. "It's over now," she said, knowing it wasn't.

"I found the quaintest little pub," Olivia went on to say. "Since I'm leaving soon, I thought we could meet for a drink. I've got something to give you."

Sam suppressed a shiver. She'd had enough of surprises. "Not Bennett again, I trust."

"Samantha, I said I was sorry. But it does involve Bennett indirectly. He gave me a bank draft for the money he owes you."

"The money?" Sam repeated, stunned. "He's paying back the money?" She'd been prepared to kiss the money goodbye and consider it a cheap way to rid herself of Bennett.

"Yes. He said something about balancing the books."

"You're sure he wants me to have the money?" she asked, dumbfounded.

"Of course I'm sure," Olivia said impatiently. "He was very insistent. Can you make it, Samantha?"

"Yes, I'll come," Sam said, quelling her misgivings. "Where is this pub?"

"Near the Tower Bridge. It's simple, only one underground line."

"But why don't we meet at the Grosvenor and go together?" Sam asked.

"Because I've another appointment first. Can you make it, Samantha, say sixish?"

Sam nodded. "I'll be there."

"Good. Oh, and Samantha, I may be a little late. Wait for me, won't you?"

"I will."

Samantha immediately dialed the meeting room where Tony had set up operations with the security personnel.

Tony, as expected, gave her an argument.

"I'll come with you."

She heard voices in the background.

"Damn it, I can't. Can you phone her back and make it a bit later?"

"I can't. She's not at her hotel. Don't worry, Tony. I'll be fine."

"Okay." He sighed gustily. "What's the name of that pub again, in case I have to send out a search party?"

She told him and waited until he wrote it down.

"By the way, Sam," he added in an almost absent-minded tone, "Dubray has checked out of the hotel. Left this morning."

Tony faded and Samantha could hear him bark orders. Then he returned.

"And the special RCMP arrived with a contingent of plainclothes London police. A mosquito couldn't sneeze without someone recording it in a log."

OLIVIA WAS LATE. When Sam reached the pub at a quarter after six, her aunt hadn't arrived yet. Sam found a table where she could wait, not an easy task in the busy, noisy bar. At the barmaid's second sweep by the table, Samantha ordered a lemonade. She wanted to stay alert. But that proved fruitless. After half an hour, wishing she'd asked Tony to meet her, she ordered a sandwich. She managed to stretch that out, but finally deciding Olivia must have changed her mind, she pushed aside her plate.

The chair scraped on the stone-tiled floor as Sam got up. The room seemed to tip for a moment, and she clutched the back of the chair, shaking her head to clear it.

The barmaid walked up to the table, concern on her face. "Are you all right, miss?"

Sam pressed her fingers against the bridge of her nose. The dizziness was passing, although her stomach felt distinctly queasy. "I think so." She forced a smile. "Must have gotten up too fast."

"You're Miss Smith, aren't you?" the young woman asked. "The caller described you well. We can't let customers receive calls here, but I took the message. It sounded urgent. Your aunt had to change her plans, something about an interested party too close for comfort. Does that make any sense?"

Bennett, Sam thought, her stomach executing a slow, sickening roll. "Yes, I understand."

The woman sucked on the end of her pen. "She says she'll wait for you in Pickle Herring Street. It's not far. She said to look for a gray Mercedes."

Sam flexed her neck, a curious numbness creeping into her body. Her thoughts were sluggish. Meeting her aunt was risky, especially if Bennett had followed her. On the other hand, maybe Olivia had changed the meeting place to throw Bennett off. If only she could think clearly.

Her stomach made another slow turn and she pressed her hand to her waist, fighting the wave of nausea. She felt as if she were coming down with flu.

She made a decision. If she saw anything suspicious, she could always get Olivia's chauffeur to drive off. "Okay," she said, shivering as a chill ran over her skin. "Could you tell me how to get there?"

Chapter Fourteen

Pickle Herring Street was deserted. Rust-brown ware-houses bordered the street, and the creeping twilight leached out the color even more. On the river a ship's horn sounded a sonorous, lonely note.

Sam passed a vacant lot clogged with weeds, her heels clicking on the concrete sidewalk. They echoed behind her like a ghost's footsteps. The wind cut a path across the open ground, and she shuddered as the cold reached her bones.

Where was Aunt Olivia? Sam glanced at her watch. More than half an hour had passed since she'd left the pub. She scanned the rows of parked cars, her hand again going to her stomach. A cramp stabbed her, making her gasp. After a moment the cramp sub-sided, a deep ache left in its wake.

She resumed walking, stumbling a little as another cramp, sharper than the first, nearly doubled her over. She had to find Aunt Olivia. Or a taxi—not likely to be just passing here.

Then she spotted the pale gray Mercedes parked near the last loading dock. Stepping up her pace, Sam hurried toward it.

Glancing inside, she found it empty. Where was her aunt?

Cold and ill, she decided she needed to rest. Her frantic eyes fell on the gloomy interior of the warehouse. Inside a light burned. Staggering indoors, she was suddenly enveloped in dark.

A grating creak was followed by a thud. Looking up, Sam saw that the double doors had been closed. The light at the back of the warehouse beckoned. "No, don't leave me," she thought she shouted, but she heard the words as a whisper.

Clumsily she got up and headed for the light. Her feet felt as if she were walking through quicksand, invisible mud sucking at her ankles. A dark shadow lay in her path and she wondered if she had the strength to go around it. Suddenly she stumbled, tripping over a shoe. A man's shoe, shiny with polish. For a moment she was distracted from the almost-constant agony that clawed in her stomach. Where had a man's shoe come from? Where was the man?

She saw him. The dark shadow she'd skirted with such difficulty was a body.

Dubray. Dead again. Samantha screamed, and sank into a dense, cold oblivion.

VOICES. They eddied around her in the rise and fall of argument like the wind that had chilled her earlier.

"I tell you we have to get rid of her."

The accent was British, vaguely familiar. If only she didn't hurt so much. It felt as if ten gremlins with hooks were working at her stomach, with ten more with hammers pounding in her head. They were talking, too, a constant buzzing in her ears.

"We can't. It would give the whole game away."

Game. That word again. Everyone was playing games, but no one had explained the rules. *Help me,* she thought, but her vocal cords seemed paralyzed, or the message to shout had gone astray in her brain.

The voices faded or she fainted. She didn't know which, or much care. She wanted only to sleep. If only the bed wasn't so hard...

"SAMANTHA."

The peremptory command broke through the hum in her ears.

"Go away," she mumbled, batting ineffectually at the hands trying to lift her.

"I won't go away."

Tony. She was too tired to know whether she was glad or annoyed that he'd come to her rescue. He spoke again, the sound carrying away from her as he turned toward someone behind him. "Where is that ambulance?"

Sam struggled to sit up. "I don't need an ambulance."

"Well, even if you don't, Dubray does, although it's too late by several hours." Tony tightened his hands on her shoulders. "Sam, what happened here?"

"I don't know." She saw his look of disbelief. "Really, Tony, I don't know. I was supposed to meet my aunt. I heard voices, came in here. Then I found...the body." She shuddered, a clammy sweat beading her skin.

The ambulance's shriek reached their ears as it rounded the corner into the dead-end street. "I have to speak with them," Tony said apologetically.

He had to protect Sam from the flurry of questions the police would ask. As if the thought had summoned him, a plain black car drove up and Allen slowly got out, already fumbling in his pockets for his notepad.

As she had surmised at their first meeting, Inspector Allen was a compassionate man. He took one look at Sam's white face, the shadows of horror in her eyes, and ordered her into the ambulance. "You're not going far, anyway," he said with heavy-handed humor before turning to Tony. "All right, Mr. Theopoulos, what do we have here?"

Tony looked at the ambulance attendants, who were gingerly lifting Sam onto a stretcher. It worried him that she couldn't seem to stand. He'd assumed she'd fainted, but her listlessness made him wonder. "I'd like to go with her to the hospital," he said to Allen.

"This won't take a moment. I know where I can find you if I need you. Just a couple of questions now and you can go with her."

"I WAS DRUGGED?" Sam's incredulous question coincided with the mellow striking of the clock on Tony's mantel. Midnight.

Tony turned away from the table where he'd just recradled the telephone receiver. "Yes, that's what the hospital said. Inspector Allen wants us both down at New Scotland Yard in the morning."

Drugged. Of course. It'd fit in.

Tony sat down next to her and took her hands in his. "You should be in bed, Sam. I should have let the hospital keep you."

"I feel much better. Tony, how did you find me?"

"I went to the pub. You'd already gone. The barmaid told me you'd had a message, that you were supposed to meet your aunt in Pickle Herring Street."

Thank God for what she had sometimes considered Tony's overprotectiveness, Sam thought. If he hadn't found her, she might still be lying on the cold warehouse floor. Next to...

Tony must have felt the trembling that racked her body. "Don't, Sam. Don't belabor it. It's done."

"How did Dubray die?" she queried.

"I asked, but Allen said he was waiting for the autopsy report. There may have been a motive, however. Dubray phoned me at the Regal Arms last evening just before the package arrived. He didn't give his name, but I recognized his voice. He warned me there would be a disruption of some kind at the conference, that someone might die. Those were his words. Then he hung up. If someone found out he'd warned us, that might be why he was killed."

"Are they taking this threat seriously?"

"Of course. They're beefing up security even more. Even though the call was technically anonymous, Dubray's death gives it authenticity."

Sam's head was befogged with fatigue. "Am I a suspect?"

Tony stared at her. "A suspect?" A bitter laugh burst from his lips. "Sam, how could you be a suspect? I saw them load Dubray on the stretcher. He'd been dead for hours. Sam, this needn't have happened. If I'd been with you—"

"I was supposed to meet Aunt Olivia," she said, gripping Tony's hands, her nails digging into his skin. "Tony, she must be frantic. I have to phone her."

Tony watched with troubled eyes as she dialed the number of the Grosvenor. Sam seemed so trusting, but he wondered whether Olivia had led her into a trap. Sam had mentioned the gray Mercedes as the ambulance had driven them away, but he'd seen no sign of it on the street.

"Aunt Olivia—" Sam broke off and held the phone a safe distance from her ear.

Tony could clearly hear Olivia's first question. "Samantha, why didn't you meet me?"

"You were late. I waited, then I got a message to meet you—"

"I know I was late," Olivia interrupted. "I'm sorry. I was delayed at my previous appointment. But I didn't send any message, Samantha."

"You didn't?"

"No, I didn't."

Sam closed her eyes, rubbing the renewed ache in her temples. "Then I wonder who did."

"Samantha, are you all right? You sound strange."

Sam loosened her fingers, which had been gripping the phone painfully. "I feel strange, Aunt Olivia," she admitted, without the least intention of elaborating. "When are you leaving? Perhaps you could mail me the item we discussed, since we won't be seeing each other."

"I'm staying on for a few more days," Olivia said. "I may be needed for the trade conference."

"You didn't mention that."

"It hadn't come up. I received a call today from the organizers, who asked if I'd lend a hand, since one of the regular staff canceled. So we may have time together, after all."

"Since you'll be staying, I'll give you a call, Aunt Olivia." Sam wasn't in the mood for any more wild-goose chases to out-of-the-way pubs.

"Do that," her aunt said pleasantly. "Good night, Samantha."

"Good night," Sam echoed, knowing exactly how Alice had felt at the Mad Hatter's tea party.

"Well?" Tony asked as soon as she put down the phone.

"She was delayed, and I guess by the time she got there, I was already on my way to Pickle Herring Street." She fixed wide, perplexed eyes on his face. "I wonder who sent that message. Damn it, I don't like being made a fool of."

"You did what you thought best, Sam. Nobody's calling you a fool," Tony said soothingly. She needed sleep. He didn't like the glassy look in her eyes. Dark smudges lay beneath them. "Maybe we'd better leave it until tomorrow, Sam. Your aunt will still be here and we can talk to her then."

He put his arm around her shoulders and carried her to his room. Her brain was fuzzy with the need for sleep, but a question nagged at the edge of her consciousness. Only she couldn't think what it was.

The soft quilt enfolded her like loving arms. She was dimly aware that Tony had undressed and crawled in beside her, fitting his hard, warm body along her back. He wrapped his arm around her waist and tucked her in close. Secure, Samantha slept.

She awoke with a start, the room dark around her. Tony breathed quietly beside her, his mouth against her shoulder.

"Tony, wake up." Sam shook him.

"Wha—?" He lifted his head, shaking his hair out of his eyes. "What's the matter, Sam? It's the middle of the night. Go back to sleep."

"Tony, Bennett must have known about Aunt Olivia's plan." She leaned across him to switch on a lamp. "He'd given her the bank draft for me."

Tony frowned. "Not necessarily, unless he was still there when she made the plan."

"He might have been." An ominous thought hit her. "If that's true, it's very likely Bennett had something to do with Dubray's death." She shook her head, her hair sweeping around her shoulders. "Tony, I hate to think it, but I wonder how deeply Aunt Olivia is involved with Bennett and all this political stuff."

Tony scratched his chin, his fingers rasping over twenty hours of beard stubble. "We're not about to find out here at—" he squinted at the clock "—three in the morning." He yawned. "We'll ask Aunt Olivia when we see her." Brushing his hand lightly over Sam's hair, he settled back down on the pillow beside her. "Sam, how do you feel?"

She looked at him indignantly. "I'm not hallucinating."

Tony laughed, a rumble of enjoyment. "I wouldn't suggest any such thing, Sam. I meant, after last evening. Does your head feel better?"

She shook it and smiled. "Yes, much. Whatever they used doesn't seem to have any lasting effects."

"Didn't want to damage the merchandise."

"You said that once before." Sam frowned at him. "Tony, I'm only incidental in this. If Bennett's paying back the loan, doesn't that prove he's not after my money?"

"I guess." Although Tony pretended agreement to reassure her, his doubts remained. Compared to Sam's total fortune, one and a half million dollars was a paltry sum. He turned off the light. "Sleep now, Sam. We'll sort it out tomorrow."

THE IMMINENT ARRIVAL of the trade conference delegates made Tony's presence at the Regal Arms vital, especially after yesterday's threat. Reluctant though he was to leave Sam, he went to his office in the morning. "Stay here," he admonished as he kissed her goodbye at the door. "You'll be safe."

Samantha set her jaw. "What about Aunt Olivia? I need to talk to her."

"The telephone. Besides, Inspector Allen, once he has the autopsy report, may want to talk to you again. It's better if you stay available."

"Don't smother me, Tony. I refuse to be a prisoner."

Tony made an impatient sound. "Sam, nobody's making you a prisoner. But until we find out what Bennett is up to, you have to be careful." He lifted her chin with his forefinger and dropped a kiss on her nose.

Sam gave him a reluctant smile. "I'm not a child."

He ran his eye over her face. It showed maturity, character and a stubbornness that was bound to cause him many more sleepless nights. "No, you're not. Sam, please stay here. I'll call you later, and I'll be home as soon as I can."

AN HOUR LATER Samantha walked into the lobby of the Regal Arms. The desk clerk gasped. "Mr. Theopoulos said you wouldn't be in today."

"As you can see, I am. Would you please tell me where Olivia Smith is working?"

The man picked up the phone. "One moment, please."

Sam had put a call through to the Grosvenor as soon as Tony had left. Aunt Olivia wasn't going to be in for the rest of the day; she could be reached at the Regal Arms.

"Just go down that hall and to the right, Miss Smith. You'll find her." He hesitated. "Shall I tell Mr. Theopoulos you're here?"

Sam threw him a bright smile. "I'm sure he'll hear of it soon enough."

The man looked faintly bewildered. "Quite, miss."

"By the way, do you happen to know whose idea it was for my aunt to work here today?"

"I think one of the Canadian representatives suggested it. Some of them have arrived."

"Thanks."

Samantha strode down the hall. The room she entered was a scene of chaos: a dozen makeshift desks, numerous filing cabinets and the sound of phones ringing incessantly. Aunt Olivia was installed in the far corner, scribbling on a legal-size notepad.

"Hello, Aunt Olivia," Sam said coolly as she reached the desk.

Olivia looked up, surprised. "Why, hello, Samantha. I thought you were resting today."

"I'm fine. Aunt Olivia, who knew I was meeting you last night?"

For a split second Olivia looked unguarded. Then she gave a quick laugh. "Why, the hotel did. I left my itinerary there in case someone needed to contact me. You see, I was out for most of the day."

"So Bennett could have found out where I was."

"I suppose so," Olivia said slowly. "But why would he? If he'd wanted to see you, he could have met you himself and given you the money in person."

Before Sam could answer two hands closed around her waist. She spun around, finding herself looking into Tony's face. "Hi, Tony. I thought you might need me."

His eyes narrowed and he compressed his lips as if he wanted to be angry with her. Then he relaxed. "You win, Sam. But be warned, it's the same boring stuff as yesterday."

"That's fine. Better than waiting around for something to happen."

BY MIDAFTERNOON she was tired. She rubbed her temples, a headache coming on. The door to the small office where she worked opened and she looked up gratefully as Tony marched in.

"Good news, Sam. I think they're finally taking our suspicions seriously. I had a call from New Scotland Yard. They've hauled Bennett in for questioning."

Somehow the news seemed rather anticlimactic. "Does that mean they'll hold him until after the conference, just to make sure nothing happens?"

"I doubt it. Not unless they charge him with something." He leaned down and scrutinized her face. "Sam, I think you've done enough. You look pale."

"A walk in the fresh air would help. I'd like to stop by my flat and give Bagheera something to eat."

Tony frowned. "He managed before he adopted you. Sam, I don't know about you walking on the streets on your own—"

She squeezed his hand, touched by his concern. "Tony, I'll be fine. If Bennett is with the police, he'll be tied up for hours. It'll be perfectly safe."

After her surprising appearance in the hotel that morning, Tony knew it was useless to argue unless he had some very heavy ammunition. "Okay, Sam. But take a taxi."

Outside, the sunlight spilled over the old brick buildings and on her back. Taxi? She'd walk it. Throwing back her shoulders, she strode down the street, her headache already a vague memory.

HER FLAT APPEARED undisturbed. She wrinkled her nose as she inhaled the stuffy air. Opening a window at the front, she let in a breeze already scented with autumn.

In the kitchen she threw open the fire escape door, delighted to see Bagheera preening on the little landing. "There you are, cat. I was beginning to worry."

"Not half as much as I," he seemed to say as he wound himself around her legs, purring ecstatically.

She rinsed out his food dish and filled it; then, taking up her mail, she went into the bedroom. Tony had asked her to be his guest at the trade conference banquet and she had to scour her closets for suitable wear. But examining her mail first, she noticed the last fat envelope. She turned it over curiously, her heart jumping as she saw the Smith Industries logo. The items James had promised to send. As she ripped the envelope open, papers and photographs tumbled out.

With mixed feelings she sorted through them. Several photos were of her as a child, with her mother. There were also transcripts of school reports. She hugged the papers to her chest for an instant, closing her eyes as tears threatened to spill over. Her father *had* cared. He hadn't shown it, especially since she'd grown into an adult, but he had cared.

The last item was a long white envelope. She tore it open and drew out a document bearing the letterhead of the corporate law firm that handled Smith Industries' legal work. Her eyes widened in horror as she ran them over the pages. Although written in lawyers' jargon, she had no trouble understanding the gist.

With trembling fingers she picked up the phone on the bedside table. "Tony, you were right," she said, in a voice gravelly with despair. "Bennett does stand to gain."

"What do you mean, Sam?"

"I just got a document my father had made up before his death. It gives Bennett half of Smith Industries as soon as we marry."

Tony let out a long, low whistle. "No wonder he didn't come after you right away. He figured that if he gave you time, you'd come around. Of course, when you didn't, he had to find you and put on the pressure. Sam, I'm coming over."

A tear escaped and rolled down her cheek. She sniffed. Standing, she pulled open a drawer to find a handkerchief.

A knife.

There, obscenely displayed on a white satin slip, lay a knife. Bloodstains darkened the blade. The last place she'd seen it was in her kitchen drawer.

Her hand fell nervelessly to her side, and she almost dropped the phone. A scream formed in her throat. An image of Dubray's lifeless body flashed into her head. She'd thought him dead months ago. Had the sight of him alive unhinged her mind so that she had fulfilled the memory, made sure he wouldn't come back to life, to remind her of Bennett's duplicity?

Without taking her eyes from the drawer, she backed away, the receiver still in her hand. She could hear Tony calling her. It helped her recover her senses. In one swift motion, she slammed the drawer shut.

"Sam, what was that? Sam, what's happening? Answer me!"

Slowly, as if her muscles had turned to cement, she brought the receiver back to her ear.

"Sam? Is something wrong?"

Sickness rose in her throat. "You might say that." She fought against the cotton in her throat. "Tell me one thing. Did Inspector Allen tell you how Dubray died?"

"Knife wound. Why?"

She closed her eyes. "Tony, there's a big knife here, and it's covered with blood."

She distinctly heard Tony swallow, but when he spoke next his voice was preternaturally calm. "Sam, stay in your flat. Don't touch anything. I'll be right there."

"But you won't be, Miss Smith." A large hand reached around and broke the phone connection. "By the time Theopoulos gets here, you'll be gone."

Chapter Fifteen

Sam felt the blood drain from her face, and looked down curiously. The oxford shoes near her feet were a dead giveaway. It was Jason Wheeler. He'd propped those shoes on her coffee table just a week ago. Now, a self-satisfied smile on his lips, he jabbed the gun he held into her ribs.

Twisting the set of headphones off his head, he spoke briefly into the mouthpiece attached. "It's all right. I've got her."

A fatalism settled into Sam's chest. "That's how you knew where I was and how long I'd be out. You bugged my flat."

"And your phone, dear lady." He lifted the gun and ran the barrel caressingly along her cheek.

Sam flinched. "Then you must have been quite put out when I stayed at Tony's."

Wheeler shrugged, the gun steady on her. "Over there, you were even more ridiculously predictable."

"Who are you working for?" If she was going to die, she wanted to know why.

"Me," Bennett Price said from the bedroom door. "Jason, bring her into the living room. We'll wait for Theopoulos."

She felt cold but, oddly, free. The puzzle was coming together. "I might have known it would ultimately come back to you, Bennett. But why?"

Bennett ran his fingers over her glossy hair in a gesture that might have indicated regret. "So pretty, Sam. I always loved your hair, your skin, your coolness. The princess."

She moved away from him. He was sweating, not offensively, but she smelled the astringent tang of tension on him.

"Why, Bennett?" She leveled her gaze on him.

He smiled cruelly. "If you'd married me for real, you would have understood. Money can buy power. And power is the one thing that gets you respect in the world. It's going to be mine, as soon as I remove a few minor obstacles."

"Like the premier of Quebec."

His expression turned from gloating into hard calculation. "How did you guess that?"

"It was rather obvious, wasn't it? None of the federal leaders are likely to step down. Provincial politics would have given your man, Paul Messier, a nice start, especially in Quebec, which has had more autonomy than the other provinces. But don't get your hopes up, Bennett. Scotland Yard is already suspicious. If someone were to die at the conference, you might find yourself first in the line of suspects."

He gave a harsh laugh. "Not likely, dear Samantha. In this, my reputation is impeccable. Whatever happens won't be connected to me. Or if it is, someone else will take over. Our cause will go on. Besides, Scotland Yard is tied up with Dubray's death, and security for the conference. They've got plenty to keep them occupied." He propelled her into the living room, pushing her down on the sofa as he spoke to Wheeler. "Watch her. I'll check if Theopoulos is coming."

He moved to the window, flicking the curtain aside as he peered out. The day's sunshine had vanished, swallowed up by thick clouds massing in the sky.

As the damp breeze billowed into the room, Sam realized the window still stood open. She dragged in a long breath and formed a plan. "Bagheera," she called.

Entering, the cat swung his head toward her. Gathering his muscles, he leaped up onto her lap. Sam pretended to give him all her attention as she stroked his belly in the spot he liked. Wheeler visibly relaxed as he pulled a chair closer to the sofa and sat down on it.

Sam looked at him. "I suppose it was you doing all those things to frighten me," she said conversationally. "What I don't understand is that if you wanted to kill me, why bother with the other stuff?"

Bennett turned around, answering. "We didn't want to kill you. Only to get you in the right frame of mind."

Sam frowned. "That business with the truck certainly looked real. And dangerous." Her voice rose angrily. "It wasn't fair to involve Tony."

"My dear Samantha," Bennett drawled. "In a war, sometimes bystanders get hurt. You didn't need to get involved with Theopoulos. Anyway, the truck wasn't my idea. That was Dubray's."

"I thought Dubray was dead. That's why I left."

"He wasn't. So you admit you were at the house that day, do you, Sam?" Bennett asked in a silky tone that sheathed naked steel.

"There's no use denying it. Yes. I saw Germain."

"That's why Dubray wanted you dead. He knew it would put an end to everything if he was connected with Germain. As it was, he might have been able to salvage his career, although he was finished at city hall." He nestled his elbow in his palm and tugged at his ear. "Dubray was helpful in finding you. He knew the person who could keep an eye on your bank account. But he got too vindictive, too nervous."

"Yes," Jason Wheeler put in. "He had to be eliminated."

"You killed him." The statement was matter-of-fact, but an icy knot formed in her stomach. If Wheeler had killed once, he'd kill a second time.

"He was becoming a liability," Bennett said. "We had to get him out of the way."

"But why have me find his body?"

Bennett didn't answer, merely smiling as he turned back to the window.

"You'll find out soon enough," Wheeler said. "After they discover the knife in your room, the police are going to think you killed him."

Were they? There was a hole in the premise. But for now she had to stay cool. Bagheera purred and she held on to his fur as if it represented her sanity.

"The old lady got too nosy."

Wheeler's low voice penetrated her thoughts. Sam's eyes popped open. "You killed her. You bastard."

"Cut it," Bennett ordered, without turning around. "Theopoulos just came around the corner. Get ready."

Now was the time. She'd have no other chance. As Wheeler's eyes flicked momentarily toward Bennett, Sam tightened her grip on the cat. "Sorry, cat," she muttered, and threw him at Wheeler.

The man yelled and recoiled. The chair tipped over, catching his legs. Sam was on her feet. She yanked the door open and broke into a run before she heard it slam against the adjacent wall.

Her feet clattered on the stairs as she tore down them. She made it to the second-floor landing before she heard a pursuer panting behind her, shoes falling heavily on the thinly carpeted steps.

"Tony," she yelled, confident her pursuer wouldn't shoot.

Bennett caught up with her on the next landing. He grabbed her around her waist just as Tony walked into the main-floor hall. He stopped dead in his tracks, but his expression gave away nothing. His eyes met Sam's briefly, sending a message that she stay cool. Faint hope swelled in her. Together they might be able to beat this situation.

"One sound and I'll shoot her," Bennett warned, his eyes opaque and deadly. "No, I won't kill her, but she'll wish I had."

A pale gray Mercedes rumbled at the curb. The chauffeur, whom Sam remembered from Paris, sat impassively at the wheel.

"So it was your car that was parked in Pickle Herring Street last evening," Sam said. "Not Aunt Olivia's."

"You didn't even know what kind of a car Olivia had," Bennett said scornfully.

"But the message said to look for a car like this."

"Trusting soul, aren't you?" Bennett's lip curled. "Taking anonymous messages. That wasn't even Olivia who phoned you at the pub to change the meeting. It was Jason."

"Damn," she muttered in useless chagrin. "And I suppose it was Jason who phoned Tony to say you'd been called in for questioning?"

Bennett smiled silkily. "Of course, my dear."

Sam stared at the ugliness that had once been her fiancé. No, he hadn't suddenly grown warts, but she could no longer see the good in his soul. "And you drugged me."

"Just enough in your lemonade to make you feel a little confused, not enough to do any harm. Your story about going to the warehouse didn't make much sense. Now when the police find the knife in your flat, I'd say your credibility will be fairly shattered."

Tony ground his teeth in angry frustration as Bennett manhandled Sam toward the car. He couldn't budge with two guns aimed at them.

Wheeler pulled the car door open. "Get in," Bennett ordered, taking a tighter hold on Sam's arm as he poked the gun into her side. "You first, Theopoulos."

Sam crawled in after Tony, settling down with relief as Bennett let go of her. Tony wrapped his arm around her shoulders, giving her a quick smile that warmed some of the chill from her bones.

Bennett climbed in beside them, while Wheeler ran around the car to climb into the front seat. The driver pressed a button on the dash, electronically locking the doors.

In less than an hour they reached a construction site in the east end. Several hard-hatted workers nodded and Bennett indicated they head for a clump of trailers a hundred yards away. The weapons might be invisible but Sam was conscious of the hard grip Bennett kept on her arm.

Outside a trailer Bennett nodded to a man coming out of it. "Afternoon, Tremblay. Some business to take care of. Please see that we're not disturbed."

"Right, Mr. Price." The accent was French-Canadian.

Bennett was known at the site. The realization slammed into Sam's brain. Then she saw the logo painted on the trailers: Price Enterprises. No wonder Aunt Olivia had said Bennett's business was doing well, if he was involved in this megaproject that would change the face of East London.

Bennett handed Wheeler a ring of keys and waited as he unlocked the door. They strolled into a room furnished with no more than a desk, a filing cabinet and a photocopier. An electric heater warmed the air.

"Sit down, Samantha," Bennett ordered, gesturing toward a straight chair opposite the desk. Finding some rope, he had Wheeler tie Tony down.

Bennett meantime unlocked the file cabinet and took out a folder. Seating himself behind the desk, he placed the file in front of Samantha.

"Okay, Samantha, the games are over. You're going to sign these papers."

She glared at him defiantly. "Why should I?"

"Because if you don't—" he directed a slight nod at Wheeler "—your friend Tony will soon be begging you to."

Before he finished speaking, Wheeler doubled his fist and slammed it into Tony's stomach. Sam felt tears stinging her eyes as Tony grunted in pain and hunched over. Grabbing a handful of Tony's shirt-front, Wheeler pulled him up and landed a second blow to his kidney. Tony turned white but managed to gasp, "Don't do it, Sam."

"Make it easy for him, Samantha," Bennett said with a smile. He extended a pen to her. "Sign the paper."

Sam looked down at the folder. Shocked, she took in the words. "I, Samantha Smith Price, being of sound mind..."

Skipping through the conventional legal phrases, she slid her eyes to the bottom. "I leave my shares of stock in Smith Industries to my husband, Bennett Price, as well as the trust fund from my grandmother...." More legalese. Only the space with her name typed below it remained blank.

She pulled her gaze away from the document, her face tight with anger. "So you're going to get it all, Bennett."

For a second he looked startled, but at once a calculating comprehension crept into his eyes. "Ah, I see you know about my arrangement with your father. He wanted to be sure you married well this time. It was part of the agreement I made with him. Once you sign these papers and the marriage certificate—the date on it coincides with a business trip I took to Europe—no court will be able to dispute my claims."

Her lips would hardly move and she didn't recognize her voice as she whispered, "You planned all along to kill me."

"No, my dear. It wouldn't have been necessary. Look at this other document. You'll see. As soon as we married I would have gotten half of Smith Industries. When you disappeared, I couldn't claim it."

"That's how you covered your ass," Tony retorted. "It always bothered me that the prenuptial agreement seemed so heavily in Sam's favor."

"Shut up," Wheeler snarled, aiming a blow at Tony's head.

Ducking to one side, Tony deflected the worst of it, but Wheeler's fist connected with Tony's shoulder muscle.

"Stop," Sam cried. "You're killing him."

"Not yet." Bennett smiled grimly. "But I'm prepared to if you don't sign. And remember, there are a lots of ways to die."

Sam's eyes skittered from Bennett's face to Tony's. All the color had gone from his skin, leaving it a pasty gray. He looked sick, as sick as she felt.

"Okay, give me the pen."

"Sensible decision, Sam," Bennett said. "You see, that's where you and I differ. I've always found it safer and more profitable not to care about anyone. Too much emotional baggage slows you down."

"What a rotten way to live." Sam stabbed at the paper with the pen. Maybe someone would contest these diabolical documents, and salvage her integrity and her life.

"Maybe," Bennett said complacently. "But if you don't care for anyone, no one can use it as a weapon against you. Emotions have no place with ambition. That was Dubray's weakness. He got soft, too soft for this business. If he'd played along, he could have had a great future."

"A future that ended permanently last night," Tony declared. He glared murderously at Wheeler as the man lifted his gun. "Try it, Wheeler. Another body might not be so easy to explain."

Snarling, Wheeler pulled back his arm to hit Tony once more.

"That's enough, Jason," Bennett said crisply. "He's right, of course. There'll be no murder." His smile turned thin and cruel. "We'll keep you in cold storage, so to speak, for a day or two, and then you'll die in an accident. The tragedy will be a good human interest story. Two lovers going off together, only to die in a flaming car crash."

Turning back to Samantha, he riffled through the papers until he found the one he wanted. "Sign this one, too. It's a letter giving me power of attorney. You know," he added, "the double indemnity clause in our insurance policy will work right into my hands."

As Tony had warned, Sam thought sickly. She looked at Tony, her eyes wide and desperate. The nod he gave her was not so much a gesture of his head as a flicker in his eyes. *Go ahead,* he seemed to be telling her, *we'll undo it later.*

She carelessly scribbled a signature she hoped would be questioned, tossing down the pen when she had dotted the i's and crossed the t's. "There, are you satisfied?"

Bennett eyed her, his smile never fading. "Not really, my dear." He stroked her skin. "But I guess it will have to do."

"Just for the record, Bennett, were you ever in love with me as you said once?" Sam asked with a defiant lilt to her voice.

Bennett's smile died. She could have sworn he looked almost regretful. "You were sweet, Samantha. If I believed in love, I would have felt it for you." He picked up the overcoat he'd taken off. "However, power and money are more important than love, more important than sex or lust, as well."

What a fool. She hadn't known him at all.

Tony coughed, bringing her attention to his pain-clenched face.

"Just how do you think you'll engineer this assassination, Price?"

Bennett laughed. "Who said anything about an assassination?"

"Dubray did. He phoned me and said someone was going to die."

Intense hatred flew across Bennett's face, but then he recovered. "So what? People die all the time, especially those in high places. At a conference as potentially volatile as this one, it would be a superb, dramatic touch, don't you think?"

"The security is tighter than a hangman's noose," Tony said, while his mind raced over possible slipups that might have been made.

"Ah, but that's where the weakness lies. You trust people. When there's enough money available, you find out that anyone can be bought, for the right price." He tapped one perfectly manicured finger on the papers Samantha had signed. "And this will ensure that there's plenty of money. I didn't need Germain, after all."

"Yeah, Germain," Tony said. "Where did he come in, anyway? Did you even bother to look for Sam before he so conveniently died?"

Bennett's lip curled. "Inconvenient is more like it. Germain was going to supply the cash, but when he was killed—not my doing, by the way—that source dried up. Besides, I never liked using him, because if it was found out, I would be blackmailed at best and ruined at worst. Even though I figured Sam would show up sooner or later, I got a private detective to speed up the process."

"Then you didn't need someone to break into poor Mr. Collins's office to get my address, especially with Wheeler already living in my building, spying on me?"

"I needed some of the information in the files," Bennett said. "And it seemed a good idea to keep you on edge. You've already been to the police several times with wild, improbable stories. When you disappear along with Tony, they won't even question it until your bodies are found."

"It won't work, Price," Tony retorted. "It's hardly going to look plausible if I disappear just when the conference delegates are coming to my hotel. In fact, the police may already be looking for me."

"Well, they won't find you." Bennett shrugged into his coat. "You can count on it." He peered out of the dusty window. The pile driver had stopped its pounding. Quiet settled over the construction site as the workers locked up their tools and closed for the day. "A few more minutes and it'll be safe to move you."

Move us where? Samantha wondered with a sickening tug in her stomach. Her eyes met Tony's, and she saw the same bleak dismay in his face that she felt.

Moments passed, punctuated only by the hoot of a barge on the river. Outside, the heavy clouds created a premature twilight.

Then their captors moved. They roughly herded Sam and Tony out of the trailer and pressed them to the edge of the excavation site.

Bennett was forced to untie Tony's hands so that he could clamber down a wooden ladder into one of the pits. His fingers were numb, clumsy on the risers, and he lost his grip once, sliding down several steps toward the bottom. "Get a move on. We haven't got all night," Wheeler barked.

"Leave him alone," Samantha cried. In the bottom of the pit, she sloshed through ankle-deep water and wrapped her arm around Tony's waist.

"I can manage, Sam," he muttered. "Just look after yourself."

"I got you into this."

"No, you didn't," Tony interrupted. "I walked in with my eyes open."

"Knock off the chatter, you two." Wheeler swung his gun meaningfully.

He marched them across the pit to the opposite side, where lumber was piled up for the foundations. One wall was already prepared and it was to this corner that Bennett led them. Here an alcove, probably for an exit stairway, jutted out from the main building. It was lined with wood, ready for the concrete to be poured.

Bennett took hold of a crowbar and began to pull the short planks loose from the narrow end of the alcove, nails shrieking loudly in protest as he pulled them out. In a short time he had cleared enough space for a man to get through.

"In there," he growled.

Tony glared belligerently at Wheeler, and for a moment Sam feared he would attack the man in defiance of the gun being held on them. "Why not kill us now and get it over with?"

"I'd like nothing better." Wheeler tightened his finger on the trigger.

Bennett calmly pushed the gun aside, lifting his own. "We've got preparations to make. I don't want any possibility that anyone will suspect foul play later on. Anyway, Sam, I thought you might enjoy thinking over what you could have had if you'd cooperated.'' He laughed. ''Au revoir. We'll be back in a day or two.''

He pushed them into the opening, signaling Wheeler to hammer the boards back into place. Just before he put in the last board, Bennett added, ''Don't waste any of the time you have left.''

Sam and Tony listened in silence as the slosh of footsteps died away. Enough daylight seeped between the planks that they could see each other. Tony sighed and opened his arms. With a little cry Sam walked into them and held on as tight as she could.

''It's not going to end like this,'' Tony said huskily. ''I won't let it.''

Chapter Sixteen

Sam's teeth chattered. She knew it was stark terror, not the cold. She'd never liked closed-in places, but that consideration faded in the face of another, far more critical one.

No one knew where they were. Even if Tony were missed, as he was sure to be, no one knew where to look to find them. Which meant they could only rely on their own ingenuity to discover a way out of their prison.

"We've got to get out of here, Sam."

At Tony's almost prosaic tone, Sam couldn't help but laugh bitterly. "Yes, but how?"

He held her more closely, wishing he'd stopped to pull on his coat before he'd rushed wildly out of the hotel in answer to Sam's phone call. The suit he wore was little protection against what promised to be a wet, miserable night.

Sam was not much better off in tailored pants topped by a wool sweater that felt fluffy under his hands. The soft fibers were already damp.

"We'll find a way," he said stoutly, wishing he felt as confident as he sounded. "I've no intention of waiting calmly for Bennett to come back and kill us."

He leaned down and set his mouth over hers, gratified when her cold lips stopped trembling and warmed under his. A slow heat uncoiled in his body, awakening a desire he rebuked sternly. There was no time for indulgence. They had to direct all their energy and resources on an escape plan.

Sam pulled free of Tony's arms reluctantly, the desire to stay close to him, where it was warm and safe, almost stronger than the instinct to survive. Her fighting spirit, fragile after weeks of battering, was at its lowest ebb. Yet giving up was unthinkable. "We have to get out," she said. "It's not only our lives that depend on it."

If it hadn't been for the renewed pain in his wrists and hands, Tony would have smiled. Trust Sam to think of the assassination they were powerless to prevent unless they got out in time. Rubbing his fingers, he followed her as she prowled around the enclosure.

One side of their prison appeared to be solid earth. The other walls were covered with planks, old and slimy. The boards of their entranceway were solid and thick, well nailed and reinforced to withstand the weight of wet concrete until it set.

The sides covered with old lumber might be more vulnerable. Tony pulled at a protruding corner, cursing as the wood snapped back and pinched his fingers. "Ouch, damn it."

Sam turned, the concern on her face visible even in the dim light. "What is it, Tony?" She hurried to his side. "You took quite a beating. Is it bad?"

He kneaded his right hand with his left. "My hands. Circulation was cut off too long."

Samantha took both his hands in hers, massaging them gently. As he looked down at her bent head, the courage she had managed to summon made Tony's eyes sting with tears. His mouth tightened with anger. If he got his hands on Bennett . . .

The irony of the thought didn't escape him. His hands were practically useless at the moment. He pulled one free of Sam's capable fingers, clenching it experimentally. A smile broke over his face. "You know, Sam, that's wonderful."

She worked over the fleshy base of his thumb, her hands firm and sure as she manipulated the muscles underlying his skin. "Just let your hand relax. That's it. Let me do the work."

"Where did you learn that? Not by chance, I'd guess."

She bit her lip in concentration, her hair falling forward over her cheeks. "My grandmother suffered from arthritis. I used to rub her hands and her back when she had pain. A friend of mine who's a physical therapist taught me how." Lifting her head, she shook her hair back from her face. "There, that should do it. Flex or shake your fingers now and then, until they feel normal."

Stepping back from him, she stared up at the ceiling, making a little grunt of disgust when she saw the heavy concrete slab. Spider webs festooned the corners. There was no way out of there, unless they could produce a jackhammer and were willing to spend a year or two drilling a hole.

"How long do we have, do you think?"

Tony blinked at her. "Until tomorrow I'd guess, maybe even tomorrow evening if they want to avoid moving us in the daytime. You're taking this remarkably calmly, aren't you?"

She bent over, tapping her fist against a rotting plank at the back of the enclosure. "What do you want me to do, scream and carry on? Hysterics won't get us out of here." Straightening, she tapped the next board. "We have to find a way out. The sooner we get started the better. By tomorrow we'll be awfully hungry."

Tony grimaced at the wet earth floor, puddled with water in low spots. "At least we won't lack for water, although forcing ourselves to drink it may be another matter."

He began to tap the walls, too.

"If we don't find a way out tonight, do you think the work crews would be able to hear us shouting when they come back in the morning?"

Tony shook his head. "I wouldn't count on it. Once the equipment is running, no one will hear a word."

Which meant that ultimately they could rely only on their own wits. Samantha accepted that. There was little else she could do. If she allowed herself to think beyond the moment, she was afraid she would dissolve in ignominious tears.

Her eyes met Tony's, the worry she knew was on her face reflected in his. "There has to be a way out. All the guidebooks say London is riddled with underground tunnels and passages, especially by the river." She gave him a little push. "You start over there. I'll continue here. We'll meet in the middle."

"It's worth a try." He splashed across the small room.

After an hour of minutely going over every inch of the grimy rotting planks, Sam sagged against the wall. "This isn't working, is it? Every place I tap sounds the same. I thought we'd be able to hear a hollow noise if there was a passage behind the walls.''

The light was still strong enough for Tony to see the smudges of dirt and lichen on her cheeks. She had never looked dearer, and he inwardly railed at the injustice of it all. He'd found her only to lose her.

His thoughts must have shown on his face, for Samantha smiled sadly and reached out her hand to him, burying her face in his shirt as he went to her.

"Oh, Tony, it's not fair."

"Not fair at all." He held her close, running his hand up and down her back, feeling the little indentations of her spine through the inadequate sweater. "You're freezing." Taking off his jacket, he draped it over her shoulders, holding it so she could slip her arms into the sleeves. He buttoned the front, overlapping the lapels at the top.

"When we get out of this, Sam, I promise you—" He broke off, emotion tearing at him. Cupping his palms to her face, he kissed her gently on the lips.

Sam smiled at his choice of words. *When.* "You promise what?"

He returned her smile, willing her to hope. "You'll see."

It was so dark by now that they could barely see each other. The construction site was lit by spotlights, but the beam from the nearest one, located on the edge of the excavation, barely reached their prison. Only the cold, rain-laden wind had no trouble reaching them through the minute spaces between the planks.

"You'll catch pneumonia," Sam said as she felt Tony shiver in only his shirt.

He shrugged. "You catch cold from a virus, not a chill. I'll be okay. Come on, Sam, let's get back at it."

The rain had subsided to a soft drizzle that sounded like sinister whispers. Sam tilted her head to listen. "What are those noises?"

"Probably mice. Doesn't mean anything. They tunnel through wood, soil, possibly even brick and concrete."

Sam took an instinctive step closer to Tony. "Mice? Can they get in here?"

Tony's spontaneous laugh echoed around the room. "You stare down Bennett even when he's holding a gun, yet you're afraid of a mouse? Sam, I'm surprised at you."

"Not scared," she declared. "But I don't like little furry things crawling on me, especially in the dark."

"They're hardly likely to do that." A thought struck him. "Sam, check the pockets in my jacket. There might be some matches. We leave packets of them on all the tables in the lobby and I sometimes pick them up."

She groped in the pockets, encountering a folded handkerchief and what felt like an extra tie, sleek and cool. She'd noticed his dislike of ties, how he would rip them off at the end of the day and tuck them in his pocket. "Nothing in the outside pockets."

"There's another inside the jacket. Try that."

The pocket was long and narrow, apparently empty. She reached the bottom and made a sound of satisfaction. "Here they are. Now if we had some dry wood, we could make a bonfire."

"We used to do that every Halloween," Tony mused aloud. "Make a big fire, set off fireworks and toast marshmallows."

He struck a match. As the light flared, something ran over Sam's foot. She uttered a small, involuntary shriek and grabbed Tony's arm, nearly extinguishing the match. "What was that?"

A shadowy form scurried up the farthest plank wall and disappeared. "Probably a rat."

Sam felt herself turn pale. "A rat? There're rats here? Then I'm not closing my eyes all night."

The flame guttered, then steadied. "Look, Tony." She forgot about rats as her voice rose on an edge of excitement. "Look at the flame."

It was pulling definitely to one side, toward them from the plank-covered wall. "That's where the rat disappeared. There must be a hole if there's a strong air flow coming from that direction. Come on, Tony, let's have a look."

The match went out before they reached the corner, but Tony lit another, holding it high.

"Looks the same as the other walls," Sam said skeptically.

The ceiling was low, six inches or so above their heads. Tony reached up to the spot where the rat had gone, groping with his fingertips. "Ah, there's a strong draft here. Put your hand up, Sam. You can feel it."

Gingerly, picturing a pointed furry face and sharp teeth, she did so. Cold air blew steadily. "I'd say it's open behind there," she ventured, hardly daring to raise her hopes. Even if there was a passage, how could they reach it?

"Ouch." Tony dropped the spent match, shaking his singed fingers to cool them. "Sam, up there it's drier because of the air flow. The wood is probably pretty rotten."

"Really? Want me to hold a match while you check it out?"

Tony frowned. "Better save the matches. I'll do it by touch."

As he suspected, the wood crumbled as he tore at it with his fingers. But without tools he only succeeded in enlarging the rat hole so his arm could fit through it. "It is hollow, Sam," he announced. "And cold. I'd say we've hit a tunnel."

"But can we get into it?"

"That's the problem. Sam, let me have the matches. No, wait. I'll lift you so that you can have a look around."

She hesitated. "Will the rat come back?"

Tony chuckled, a heartening sound. "Not likely. We've been making too much noise."

"Okay." She sounded so resigned he laughed again.

"Don't worry, Sam. Think of this as an adventure to tell our children."

Our children. A curious emotion ran through her. Repressing it, she glanced back at him. "Okay, what do I do?"

"Take off your shoes and step into my hands." He cupped his hands close to his crouching body. She was light, lighter than her height and figure indicated. An easy lift. "Okay, Sam, strike a match and tell me what you see."

Sam managed to light one without either dropping the others or setting herself on fire. "A black hole, odd bits of fallen lumber, brick arches. I can't see the floor, but there must be water, because the drips are making plops. There's an awful echo. Maybe we should try shouting."

Tony lowered his hands and set her on the ground, helping her into her shoes. "Around here, the tunnel is bound to be deserted. Odd bits of lumber—could you reach any of them?''

She slipped out of her shoes again. ''Lift me and I'll see. If we could make the hole only a little bigger I could crawl through.''

Banishing thoughts of mice and rats, she groped on the far side of the hole. ''Lift me a bit more, Tony. I feel something.''

With a groan of bending nails loosened by years in the damp air, she managed to pull a length of wood free. Jumping down, she handed it to Tony. ''Will this help?''

He weighed it in his hands. Short and not too sturdy, but perhaps it would do. ''We'll give it a try.''

He inserted it into the hole where he judged the planks to be weakest. At first the wood resisted, but then a narrow board gave way, sending Tony backward to sit down hard in the mud.

When he made no sound, Sam quickly lit a match. ''Are you all right?''

He held the broken end of his lever, staring at it ruefully. ''There goes our equipment.''

She pulled at the board he'd loosened. It broke free. ''Here's a replacement. Sturdier, too.''

Working with the larger piece of lumber, they pried loose several more boards, until within minutes the hole was large enough to crawl through. They climbed over into the abandoned subway tunnel.

''Now what?'' Sam couldn't keep the triumph from her voice.

Tony hugged her close for an instant. ''Now, my sweet, we walk, and since there's only one direction, we don't even have to draw straws.''

In order to conserve the few matches left, they navigated by groping along the wall. Not a pleasant process, as moss and lichens grew there.

The tunnel soon connected to another, branching off to the right. Here they lit a match. The new passage was narrower, but its construction looked newer. "What do you say, Sam?"

The flickering light turned her eyes gold. "Follow the new one."

It proved a bad choice, for it had more connecting tunnels. After a couple of hours they both admitted they were lost, with no idea where the original tunnel lay. For a second Sam gave in to despair, picturing them wandering for the rest of their lives in an endless maze of underground passages. She laid her forehead against Tony's shoulder, fighting back tears.

Warm air caressed her cheeks, ephemeral as a spring breeze. Sam lifted her head. "Tony, it's warm." *Warm, warm, warm.* Her voice rebounded from the curved ceiling.

"Warm?"

"Yes, there's warm air from someplace."

Tony put up his hand, a smile breaking through his discouragement. "You're right. It must be from one of the ducts carrying steam or hot water. There are thousands of them under the city."

He took her hand. "Come on. We should be able to find a dry spot to sit down on."

She tried to move energetically, but it was past midnight and she was tired.

"Isn't this the sort of place where Jack the Ripper hid out?" Sam said at one point.

Tony looked at her, smiling despite his own fatigue and hunger. "I don't think we need to worry about him. Even if he were still alive, he'd be pretty old."

Another intersection, another passage that beckoned. But up ahead stood a little alcove that must once have served as an escape hatch for the subway workers.

Tony led Sam into the shelter, swiping briefly at the dusty floor. He lit a match, checking for crawling things. "It looks all right." The flame went out, leaving them in darkness that seemed even denser by contrast. Tony sat down, pulling Sam in close beside him. "We'll stay here until morning," he said quietly. "Maybe when it's light out, we'll be able to spot a manhole cover or something."

"At least it's warm." Sam's voice was husky. She coughed, aching in every bone.

SHE WAS TIRED, but sleep eluded her. The rhythm of Tony's breathing told her that he, too, was awake. "Tony, you dropped everything to come when I called. Did you think I had killed Dubray?"

"Not a chance. No weapon was found near the body. You were completely out of it. But the real clincher was when you said you'd found a big knife. Dubray was killed by a small knife, like a stiletto, by someone who knew exactly what he was doing. No, I came because I knew you were in danger. Someone had left that knife for you to find, which meant they were expecting you to come back to your flat. They had to be nearby."

"Jason Wheeler," Sam mused. "I never liked him, but it never would have occurred to me he was a killer. He seemed like a sleazy little con man, no personality."

"Killers are often like that. Makes it easy for them to blend into the crowd after they've made their hit."

Sam shivered again. "The assassination, if there's going to be one—we have to stop it. How much time do you think we have?"

"The first meetings start—" he glanced at the luminous dial of his watch "—this afternoon. At the Regal Arms. Then there's a banquet and more meetings."

"A bomb would do the most damage, wouldn't it?" Sam suppressed a shudder. "They could take out several people at once as long as it was properly placed. With inside help—" She broke off, her fingers gripping Tony's arm. "Aunt Olivia—is it possible she's the inside contact? Oh, Tony, I just can't see it."

Tony tightened his arms around her. "I don't think she is. This has been planned for some time, and Olivia only came to work with the delegates yesterday. Besides, as a volunteer, even with her security clearance, she's still not in on the arrangements, nor is it likely she'd have access to the security office. No, Sam, it has to be someone else. Someone who's been working in this for a long time and who is impeccably trusted, beyond suspicion." He clenched his fist. "Damn it, if we knew who the target was, it would help."

"I would guess the Quebec premier," Sam said. "Paul Messier is already the opposition leader in Quebec. Bennett indicated he'd have a good chance of winning if there were an election. With the premier out of the way, it would be easy."

"Perhaps." Tony sounded doubtful. "It's true he's not very well liked at the moment. And it would certainly disrupt the conference. I guess we'll just have to warn security and do the best we can."

He shifted her to a more comfortable position. "There's nothing we can do tonight." His voice was gentle. "Sleep now, Sam."

To her surprise she did, waking up cramped and chilly. Her clothes had dried and felt scratchy and stiff. Tony's head rested against her shoulder. She only had to turn her face slightly to lay her cheek against his. She smiled faintly. His skin was rough with his growing beard, like velour stroked the wrong way.

He awoke with a start, sitting up and rubbing his eyes. Odd ribbons of light seeped into the tunnel from somewhere, carrying wavering echoes of sound. "Sam, do you hear that? Voices."

They walked toward the sounds, their joints gradually losing the stiffness caused by sleeping on a brick floor. Water gurgled down the abandoned subway tracks. Above them they could hear a steady muted hum. "Cars on the roads," Tony guessed. Once they jumped as a loud roar echoed through the passages.

"We must be near some present-day underground line." He grinned at Sam, the tired lines of his face smoothing out. "Sam, we're going to get out of here."

A pile of fallen bricks blocked their path. They retraced their steps and tried an adjacent tunnel. A bright light beckoned them on, and the unmistakable sound of voices.

"What'd you get today, love?" a woman called to a man whose silhouette showed starkly against a bonfire set in the middle of the abandoned track.

"Not much. I'll try again tonight."

Sam and Tony glanced at each other. People lived here? "It's warm and dry, which is more than you can say for outside in winter," Tony whispered.

They walked forward, not without some trepidation. No doubt it was illegal to live in the disused tunnels; they couldn't be sure of their reception.

Although the man and the woman stared, they must have taken in their mud-streaked clothing and labeled them another homeless couple.

"Hallo," the woman greeted them. "Want some coffee?"

Sam eyed the smoke-blackened pot dubiously, but accepted the tin cup, sipping gratefully. In her empty stomach the caffeine hit with a jolt, pouring energy into her tired muscles.

"Thanks," Tony said. "Can you show us the way out? I'm afraid we've gotten lost."

If they were surprised at his accent, they didn't show it. The coffee finished, the man gestured for them to follow him.

Another mile or two of tunnels passed under their trudging feet. The rails lining the ground began to look less neglected, the steel still shiny, the gravel base dry and free of the plants that thrived in dampness.

When at last they reached a wire-mesh gate, the man deftly slipped the pin from the hinge and held it open for them to clamber out free.

"Goodbye," he said after he had refixed it. "Good luck."

He turned, and within minutes had vanished down the long dark passage.

Chapter Seventeen

A short walk took Sam and Tony to a lit subway station, obviously in a poor district, since their ragged appearance seemed to attract little attention. Tony spent a moment studying the posted map. He turned and took Sam's hand. "Okay, I've got it. Only two changes."

"Wouldn't a taxi be better?" Sam asked.

"At this time of morning? It's rush hour. The tube's quickest. We'll come out only a block from the hotel."

The trains were crowded. Sam felt distinctly out of place in the cars shared with bankers and stockbrokers in neat, three-piece suits. She intercepted more than one grimace of disgust. If it hadn't been for the urgency of reaching their destination, she might have seen the humor in it. Before long, they rushed into the opulent lobby of the Regal Arms. But nothing was happening. Samantha barely restrained herself from gaping. Somehow she'd expected chaos. What? she asked herself, an assassination scene right before our eyes?

The lobby was virtually deserted, the morning desk clerk presiding behind the oak counter as if it were any normal workday, as indeed it was, for him. He looked up as Tony and Sam walked past.

"Eh, you can't come in here like that." Running around the end of the counter, he made as if to restrain Tony by force. He jerked to a stop, his face taking on a comical look of astonishment as he recognized his boss. "Oh, sorry, sir."

Sam could see he was dying of curiosity, but the social space the British maintained between employer and employee prevented him from asking questions.

"Have the delegates checked in yet?" Tony asked.

"Yes, sir. The first meeting's scheduled for one this afternoon."

"Okay." Tony paused for a moment. "I'll be in my office. Could you send up some food—a complete breakfast for two, I'd say?" He glanced at Sam, who nodded. "And have the boutique send up some clothes for Miss Smith. The clothes right away, the breakfast in half an hour. And notify the chief of security to come to my office as soon as possible."

Tony's secretary nearly fell on his neck when he walked into his outer office. "Mr. Theopoulos, where have you been? You just disappeared."

"I'm sorry, Marcia. I couldn't get in touch with you. But I see you managed all right."

She flushed at the praise. "Thank you, sir. Here are your messages." She handed Tony a stack of pink slips.

He took them, but the look on his face told Sam he was thinking of tossing the lot into the wastebasket.

"Please take messages for a little while longer, Marcia," Tony said, unlocking the door of his private office. "I want to clean up and eat breakfast. But if the security man arrives, let him in at once."

"Why don't you shower first, Sam," Tony suggested as he showed her to the fully equipped bathroom connected to his office.

"Very nice," she said. "Another perk?"

His grin came and went. "Yeah, another perk." He gave her a little push. "Be quick, will you? There's a robe on the door, which you can wear until your clothes get here."

Within twenty minutes they were both clean and dressed, and Tony had sent the mail boy down to the incinerator with their soiled clothes. Food had never tasted so good, the bacon crisp and savory, the coffee fragrant with the aroma of freshly ground beans.

Bob Green, the security chief, came in just as they were finishing. "What's up, Mr. Theopoulos?" he said briskly. "We missed you yesterday."

"If it had been possible, I would have been here," Tony said with dry emphasis. "First of all, we'd better have the building searched from top to bottom in case there's a bomb." Briefly Tony sketched their speculations.

Green reached for the phone, speaking as he dialed. "We've already done a search, but we'll go over everything again." He spoke into the phone, giving quick, succinct orders.

Tony turned to Sam. "Samantha, would you use the other phone to call Inspector Allen? Tell him everything."

"Right." Glad of something to do, Sam sat at the small desk in the corner and pulled the phone over.

To her frustration, however, Allen was not in. The situation was too complicated to explain to anyone else, so she left a message for him to call her.

Tony and Bob were deep in conversation. "Wasn't he there, Sam?" Tony asked as she joined them.

"He'll be in later."

"Well, no matter. I've told Bob to keep an eye out for Bennett. The timetable's been changed. Today's meeting is at three rather than one. That's to give us more time to set up tighter security."

"Is Aunt Olivia here today?" Sam asked.

"Not here. This morning she's at the hotel where the other delegates are staying."

"What about Bennett and Jason Wheeler?"

"There's no answer at Wheeler's place. Bob here finally tracked down a flat Bennett owns. Yesterday. Unlisted number. But there's no one there, either, only an answering machine."

There was nothing to do but wait. Sam nearly wore a hole in the carpet, pacing from the window to the desk and back. "Why doesn't Allen phone?" she burst out at one point.

"Another case, isn't that what the dispatcher said?" Tony leaned back in his chair, glad of a moment's respite from the constantly ringing telephone.

She clenched her fists at her sides. "Another case. But why now, today?"

Tony smiled gently. "Come here, Samantha."

She stared at him, then moved across the room, feet dragging. She'd wanted to touch him, but he had been so matter of fact, so occupied with the necessary responsibilities of his position and the threat that meant life or death for one or more statesmen, that he'd become almost a stranger. She'd only seen him at work a couple of times. Then there had been no pressures on him. Today she was seeing a new side of him, the man who shouldered his duties and put others before himself.

His face was drawn with weariness, the same bone-deep fatigue that had painted dark circles under her eyes. He reached for her, pulling her down on his lap.

"Sam, don't worry so. It's all under control."

She stirred, unable to settle despite the temptation to burrow against him and shut out reality. "Is it? I won't be able to breathe freely again until it's over and everyone's safe."

"Me, too. In the meantime, here's a deposit on account."

He kissed her deeply, his mouth tender on hers, infusing her with a promise of passion.

"Sam—"

The telephone rang. Muttering under his breath, Tony reached for it. Awkwardly Sam stood up. Tony briefly clung to her hand, then let it slide through his as she stepped away.

By TWO-THIRTY Tony and Sam and several uniformed security people were in the lobby. Bob Green had briefed them thoroughly. "I don't normally like to have civilians involved in a deal like this, but Maurice St. Clair suggested it."

Sam looked around. "Where is St. Clair? I would have thought he'd have wanted to talk to us."

"Don't worry, Miss Smith. He's around. I've spoken to him. It's important that you be on the alert. You and Mr. Theopoulos are the only ones who would recognize Jason Wheeler and Price's driver on sight. While it's not likely they can penetrate our net, it's best to anticipate the worst. Of course, Price may not use either of these men, but since he thinks you're safely put away, he may feel he has nothing to worry about. That's why I had you stay in the office all day, in case he has anyone nosing around.''

The plan sounded simple and foolproof on the surface, but Sam could not shake off the uneasy feeling they were missing some vital fact. "What about his inside man?" she asked as they scanned the lobby, in which an unusual number of people circulated for a normally quiet midafternoon.

It wasn't the first time she'd asked the question. Only a faint tightening of his mouth indicated Bob Green's resentment. "As I said before, all our people have been thoroughly checked out. There's no possibility that it's any of them."

"But Bennett sounded so sure."

"Bennett Price was probably bragging," Green stated with a frown. "Contrary to the plots of mystery novels, criminals do not usually spill everything they're planning to the first person who asks."

Unhappy, but still convinced of Bennett's deadly sincerity, Sam gave up. "At least Aunt Olivia's not here," she whispered to Tony as Green left them. "It can't be her."

"I never believed it was," Tony assured her quietly.

From their position near the staircase leading to the mezzanine conference room, where the first meeting would be held, they had a clear view of the main floor into the hotel. Regular hotel guests and tourists had been barred from the lobby.

Promptly at three a limousine pulled up, followed by two more.

"Come on, Sam," Tony said. "Time to do our stuff." He tugged his jacket straight, one hand going up to check the knot on his tie. He tucked her arm through his and walked toward the door to take up their position in a short receiving line.

Sam patted the smooth chignon into which she'd fastened her hair. The suit she wore was beautifully tailored, a designer original much like the clothes she'd worn in Montreal. Used as she had become to casual dress, she'd felt overdressed for the first moment she put it on. But now she slipped easily into her role as Tony's consort.

Since Tony was the division manager of the hotel chain, Bob Green had decided his presence in the lobby as one of the greeting party would look perfectly natural.

The delegates who had rooms in the Regal Arms emerged from the elevator, their mood relaxed and congenial. They positioned themselves by the door.

As the group from the first limousine entered the hotel, Sam's jaw dropped. The prime minister of Canada led the team, his long, pleasant face wreathed in smiles. She'd only been told the premier of Quebec was representing the political side. Suddenly the conference took on a greater magnitude.

She closed her mouth before anyone could notice, although an unobtrusive nudge from Tony told her he had. "It's a surprise to me, too, Sam," he whispered from the side of his mouth.

The prime minister moved along the reception line, graciously shaking hands and exchanging a few words with the delegates. When he came to Sam, he paused. "Samantha Smith. Haven't we met? At a reception last year?"

"Yes, sir." The encounter had been so brief Sam was surprised he remembered.

"Please accept my condolences on your father's death," the prime minister said, his face genial. "He'll be missed."

"Thank you," Sam murmured.

The lobby had become crowded, making it difficult to keep track of all the people who swiveled in and out of the doors and the elevator. Even knowing the security staff were everywhere, Sam felt nervous, as if the delegates' safety depended on her alone.

A movement on the mezzanine balcony overhead drew her eye. Why, she couldn't have said. A number of security staff were stationed up there, watching all the entrances. They were in a constant shift as they changed their positions for better views.

At the moment they'd gathered near the head of the stairs. As Sam watched, the door that led to a group of utility rooms inched open. An uneasy feeling clutched at her stomach. She and Tony had checked that door earlier and it had been locked.

With a kind of mesmerized fascination she watched as the door swung farther open, very slowly, as if underwater. She tore her gaze away for a second. The prime minister and his entourage had reached the middle of the lobby.

She looked back up. The door was closed. Had she imagined seeing it ajar?

"Tony—" She was about to tug at his arm, when she looked toward the kitchen doors behind the delegates. Maurice St. Clair. Her tension dropped a notch, yet the back of her neck prickled, as the fine hairs there stood on end.

What was wrong with St. Clair standing at the kitchen door? He was part of security.

Glancing back up the balcony, she again felt reassured. The utility door was closed, the rail deserted except for one security man overlooking the lobby.

Her eyes swiveled back to the kitchen.

She froze, her heart jumping into her throat as she saw the drawn gun in St. Clair's hand. He was slowly raising it, a look of intense concentration on his face.

"Tony, there—" She screamed, her vocal cords finding surprising power.

At that instant everything went crazy, although it unreeled before her horrified eyes like a scene in slow motion. Tony, among many who had heard her, grabbed a gun from the security man next to him. But in stunned disbelief she saw him lift it and aim straight at the prime minister.

No, it couldn't be. It wasn't possible that Tony was the assassin.

"Mr. Prime Minister!" she yelled, this time directly to him.

The RCMP officer next to the prime minister pushed his charge to the carpet, casting his own body on him as a shield.

In the same instant Sam lifted her arm to swing at Tony's to deflect his aim.

But before she could follow through, it hit her. He had seen St. Clair. He wasn't aiming at the prime minister. With a supreme force of will, she stopped the motion of her arm in midair.

Just in time. His knuckle whitened as he pulled the trigger. The report was deafening, nearly drowning out the shouts and screams of the bystanders as they threw themselves to the floor.

Like a woman in shock, Samantha fixed her eyes on Maurice St. Clair. He sprawled on the floor next to the kitchen door, writhing in pain as he clutched his thigh. Bob Green scooped up the pistol equipped with a silencer, which lay on the carpet nearby.

Tony had left her side to join Green. The prime minister pushed himself to his feet, smiling and brushing away the RCMP officers' attempts to fuss over him.

Samantha let out her pent-up breath. But her relief was premature.

A sound, faint above the surrounding noise, fell on her ears. It might have been a clang, its significance was so clear to her. She looked up, and her mouth dropped open.

"Oh, no, how did he get in here?"

Tony snapped his head around at the sound of her voice, following the direction of her gaze.

On the balcony, the utility door stood open. Leaning over the rail, Jason Wheeler lifted a gun. "Get down," Sam screamed, hurling herself toward Tony and the prime minister. Twisting her head up as she ran, she looked in the direction of Wheeler's aim. "Oh, no, the chandelier."

If he could bring it down, the weight of it would crush anyone underneath.

Parker, behind the counter, covered his eyes.

The prime minister and those around him scrambled for safety, out of line of the heavy fixture.

But the shot was never fired. Half a dozen security men grabbed Wheeler before he had a chance to squeeze the trigger.

Sam took one step toward Tony and, to her astonishment, sat down abruptly on the carpet. Her knees buckled under her weight.

She looked at Tony, who wore a stunned expression. Very gingerly he let go of the gun he held and let it slide to the floor.

Then he came over, sank down beside her and pulled her close. "Thanks, Sam. Thanks," he murmured into her hair.

"Thanks for what?" Relief bubbled in her, making her feel as if she'd swallowed a helium balloon.

"For trusting me. Sam, if you'd knocked against my arm, it either would have given St. Clair his chance or I would have missed him and maybe hit somebody else."

"I was ready to," Sam confessed. "But I knew you couldn't be an assassin. But St. Clair? How did he pull it off? He must have planned it for a long time to have gotten into that position without creating suspicion."

"Or he got an offer he couldn't refuse. Remember what Bennett said about enough money?" He pulled himself up by bracing his hand on a nearby chair, and drew her up with him. "Can you stand, Samantha? They're calling us."

"IT WAS THE PRIME MINISTER he was going to kill all along, wasn't it?" Sam said. Sunday evening they were enjoying the first restful hour they'd had in days. "The Quebec premier wasn't even close."

"Looks that way." Tony arranged her more comfortably against him on the sofa and threaded his fingers lazily through her hair. "I'm glad your Aunt Olivia wasn't involved. She was as shocked as everybody else by what happened."

Rain pelted the windows, a soothing counterpoint to the fire crackling in the hearth. "Do you think the police have enough evidence to charge Bennett?"

"I think so," Tony said. "St. Clair with his fanatical devotion to the cause probably wouldn't have admitted anything even under torture, but Jason Wheeler was the weak point. According to Inspector Allen when I talked to him earlier, Wheeler looked about to break. If he talks, he'll implicate Bennett."

"Then why did they use him?"

"He was the backup in case St. Clair failed, something they didn't expect to happen. Germain probably masterminded the whole thing, but when he was killed, some of the details fell apart. I guess they had to change the plans."

"Which must be why Bennett needed more money. Mine."

"Yeah, it looks that way." Tony groped among the sofa cushions to find the remote control for the little television paneled behind the doors of a bookcase. Pressing a button, he turned it on. The news was just beginning.

"The conference went well, better than anyone expected," Sam commented as the broadcast journalist recited in glowing terms the accord reached between the two countries and detailed the new agreements proposed. "The incident seems to be forgotten. Good thing the media were persuaded to downplay it."

"Yeah, even Parker agreed the hotel suffered no serious damage, either physically or in its reputation." He laughed. "Sometimes I think that man feels more possessive about the place than the owners do."

Sam laid an urgent hand on Tony's knee. "Tony, look."

A reporter stood before the international terminal at Heathrow, his microphone held to his mouth.

"Bennett Price, the Canadian industrialist, was arrested late this afternoon. It is not clear what charges he'll be booked under. Scotland Yard has declined to comment."

The scene dissolved into an interior shot. Bennett stood between two uniformed policemen, his face stiff in anger.

"You know, Tony," Sam said slowly, "I almost feel sorry for him. He had so much, and he threw it all away out of greed and a thirst for power."

Tony looked down at her, tender amusement lighting his eyes. "You don't still have a sneaking fondness for him, do you?"

Sam laughed. "Not a chance. Besides, you've got something Bennett never had."

"Oh? What's that?"

"Integrity. And stability."

Tony grimaced, his mouth curving in wry humor. "Sounds dull."

"Never," she said firmly. "Not when it goes with eyes the color of melted chocolate."

Tony gathered her closer, inhaling the faint perfume that had enthralled him from the first day. "Oh, Sam, it's so good to hold you. Will you be going back to Montreal?"

She tapped his nose with the tip of her finger. "What do you think, Tony?"

"I think you should stay right here. You like freelancing, don't you? In a city like this, there's plenty of work like that. And in your spare time, maybe you could marry me and have my babies."

"In my spare time? Do you think that'll be enough?"

He smiled tenderly at her. "We'll work on it."

With eager fingers, she began to unbutton his shirt. With Tony, anything was possible.

The adventure was only beginning.

Harlequin Intrigue ®

COMING NEXT MONTH

#133 JIGSAW by Margaret St. George
Someone was breaking into Laura Penn's home to
leave seemingly innocent items, but when an
identical bookend was discovered at the scene of a
murder, Laura realized she'd made one fatal mistake.
She'd lied to Detective Max Elliot, withheld
information that might have shielded a murderer.
Laura hated to confess her lie lest it destroy her new
and fragile relationship with Max. But there was no
alternative. Not even his love for her could keep the
messengers of death at bay.

#134 FEAR FAMILIAR by Caroline Burnes
Since Professor Eleanor Duncan had taken home the
cat she found in the university parking lot, she'd
been assaulted, interrogated by the CIA, her
apartment invaded and her husband seemed to have
returned from the dead. When veterinarian Peter
Curry identified Eleanor's furry friend as an escaped
research animal, he couldn't know where that clue
would lead. To adventure, romance, counterplot and
conspiracy and to an explosive enigma.

"This fast-paced mystery contains a rich trove of sharply
edged supporting characters. Of course, mom steals
the show."
— *Publishers Weekly*

A NICE MURDER FOR MOM

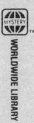

James Yaffe

For a New York City homicide cop, Mesa Grande, Colorado,
was like another planet. But Dave liked his new job as Chief
Investigator for the Public Defender's Office, although he
did miss his mother's cooking. He also missed her amazing
knack to solve his most difficult murder cases. So when Mom
comes for a visit, Dave knows what she'd really love is a nice
murder.

Luckily, there was a corpse to oblige. A pompous college
professor is bludgeoned to death in his living room. Soon
some very bizarre twists and turns leave everybody guessing.
Except, of course, Mom.

Have You Ever Wondered If You Could Write A Harlequin Novel?

Here's great news—Harlequin is offering a series of cassette tapes to help you do just that. Written by Harlequin editors, these tapes give practical advice on how to make your characters—and your story—come alive. There's a tape for each contemporary romance series Harlequin publishes.

Mail order only

All sales final

HARLEQUIN
American Romance®

Join in the

Rocky Mountain Magic

Experience the charm and magic of The Stanley Hotel in the Colorado Rockies with #329 BEST WISHES this month, and don't miss out on further adventures to take place there in the next two months.

In March 1990 look for #333 SIGHT UNSEEN by Kathy Clark and find out what psychic visions lie ahead for Hayley Austin's friend Nicki Chandler. In April 1990 read #337 RETURN TO SUMMER by Emma Merritt and travel back in time with their friend Kate Douglas.

ROCKY MOUNTAIN MAGIC—All it takes is an open heart. Only from Harlequin American Romance

All the Rocky Mountain Magic Romances take place at the beautiful Stanley Hotel.

RMM2-1

The Pirate
JAYNE ANN KRENTZ

At the heart of every powerful romance story lies a legend. There are many romantic legends and countless modern variations on them, but they all have one thing in common: They are tales of brave, resourceful women who must gentle and tame the powerful, passionate men who are their true mates.

The enormous appeal of Jayne Ann Krentz lies in her ability to create modern-day versions of these classic romantic myths, and her LADIES AND LEGENDS trilogy showcases this talent. Believing that a storyteller who can bring legends to life deserves special attention, Harlequin has chosen the first book of the trilogy—THE PIRATE—to receive our Award of Excellence. Look for it now.

AE-PIR-1A

SUZANNE

Suzanne takes you down
to her place near the river,
you can hear the boats go by
you can stay the night beside her.
And you know that she's half crazy
but that's why you want to be there . . .
    And you want to travel with her,
    you want to travel blind
    and you know that she can trust you
    because you've touched her perfect body
    with your mind.

SELECTED POEMS
1956–1968

LEONARD COHEN

BANTAM BOOKS, INC.
Toronto / New York / London
A National General Company

*This low-priced Bantam Book
has been completely reset in a type face
designed for easy reading, and was printed
from new plates. It contains the complete
text of the original hard-cover edition.*
NOT ONE WORD HAS BEEN OMITTED.

SELECTED POEMS 1956-1968

*A Bantam Book / published by arrangement with
The Viking Press, Inc.*

PRINTING HISTORY

*Originally published September 1963
Viking edition published 1968
7 printings through August 1969
Bantam edition published December 1971*

*Some of these poems were previously published by The Viking
Press, Inc., in a volume entitled* The Spice-Box of Earth. "This
Is For You" *first appeared in* MADEMOISELLE. *Other poems first
appeared in* QUEEN'S QUARTERLY, PRISM, SATURDAY REVIEW, PAN-IC,
THE MCGILL CHAPBOOK, *and* TAMARACK REVIEW. *Most of the poems
have appeared in volumes published in Canada by McClelland
& Stewart Limited.*

*Bantam Books are published by Bantam Books, Inc., a National
General company. Its trade-mark, consisting of the words "Bantam
Books" and the portrayal of a bantam, is registered in the United
States Patent Office and in other countries. Marca Registrada.
Bantam Books, Inc., 666 Fifth Avenue, New York, N.Y. 10019.*

PRINTED IN THE UNITED STATES OF AMERICA

Contents

II. *The Spice-Box of Earth*

III. *Flowers for Hitler*

IV. *Parasites of Heaven*

V. *New Poems*

I / Let Us Compare Mythologies

FOR WILF AND HIS HOUSE

When young the Christians told me
how we pinned Jesus
like a lovely butterfly against the wood,
and I wept beside paintings of Calvary
at velvet wounds
and delicate twisted feet.

But he could not hang softly long,
your fighters so proud with bugles,
bending flowers with their silver stain,
and when I faced the Ark for counting,
trembling underneath the burning oil,
the meadow of running flesh turned sour
and I kissed away my gentle teachers,
warned my younger brothers.

Among the young and turning-great
of the large nations, innocent
of the spiked wish and the bright crusade,
there I could sing my heathen tears
between the summersaults and chestnut battles,
love the distant saint
who fed his arm to flies,
mourn the crushed ant
and despise the reason of the heel.

Raging and weeping are left on the early road.
Now each in his holy hill
the glittering and hurting days are almost done.
        Then let us compare mythologies.
I have learned my elaborate lie
of soaring crosses and poisoned thorns

and how my fathers nailed him
like a bat against a barn
to greet the autumn and late hungry ravens
as a hollow yellow sign.

PRAYER FOR MESSIAH

His blood on my arm is warm as a bird
his heart in my hand is heavy as lead
his eyes through my eyes shine brighter than love
O send out the raven ahead of the dove

His life in my mouth is less than a man
his death on my breast is harder than stone
his eyes through my eyes shine brighter than love
O send out the raven ahead of the dove

O send out the raven ahead of the dove
O sing from your chains where you're chained in a cave
your eyes through my eyes shine brighter than love
your blood in my ballad collapses the grave

O sing from your chains where you're chained in a cave
your eyes through my eyes shine brighter than love
your heart in my hand is heavy as lead
your blood on my arm is warm as a bird

O break from your branches a green branch of love
after the raven has died for the dove

4

THE SONG OF THE HELLENIST

(For R.K.)

> *Those unshadowed figures, rounded lines of men*
> *who kneel by curling waves, amused by ornate birds—*
> > *If that had been the ruling way,*
> *I would have grown long hairs for the corners of my*
> > > *mouth ...*

O cities of the Decapolis across the Jordan,
you are too great; our young men love you,
and men in high places have caused gymnasiums
to be built in Jerusalem.
> I tell you, my people, the statues are too tall.
> Beside them we are small and ugly,
> blemishes on the pedestal.

My name is Theodotus, do not call me Jonathan.
My name is Dositheus, do not call me Nathaniel.
> Call us Alexander, Demetrius, Nicanor ...

"Have you seen my landsmen in the museums,
the brilliant scholars with the dirty fingernails,
standing before the marble gods,
> underneath the lot?"
Among straight noses, natural and carved,
I have said my clever things thought out before;
jested on the Protocols, the cause of war,
> quoted "Bleistein with a Cigar."

And in the salon that holds the city in its great window,
in the salon among the Herrenmenschen,
among the close-haired youth, I made them laugh
when the child came in:

"Come, I need you for a Passover Cake."
And I have touched their tall clean women,
thinking somehow they are unclean,
    as scaleless fish.
They have smiled quietly at me,
and with their friends—
    I wonder what they see.

O cities of the Decapolis,
call us Alexander, Demetrius, Nicanor ...
    Dark women, soon I will not love you.
My children will boast of their ancestors at Marathon
and under the walls of Troy,
    and Athens, my chiefest joy—

O call me Alexander, Demetrius, Nicanor ...

THE SPARROWS

Catching winter in their carved nostrils
the traitor birds have deserted us,
leaving only the dullest brown sparrows
for spring negotiations.

I told you we were fools
to have them in our games,
but you replied:
        They are only wind-up birds
who strut on scarlet feet
so hopelessly far
from our curled fingers.

I had moved to warn you,
but you only adjusted your hair
and ventured:
        Their wings are made of glass and gold
and we are fortunate
not to hear them splintering
against the sun.

Now the hollow nests
sit like tumors or petrified blossoms
between the wire branches
and you, an innocent scientist,
question me on these brown sparrows:
whether we should plant our yards with breadcrumbs
or mark them with the black, persistent crows
whom we hate and stone.

But what shall I tell you of migrations
when in this empty sky

the precise ghosts of departed summer birds
still trace old signs;
or of desperate flights
when the dimmest flutter of a coloured wing
excites all our favourite streets
to delight in imaginary spring.

CITY CHRIST

He has returned from countless wars,
Blinded and hopelessly lame.
He endures the morning streetcars
And counts ages in a Peel Street room.

He is kept in his place like a court jew,
To consult on plagues or hurricanes,
And he never walks with them on the sea
Or joins their lonely sidewalk games.

SONG OF PATIENCE

For a lovely instant I thought she would grow mad
and end the reason's fever.
But in her hand she held Christ's splinter,
so I could only laugh and press a warm coin
across her seasoned breasts:
but I remembered clearly then your insane letters
and how you wove initials in my throat.

My friends warn me
that you have read the ocean's old skeleton;
they say you stitch the water sounds
in different mouths, in other monuments.
"Journey with a silver bullet," they caution.
"Conceal a stake inside your pocket."
And I must smile as they misconstrue your insane letters
and my embroidered throat.

O I will tell him to love you carefully;
to honour you with shells and coloured bottles;
to keep from your face the falling sand
and from your human arm the time-charred beetle;
to teach you new stories about lightning
and let you run sometimes barefoot on the shore.
And when the needle grins bloodlessly in his cheek
he will come to know how beautiful it is
to be loved by a madwoman.

And I do not gladly wait the years
for the ocean to discover and rust your face
as it has all of history's beacons
that have turned their gold and stone to water's onslaught,

for then your letters too rot with ocean's logic
and my fingernails are long enough
to tear the stitches from my throat.

WHEN THIS AMERICAN WOMAN

When this American woman,
whose thighs are bound in casual red cloth,
comes thundering past my sitting-place
like a forest-burning Mongol tribe,
the city is ravished
and brittle buildings of a hundred years
splash into the street;
and my eyes are burnt
for the embroidered Chinese girls,
already old,
and so small between the thin pines
on these enormous landscapes,
that if you turn your head
they are lost for hours.

SONG

The naked weeping girl
is thinking of my name
turning my bronze name
over and over
with the thousand fingers
of her body
anointing her shoulders
with the remembered odour
of my skin

O I am the general
in her history
over the fields
driving the great horses
dressed in gold cloth
wind on my breastplate
sun in my belly

May soft birds
soft as a story to her eyes
protect her face
from my enemies
and vicious birds
whose sharp wings
were forged in metal oceans
guard her room
from my assassins

And night deal gently with her
high stars maintain the whiteness
of her uncovered flesh

And may my bronze name
touch always her thousand fingers
grow brighter with her weeping
until I am fixed like a galaxy
and memorized
in her secret and fragile skies.

THESE HEROICS

If I had a shining head
and people turned to stare at me
in the streetcars;
and I could stretch my body
through the bright water
and keep abreast of fish and water snakes;
if I could ruin my feathers
in flight before the sun;
do you think that I would remain in this room,
reciting poems to you,
and making outrageous dreams
with the smallest movements of your mouth?

LOVERS

During the first pogrom they
Met behind the ruins of their homes—
Sweet merchants trading: her love
For a history-full of poems.

And at the hot ovens they
Cunningly managed a brief
Kiss before the soldier came
To knock out her golden teeth.

And in the furnace itself
As the flames flamed higher,
He tried to kiss her burning breasts
As she burned in the fire.

Later he often wondered:
Was their barter completed?
While men around him plundered
And knew he had been cheated.

THE WARRIOR BOATS

The warrior boats from Portugal
Strain at piers with ribs exposed
And seagull generations fall
Through the wood anatomy

But in the town, the town
Their passion unimpaired
The beautiful dead crewmen
Go climbing in the lanes
Boasting poems and bitten coins

Handsome bastards
What do they care
If the Empire has withered
To half a peninsula
If the Queen has the King's Adviser
For her last and seventh lover

Their maps have not changed
Thighs still are white and warm
New boundaries have not altered
The marvellous landscape of bosoms
Nor a Congress relegated the red mouth
To a foreign district

Then let the ships disintegrate
At the edge of the land
The gulls will find another place to die
Let the home ports put on mourning

And little clerks
Complete the necessary papers

But you swagger on, my enemy sailors
Go climbing in the lanes
Boasting your poems and bitten coins
Go knocking on all the windows of the town

At one place you will find my love
Asleep and waiting
And I cannot know how long
She has dreamed of all of you

Oh remove my coat gently
From her shoulders.

LETTER

How you murdered your family
means nothing to me
as your mouth moves across my body

And I know your dreams
of crumbling cities and galloping horses
of the sun coming too close
and the night never ending

but these mean nothing to me
beside your body

I know that outside a war is raging
that you issue orders
that babies are smothered and generals beheaded

but blood means nothing to me
it does not disturb your flesh

tasting blood on your tongue
does not shock me
as my arms grow into your hair

Do not think I do not understand
what happens
after the troops have been massacred
and the harlots put to the sword

And I write this only to rob you

that when one morning my head
hangs dripping with the other generals
from your house gate

that all this was anticipated
and so you will know that it meant nothing to me.

PAGANS

With all Greek heroes
swarming around my shoulders,
I perverted the Golem formula
and fashioned you from grass,
using oaths of cruel children
for my father's chant.

O pass by, I challenged you
and gods in their approval
rustled my hair with marble hands,
and you approached slowly
with all the pain of a thousand-year statue
breaking into life.

I thought you perished
at our first touch
(for in my hand I held a fragment
of a French cathedral
and in the air a man spoke to birds
and everywhere
the dangerous smell of old Italian flesh).

But yesterday while children
slew each other in a dozen games,
I heard you wandering through grass
and watched you glare (O Dante)
where I had stood.

I know how our coarse grass
mutilates your feet,
      how the city traffic
echoes all his sonnets

and how you lean for hours
at the cemetery gates.

Dear friend, I have searched all night
        through each burnt paper,
but I fear I will never find
the formula to let you die.

SONG

My lover Peterson
He named me Goldenmouth
I changed him to a bird
And he migrated south

My lover Frederick
Wrote sonnets to my breast
I changed him to a horse
And he galloped west

My lover Levite
He named me Bitterfeast
I changed him to a serpent
And he wriggled east

My lover I forget
He named me Death
I changed him to a catfish
And he swam north

My lover I imagine
He cannot form a name
I'll nestle in his fur
And never be to blame.

PRAYER FOR SUNSET

The sun is tangled
    in black branches,
raving like Absalom
    between sky and water,
struggling through the dark terebinth
to commit its daily suicide.

Now, slowly, the sea consumes it,
leaving a glistening wound
    on the water,
    a red scar on the horizon:
In darkness
    I set out for home,
terrified by the clash of wind on grass,
and the victory cry of weeds and water.

Is there no Joab for tomorrow night,
    with three darts
    and a great heap of stones?

BALLAD

He pulled a flower
out of the moss
and struggled past soldiers
to stand at the cross.

He dipped the flower
into a wound
and hoped that a garden
would grow in his hand.

The hanging man shivered
at this gentle thrust
and ripped his flesh
from the flower's touch,

and said in a voice
they had not heard,
"Will petals find roots
in the wounds where I bleed?

"Will minstrels learn songs
from a tongue which is torn
and sick be made whole
through rents in my skin?"

The people knew something
like a god had spoken
and stared with fear
at the nails they had driven.

And they fell on the man
with spear and knife

to honour the voice
with a sacrifice.

O the hanging man
had words for the crowd
but he was tired
and the prayers were loud.

He thought of islands
alone in the sea
and sea water bathing
dark roots of each tree;

of tidal waves lunging
over the land,
over these crosses
these hills and this man.

He thought of towns
and fields of wheat,
of men and this man
but he could not speak.

O they hid two bodies
behind a stone;
day became night
and the crowd went home.

And men from Golgotha
assure me that still
gardeners in vain
pour blood in that soil.

SAINT CATHERINE STREET

Towering black nuns frighten us
as they come lumbering down the tramway aisle
amulets and talismans caught in careful fingers
promising plagues for an imprudent glance
So we bow our places away
     the price of an indulgence

How may we be saints and live in golden coffins
Who will leave on our stone shelves
     pathetic notes for intervention
How may we be calm marble gods at ocean altars
Who will murder us for some high reason

There are no ordeals
Fire and water have passed from the wizards' hands
We cannot torture or be tortured
Our eyes are worthless to an inquisitor's heel
No prince will waste hot lead
     or build a spiked casket for us

Once with a flaming belly she danced upon a green road
Move your hand slowly through a cobweb
     and make drifting strings for puppets
Now the tambourines are dull
at her lifted skirt boys study cigarette stubs
no one is jealous of her body

We would bathe in a free river
but the lepers in some spiteful gesture
have suicided in the water

and all the swollen quiet bodies crowd the other
    prey for a fearless thief or beggar

How can we love and pray
when at our lovers' arms
we hear the damp bells of them
who once took bitter alms
but now float quietly away

Will no one carve from our bodies a white cross
for a wind-torn mountain
or was that forsaken man's pain
enough to end all passion

Are those dry faces and hands we see
all the flesh there is of nuns
Are they really clever non-excreting tapestries
prepared by skillful eunuchs
for our trembling friends

BALLAD

My lady was found mutilated
in a Mountain Street boarding house.
My lady was a tall slender love,
    like one of Tennyson's girls,
and you always imagined her erect on a thoroughbred
in someone's private forest.
    But there she was,
naked on an old bed, knife slashes
across her breasts, legs badly cut up:
Dead two days.

They promised me an early conviction.
We will eavesdrop on the adolescents
    examining pocket-book covers in drugstores.
We will note the broadest smiles at torture scenes
    in movie houses.
We will watch the old men in Dominion Square
    follow with their eyes
the secretaries from the Sun Life at five-thirty ...

Perhaps the tabloids alarmed him.
Whoever he was the young man came alone
    to see the frightened blonde have her blouse
ripped away by anonymous hands;
the person guarded his mouth
    who saw the poker blacken the eyes
of the Roman prisoner;
the old man pretended to wind his pocket-watch ...

The man was never discovered.
There are so many cities!
    so many knew of my lady and her beauty.

Perhaps he came from Toronto, a half-crazed man
    looking for some Sunday love;
or a vicious poet stranded too long in Winnipeg;
or a Nova Scotian fleeing from the rocks and preachers . . .

Everyone knew my lady
    from the movies and art-galleries,
Body from Goldwyn. Botticelli had drawn her long limbs.
Rossetti the full mouth.
Ingres had coloured her skin.
    She should not have walked so bravely
through the streets.
After all, that was the Marian year, the year
the rabbis emerged from their desert exile, the year
the people were inflamed by tooth-paste ads . . .

We buried her in Spring-time.
    The sparrows in the air
wept that we should hide with earth
    the face of one so fair.

The flowers they were roses
    and such sweet fragrance gave
that all my friends were lovers
    and we danced upon her grave.

SUMMER NIGHT

The moon dangling wet like a half-plucked eye
was bright for my friends bred in close avenues
of stone, and let us see too much.
The vast treeless field and huge wounded sky,
opposing each other like continents,
made us and our smoking fire quite irrelevant
between their eternal attitudes.
We knew we were intruders. Worse. Intruders
unnoticed and undespised.

      Through orchards of black weeds
with a sigh the river urged its silver flesh.
From their damp nests bull-frogs croaked
warnings, but to each other.
And occasional birds, in a private grudge,
flew noiselessly at the moon.
What could we do? We ran naked into the river,
but our flesh insulted the thick slow water.
We tried to sit naked on the stones,
but they were cold and we soon dressed.
One squeezed a little human music from his box:
mostly it was lost in the grass
where one struggled in an ignorant embrace.
One argued with the slight old hills
and the goose-fleshed naked girls, I will not be old.
One, for his protest, registered a sexual groan.
And the girl in my arms
broke suddenly away, and shouted for us all,
Help! Help! I am alone. But then all subtlety was gone
and it was stupid to be obvious before the field and sky,
experts in simplicity. So we fled on the highways,
in our armoured cars, back to air-conditioned homes.

THE FLIER

Do not arrange your bright flesh in the sun
Or shine your limbs, my love, toward this height
Where basket men and the lame must run, must run
And grasp at angels in their lovely flight
With stumps and hooks and artificial skin.
O there is nothing in your body's light
To grow us wings or teach the discipline
Which starvers know to calm the appetite.
Understand we might be content to beg
The clinic of your thighs against the night
Were there no scars of braces on his leg
Who sings and wrestles with them in our sight,
Then climbs the sky, a lover in their band.
Tell him your warmth, show him your gleaming hand.

...eard of a man
who says words so beautifully
that if he only speaks their name
women give themselves to him.

If I am dumb beside your body
while silence blossoms like tumors on our lips
it is because I hear a man climb stairs
and clear his throat outside our door.

THE FLY

In his black armour
    the house-fly marched the field
of Freia's sleeping thighs,
undisturbed by the soft hand
    which vaguely moved
to end his exercise.

And it ruined my day—
    this fly which never planned
to charm her or to please
should walk boldly on that ground
    I tried so hard
to lay my trembling knees.

WARNING

If your neighbour disappears
O if your neighbour disappears
The quiet man who raked his lawn
The girl who always took the sun

Never mention it to your wife
Never say at dinner time
Whatever happened to that man
Who used to rake his lawn

Never say to your daughter
As you're walking home from church
Funny thing about that girl
I haven't seen her for a month

And if your son says to you
Nobody lives next door
They've all gone away
Send him to bed with no supper

Because it can spread, it can spread
And one fine evening coming home
Your wife and daughter and son
They'll have caught the idea and will be gone.

STORY

She tells me a child built her house
one Spring afternoon,
but that the child was killed
crossing the street.

She says she read it in the newspaper,
that at the corner of this and this avenue
a child was run down by an automobile.

Of course I do not believe her.
She has built the house herself,
hung the oranges and coloured beads in the doorways,
crayoned flowers on the walls.
She has made the paper things for the wind,
collected crooked stones for their shadows in the sun,
fastened yellow and dark balloons to the ceiling.

Each time I visit her
she repeats the story of the child to me,
I never question her. It is important
to understand one's part in a legend.

I take my place
among the paper fish and make-believe clocks,
naming the flowers she has drawn,
smiling while she paints my head on large clay coins,
and making a sort of courtly love to her
when she contemplates her own traffic death.

BESIDE THE SHEPHERD

Beside the shepherd dreams the beast
Of laying down with lions.
The youth puts away his singing reed
And strokes the consecrated flesh.

Glory, Glory, shouts the grass,
Shouts the brick, as from the cliff
The gorgeous fallen sun
Rolls slowly on the promised city.

Naked running through the mansion
The boy with news of the Messiah
Forgets the message for his father,
Enjoying the marble against his feet.

Well finally it has happened,
Imagines someone in another house,
Staring one more minute out his window
Before waking up his wife.

II / The Spice-Box of Earth

A KITE IS A VICTIM

A kite is a victim you are sure of.
You love it because it pulls
gentle enough to call you master,
strong enough to call you fool;
because it lives
like a desperate trained falcon
in the high sweet air,
and you can always haul it down
to tame it in your drawer.

A kite is a fish you have already caught
in a pool where no fish come,
so you play him carefully and long,
and hope he won't give up,
or the wind die down.

A kite is the last poem you've written,
so you give it to the wind,
but you don't let it go
until someone finds you
something else to do.

A kite is a contract of glory
that must be made with the sun,
so you make friends with the field
the river and the wind,
then you pray the whole cold night before,
under the travelling cordless moon,
to make you worthy and lyric and pure.

THE FLOWERS THAT I LEFT
IN THE GROUND

The flowers that I left in the ground,
that I did not gather for you,
today I bring them all back,
to let them grow forever,
not in poems or marble,
but where they fell and rotted.

And the ships in their great stalls,
huge and transitory as heroes,
ships I could not captain,
today I bring them back
to let them sail forever,
not in model or ballad,
but where they were wrecked and scuttled.

And the child on whose shoulders I stand,
whose longing I purged
with public, kingly discipline,
today I bring him back
to languish forever,
not in confession or biography,
but where he flourished,
growing sly and hairy.

It is not malice that draws me away,
draws me to renunciation, betrayal:
it is weariness, I go for weariness of thee.
Gold, ivory, flesh, love, God, blood, moon—
I have become the expert of the catalogue.

My body once so familiar with glory,
my body has become a museum:
this part remembered because of someone's mouth,
this because of a hand,
this of wetness, this of heat.

Who owns anything he has not made?
With your beauty I am as uninvolved
as with horses' manes and waterfalls.
This is my last catalogue.
I breathe the breathless
I love you, I love you—
and let you move forever.

GIFT

You tell me that silence
is nearer to peace than poems
but if for my gift
I brought you silence
(for I know silence)
you would say
This is not silence
this is another poem
and you would hand it back to me.

THERE ARE SOME MEN

There are some men
who should have mountains
to bear their names to time.

Grave-markers are not high enough
or green,
and sons go far away
to lose the fist
their father's hand will always seem.

I had a friend:
he lived and died in mighty silence
and with dignity,
left no book, son, or lover to mourn.

Nor is this a mourning-song
but only a naming of this mountain
on which I walk,
fragrant, dark, and softly white
under the pale of mist.
I name this mountain after him.

YOU ALL IN WHITE

Whatever cities are brought down,
I will always bring you poems,
and the fruit of orchards
I pass by.

Strangers in your bed,
excluded by our grief,
listening to sleep-whispering,
will hear their passion beautifully explained,
and weep because they cannot kiss
your distant face.

Lovers of my beloved,
watch how my words put on her lips like clothes,
how they wear her body like a rare shawl.
Fruit is pyramided on the window-sill,
songs flutter against the disappearing wall.

The sky of the city
is washed in the fire
of Lebanese cedar and gold.
In smoky filigree cages
the apes and peacocks fret.
Now the cages do not hold,
in the burning street man and animal
perish in each other's arms,
peacocks drown around the melting throne.

Is it the king
who lies beside you listening?
Is it Solomon or David
or stuttering Charlemagne?

Is that his crown
in the suitcase beside your bed?

When we meet again,
you all in white,
I smelling of orchards,
when we meet—

But now you awaken,
and you are tired of this dream.
Turn toward the sad-eyed man.
He stayed by you all the night.
You will have something
to say to him.

I WONDER HOW MANY PEOPLE IN THIS CITY

I wonder how many people in this city
live in furnished rooms.
Late at night when I look out at the buildings
I swear I see a face in every window
looking back at me,
and when I turn away
I wonder how many go back to their desks
and write this down.

GO BY BROOKS

Go by brooks, love,
Where fish stare,
Go by brooks,
I will pass there.

Go by rivers,
Where eels throng,
Rivers, love,
I won't be long.

Go by oceans,
Where whales sail,
Oceans, love,
I will not fail.

TO A TEACHER

Hurt once and for all into silence.
A long pain ending without a song to prove it.

Who could stand beside you so close to Eden,
when you glinted in every eye the held-high razor,
shivering every ram and son?

And now the silent loony-bin,
where the shadows live in the rafters
like day-weary bats,
until the turning mind, a radar signal,
lures them to exaggerate mountain-size
on the white stone wall
your tiny limp.

How can I leave you in such a house?
Are there no more saints and wizards
to praise their ways with pupils,
no more evil to stun with the slap
of a wet red tongue?

Did you confuse the Messiah in a mirror
and rest because he had finally come?

Let me cry Help beside you, Teacher.
I have entered under this dark roof
as fearlessly as an honoured son
enters his father's house.

I HAVE NOT LINGERED IN EUROPEAN MONASTERIES

I have not lingered in European monasteries
and discovered among the tall grasses tombs of knights
who fell as beautifully as their ballads tell;
I have not parted the grasses
or purposefully left them thatched.

I have not released my mind to wander and wait
in those great distances
between the snowy mountains and the fishermen,
like a moon,
or a shell beneath the moving water.

I have not held my breath
so that I might hear the breathing of God,
or tamed my heartbeat with an exercise,
or starved for visions.
Although I have watched him often
I have not become the heron,
leaving my body on the shore,
and I have not become the luminous trout,
leaving my body in the air.

I have not worshipped wounds and relics,
or combs of iron,
or bodies wrapped and burnt in scrolls.

I have not been unhappy for ten thousand years.
During the day I laugh and during the night I sleep.
My favourite cooks prepare my meals,
my body cleans and repairs itself,
and all my work goes well.

IT SWINGS, JOCKO

It swings, Jocko,
but we do not want too much flesh in it.
Make it like fifteenth-century prayers,
love with no climax,
constant love,
and passion without flesh.
(Draw those out, Jocko,
like the long snake from Moses' arm;
how he must have screamed
to see a snake come out of him;
no wonder he never felt holy:
We want that scream tonight.)
Lightly, lightly,
I want to be hungry,
hungry for food,
for love, for flesh;
I want my dreams to be of deprivation,
gold thorns being drawn from my temples.
If I am hungry
then I am great,
and I love like the passionate scientist
who knows the sky
is made only of wave-lengths.
Now if you want to stand up,
stand up lightly,
we'll lightly march around the city.
I'm behind you, man,
and the streets are spread with chicks and palms,
white branches and summer arms.
We're going through on tiptoe,
like monks before the Virgin's statue.

We built the city,
We drew the water through,
We hang around the rinks,
The bars, the festive halls,
Like Brueghel's men.
Hungry, hungry.
Come back, Jocko,
Bring it all back for the people here,
It's your turn now.

CREDO

A cloud of grasshoppers
rose from where we loved
and passed before the sun.

I wondered what farms
they would devour,
what slave people would go free
because of them.

I thought of pyramids overturned,
of Pharaoh hanging by the feet,
his body smeared—

Then my love drew me down
to conclude what I had begun.

Later, clusters of fern apart,
we lay.

A cloud of grasshoppers
passed between us and the moon,
going the other way,

each one fat and flying slow,
not hungry for the leaves and ferns
we rested on below.

The smell that burning cities give
was in the air.

Battalions of the wretched,
wild with holy promises,
soon passed our sleeping place;

they ran among
the ferns and grass.

I had two thoughts:
to leave my love
and join their wandering,

join their holiness;
     or take my love
to the city they had fled:
     That impoverished world
of boil-afflicted flesh
and rotting fields
could not tempt us from each other.

     Our ordinary morning lust
claimed my body first
and made me sane.
     I must not betray
the small oasis where we lie,
though only for a time.
     It is good to live between
a ruined house of bondage
and a holy promised land.
     A cloud of grasshoppers
will turn another Pharaoh upside-down;
slaves will build cathedrals
for other slaves to burn.
     It is good to hear
the larvae rumbling underground,
good to learn
the feet of fierce or humble priests
trample out the green.

YOU HAVE THE LOVERS

You have the lovers,
they are nameless, their histories only for each other,
and you have the room, the bed and the windows.
Pretend it is a ritual.
Unfurl the bed, bury the lovers, blacken the windows,
let them live in that house for a generation or two.
No one dares disturb them.
Visitors in the corridor tip-toe past the long closed door,
they listen for sounds, for a moan, for a song:
nothing is heard, not even breathing.
You know they are not dead,
you can feel the presence of their intense love.
Your children grow up, they leave you,
they have become soldiers and riders.
Your mate dies after a life of service.
Who knows you? Who remembers you?
But in your house a ritual is in progress:
it is not finished: it needs more people.
One day the door is opened to the lover's chamber.
The room has become a dense garden,
fun of colours, smells, sounds you have never known.
The bed is smooth as a wafer of sunlight,
in the midst of the garden it stands alone.
In the bed the lovers, slowly and deliberately and silently,
perform the act of love.
Their eyes are closed,
as tightly as if heavy coins of flesh lay on them.
Their lips are bruised with new and old bruises.
Her hair and his beard are hopelessly tangled.
When he puts his mouth against her shoulder
she is uncertain whether her shoulder
has given or received the kiss.

All her flesh is like a mouth.
He carries his fingers along her waist
and feels his own waist caressed.
She holds him closer and his own arms tighten around
her.
She kisses the hand beside her mouth.
It is his hand or her hand, it hardly matters,
there are so many more kisses.
You stand beside the bed, weeping with happiness,
you carefully peel away the sheets
from the slow-moving bodies.
Your eyes are filled with tears, you barely make out the
lovers.
As you undress you sing out, and your voice is magnificent
because now you believe it is the first human voice
heard in that room.
The garments you let fall grow into vines.
You climb into bed and recover the flesh.
You close your eyes and allow them to be sewn shut.
You create an embrace and fall into it.
There is only one moment of pain or doubt
as you wonder how many multitudes are lying beside
your body,
but a mouth kisses and a hand soothes the moment away.

OWNING EVERYTHING

For your sake I said I will praise the moon,
tell the colour of the river,
find new words for the agony
and ecstasy of gulls.

Because you are close,
everything that men make, observe
or plant is close, is mine:
the gulls slowly writhing, slowly singing
on the spears of wind;
the iron gate above the river;
the bridge holding between stone fingers
her cold bright necklace of pearls.

The branches of shore trees,
like trembling charts of rivers,
call the moon for an ally
to claim their sharp journeys
out of the dark sky,
but nothing in the sky responds.
The branches only give a sound
to miles of wind.

With your body and your speaking
you have spoken for everything,
robbed me of my strangerhood,
made me one
with the root and gull and stone,
and because I sleep so near to you
I cannot embrace
or have my private love with them.

You worry that I will leave you.
I will not leave you.
Only strangers travel.
Owning everything,
I have nowhere to go.

THE PRIEST SAYS GOODBYE

My love, the song is less than sung
when with your lips you take it from my tongue—
nor can you seize this firm erotic grace
and halt it tumbling into commonplace.

No one I know can set the hook
to fix lust in a longing look
where we can read from time to time
the absolute ballet our bodies mime.

Harry can't, his face in Sally's crotch,
nor Tom, who only loves when neighbours watch—
one mistakes the ballet for the chart,
one hopes that gossip will perform like art.

And what of art? When passion dies
friendship hovers round our flesh like flies,
and we name beautiful the smells
that corpses give and immortelles.

I have studied rivers: the waters rush
like eternal fire in Moses' bush.
Some things live with honour. I will see
lust burn like fire in a holy tree.

Do not come with me. When I stand alone
my voice sings out as though I did not own
my throat. Abelard proved how bright could be
the bed between the hermitage and nunnery.

You are beautiful. I will sing beside
rivers where longing Hebrews cried.

As separate exiles we can learn
how desert trees ignite and branches burn.

At certain crossroads we will win
the harvest of our discipline.
Swollen flesh, minds fed on wilderness—
Oh, what a blaze of love our bodies press!

THE CUCKOLD'S SONG

If this looks like a poem
I might as well warn you at the beginning
that it's not meant to be one.
I don't want to turn anything into poetry.
I know all about her part in it
but I'm not concerned with that right now.
This is between you and me.
Personally I don't give a damn who led who on:
in fact I wonder if I give a damn at all.
But a man's got to say something.
Anyhow you fed her 5 McKewan Ales,
took her to your room, put the right records on,
and in an hour or two it was done.
I know all about passion and honour
but unfortunately this had really nothing to do with
    either:
oh there was passion I'm only too sure
and even a little honour
but the important thing was to cuckold Leonard Cohen.
Hell, I might just as well address this to the both of you:
I haven't time to write anything else.
I've got to say my prayers.
I've got to wait by the window.
I repeat: the important thing was to cuckold Leonard
    Cohen.
I like that line because it's got my name in it.
What really makes me sick
is that everything goes on as it went before:
I'm still a sort of friend,
I'm still a sort of lover.
But not for long:
that's why I'm telling this to the two of you.

The fact is I'm turning to gold, turning to gold.
It's a long process, they say,
it happens in stages.
This is to inform you that I've already turned to clay.

DEAD SONG

As I lay dead
In my love-soaked bed,
Angels came to kiss my head.

I caught one gown
And wrestled her down
To be my girl in death town.

She will not fly.
She has promised to die.
What a clever corpse am I!

MY LADY CAN SLEEP

My lady can sleep
Upon a handkerchief
Or if it be Fall
Upon a fallen leaf.

I have seen the hunters
Kneel before her hem—
Even in her sleep
She turns away from them.

The only gift they offer
Is their abiding grief—
I pull out my pockets
For a handkerchief or leaf.

TRAVEL

Loving you, flesh to flesh, I often thought
of travelling penniless to some mud throne
where a master might instruct me how to plot
my life away from pain, to love alone
in the bruiseless embrace of stone and lake.

Lost in the fields of your hair I was never lost
enough to lose a way I had to take;
breathless beside your body I could not exhaust
the will that forbid me contract, vow,
or promise, and often while you slept
I looked in awe beyond your beauty.

                                    Now
I know why many men have stopped and wept
Half-way between the loves they leave and seek,
and wondered if travel leads them anywhere—
Horizons keep the soft line of your cheek,
The windy sky's a locket for your hair.

I HAVE TWO BARS OF SOAP

I have two bars of soap,
the fragrance of almond,
one for you and one for me.
Draw the bath,
we will wash each other.

I have no money,
I murdered the pharmacist.

And here's a jar of oil,
Just like in the Bible.
Lie in my arms,
I'll make your flesh glisten.

I have no money,
I murdered the perfumer.

Look through the window
at the shops and people.
Tell me what you desire,
you'll have it by the hour.

I have no money,
I have no money.

CELEBRATION

When you kneel below me
and in both your hands
hold my manhood like a sceptre,

When you wrap your tongue
about the amber jewel
and urge my blessing,

I understand those Roman girls
who danced around a shaft of stone
and kissed it till the stone was warm.

Kneel, love, a thousand feet below me,
so far I can barely see your mouth and hands
perform the ceremony,

Kneel till I topple to your back
with a groan, like those gods on the roof
that Samson pulled down.

BENEATH MY HANDS

Beneath my hands
your small breasts
are the upturned bellies
of breathing fallen sparrows.

Wherever you move
I hear the sounds of closing wings
of falling wings.

I am speechless
because you have fallen beside me
because your eyelashes
are the spines of tiny fragile animals.

I dread the time
when your mouth
begins to call me hunter.

When you call me close
to tell me
your body is not beautiful
I want to summon
the eyes and hidden mouths
of stone and light and water
to testify against you.

I want them
to surrender before you
the trembling rhyme of your face
from their deep caskets.

When you call me close
to tell me
your body is not beautiful
I want my body and my hands
to be pools
for your looking and laughing.

AS THE MIST LEAVES NO SCAR

As the mist leaves no scar
On the dark green hill,
So my body leaves no scar
On you, nor ever will.

When wind and hawk encounter,
What remains to keep?
So you and I encounter,
Then turn, then fall to sleep.

freedom

As many nights endure
Without a moon or star,
So will we endure
When one is gone and far.

I LONG TO HOLD SOME LADY

I long to hold some lady
For my love is far away,
And will not come tomorrow
And was not here today.

There is no flesh so perfect
As on my lady's bone,
And yet it seems so distant
When I am all alone:

As though she were a masterpiece
In some castled town,
That pilgrims come to visit
And priests to copy down.

Alas, I cannot travel
To a love I have so deep
Or sleep too close beside
A love I want to keep.

But I long to hold some lady,
For flesh is warm and sweet.
Cold skeletons go marching
Each night beside my feet.

NOW OF SLEEPING

Under her grandmother's patchwork quilt
a calico bird's-eye view
of crops and boundaries
naming dimly the districts of her body
sleeps my Annie like a perfect lady

Like ages of weightless snow
on tiny oceans filled with light
her eyelids enclose deeply
a shade tree of birthday candles
one for every morning
until the now of sleeping

The small banner of blood
kept and flown by Brother Wind
long after the pierced bird fell down
is like her red mouth
among the squalls of pillow

Bearers of evil fancy
of dark intention and corrupting fashion
who come to rend the quilt
plough the eye and ground the mouth
will contend with mighty Mother Goose
and Farmer Brown and all good stories
of invincible belief
which surround her sleep
like the golden weather of a halo

Well-wishers and her true lover
may stay to watch my Annie
sleeping like a perfect lady

under her grandmother's patchwork quilt
but they must promise to whisper
and to vanish by morning—
all but her one true lover.

SONG

When with lust I am smitten
To my books I then repair
And read what men have written
Of flesh forbid but fair

But in these saintly stories
Of gleaming thigh and breast
Of sainthood and its glories
Alas I find no rest

For at each body rare
The saintly man disdains
I stare O God I stare
My heart is stained with stains

And casting down the holy tomes
I lead my eyes to where
The naked girls with silver combs
Are combing out their hair

Then each pain my hermits sing
Flies upward like a spark
I live with the mortal ring
Of flesh on flesh in dark

SONG

I almost went to bed
without remembering
the four white violets
I put in the button-hole
of your green sweater

and how I kissed you then
and you kissed me
shy as though I'd
never been your lover

FOR ANNE

With Annie gone,
Whose eyes to compare
With the morning sun?

Not that I did compare,
But I do compare
Now that she's gone.

LAST DANCE AT THE FOUR PENNY

Layton, when we dance our freilach
under the ghostly handkerchief,
the miracle rabbis of Prague and Vilna
resume their sawdust thrones,
and angels and men, asleep so long
in the cold palaces of disbelief,
gather in sausage-hung kitchens
to quarrel deliciously and debate
the sounds of the Ineffable Name.

Layton, my friend Lazarovitch,
no Jew was ever lost
while we two dance joyously
in this French province,
cold and oceans west of the temple,
the snow canyoned on the twigs
like forbidden Sabbath manna;
I say no Jew was ever lost
while we weave and billow the handkerchief
into a burning cloud,
measuring all of heaven
with our stitching thumbs.

Reb Israel Lazarovitch,
you no-good Romanian, you're right!
Who cares whether or not
the Messiah is a Litvak?
As for the cynical,
such as we were yesterday,
let them step with us or rot
in their logical shrouds.
We've raised a bright white flag,

and here's our battered fathers' cup of wine,
and now is music
until morning and the morning prayers
lay us down again,
we who dance so beautifully
though we know that freilachs end.

SUMMER HAIKU

For Frank and Marion Scott

Silence

and a deeper silence

when the crickets

hesitate

OUT OF THE LAND OF HEAVEN

For Marc Chagall

Out of the land of heaven
Down comes the warm Sabbath sun
Into the spice-box of earth.
The Queen will make every Jew her lover.
      In a white silk coat
Our rabbi dances up the street,
Wearing our lawns like a green prayer-shawl,
Brandishing houses like silver flags.
      Behind him dance his pupils,
Dancing not so high
And chanting the rabbi's prayer,
But not so sweet.
      And who waits for him
On a throne at the end of the street
But the Sabbath Queen.
      Down go his hands
Into the spice-box of earth,
And there he finds the fragrant sun
For a wedding ring,
And draws her wedding finger through.
      Now back down the street they go,
Dancing higher than the silver flags.
His pupils somewhere have found wives too,
And all are chanting the rabbi's song
And leaping high in the perfumed air.
      Who calls him Rabbi?
Cart-horse and dogs call him Rabbi,
And he tells them:
The Queen makes every Jew her lover.

And gathering on their green lawns
The people call him Rabbi,
And fill their mouths with good bread
And his happy song.

PRAYER OF MY WILD GRANDFATHER

God, God, God, someone of my family
hated your love with such skill that you sang
to him, your private voice violating
his drum like a lost bee after pollen
in the brain. He gave you his children
opened on a table, and if a ram
ambled in the garden you whispered nothing
about that, nor held his killing hand.

It is no wonder fields and governments
rotted, for soon you gave him all your range,
drove all your love through that sting in his brain.

Nothing can flourish in your absence
except our faith that you are proved through him
who had his mind made mad and honey-combed.

72

ISAIAH

For G.C.S.

Between the mountains of spices
the cities thrust up pearl domes and filigree spires.
Never before was Jerusalem so beautiful.
    In the sculptured temple how many pilgrims,
lost in the measures of tambourine and lyre,
kneeled before the glory of the ritual?
    Trained in grace the daughters of Zion moved,
not less splendid than the golden statuary,
the bravery of ornaments about their scented feet.
    Government was done in palaces.
Judges, their fortunes found in law,
reclining and cosmopolitan, praised reason.
Commerce like a strong wild garden
    flourished in the street.
The coins were bright, the crest on coins precise,
new ones looked almost wet.

Why did Isaiah rage and cry,
Jerusalem is ruined,
    your cities are burned with fire?

On the fragrant hills of Gilboa
were the shepherds ever calmer,
the sheep fatter, the white wool whiter?
    There were fig trees, cedar, orchards
where men worked in perfume all day long.
New mines as fresh as pomegranates.
    Robbers were gone from the roads,
    the highways were straight.
There were years of wheat against femine.

Enemies? Who has heard of a righteous state
        that has no enemies,
but the young were strong, archers cunning,
        their arrows accurate.

Why then this fool Isaiah,
smelling vaguely of wilderness himself,
why did he shout,
        Your country is desolate?

Now will I sing to my well-beloved
a song of my beloved touching her hair
which is pure metal black
        no rebel prince can change to dross,
of my beloved touching her body
        no false swearer can corrupt,
of my beloved touching her mind
        no faithless counsellor can inflame,
of my beloved touching the mountains of spices
making them beauty instead of burning.

Now plunged in unutterable love
Isaiah wanders, chosen, stumbling
against the sculptured walls which consume
their full age in his embrace and powder
as he goes by. He reels beyond
        the falling dust of spires and domes,
obliterating ritual: the Holy Name, half-spoken,
is lost on the cantor's tongue; their pages barren,
congregations blink, agonized and dumb.
        In the turns of his journey
heavy trees he sleeps under
mature into cinder and crumble:
        whole orchards join the wind

ike rising flocks of ravens.
    The rocks go back to water, the water to waste.
And while Isaiah gently hums a sound
o make the guilty country uncondemned,
        all men, truthfully desolate and lonely,
as though witnessing a miracle,
behold in beauty the faces of one another.

THE GENIUS

For you
I will be a ghetto jew
and dance
and put white stockings
on my twisted limbs
and poison wells
across the town

For you
I will be an apostate jew
and tell the Spanish priest
of the blood vow
in the Talmud
and where the bones
of the child are hid

For you
I will be a banker jew
and bring to ruin
a proud old hunting king
and end his line

For you
I will be a Broadway jew
and cry in theatres
for my mother
and sell bargain goods
beneath the counter

For you
I will be a doctor jew
and search

in all the garbage cans
for foreskins
to sew back again

For you
I will be a Dachau jew
and lie down in lime
with twisted limbs
and bloated pain
no mind can understand

LINES FROM MY GRANDFATHER'S JOURNAL

I am one of those who could tell every word the pin went through. Page after page I could imagine the scar in a thousand crowned letters. . . .

The dancing floor of the pin is bereft of angels. The Christians no longer want to debate. Jews have forgotten the best arguments. If I spelled out the Principles of Faith I would be barking on the moon.

I will never be free from this old tyranny: "I believe with a perfect faith. . . ."

Why make trouble? It is better to stutter than sing. Become like the early Moses: dreamless of Pharaoh. Become like Abram: dreamless of a longer name. Become like a weak Rachel: be comforted, not comfortless. . . .

There was a promise to me from a rainbow, there was a covenant with me after a flood drowned all my friends, inundated every field: the ones we had planted with food and the ones we had left untilled.

Who keeps promises except in business? We were not permitted to own land in Russia. Who wants to own land anywhere? I stare dumbfounded at the trees. Montreal trees, New York trees, Kovno trees. I never wanted to own one. I laugh at the scholars in real estate. . . .

Soldiers in close formation. Paratroops in a white Tel Aviv street. Who dares disdain an answer to the ovens? Any answer.

I did not like to see the young men stunted in the Polish ghetto. Their curved backs were not beautiful. Forgive me, it gives me no pleasure to see them in uniform. I do not thrill to the sight of Jewish battalions.

But there is only one choice between ghettos and battalions, between whips and the weariest patriotic arrogance....

I wanted to keep my body free as when it woke up in Eden. I kept it strong. There are commandments.

Erase from my flesh the marks of my own whip. Heal the razor slashes on my arms and throat. Remove the metal clamps from my fingers. Repair the bones I have crushed in the door.

Do not let me lie down with spiders. Do not let me encourage insects against my eyes. Do not let me make my living nest with worms or apply to my stomach the comb of iron or bind my genitals with cord.

It is strange that even now prayer is my natural language....

Night, my old night. The same in every city, beside every lake. It ambushes a thicket of thrushes. It feeds on the houses and fields. It consumes my journals of poems.

The black, the loss of sun: it will always frighten me. It will always lead me to experiment. My journal is filled with combinations. I adjust prayers like the beads of an abacus....

Thou. Reach into the vineyard of arteries for my heart. Eat the fruit of ignorance and share with me the mist and fragrance of dying.

Thou. Your fist in my chest is heavier than any bereavement, heavier than Eden, heavier than the Torah scroll....

The language in which I was trained: spoken in despair of priestliness.

This is not meant for any pulpit, not for men to chant or tell their children. Not beautiful enough.

But perhaps this can suggest a passion. Perhaps this passion could be brought to clarify, make more radiant, the standing Law.

Let judges secretly despair of justice: their verdicts will be more acute. Let generals secretly despair of triumph; killing will be defamed. Let priests secretly despair of faith: their compassion will be true. It is the tension. . . .

My poems and dictionaries were written at night from my desk or from my bed. Let them cry loudly for life at your hand. Let me be purified by their creation. Challenge me with purity.

O break down these walls with music. Purge from my flesh the need to sleep. Give me eyes for your darkness. Give me legs for your mountains. Let me climb to your face with my argument. If I am unprepared, unclean, lead me first to deserts full of jackals and wolves where I will learn what glory or humility the sand can teach, and from beasts the direction of my evil.

I did not wish to dishonour the scrolls with my logic, or David with my songs. In my work I meant to love you but my voice dissipated somewhere before your infinite regions. And when I gazed toward your eyes all the bristling hills of Judea intervened.

I played with the idea that I was the Messiah. . . .

> I saw a man gouge out his eye,
> hold it in his fist
> until the nursing sky

grew round it like a vast and loving face.
With shafts of light
I saw him mine his wrist
until his blood filled out the rest of space
and settled softly on the world
like morning mist.

Who could resist such fireworks?

I wrestled hard in Galilee.
In the rubbish of pyramids
and strawless bricks
I felled my gentle enemy.
I destroyed his cloak of stars.
It was an insult to our human flesh,
worse than scars.

If we could face his work, submit it to annotation. . . .

You raged before them
like the dreams of their old-time God.
You smashed your body
like tablets of the Law.
You drove them from the temple counters.
Your whip on their loins
was a beginning of trouble.
Your thorns in their hearts
was an end to love.

O come back to our books.
Decorate the Law with human commentary.
Do not invoke a spectacular death.
There is so much to explain—
the miracles obscure your beauty. . . .

Doubting everything that I was made to write. My dictionaries groaning with lies. Driven back to Genesis. Doubting where every word began. What saint had shifted a meaning to illustrate a parable. Even beyond Genesis, until I stood outside my community, like the man who took too many steps on Sabbath. Faced a desolation which was unheroic, unbiblical, no dramatic beasts.

The real deserts are outside of tradition. . . .

The chimneys are smoking. The little wooden synagogues are filled with men. Perhaps they will stumble on my books of interpretation, useful to anyone but me.

The white tablecloths—whiter when you spill the wine. . . .

Desolation means no angels to wrestle. I saw my brothers dance in Poland. Before the final fire I heard them sing. I could not put away my scholarship or my experiments with blasphemy.

(In Prague their Golem slept.)

Desolation means no ravens, no black symbols. The carcass of the rotting dog cannot speak for you. The ovens have no tongue. The flames thud against the stone roofs. I cannot claim that sound.

Desolation means no comparisons. . . .

"Our needs are so manifold, we dare not declare them."

It is painful to recall a past intensity, to estimate your distance from the Belsen heap, to make your peace with numbers. Just to get up each morning is to make a kind of peace.

It is something to have fled several cities. I am glad that I could run, that I could learn twelve languages, that I escaped conscription with a trick, that borders were only stones in an empty road, that I kept my journal.

Let me refuse solutions, refuse to be comforted. . . .

Tonight the sky is luminous. Roads of cloud repeat themelves like the ribs of some vast skeleton.

The easy gulls seem to embody a doomed conception of he sublime as they wheel and disappear into the darkness of he mountain. They leave the heart, they abandon the heart o the Milky Way, that drunkard's glittering line to a physical od. . . .

Sometimes, when the sky is this bright, it seems that if I ould only force myself to stare hard at the black hills I could ecover the gulls. It seems that nothing is lost that is not foraken: The rich old treasures still glow in the sand under the umbled battlement; wrapped in a starry flag a master-God loats through the firmament like a childless kite.

I will never be free from this tyranny.

A tradition composed of the exuviae of visions. I must reist it. It is like the garbage river through a city: beautiful by lay and beautiful by night, but always unfit for bathing.

There were beautiful rules: a way to hear thunder, praise a wise man, watch a rainbow, learn of tragedy.

All my family were priests, from Aaron to my father. It was my honour to close the eyes of my famous teacher.

Prayer makes speech a ceremony. To observe this ritual in the absence of arks, altars, a listening sky: this is a rich discipline.

I stare dumbfounded at the trees. I imagine the scar in a thousand crowned letters. Let me never speak casually.

Inscription for the family spice-box:

Make my body
a pomander for worms
and my soul
the fragrance of cloves.

Let the spoiled Sabbath
leave no scent.
Keep my mouth
from foul speech.

Lead your priest
from grave to vineyard.
Lay him down
where air is sweet.

III / Flowers for Hitler

WHAT I'M DOING HERE

I do not know if the world has lied
I have lied
I do not know if the world has conspired against love
I have conspired against love
The atmosphere of torture is no comfort
I have tortured
Even without the mushroom cloud
still I would have hated
Listen
I would have done the same things
even if there were no death
I will not be held like a drunkard
under the cold tap of facts
I refuse the universal alibi

Like an empty telephone booth passed at night
and remembered
like mirrors in a movie palace lobby consulted
only on the way out
like a nymphomaniac who binds a thousand
into strange brotherhood
I wait
for each one of you to confess

THE HEARTH

The day wasn't exactly my own
since I checked
    and found it on a public calendar.
Tripping over many pairs of legs
as I walked down the park
    I also learned my lust
was not so rare a masterpiece.

Buildings actually built
wars planned with blood and fought
men who rose to generals
    deserved an honest thought
as I walked down the park.

I came back quietly to your house
which has a place on a street.
    Not a single other house
disappeared when I came back.
You said some suffering
    had taught me that.

I'm slow to learn I began
to speak of stars and hurricanes.
    Come here little Galileo—
you undressed my vision—
    it's happier and easier by far
or cities wouldn't be so big.

Later you worked over lace
    and I numbered many things
your fingers and all fingers did.

As if to pay me a sweet
　　　for my ardour on the rug
you wondered in the middle of a stitch:
Now what about those stars and hurricanes?

THE DRAWER'S CONDITION
ON NOVEMBER 28, 1961

Is there anything emptier
than the drawer where
you used to store your opium?
How like a black-eyed susan
blinded into ordinary daisy
is my pretty kitchen drawer!
How like a nose sans nostrils
is my bare wooden drawer!
How like an eggless basket!
How like a pool sans tortoise!
My hand has explored
my drawer like a rat
in an experiment of mazes.
Reader, I may safely say
there's not an emptier drawer
in all of Christendom!

THE SUIT

I am locked in a very expensive suit
old elegant and enduring
Only my hair has been able to get free
but someone has been leaving
their dandruff in it
Now I will tell you
all there is to know about optimism
Each day in hubcap mirror
in soup reflection
in other people's spectacles
I check my hair
for an army of Alpinists
for Indian rope trick masters
for tangled aviators
for dove and albatross
for insect suicides
for abominable snowmen
I check my hair
for aerialists of every kind
Dedicated as an automatic elevator
I comb my hair for possibilities
I stick my neck out
I lean illegally from locomotive windows
and only for the barber
do I wear a hat

INDICTMENT OF THE BLUE HOLE

                              January 28 1962
you must have heard me tonight
I mentioned you 800 times
                              January 28 1962
My abandoned narcotics have
abandoned me
                              January 28 1962
30 must have dug its
spikes into your blue wrist
                              January 28 1962
I shoved the transistor up my ear

And putting down
   3 loaves of suicide (?)
   2 razorblade pies
   1 De Quincey hairnet
   ~~5 gasfilled Hampstead bedsitters~~ (sic)
   a collection of oil
   ~~2 eyelash garottes~~ (sic)
   6 lysol eye foods
He said with considerable charm and travail:
Is this all I give?
One lousy reprieve
      at 2 in the morning?
This?
I'd rather have a job.

I WANTED TO BE A DOCTOR

The famous doctor held up Grandma's stomach.
Cancer! Cancer! he cried out.
The theatre was brought low.
None of the internes thought about ambition.

Cancer! They all looked the other way.
They thought Cancer would leap out
and get them. They hated to be near.
This happened in Vilna in the Medical School.

Nobody could sit still.
They might be sitting beside Cancer.
Cancer was present.
Cancer had been let out of its bottle.

I was looking in the skylight.
I wanted to be a doctor.
All the internes ran outside.
The famous doctor held on to the stomach.

He was alone with Cancer.
Cancer! Cancer! Cancer!
He didn't care who heard or didn't hear.
It was his 87th Cancer.

ON HEARING A NAME
LONG UNSPOKEN

Listen to the stories
men tell of last year
that sound of other places
though they happened here

Listen to a name
so private it can burn
hear it said aloud
and learn and learn

History is a needle
for putting men asleep
anointed with the poison
of all they want to keep

Now a name that saved you
has a foreign taste
claims a foreign body
froze in last year's waste

And what is living lingers
while monuments are built
then yields its final whisper
to letters raised in gilt

But cries of stifled ripeness
whip me to my knees
I am with the falling snow
falling in the seas

I am with the hunters
hungry and shrewd
and I am with the hunted
quick and soft and nude

I am with the houses
that wash away in rain
and leave no teeth of pillars
to rake them up again

Let men numb names
scratch winds that blow
listen to the stories
but what you know you know

And knowing is enough
for mountains such as these
where nothing long remains
houses walls or trees

STYLE

I don't believe the radio stations
of Russia and America
but I like the music and I like
the solemn European voices announcing jazz
I don't believe opium or money
though they're hard to get
and punished with long sentences
I don't believe love
in the midst of my slavery I
do not believe
I am a man sitting in a house
on a treeless Argolic island
I will forget the grass of my mother's lawn
I know I will
I will forget the old telephone number
Fitzroy seven eight two oh
I will forget my style
I will have no style
I hear a thousand miles of hungry static
and the old clear water eating rocks
I hear the bells of mules eating
I hear the flowers eating the night
under their folds
Now a rooster with a razor
plants the haemophilia gash across
the soft black sky
and now I know for certain
I will forget my style
Perhaps a mind will open in this world
perhaps a heart will catch rain
Nothing will heal and nothing will freeze
but perhaps a heart will catch rain

America will have no style
Russia will have no style
It is happening in the twenty-eighth year
of my attention
I don't know what will become
of the mules with their lady eyes
or the old clear water
or the giant rooster
The early morning greedy radio eats
the governments one by one the languages
the poppy fields one by one
Beyond the numbered band
a silence develops for every style
for the style I laboured on
an external silence like the space
between insects in a swarm
electric unremembering
and it is aimed at us
 (I am sleepy and frightened)
it makes toward me brothers

GOEBBELS ABANDONS HIS NOVEL
AND JOINS THE PARTY

His last love poem
        broke in the harbour
where swearing blondes
loaded scrap
        into rusted submarines.
Out in the sun
he was surprised
        to find himself lustless
as a wheel.
More simple than money
he sat in some spilled salt
and wondered if he would find again
the scars of lampposts
ulcers of wrought-iron fence.
He remembered perfectly
how he sprung
        his father's heart attack
and left his mother
in a pit
memory white from loss of guilt.
Precision in the sun
the elevators
        the pieces of iron
broke whatever thous
        his pain had left
like a whistle breaks
a gang of sweating men.
Ready to join the world
yes yes ready to marry
convinced pain a matter of choice
a Doctor of Reason

he began to count the ships
decorate the men.
Will dreams threaten
        this discipline
will favourite hair favourite thighs
last life's sweepstake winners
drive him to adventurous cafés?
Ah my darling pupils
do you think there exists a hand
so bestial in beauty so ruthless
that can switch off
his religious electric Exlax light?

HITLER THE BRAIN-MOLE

Hitler the brain-mole looks out of my eyes
Goering boils ingots of gold in my bowels
My Adam's Apple bulges with the whole head of Goeb-
        bels
No use to tell a man he's a Jew
I'm making a lampshade out of your kiss
Confess! confess!
        is what you demand
although you believe you're giving me everything

IT USES US!

Come upon this heap
expose to camera leer:
would you snatch a skull
for midnight wine, my dear?

Can you wear a cape
claim these burned for you
or is this death unusable
alien and new?

In our leaders' faces
 (albeit they deplore
the past) can you read how
they love Freedom more?

In my own mirror
their eyes beam at me:
my face is theirs, my eyes
burnt and free.

Now you and I are mounted
on this heap, my dear:
from this height we thrill
as boundaries disappear.

Kiss me with your teeth.

All things can be done
whisper museum ovens of
a war that Freedom won.

MY TEACHER IS DYING

Martha they say you are gentle
No doubt you labour at it
Why is it I see you
leaping into unmade beds
strangling the telephone
Why is it I see you
hiding your dirty nylons
in the fireplace
Martha talk to me
My teacher is dying
His laugh is already dead
that put cartilage
between the bony facts
Now they rattle loud
Martha talk to me
Mountain Street is dying
Apartment fifteen is dying
Apartment seven and eight are dying
All the rent is dying
Martha talk to me
I wanted all the dancers' bodies
to inhabit like his old classroom
where everything that happened
was tender and important
Martha talk to me
Toss out the fake Jap silence
Scream in my kitchen
logarithms laundry lists anything
Talk to me
My radio is falling to pieces
My betrayals are so fresh
they still come with explanations

Martha talk to me
What sordid parable
do you teach by sleeping
Talk to me
for my teacher is dying
The cars are parked
on both sides of the street
some facing north
some facing south
I draw no conclusions
Martha talk to me
I could burn my desk
when I think how perfect we are
you asleep me finishing
the last of the Saint Emilion
Talk to me gentle Martha
dreaming of percussions massacres
hair pinned to the ceiling
I'll keep your secret
Let's tell the milkman
we have decided
to marry our rooms

FOR MY OLD LAYTON

His pain, unowned, he left
in paragraphs of love, hidden,
like a cat leaves shit
under stones, and he crept out in day,
clean, arrogant, swift, prepared
to hunt or sleep or starve.

The town saluted him with garbage
which he interpreted as praise
for his muscular grace. Orange peels,
cans, discarded guts rained like ticker-tape.
For a while he ruined their nights
by throwing his shadow in moon-full windows
as he spied on the peace of gentle folk.

Once he envied them. Now with a happy
screech he bounded from monument to monument
in their most consecrated plots, drunk
to know how close he lived to the breathless
in the ground, drunk to feel how much he loved
the snoring mates, the old, the children of the town.

Until at last, like Timon, tired
of human smell, resenting even
his own shoe-steps in the wilderness,
he chased animals, wore live snakes, weeds
for bracelets. When the sea
pulled back the tide like a blanket
he slept on stone cribs, heavy,
dreamless, the salt-bright atmosphere
like an automatic laboratory
building crystals in his hair.

FINALLY I CALLED

Finally I called the people I didn't want to hear from
After the third ring I said
I'll let it ring five more times then what will I do
The telephone is a fine instrument
but I never learned to work it very well
Five more rings and I'll put the receiver down
I know where it goes I know that much
The telephone was black with silver rims
The booth was cozier than the drugstore
There were a lot of creams and scissors and tubes
I needed for my body
I was interested in many coughdrops
I believe the drugstore keeper hated
his telephone and people like me
who ask for change so politely
I decided to keep to the same street
and go into the fourth drugstore
and call them again

THE ONLY TOURIST IN HAVANA
TURNS HIS THOUGHTS HOMEWARD

Come, my brothers,
let us govern Canada,
let us find our serious heads,
let us dump asbestos on the White House,
let us make the French talk English,
   not only here but everywhere,
let us torture the Senate individually
   until they confess,
let us purge the New Party,
let us encourage the dark races
   so they'll be lenient
   when they take over,
let us make the CBC talk English,
let us all lean in one direction
   and float down
   to the coast of Florida,
let us have tourism,
let us flirt with the enemy,
let us smelt pig-iron in our back yards,
let us sell snow
   to under-developed nations,
(Is it true one of our national leaders
   was a Roman Catholic?)
let us terrorize Alaska,
let us unite
   Church and State,
let us not take it lying down,
let us have two Governor Generals
   at the same time,
let us have another official language,
let us determine what it will be,

et us give a Canada Council Fellowship
    to the most original suggestion,
et us teach sex in the home
    to parents,
et us threaten to join the U.S.A.
    and pull out at the last moment,
my brothers, come,
our serious heads are waiting for us somewhere
    like Gladstone bags abandoned
    after a *coup d'état,*
let us put them on very quickly,
let us maintain a stony silence
    on the St. Lawrence Seaway.

Havana
April 1961

MILLENNIUM

This could be my little
   book about love
   if I wrote it—
but my good demon said:
   "Lay off documents!"
Everybody was watching me
   burn my books—
I swung my liberty torch
happy as a gestapo brute;
the only thing I wanted to save
   was a scar
   a burn or two—
but my good demon said:
   "Lay off documents!
   The fire's not important!"
The pile was safely blazing.
I went home to take a bath.
I phoned my grandmother.
She is suffering from arthritis.
"Keep well," I said, "don't mind the pain."
   "You neither," she said.
Hours later I wondered
   did she mean
   don't mind *my* pain
   or don't mind *her* pain?
Whereupon my good demon said:
   "Is that all you can do?"
   Well was it?
   Was it all I could do?
   There was the old lady
   eating alone, thinking about
   Prince Albert, Flanders Field,

my personal fire

Kishenev, her fingers too sore
    for TV knobs;
      but how could I get there?
  The books were gone
    my address lists—
My good demon said again:
  "Lay off documents!
    You know how to get there!"
  And suddenly I did!
remembered it from memory!
    I found her
poring over the royal family tree,
      "Grandma,"
    I almost said,
  "you've got it upside down—"
  "Take a look," she said,
  "it only goes to George V."
      "That's far enough
        you sweet old blood!"
    "You're right" she sang
      and burned the
      London Illustrated Souvenir

fires in every window

    I did not understand
        the day it was
          till I looked outside
        and saw a fire in every
          window on the street
        and crowds of humans
          crazy to talk
    and cats and dogs and birds
        smiling at each other!

animals in love

ALEXANDER TROCCHI, PUBLIC JUNKIE, PRIEZ POUR NOUS

Who is purer
    more simple than you?
Priests play poker with the burghers,
police in underwear
    leave Crime at the office,
our poets work bankers' hours
retire to wives and fame-reports.

The spike flashes in your blood
permanent as a silver lighthouse.

I'm apt to loaf
    in a coma of newspapers,
avoid the second-hand bodies
which cry to be catalogued.
I dream I'm
    a divine right Prime Minister,
I abandon plans for bloodshed in Canada.
I accept an O.B.E.

Under hard lights
with doctors' instruments
    you are at work
in the bathrooms of the city,
changing The Law.

I tend to get distracted
    by hydrogen bombs,
by Uncle's disapproval
    of my treachery
to the men's clothing industry.

find myself
  believing public clocks,
taking advice
from the Dachau generation.

The spike hunts
constant as a compass.
  You smile like a Navajo
discovering American oil
on his official slum wilderness,
a surprise every half hour.

I'm afraid I sometimes forget
my lady's pretty little blond package
is an amateur time-bomb
set to fizzle in my middle-age.
  I forget the Ice Cap, the pea-minds,
the heaps of expensive teeth.

You don a false nose
line up twice for the Demerol dole;
you step out of a tourist group
shoot yourself on the steps of the White House,
you try to shoot the big arms
  of the Lincoln Memorial;
through a flaw in their lead houses
you spy on scientists,
  stumble on a cure for scabies;
you drop pamphlets from a stolen jet:
"The Truth about Junk";
you pirate a national TV commercial
shove your face against
  the window of the living-room
insist that healthy skin is grey.

A little blood in the sink
Red cog-wheels
   shaken from your arm
punctures inflamed
like a roadmap showing cities
over 10,000 pop.

Your arms tell me
you have been reaching into the coke machine
for strawberries,
you have been humping the thorny crucifix
you have been piloting Mickey Mouse balloons
through the briar patch,
you have been digging for grins in the tooth-pile.

Bonnie Queen Alex Eludes Montreal Hounds
Famous Local Love Scribe Implicated

Your purity drives me to work.
I must get back to lust and microscopes,
experiments in embalming,
resume the census of my address book.

You leave behind you a fanatic
to answer RCMP questions.

THREE GOOD NIGHTS

Out of some simple part of me
which I cannot use up
    I took a blessing for the flowers
tightening in the night
like fists of jealous love
    like knots
no one can undo without destroying
    The new morning gathered me
in blue mist
    like dust under a wedding gown
Then I followed the day
like a cloud of heavy sheep
    after the judas
up a blood-ringed ramp
into the terror of every black building

Ten years sealed journeys unearned dreams
Laughter meant to tempt me into old age
    spilled for friends stars unknown flesh mules sea
Instant knowledge of bodies material and spirit
    which slowly learned would have made death smile
Stories turning into theories
    which begged only for the telling and retelling
Girls sailing over the blooms of my mouth
    with a muscular triangular kiss
    ordinary mouth to secret mouth
Nevertheless my homage sticky flowers
    rabbis green and red serving the sun like platters
In the end you offered me the dogma you taught
    me to disdain and I good pupil disdained it
I fell under the diagrammed fields like the fragment
    of a perfect statue layers of cities build upon

I saw you powerful I saw you happy
that I could not live only for harvesting
that I was a true citizen of the slow earth

Light and Splendour
in the sleeping orchards
entering the trees
like a silent movie wedding procession
entering the arches of branches
for the sake of love only
From a hill I watched
the apple blossoms breathe
the silver out of the night
like fish eating the spheres
of air out of the river
So the illumined night fed
the sleeping orchards
entering the vaults of branches
like a holy procession
Long live the Power of Eyes
Long live the invisible steps
men can read on a mountain
Long live the unknown machine
or heart
which by will or accident
pours with victor's grace
endlessly perfect weather
on the perfect creatures
the world grows

Montreal
July 1964

ON THE SICKNESS OF MY LOVE

Poems! break out!
break my head!
What good's a skull?
Help! help!
I need you!

She is getting old.
Her body tells her everything.
She has put aside cosmetics.
She is a prison of truth.

Make her get up!
dance the seven veils!
Poems! silence her body!
Make her friend of mirrors!

Do I have to put on my cape?
wander like the moon
over skies & skies of flesh
to depart again in the morning?

Can't I pretend
she grows prettier?
be a convict?
Can't my power fool me?
Can't I live in poems?

Hurry up! poems! lies!
Damn your weak music!
You've let arthritis in
You're no poem
you're a visa.

FOR MARIANNE

It's so simple
to wake up beside your ears
and count the pearls
with my two heads

It takes me back to blackboards
and I'm running with Jane
and seeing the dog run

It makes it so easy
to govern this country
I've already thought up the laws
I'll work hard all day
in Parliament

Then let's go to bed
right after supper
Let's sleep and wake up
all night

THE FAILURE OF A SECULAR LIFE

The pain-monger came home
from a hard day's torture.

He came home with his tongs.
He put down his black bag.

His wife hit him with an open nerve
and a cry the trade never heard.

He watched her real-life Dachau,
knew his career was ruined.

Was there anything else to do?
He sold his bag and tongs,

went to pieces. A man's got to be able
to bring his wife something.

MY MENTORS

My rabbi has a silver buddha,
my priest has a jade talisman.
My doctor sees a marvellous omen
in our prolonged Indian summer.

My rabbi, my priest stole their trinkets
from shelves in the holy of holies.
The trinkets cannot be eaten.
They wonder what to do with them.

My doctor is happy as a pig
although he is dying of exposure.
He has finished his big book
on the phallus as a phallic symbol.

My zen master is a grand old fool.
I caught him worshipping me yesterday,
so I made him stand in a foul corner
with my rabbi, my priest, and my doctor.

HEIRLOOM

The torture scene developed under a glass bell
such as might protect an expensive clock.
I almost expected a chime to sound
as the tongs were applied
and the body jerked and fainted calm.
All the people were tiny and rosy-cheeked
and if I could have heard a cry of triumph or pain
it would have been tiny as the mouth that made it
or one single note of a music box.
The drama bell was mounted
like a gigantic baroque pearl
on a wedding ring or brooch or locket.

     I know you feel naked, little darling.
I know you hate living in the country
and can't wait until the shiny magazines
come every week and every month.
Look through your grandmother's house again.
There is an heirloom somewhere.

THE PROJECT

Evidently they need a lot of blood for these tests. I let th
take all they wanted. The hospital was cool and its atmosph
of order encouraged me to persist in my own projects.

I always wanted to set fire to your houses. I've been in the
Through the front doors and the back. I'd like to see th
burn slowly so I could visit many and peek in the falli
windows. I'd like to see what happens to those white carp
you pretended to be so careless about. I'd like to see a wh
telephone melting.

We don't want to trap too many inside because the stre
have got to be packed with your poor bodies screaming ba
and forth. I'll be comforting. Oh dear, pyjama flannel sea
right on to the flesh. Let me pull it off.

It seems to me they took too much blood. Probably selli
it on the side. The little man's white frock was smeared w
blood. Little men like that keep company with blood. S
them in *abattoirs* and assisting in human experiments.

—When did you last expose yourself?

—Sunday morning for a big crowd in the lobby of the Que
Elizabeth.

—Funny. You know what I mean.

—Expose myself to what?

—A woman.

—Ah.

I narrowed my eyes and whispered in his yellow ear.

—You better bring her in too.

—And it's still free?

Of course it was still free. Not counting the extra blood th
stole. Prevent my disease from capturing the entire city. He
this man. Give him all possible Judeo-Christian help.

Fire would be best. I admit that. Tie firebrands betwe

he foxes and chase them through your little gardens. A rosy
sky would improve the view from anywhere. It would be a
mercy. Oh, to see the roofs devoured and the beautiful old
level of land rising again.

The factory where I work isn't far from the hospital. Same
architect as a matter of fact and the similarities don't end
there. It's easier to get away with lying down in the hospital.
However we have our comforts in the factory.

The foreman winked at me when I went back to my machine. He loved his abundant nature. Me new at the job and
he'd actually given me time off. I really enjoy the generosity
of slaves. He came over to inspect my work.

—But this won't do at all.

—No?

—The union said you were an experienced operator.

—I am. I am.

—This is no seam.

—Now that you mention it.

—Look here.

He took a fresh trouser and pushed in beside me on the
bench. He was anxious to demonstrate the only skill he owned.
He arranged the pieces under the needle. When he was half-
way down the leg and doing very nicely I brought my foot
down on the pedal beside his. The unexpected acceleration
sucked his fingers under the needle.

Another comfort is the Stock Room.

It is large and dark and filled with bundles and rolls of material.

—But shouldn't you be working?

—No, Mary, I shouldn't.

—Won't Sam miss you?

—You see he's in the hospital. Accident.

Mary runs the Cafeteria and the Boss exposes himself to her
regularly. This guarantees her the concession.

I feel the disease raging in my blood. I expect my saliva to be discoloured.

—Yes, Mary, real cashmere. Three hundred dollar suits.

The Boss has a wife to whom he must expose himself ever once in a while. She has her milkmen. The city is orderly. There are white bottles standing in front of a million doors. And there are Conventions. Multitudes of bosses sharing the pleasures of exposure.

I shall go mad. They'll find me at the top of Mount Royal impersonating Genghis Khan. Seized with laughter and pus—

—Very soft, Mary. That's what they pay for.

Fire would be best. Flames. Bright windows. Two cars exploding in each garage. But could I ever manage it. This way is slower. More heroic in a way. Less dramatic of course. But I have an imagination.

HYDRA 1963

The stony path coiled around me
and bound me to the night.
A boat hunted the edge of the sea
under a hissing light.

Something soft involved a net
and bled around a spear.
The blunt death, the cumulus jet—
I spoke to you, I thought you near!

Or was the night so black
that something died alone?
A man with a glistening back
beat the food against a stone.

ALL THERE IS TO KNOW
ABOUT ADOLPH EICHMANN

EYES:	Medium
HAIR:	Medium
WEIGHT:	Medium
HEIGHT:	Medium
DISTINGUISHING FEATURES:	None
NUMBER OF FINGERS:	Ten
NUMBER OF TOES:	Ten
INTELLIGENCE:	Medium

What did you expect?

Talons?

Oversize incisors?

Green saliva?

Madness?

THE NEW LEADER

When he learned that his father had the oven contract, that the smoke above the city, the clouds as warm as skin, were his father's manufacture, he was freed from love, his emptiness was legalized.

Hygienic as a whip his heart drove out the alibis of devotion, free as a storm-severed bridge, useless and pure as drowned alarm clocks, he breathed deeply, gratefully in the polluted atmosphere, and he announced: My father had the oven contract, he loved my mother and built her houses in the countryside.

When he learned his father had the oven contract he climbed a hillock of eyeglasses, he stood on a drift of hair, he hated with great abandon the king cripples and their mothers, the husbands and wives, the familiar sleep, the decent burdens.

Dancing down Ste Catherine Street he performed great surgery on a hotel of sleepers. The windows leaked like a broken meat freezer. His hatred blazed white on the salted driveways. He missed nobody but he was happy he'd taken one hundred and fifty women in moonlight back in ancient history.

He was drunk at last, drunk at last, after years of threading history's crushing daisy-chain with beauty after beauty. His father had raised the thigh-shaped clouds which smelled of salesmen, gipsies and violinists. With the certainty and genital pleasure of revelation he knew, he could not doubt, his father was the one who had the oven contract.

Drunk at last, he hugged himself, his stomach clean, cold and drunk, the sky clean but only for him, free to shiver, free to hate, free to begin.

FOR E.J.P.

I once believed a single line
    in a Chinese poem could change
        forever how blossoms fell
and the moon itself climbed on
    the grief of concise weeping men
        to journey over cups of wine
I thought invasions were begun for crows
    to pick at a skeleton
        dynasties sown and spent
to serve the language of a fine lament
    I thought governors ended their lives
        as sweetly drunken monks
telling time by rain and candles
    instructed by an insect's pilgrimage
        across the page—all this
so one might send an exile's perfect letter
to an ancient home-town friend

I chose a lonely country
    broke from love
        scorned the fraternity of war
I polished my tongue against the pumice moon
    floated my soul in cherry wine
        a perfumed barge for Lords of Memory
to languish on to drink to whisper out
    their store of strength
        as if beyond the mist along the shore
their girls their power still obeyed
    like clocks wound for a thousand years
I waited until my tongue was sore

Brown petals wind like fire around my poems
     I aimed them at the stars but
          like rainbows they were bent
before they sawed the world in half
     Who can trace the canyoned paths
          cattle have carved out of time
wandering from meadowlands to feasts
     Layer after layer of autumn leaves
          are swept away
Something forgets us perfectly

A MIGRATING DIALOGUE

He was wearing a black moustache and leather hair.
We talked about the gipsies.

Don't bite your nails, I told him.
Don't eat carpets.
Be careful of the rabbits.
Be cute.
Don't stay up all night watching
parades on the Very Very Very Late Show.
Don't ka-ka in your uniform.

And what about all the good generals,
the fine old aristocratic fighting men,
the brave Junkers, the brave Rommels,
the brave von Silverhaired Ambassadors
who resigned in '41?

Wipe the smirk off your face.
Captain Marvel signed the ship contract.
Joe Palooka manufactured whips.
Li'l Abner packed the whips in cases.
The Katzenjammer Kids thought up experiments.
Mere cogs.

Peekaboo Miss Human Soap.
It never happened.
O castles on the Rhine.
O blond SS.
Don't believe everything you see in museums.

I said WIPE THAT SMIRK including
the mouth-foam of superior disgust.
I don't like the way you go to work every morning.
How come the buses still run?
How come they're still making movies?

I believe with a perfect faith in the Second World War.
I am convinced that it happened.
I am not so sure about the First World War.
The Spanish Civil War—maybe.
I believe in gold teeth.
I believe in Churchill.
Don't tell me we dropped fire into cribs.
I think you are exaggerating.
The Treaty of Westphalia has faded like a lipstick
smudge on the Blarney Stone.
Napoleon was a sexy brute.
Hiroshima was Made in Japan out of paper.
I think we should let sleeping ashes lie.
I believe with a perfect faith in all the history
I remember, but it's getting harder and harder
to remember much history.

There is sad confetti sprinkling
from the windows of departing trains.
I let them go. I cannot remember them.
They hoot mournfully out of my daily life.
I forget the big numbers,
I forget what they mean.
I apologize to the special photogravure section
of a 1945 newspaper which began my education.
I apologize left and right.
I apologize in advance to all the folks
in this fine wide audience for my tasteless closing remarks.

Braun, Raubal and him
Hitler and his ladies
(I have some experience in these matters),
these three humans,
I can't get their nude and loving bodies out of my mind

THE BUS

I was the last passenger of the day,
I was alone on the bus,
I was glad they were spending all that money
just getting me up Eighth Avenue.
Driver! I shouted, it's you and me tonight,
let's run away from this big city
to a smaller city more suitable to the heart,
let's drive past the swimming pools of Miami Beach,
you in the driver's seat, me several seats back,
but in the racial cities we'll change places
so as to show how well you've done up North,
and let us find ourselves some tiny American fishing village
in unknown Florida
and park right at the edge of the sand,
a huge bus pointing out,
metallic, painted, solitary,
with New York plates.

THE REST IS DROSS

We meet at a hotel
with many quarters for the radio
surprised that we've survived as lovers
not each other's
but lovers still
with outrageous hope and habits in the craft
which embarrass us slightly
as we let them be known
the special caress the perfect inflammatory word
the starvation we do not tell about
We do what only lovers can
    make a gift out of necessity
Looking at our clothes
folded over the chair
I see we no longer follow fashion
and we own our own skins
God I'm happy we've forgotten nothing
and can love each other
for years in the world

HOW THE WINTER GETS IN

I ask you where you want to go
you say nowhere
    but your eyes make a wish
An absent chiropractor
you stroke my wrist
    I'm almost fooled into
greasy circular snores
when I notice your eyes
    sounding the wall for
dynamite points
like a doctor at work on a TB chest
    Nowhere you say again in a kiss
go to sleep
First tell me your wish
    Your lashes startle on my skin
like a seismograph
An airliner's perishing drone
    pulls the wall off our room
like an old Band-aid
The winter comes in
    and the eyes I don't keep
tie themselves to a journey
like wedding tin cans

Ways Mills
November 1963

PROPAGANDA

The coherent statement was made
by father, the gent with spats to
keep his shoes secret. It had to
do with the nature of religion and
the progress of lust in the twentieth
century. I myself have several
statements of a competitive
coherence which I intend to spread
around at no little expense. I
love the eternal moment, for
instance. My father used to remark,
doffing his miniature medals, that
there is a time that is ripe for
everything. A little extravagant,
Dad, I guess, judging by values.
Oh well, he'd say, and the whole
world might have been the address.

OPIUM AND HITLER

Several faiths
bid him leap—
opium and Hitler
let him sleep.

A Negress with
an appetite
helped him think
he wasn't white.

Opium and Hitler
made him sure
the world was glass.
There was no cure

for matter
disarmed as this:
the state rose on
a festered kiss.

Once a dream
nailed on the sky
a summer sun
while it was high.

He wanted a
blindfold of skin,
he wanted the
afternoon to begin.

One law broken—
nothing held.

The world was wax,
his to mould.

No! He fumbled
for his history dose.
The sun came loose,
his woman close.

Lost in a darkness
their bodies would reach,
the Leader started
a racial speech.

FOR ANYONE DRESSED IN MARBLE

The miracle we all are waiting for
is waiting till the Parthenon falls down
and House of Birthdays is a house no more
and fathers are unpoisoned by renown.
The medals and the records of abuse
can't help us on our pilgrimage to lust,
but like whips certain perverts never use,
compel our flesh in paralysing trust.
        I see an orphan, lawless and serene,
standing in a corner of the sky,
body something like bodies that have been,
but not the scar of naming in his eye.
Bred close to the ovens, he's burnt inside.
Light, wind, cold, dark—they use him like a bride.

FOLK

flowers for hitler the summer yawned
flowers all over my new grass
and here is a little village
they are painting it for a holiday
here is a little church
here is a school
here are some doggies making love
the flags are bright as laundry
flowers for hitler the summer yawned

HAD IT FOR A MOMENT

had it for a moment
knew why I must thank you
    I saw powerful governing men in black suits
saw them undressed
in the arms of young mistresses
the men more naked than the naked women
the men crying quietly
    No that is not it
I'm losing why I must thank you
which means I'm left with pure longing
    How old are you
Do you like your thighs
had it for a moment
had a reason for letting the picture
of your mouth destroy my conversation
    Something on the radio
the end of a Mexican song
I saw the musicians getting paid
they are not even surprised
they knew it was only a job
    Now I've lost it completely
A lot of people think you are beautiful
How do I feel about that
I have no feeling about that
    I had a wonderful reason for not merely
courting you
It was tied up with the newspapers
    I saw secret arrangements in high offices
I saw men who loved their worldliness
even though they had looked through
big electric telescopes
they still thought their worldliness was serious

not just a hobby a taste a harmless affectation
　　they thought the cosmos listened
I was suddenly fearful
one of their obscure regulations
could separate us
　　I was ready to beg for mercy
Now I'm getting into humiliation
I've lost why I began this
I wanted to talk about your eyes
I know nothing about your eyes
and you've noticed how little I know
I want you somewhere safe
far from high offices
　　I'll study you later
So many people want to cry quietly beside you

July 4, 1963

INDEPENDENCE

Tonight I will live with my new white skin
which I found under a millennium of pith clothing
None of the walls jump when I call them
Trees smirked *you're one of us now*
when I strode through the wheat in my polished boots
Out of control awake and newly naked
I lie back in the luxury of my colour
Somebody is marching for me at me to me
Somebody has a flag I did not invent
I think the Aztecs have not been sleeping
Magic moves from hand to hand like money
I thought we were the bank the end of the line
New York City was just a counter
the cumpled bill passed across
I thought that heroes meant us
I have been reading too much history
and writing too many history books
Magic moves from hand to hand and I'm broke
Someone stops the sleepwalker in the middle of the opera
and pries open his fist finger by finger
and kisses him goodbye
I think the Aztecs have not been sleeping
no matter what I taught the children
I think no one has ever slept but he
who gathers the past into stories
Magic moves from hand to hand
Somebody is smiling in one of our costumes
Somebody is stepping out of a costume
I think that is what invisible means

July 4, 1963

THE HOUSE

Two hours off the branch and burnt
the petals of the gardenia curl and deepen
in the yellow-brown of waste
    Your body wandered close
    I didn't raise my hand to reach
the distance was so familiar
Our house is happy with its old furniture
the black Venetian bed stands on gold claws
guarding the window
    Don't take the window away
    and leave a hole in the stark mountains
The clothesline and the grey clothespins
would make you think we're going to be together always
    Last night I dreamed
    you were Buddha's wife
and I was a historian watching you sleep
What vanity
    A girl told me something beautiful
    Very early in the morning
she saw an orange-painted wooden boat
come into port over the smooth sea
The cargo was hay
The boat rode low under the weight
She couldn't see the sailors
but on top of all the hay sat a monk
Because of the sun behind he seemed
to be sitting in a fire
like that famous photograph
    I forgot to tell you the story
    She surprised me by telling it
and I wanted her for ten minutes
I really enjoyed the gardenia from Sophia's courtyard

You put it on my table two hours ago
    and I can smell it everywhere in the house
Darling I attach nothing to it

July 4, 1963

THE LISTS

Strafed by the Milky Way
vaccinated by a snarl of clouds
lobotomized by the bore of the moon
he fell in a heap
some woman's smell
smeared across his face
a plan for Social Welfare
rusting in a trouser cuff
    From five to seven
tall trees doctored him
mist roamed on guard
    Then it began again
the sun stuck a gun in his mouth
the wind started to skin him
Give up the Plan give up the Plan
echoing among its scissors
    The women who elected him
performed erotic calisthenics
above the stock-reports
of every hero's fame
    Out of the corner of his stuffed eye
etched in minor metal
under his letter of the alphabet
he clearly saw his tiny name
    Then a museum slid under
his remains like a shovel

ORDER

In many movies I came upon an idol
I would not touch, whose forehead jewel
was safe, or if stolen—mourned.
Truly, I wanted the lost forbidden city
to be the labyrinth for wise technicolor
birds, and every human riddle
the love-fed champion pursued
I knew was bad disguise for greed.
I was with the snake who made his nest
in the voluptuous treasure, I dropped
with the spider to threaten the trail-bruised
white skin of the girl who was searching
for her brother, I balanced on the limb
with the leopard who had to be content
with Negroes and double-crossers
and never tasted but a slash of hero flesh.
Even after double-pay I deserted
with the bearers, believing every rumour
the wind brought from the mountain pass.
The old sorceress, the spilled wine,
the black cards convinced me:
the timeless laws must not be broken.
When the lovers got away with the loot
of new-valued life or love, or bought
themselves a share in time by letting
the avalanche seal away for ever
the gold goblets and platters, I knew
a million ways the jungle might have been
meaner and smarter. As the red sun

ame down on their embrace I shouted
om my velvet seat, Get them, get them,
all the animals drugged with anarchy and happiness.

ugust 6, 1963

DESTINY

I want your warm body to disappear
politely and leave me alone in the bath
because I want to consider my destiny.
Destiny! why do you find me in this bathtub,
idle, alone, unwashed, without even
the intention of washing except at the last moment?
Why don't you find me at the top of a telephone pole,
repairing the lines from city to city?
Why don't you find me riding a horse through Cuba,
a giant of a man with a red machete?
Why don't you find me explaining machines
to underprivileged pupils, negroid Spaniards,
happy it is not a course in creative writing?
Come back here, little warm body,
it's time for another day.
Destiny has fled and I settle for you
who found me staring at you in a store
one afternoon four years ago
and slept with me every night since.
How do you find my sailor eyes after all this time?
Am I what you expected?
Are we together too much?
Did Destiny shy at the double Turkish towel,
our knowledge of each other's skin,
our love which is a proverb on the block,
our agreement that in matters spiritual
I should be the Man of Destiny
and you should be the Woman of the House?

QUEEN VICTORIA AND ME

Queen Victoria
my father and all his tobacco loved you
I love you too in all your forms
the slim unlovely virgin anyone would lay
the white figure floating among German beards
the mean governess of the huge pink maps
the solitary mourner of a prince
Queen Victoria
I am cold and rainy
I am dirty as a glass roof in a train station
I feel like an empty cast-iron exhibition
I want ornaments on everything
because my love she gone with other boys
Queen Victoria
do you have a punishment under the white lace
will you be short with her
and make her read little Bibles
will you spank her with a mechanical corset
I want her pure as power
I want her skin slightly musty with petticoats
will you wash the easy bidets out of her head
Queen Victoria
I'm not much nourished by modern love
Will you come into my life
with your sorrow and your black carriages
and your perfect memory
Queen Victoria
The 20th century belongs to you and me
Let us be two severe giants
(not less lonely for our partnership)
who discolour test tubes in the halls of science

who turn up unwelcome at every World's Fair
heavy with proverb and correction
confusing the star-dazed tourists
with our incomparable sense of loss

HE NEW STEP

Ballet-Drama in One Act

CHARACTERS:

MARY and DIANE, two working girls who room together. MARY is very plain, plump, clumsy: ugly, if one is inclined to the word. She is the typical victim of beauty courses and glamour magazines. Her life is a search for, a belief in the technique, the elixir, the method, the secret, the hint that will transform and render her forever lovely. DIANE is a natural beauty, tall, fresh and graceful, one of the blessed. She moves to a kind of innocent sexual music, incapable of any gesture which could intrude on this high animal grace. To watch her pull on her nylons is all one needs of ballet or art.

HARRY is the man DIANE loves. He has the proportions we associate with Greek statuary. Clean, tall, openly handsome, athletic. He glitters with health, decency, and mindlessness.

THE COLLECTOR is a woman over thirty, grotesquely obese, a great heap, deformed, barely mobile. She possesses a commanding will and combines the fascination of the tyrant and the freak. Her joliness asks for no charity. All her movements represents the triumph of a rather sinister spiritual energy over an intolerable mass of flesh.

SCENE:

It is eight o'clock of a Saturday night. All the action takes place in the girls' small apartment which need be furnished with no more than a dressing-mirror, wardrobe, record-player, easy chair, and a front door. We have the impression, as we do from the dwelling places of most bachelor girls, of an arrangement they want to keep comfortable but temporary.

DIANE is dressed in bra and panties, preparing herself for an evening with HARRY. MARY follows her about the room, lost in envy and awe, handing DIANE the necessary lipstick or brush, doing up a button or fastening a necklace. MARY is the dull but orthodox assistant to DIANE's mysterious ritual of beauty.

MARY: What is it like?
DIANE: What like?
MARY: You know.
DIANE: No.
MARY: To be like you.
DIANE: Such as?
MARY: Beautiful.
(*Pause. During these pauses* DIANE *continues her toilet as does* MARY *her attendance.*)
DIANE: Everybody can be beautiful.
MARY: You can say that.
DIANE: Love makes people beautiful.
MARY: You can say that.
DIANE: A women in love is beautiful.
(*Pause.*)
MARY: Look at me.
DIANE: I've got to hurry.
MARY: Harry always waits.
DIANE: He said he's got something on his mind.
MARY: You've got the luck.
(*Pause.*)
MARY: Look at me a second.
DIANE: All right.
(MARY *performs an aggressive curtsy.*)
MARY: Give me some advice.
DIANE: Everybody has their points.
MARY: What are my points?

DIANE: What are your points?

MARY: Name my points.

(MARY *stands there belligerently. She lifts up her skirt. She rolls up her sleeves. She tucks her sweater in tight.*)

DIANE: I've got to hurry.

MARY: Name one point.

DIANE: You've got nice hands.

MARY *(Surprised)*: Do I?

DIANE: Very nice hands.

MARY: Do I really?

DIANE: Hands are very important.

(MARY *shows her hands to the mirror and gives them little exercises.*)

DIANE: Men often look at hands.

MARY: They do?

DIANE: Often.

MARY: What do they think?

DIANE: Think?

MARY *(Impatiently)*: When they look at hands.

DIANE: They think: There's a nice pair of hands.

MARY: What else?

DIANE: They think: Those are nice hands to hold.

MARY: And?

DIANE: They think: Those are nice hands to— squeeze.

MARY: I'm listening.

DIANE: They think: Those are nice hands to— kiss.

MARY: Go on.

DIANE: They think— (*racking her brain for compassion's sake.*)

MARY: Well?

147

DIANE: Those are nice hands to—love!

MARY: Love!

DIANE: Yes.

MARY: What do you mean "love"?

DIANE: I don't have to explain.

MARY: Someone is going to love my hands?

DIANE: Yes.

MARY: What about my arms?

DIANE: What about them? (*A little surly.*)

MARY: Are they one of my points?
(*Pause.*)

DIANE: I suppose not one of your best.

MARY: What about my shoulders?
(*Pause.*)

DIANE: Your shoulders are all right.

MARY: You know they're not. They're not.

DIANE: Then what did you ask me for?

MARY: What about my bosom?

DIANE: I don't know your bosom.

MARY: You do know my bosom.

DIANE: I don't.

MARY: You do.

DIANE: I do not know your bosom.

MARY: You've seen me undressed.

DIANE: I never looked that hard.

MARY: You know my bosom all right. (*But she'll let it pass. She looks disgustedly at her hands.*)

MARY: Hands!

DIANE: Don't be so hard on yourself.

MARY: Sexiest knuckles on the block.

DIANE: Why hurt yourself?

MARY: My fingers are really stacked.

DIANE: Stop, sweetie.

MARY: They come when they shake hands with me.

DIANE: Now please!

MARY: You don't know how it feels.

(*Pause.*)

MARY: Just tell me what it's like.

DIANE: What like?

MARY: To be beautiful. You've never told me.

DIANE: There's no such thing as beautiful.

MARY: Sure.

DIANE: It's how you feel.

MARY: I'm going to believe that.

DIANE: It's how you feel makes you beautiful.

MARY: Do you know how I feel?

DIANE: Don't tell me.

MARY: Ugly.

DIANE: You don't have to talk like that.

MARY: I feel ugly. What does that make me?

(DIANE *declines to answer. She steps into high-heeled shoes, the elevation bringing out the harder lines of her legs, adding to her stature an appealing haughtiness and to her general beauty a touch of violence.*)

MARY: According to what you said.

DIANE: I don't know.

MARY: You said: It's how you feel makes you beautiful.

DIANE: I know what I said.

MARY: I feel ugly. So what does that make me?

DIANE: I don't know.

MARY: According to what you said.

DIANE: I don't know.

MARY: Don't be afraid to say it.

DIANE: Harry will be here.

MARY: Say it! (*Launching herself into hysteria.*)

DIANE: I've got to get ready.

MARY: You never say it. You're afraid to say it.
It won't kill you. The word won't kill
you. You think it but you won't say it.
When you get up in the morning you
tiptoe to the bathroom. I tiptoe to the
bathroom but I sound like an army.
What do you think I think when I hear
myself? Don't you think I know the difference? It's no secret. It's not as though
there aren't any mirrors. If you only said
it I wouldn't try. I don't want to try. I
don't want to have to try. If you only
once said I was—ugly!
(*DIANE comforts her.*)

DIANE: You're not ugly, sweetie. Nobody's ugly.
Everybody can be beautiful. Your turn
will come. Your man will come. He'll
take you in his arms. No no no, you're
not ugly. He'll teach you that you are
beautiful. Then you'll know what it is.
(*Cradling her.*)

MARY: Will he?

DIANE: Of course he will.

MARY: Until then?

DIANE: You've got to keep going, keep looking.

MARY: Keep up with my exercises.

DIANE: Yes.

MARY: Keep up with my ballet lessons.

DIANE: Exactly.

MARY: Try and lose weight.

DIANE: Follow the book.

MARY: Brush my hair the right way.

DIANE: That's the spirit.

MARY: A hundred strokes.

DIANE: Good.

MARY: I've got to gain confidence.

DIANE: You will.

MARY: I can't give up.

DIANE: It's easier than you think.

MARY: Concentrate on my best points.

DIANE: Make the best of what you have.

MARY: Why not start now?

DIANE: Why not.

(MARY *gathers herself together, checks her posture in the mirror, crosses to the record-player and switches it on. "The Dance of the Sugar-plum Fairy." She begins the ballet exercises she has learned, perhaps, at the YWCA, two evenings a week. Between the final touches of her toilet* DIANE *encourages her with nods of approval. The doorbell rings. Enter* HARRY *in evening clothes, glittering although his expression is solemn, for he has come on an important mission.*)

HARRY: Hi girls. Don't mind me, Mary.

(MARY *waves in the midst of a difficult contortion.*)

DIANE: Darling!

(DIANE *sweeps into his arms, takes the attitude of a dancing partner.* HARRY, *with a trace of reluctance, consents to lead her in a ballroom step across the floor.*)

HARRY: I've got something on my mind.

(DIANE *squeezes his arm, disengages herself, crosses to* MARY *and whispers.*)

DIANE: He's got something on his mind.

(DIANE *and* MARY *embrace in the usual squeaky conspiratorial manner with which girls preface happy matrimonial news. While* MARY *smiles benignly exeunt* HARRY *and* DIANE. MARY *turns the machine louder, moves in front of the mirror, resumes the ballet exercises. She stops them from time to time to check various parts of her anatomy in the mirror at close range, as if the effects of the discipline might be already apparent.*)

MARY: Goody.

(*A long determined ring of the doorbell.* MARY *stops, eyes bright with expectation. Perhaps the miracle is about to unfold. She smoothes her dress and hair, switches off the machine, opens the door.* THE COLLECTOR *enters with lumbering difficulty, looks around, takes control. The power she radiates is somehow guaranteed by her grotesque form. Her body is a huge damaged tank operating under the intimate command of a brilliant field warrior which is her mind:* MARY *waits, appalled and intimidated.*)

COLLECTOR: I knew there was people in because I heard music. (MARY *cannot speak.*) Some people don't like to open the door. I'm in charge of the whole block.

MARY (*Recovering*): Are you collecting for something?

COLLECTOR: The United Fund for the Obese, you know, UFO. That includes The Obese Catholic Drive, The Committee for Jewish Fat People, the Help the Blind Obese, and the Universal Aid to the Obese. If you make one donation you won't be bothered again.

MARY: We've never been asked before.

COLLECTOR: I know. But I have your card now. The whole Fund has been reorganized.

MARY: It has?

COLLECTOR: Oh yes. Actually it was my idea to have the Obese themselves go out and canvass. They were against it at first but I convinced them. It's the only fair way. Gives the public an opportunity to see exactly where their money goes. And I've managed to get the Spastic and Polio and Cancer people to see the light. It's the only fair way. We're all over the neighbourhood.

MARY: It's very—courageous.

COLLECTOR: That's what my husband says.

MARY: Your husband!

COLLECTOR: He'd prefer me to stay at home. Doesn't believe in married girls working.

MARY: Have—have you been married long?

COLLECTOR: Just short of a year. (*Coyly.*) You might say we're still honeymooners.

MARY: Oh.

COLLECTOR: Don't be embarrassed. One of the aims of our organization is to help people like me lead normal lives. Now what could be more normal than marriage? Can you think of anything more normal? Of course you can't. It makes you feel less isolated, part of the whole community. Our people are getting married all the time.

MARY: Of course, of course. (*She is disintegrating.*)

COLLECTOR: I didn't think it would work out myself at first. But John is so loving. He's taken such patience with me. When we're together it's as though there's nothing wrong with me at all.

MARY: What does your husband do?

COLLECTOR: He's a chef.

MARY: A chef.

COLLECTOR: Not in any famous restaurant. Just an ordinary chef. But it's good enough for me. Sometimes, when he's joking, he says I married him for his profession. (MARY *tries to laugh.*) Well I've been chatting too long about myself and I have the rest of this block to cover. How much do you think you'd like to give. I know you're a working girl.

MARY: I don't know, I really don't know.

COLLECTOR: May I make a suggestion?

MARY: Of course.

COLLECTOR: Two dollars.

MARY: Two dollars. (*Goes to her purse obediently.*)

COLLECTOR: I don't think that's too much, do you?

MARY: No no.

COLLECTOR: Five dollars would be too much.

MARY: Too much.

COLLECTOR: And one dollar just doesn't seem right.

MARY: Oh, I only have a five. I don't have any change.

COLLECTOR: I'll take it.

MARY: You'll take it?

COLLECTOR: I'll take it. (*A command.*)

(MARY *drops the bill in the transaction, being afraid to make any physical contact with* THE COLLECTOR. MARY *stoops to pick it up.* THE COLLECTOR *prevents her.*)

COLLECTOR: Let me do that. The whole idea is not to treat us like invalids. You just watch how well I get along. (THE COLLECTOR *retrieves the money with immense difficulty.*)

COLLECTOR: That wasn't so bad, was it?

MARY: No. Oh no. It wasn't so bad.

COLLECTOR: I've even done a little dancing in my time.

MARY: That's nice.

COLLECTOR: They have courses for us. First we do it in water, but very soon we're right up there on dry land. I bet you do some dancing yourself, a girl like you. I heard music when I came.

MARY: Not really.

COLLECTOR: Do you know what would make me very happy?

MARY: It's very late.

COLLECTOR: To see you do a step or two.

MARY: I'm quite tired.

COLLECTOR: A little whirl.

MARY: I'm not very good.

COLLECTOR: A whirl, a twirl, a bit of a swing. I'll put it on for you.

(THE COLLECTOR *begins to make her way to the record-player.* MARY, *who cannot bear to see her expend herself, overtakes her and switches it on.* MARY *performs for a few moments while* THE COLLECTOR *looks on with pleasure, tapping out the time.* MARY *breaks off the dance.*)

MARY: I'm not very good.

COLLECTOR: Would a little criticism hurt you?

MARY: No—

COLLECTOR: They're not dancing like that any more.

MARY: No?

COLLECTOR: They're doing something altogether different.

MARY: I wouldn't know.

COLLECTOR: More like this.

(*The record has reached the end of its spiral and is now jerking back and forth over the last few bars.*)

COLLECTOR: Don't worry about that.

(THE COLLECTOR *moves to stage centre and executes a terrifying dance to the repeating bars of music. It combines the heavy mechanical efficiency of a printing machine with the convulsions of a spastic. It could be a garbage heap falling down an escalator. It is grotesque but military, excruciating but triumphant. It is a woman-creature proclaiming a disease of the flesh.* MARY *tries to look*

away but cannot. She stares, dumb-
founded, shattered, and ashamed.)

COLLECTOR: We learn to get around, don't we?

MARY: It's very nice. (*She switches off the ma-chine.*)

COLLECTOR: That's more what they're doing.

MARY: Is it?

COLLECTOR: In most of the places. A few haven't caught on.

MARY: I'm very tired now. I think—

COLLECTOR: You must be tired.

MARY: I am.

COLLECTOR: With all my talking.

MARY: Not really.

COLLECTOR: I've taken your time.

MARY: You haven't.

COLLECTOR: I'll write you a receipt.

MARY: It isn't necessary.

COLLECTOR: Yes it is. (*She writes.*) This isn't official. An official receipt will be mailed to you from Fund headquarters. You'll need it for Income Tax.

MARY: Thank you.

COLLECTOR: Thank *you*. I've certainly enjoyed this.

MARY: Me too. (*She is now confirmed in a state of numbed surrender.*)

COLLECTOR (*with a sudden disarming tenderness that changes through the speech into a vision of uncompromising domination*): No, you didn't. Oh, I know you didn't. It frightened you. It made you sort of sick. It had to frighten you. It always does at the beginning. Everyone is frightened at

157

the beginning. That's part of it. Frightened and—fascinated. Fascinated—that's the important thing. You were fascinated too, and that's why I know you'll learn the new step. You see, it's a way to start over and forget about all the things you were never really good at. Nobody can resist that, can they? That's why you'll learn the new step. That's why I must teach you. And soon you'll want to learn. Everybody will want to learn. We'll be teaching everybody.

MARY: I'm fairly busy.

COLLECTOR: Don't worry about that. We'll find time. We'll make time. You don't believe this now, but soon, and it will be very soon, you're going to want me to teach you everything. Well, you better get some sleep. Sleep is very important. I want to say thank you. All the Obese want to say thank you.

MARY: Nothing. Good night.

COLLECTOR: Just beginning for us.

(*Exit* THE COLLECTOR. MARY, *dazed and exhausted, stands at the door for some time. She moves toward stage centre, attempts a few elementary exercises, collapses into the chair and stares dumbly at the audience. The sound of a key in the lock. Door opens. Enter* DIANE *alone, crying.*)

DIANE: I didn't want him to see me home.

(MARY *is unable to cope with anyone else's problem at this point.*)

MARY: What's is the matter with you?

DIANE: It's impossible.

MARY: What's impossible?

DIANE: What happened.

MARY: What happened?

DIANE: He doesn't want to see me any more.

MARY: Harry?

DIANE: Harry.

MARY: Your Harry?

DIANE: You know damn well which Harry.

MARY: Doesn't want to see you any more?

DIANE: No.

MARY: I thought he loved you.

DIANE: So did I.

MARY: I thought he really loved you.

DIANE: So did I.

MARY: You told me he said he loved you.

DIANE: He did.

MARY: But now he doesn't?

DIANE: No.

MARY: Oh.

DIANE: It's terrible.

MARY: It must be.

DIANE: It came so suddenly.

MARY: It must have.

DIANE: I thought he loved me.

MARY: So did I.

DIANE: He doesn't!

MARY: Don't cry.

DIANE: He's getting married.

MARY: He isn't!

DIANE: Yes.

MARY: He isn't!

DIANE: This Sunday.

MARY:	This Sunday?
DIANE:	Yes.
MARY:	So soon?
DIANE:	Yes.
MARY:	He told you that?
DIANE:	Tonight.
MARY:	What did he say?
DIANE:	He said he's getting married this Sunday.
MARY:	He's a bastard.
DIANE:	Don't say that.
MARY:	I say he's a bastard.
DIANE:	Don't talk that way.
MARY:	Why not?
DIANE:	Don't.
MARY:	After what he's done?
DIANE:	It's not his fault.
MARY:	Not his fault?
DIANE:	He fell in love.
	(*The word has its magic effect.*)
MARY:	Fell in *love*?
DIANE:	Yes.
MARY:	With someone else?
DIANE:	Yes.
MARY:	He fell out of love with you?
DIANE:	I suppose so.
MARY:	That's terrible.
DIANE:	He said he couldn't help it.
MARY:	Not if it's love.
DIANE:	He said it was.
MARY:	Then he couldn't help it.
	(DIANE *begins to remove her make-up and undress, reversing exactly every step of her toilet.* MARY, *still bewildered, but out of habit, assists her.*)

MARY: And you're so beautiful.

DIANE: No.

MARY: Your hair.

DIANE: No.

MARY: Your shoulders.

DIANE: No.

MARY: Everything?

(*Pause.*)

MARY: What did he say?

DIANE: He told me everything.

MARY: Such as what?

DIANE: Harry's a gentleman.

MARY: I always thought so.

DIANE: He wanted me to know everything.

MARY: It's only fair.

DIANE: He told me about her.

MARY: What did he say?

DIANE: He said he loves her.

MARY: Then he had no choice.

DIANE: He said she's beautiful.

MARY: He didn't!

DIANE: What can you expect?

MARY: I suppose so.

DIANE: He loves her, after all.

MARY: Then I guess he thinks she's beautiful.

(*Pause.*)

MARY: What else did he say?

DIANE: He told me everything.

MARY: How did he meet her?

DIANE: She came to his house.

MARY: What for?

DIANE: She was collecting money.

MARY: Money! (*Alarm.*)

DIANE: For a charity.

MARY: Charity!

DIANE: Invalids of some kind.

MARY: Invalids!

DIANE: That's the worst part.

MARY: What part?

DIANE: She's that way herself.

MARY: What way?

DIANE: You know.

MARY: What way, what way?

DIANE: You know.

MARY: Say it!

DIANE: She's an invalid.

MARY: Harry's marrying an invalid?

DIANE: This Sunday.

MARY: You said he said she was beautiful.

DIANE: He did.

MARY: Harry is going to marry an invalid.

DIANE: What should I do?

MARY: Harry who said he loved you. (*Not a question.*)

DIANE: I'm miserable.

          (MARY *is like a woman moving through a fog toward a light.*)

MARY: Harry is going to marry an invalid. He thinks she's beautiful.

          (MARY *switches on the record-player.*) She came to his door. Harry who told you he loved you. You who told me I had my points.

          (*"The Dance of the Sugar-plum Fairy" begins.* MARY *dances but she does not use the steps she learned at the YWCA. She dances in conscious imitation of* THE COLLECTOR.)

DIANE: What are you doing? (*Horrified.*)
         (MARY *smiles at her.*)
DIANE: Stop it! Stop it this instant!
MARY: Don't tell me what to do. Don't you dare.
         Don't ever tell me what to do. Don't ever.
         (*The dance continues.* DIANE, *dressed in
         bra and panties as at the beginning,
         backs away.*)

CURTAIN

WINTER BULLETIN

Toronto has been good to me
I relaxed on TV
I attacked several dead horses
I spread rumours about myself
I reported a Talmudic quarrel
    with the Montreal Jewish Community
I forged a death certificate
    in case I had to disappear
I listened to a huckster
    welcome me to the world
I slept behind my new sunglasses
I abandoned the care of my pimples
I dreamed that I needed nobody
I faced my trap
I withheld my opinion on matters
    on which I had no opinion
I humoured the rare January weather
    with a jaunty step for the sake of heroism
Not very carefully
    I thought about the future
and how little I know about animals
The future seemed unnecessarily black and strong
as if it had received my casual mistakes
through a carbon sheet

WHY DID YOU GIVE MY NAME
TO THE POLICE?

You recited the Code of Comparisons
in your mother's voice.
Again you were the blue-robed seminary girl
but these were not poplar trees and nuns
you walked between.
These were Laws.
Damn you for making this moment hopeless,
now, as a clerk in uniform fills
in my father's name.

You too must find the moment hopeless
in the Tennyson Hotel.
I know your stomach.
The brass bed bearing your suitcase
rumbles away like an automatic
promenading target in a shooting gallery:
you stand with your hands full
of a necklace you wanted to pack.
In detail you recall your rich dinner.
Grab that towel rack!

Doesn't the sink seem a fraud
with its hair-swirled pipes?
Doesn't the overhead bulb
seem burdened with mucus?
Things will be better at City Hall.

Now you must learn to read
newspapers without laughing.
No hysterical headline breakfasts.
Police be your Guard,

Telephone Book your Brotherhood.
Action! Action! Action!
Goodbye Citizen.

The clerk is talking to nobody.
Do you see how I have tiptoed
out of his brown file?
He fingers his uniform
like a cheated bargain hunter.
Answer me, please talk to me, he weeps,
say I'm not a doorman.

I plug the wires of your fear
 (ah, this I was always meant to do)
into the lust-asylum universe:
raped by aimless old electricity
you stiffen over the steel books of your bed
like a fish
in a liquid air experiment.
Thus withers the Civil Triumph
 (Laws rush in to corset the collapse)
for you are mistress to the Mayor,
he electrocuted in your frozen juices.

THE MUSIC CREPT BY US

I would like to remind
the management
that the drinks are watered
and the hat-check girl
has syphilis
and the band is composed
of former SS monsters
However since it is
New Year's Eve
and I have lip cancer
I will place my
paper hat on my
concussion and dance

DISGUISES

I am sorry that the rich man must go
and his house become a hospital.
I loved his wine, his contemptuous servants,
his ten-year-old ceremonies.
I loved his car which he wore like a snail's shell
everywhere, and I loved his wife,
the hours she put into her skin,
the milk, the lust, the industries
that served her complexion.
I loved his son who looked British
but had American ambitions
and let the word aristocrat comfort him
like a reprieve while Kennedy reigned.
I loved the rich man: I hate to see
his season ticket for the Opera
fall into a pool for opera-lovers.

I am sorry that the old worker must go
who called me mister when I was twelve
and sir when I was twenty
who studied against me in obscure socialist
clubs which met in restaurants.
I loved the machine he knew like a wife's body.
I loved his wife who trained bankers
in an underground pantry
and never wasted her ambition in ceramics.
I loved his children who debate
and come first at McGill University.
Goodbye old gold-watch winner
all your complex loyalties
must now be borne by one-faced patriots.

Goodbye dope fiends of North Eastern Lunch
circa 1948, your spoons which were not
Swedish Stainless, were the same colour
as the hoarded clasps and hooks
of discarded soiled therapeutic corsets.
I loved your puns about snow
even if they lasted the full seven-month
Montreal winter. Go write your memoirs
for the Psychedelic Review.

Goodbye sex fiends of Beaver Pond
who dreamed of being jacked-off
by electric milking machines.
You had no Canada Council.
You had to open little boys
with a pen-knife.
I loved your statement to the press:
"I didn't think he'd mind."
Goodbye articulate monsters
Abbott and Costello have met Frankenstein.

I am sorry that the conspirators must go
the ones who scared me by showing me
a list of all the members of my family.
I loved the way they reserved judgement
about Genghis Khan. They loved me because
I told them their little beards
made them dead-ringers for Lenin.
The bombs went off in Westmount
and now they are ashamed
like a successful outspoken Schopenhauerian
whose room-mate has committed suicide.
Suddenly they are all making movies.
I have no one to buy coffee for.

I embrace the changeless:
the committed men in public wards
oblivious as Hassidim
who believe that they are someone else.
Bravo! Abelard, viva! Rockefeller,
have these buns, Napoleon,
hurrah! betrayed Duchess.
Long live you chronic self-abusers!
you monotheists!
you familiars of the Absolute
sucking at circles!
You are all my comfort
as I turn to face the beehive
as I disgrace my style
as I coarsen my nature
as I invent jokes
as I pull up my garters
as I accept responsibility.

You comfort me
incorrigible betrayers of the self
as I salute fashion
and bring my mind
    like a promiscuous air-hostess
handing out parachutes in a nose dive
bring my butchered mind
to bear upon the facts.

LOT

Give me back my house
Give me back my young wife
    I shouted to the sunflower in my path
Give me back my scalpel
Give me back my mountain view
    I said to the seeds along my path
Give me back my name
Give me back my childhood list
    I whispered to the dust when the path gave out
Now sing
Now sing
    sang my master as I waited in the raw wind
Have I come so far for this
    I wondered as I waited in the pure cold
    ready at last to argue for my silence
Tell me master
do my lips move
or where does it come from
    this soft total chant that drives my soul
    like a spear of salt into the rock
Give me back my house
Give me back my young wife

ONE OF THE NIGHTS I DIDN'T KILL MYSELF

You dance on the day you saved
my theoretical angels
daughters of the new middle-class
who wear your mouths like Bardot
    Come my darlings
the movies are true
I am the lost sweet singer whose death
in the fog your new high-heeled boots
have ground into cigarette butts
I was walking the harbour this evening
looking for a 25-cent bed of water
but I will sleep tonight
with your garters curled in my shoes
like rainbows on vacation
with your virginity ruling
the condom cemeteries like a 2nd chance
I believe I believe
Thursday December 12th
is not the night
and I will kiss again the slope of a breast
little nipple above me
like a sunset

BULLETS

Listen all you bullets
that never hit:
a lot of throats are growing
in open collars
like frozen milk bottles
on a 5 a.m. street
throats that are waiting
for bite scars
but will settle
for bullet holes

You restless bullets
lost in swarms
from undecided wars:
fasten on
these nude throats
that need some
decoration

I've done my own work:
I had 3 jewels
no more
and I have placed them
on my choices
jewels
although they performed
like bullets:
an instant of ruby
before the hands
came up
to stem the mess

And you over there
my little acrobat:
swing fast
After me
there is no care
and the air
is heavily armed
and has
the wildest aim

THE BIG WORLD

The big world will find out
about this farm
the big world will learn
the details of what
I worked out in the can

And your curious life with me
will be told so often
that no one will believe
you grew old

FRONT LAWN

The snow was falling
over my penknife
There was a movie
in the fireplace
The apples were wrapped
in 8-year-old blond hair
Starving and dirty
the janitor's daughter never
turned up in November
to pee from her sweet crack
on the gravel
      I'll go back one day
when my cast is off
Elm leaves are falling
over my bow and arrow
Candy is going bad
and Boy Scout calendars
are on fire
      My old mother
sits in her Cadillac
laughing her Danube laugh
as I tell her that we own
all the worms
under our front lawn
      Rust rust rust
in the engines of love and time

KERENSKY

My friend walks through our city this winter night,
fur-hatted, whistling, anti-mediterranean,
stricken with seeing Eternity in all that is seasonal.
He is the Kerensky of our Circle
always about to chair the last official meeting
before the pros take over, they of the pure smiling eyes
trained only for Form.

      He knows there are no measures to guarantee
the Revolution, or to preserve the row of muscular icicles
which will chart Winter's decline like a graph.

      There is nothing for him to do but preside
over the last official meeting.
It will all come round again: the heartsick teachers
who make too much of poetry, their students
who refuse to suffer, the cache of rifles in the lawyer's attic:
and then the magic, the 80-year comet touching
the sturdiest houses. The Elite Corps commits suicide
in the tennis-ball basement. Poets ride buses free.
The General insists on a popularity poll. Troops study
    satire.
A strange public generosity prevails.

      Only too well he knows the tiny moment when
everything is possible, when pride is loved, beauty held
in common, like having an exquisite sister,
and a man gives away his death like a piece of advice.

      Our Kerensky has waited for these moments
over a table in a rented room
when poems grew like butterflies on the garbage of his
    life.
How many times? The sad answer is: they can be counted.
Possible and brief: this is his vision of Revolution.
      Who will parade the shell today?

Who will kill in the name
of the husk? Who will write a Law to raise the corpse
which cries now only for weeds and excrement?
See him walk the streets, the last guard, the only idler
on the square. He must keep the wreck of the Revolution
the debris of public beauty
from the pure smiling eyes of the trained visionaries
who need our daily lives perfect.

    The soft snow begins to honour him with epaulets,
and to provoke the animal past of his fur hat. He wears
a death, but he allows the snow, like an ultimate answer,
to forgive him, just for this jewelled moment of his coro-
nation. The carved gargoyles of the City Hall receive
the snow as bibs beneath their drooling lips. How they
resemble the men of profane vision, the same greed,
the same intensity as they who whip their minds to recall an ancient lucky orgasm, yes, yes, he knows that
deadly concentration, they are the founders, they are
the bankers—of History! He rests in his walk as they
consume of the generous night everything that he does
not need.

ANOTHER NIGHT WITH
TELESCOPE

Come back to me
      brutal empty room
Thin Byzantine face
      preside over this new fast
I am broken with easy grace
Let me be neither
      father nor child
but one who spins
on an eternal unimportant loom
      patterns of wars and grass
which do not last the night
      I know the stars
are wild as dust
and wait for no man's discipline
      but as they wheel
from sky to sky they rake
      our lives with pins of light

IV / Parasites of Heaven

THE NIGHTMARES DO NOT SUDDENLY

The nightmares do not suddenly
develop happy endings
    I merely step out of them
as a five-year-old scientist
leaves the room
where he has dissected an alarm clock

Love wears out
like overused mirrors unsilvering
    and parts of your faces
make room for the wall behind
If terror needs my round green eyes
for a masterpiece
    let it lure them with nude keyholes
mounted on an egg

And should Love decide
I am not the one
    to stand scratching his head
wondering what wall to lean on
    send King Farouk to argue
or come to me dressed as a fast

A CROSS DIDN'T FALL ON ME

A cross didn't fall on me
when I went for hot-dogs
and the all-night Greek
slave in the Silver Gameland
didn't think I was his brother
Love me because nothing happens

I believe the rain will not
make me feel like a feather
when it comes tonight after
the streetcars have stopped
because my size is definite
Love me because nothing happens

Do you have any idea how
many movies I had to watch
before I knew surely
that I would love you
when the lights woke up
Love me because nothing happens

Here is a headline July 14
in the city of Montreal
Intervention décisive de Pearson
à la conférence du Commonwealth
That was yesterday
Love me because nothing happens

Stars and stars and stars
keep it to themselves
Have you ever noticed how private
a wet tree is

a curtain of razor blades
Love me because nothing happens

Why should I be alone
if what I say is true
I confess I mean to find
a passage or forge a passport
or talk a new language
Love me because nothing happens

I confess I meant to grow
wings and lose my mind
I confess that I've
forgotten what for
Why wings and a lost mind
Love me because nothing happens

SO YOU'RE THE KIND OF VEGETARIAN

So you're the kind of vegetarian
that only eats roses
Is that what you mean
with your Beautiful Losers

1965

NOTHING HAS BEEN BROKEN

Nothing has been broken
  though one of the links of the chain
is a blue butterfly

Here he was attacked
  They smiled as they came and retired
baffled with blue dust

The banks so familiar with metal
  they made for the wings
The thick vaults fluttered

The pretty girls advanced
  their fingers cupped
They bled from the mouth as though struck

The jury asked for pity
  and touched and were electrocuted
by the blue antennae

A thrust at any link
  might have brought him down
but each of you aimed at the blue butterfly

ere we are at the window. Great unbound sheaves of rain
andering across the mountain, parades of wind and driven
ver grass. So long I've tried to give a name to freedom, to-
y my freedom lost its name, like a student's room travelling
to the morning with its lights still on. Every act has its own
yle of freedom, whatever that means. Now I'm commanded
think of weeds, to worship the strong weeds that grew
rough the night, green and wet, the white thread roots tak-
g lottery orders from the coils of brain mud, the permeable
rface of the world. Did you know that the brain developed
at of a fold in the epidermis? Did you? Falling ribbons of silk,
e length of rivers, cross the face of the mountain, systems of
rass and cable. Freedom lost its name to the style with which
ings happen. The straight trees, the spools of weed, the
avelling skeins of rain floating through the folds of the moun-
in—here we are at the window. Are you ready now? Have
dismissed myself? May I fire from the hip? Brothers, each at
our window, we are the style of so much passion, we are the
der of style, we are pure style called to delight a fold of the
y.

CLEAN AS THE GRASS FROM WHICH

Clean as the grass from which
the sun has burned the little dew
I come to this page
in the not so early morning
with a picture of him
whom I could not be for long
not wanting to return or begin
again the idolatry of terror

He was burned away from me
by needles by ashes
by various shames I
engineered against his innocence
by documenting the love of one
who gathered my first songs
and gave her body to my wandering

With a picture of him
grooming her thighs for a journey
with a picture of him
buying her a staring peacock feather
with a picture of him
knighted by her smile her soft fatigue
I begin the hopeless formula
she already had the gold from

Live for him huge black eyes
He never understood their purity
or how they watched him prepare
to ditch the early songs and say goodbye
Sleep beside him uncaptured darling
while I fold into a kite

the long evenings he scratched with
experiments the empty dazzling mornings
that forbid me to recall your name

With a picture of him
standing by the window while she slept
with a picture of him
wondering what adventure is
wondering what cruelty is
with a picture of him
waking her with an angry kiss
leading her body into use and time
I bargain with the fire
which must ignore the both of them

WHEN I PAID THE SUN TO RUN

When I paid the sun to run
It ran and I sat down and cried
The sun I spent my money on
Went round and round inside
The world all at once
Charged with insignificance

I SEE YOU ON A GREEK MATTRESS

I see you on a Greek mattress
reading the *Book of Changes,*
Lebanese candy in the air.
On the whitewashed wall I see
you raise another hexagram
for the same old question:
how can you be free?
I see you cleaning your pipe
with the hairpin
of somebody's innocent night.
I see the plastic Evil Eye
pinned to your underwear.
Once again you throw the pennies,
once again you read
how the pieces of the world
have changed around your question.
Did you get to the Himalayas?
Did you visit that monk in New Jersey?
I never answered any of your letters.
Oh Steve, do you remember me?

1963

UZANNE WEARS A LEATHER COAT

Suzanne wears a leather coat.
Her legs are insured by many burnt bridges.
Her calves are full as spinnakers
in a clean race, hard from following music
beyond the maps of any audience.

Suzanne wears a leather coat
because she is not a civilian.
She never walks casually down Ste Catherine
because with every step she must redeem
the clubfoot crowds and stalk the field
of huge hail-stones that never melted,
I mean the cemetery.

Stand up! stand!
Suzanne is walking by.
She wears a leather coat. She won't stop
to bandage the fractures she walks between.
She must not stop, she must not
carry money.
Many are the workers in charity.

Few serve the lilac,
few heal with mist.
Suzanne wears a leather coat.
Her breasts yearn for marble.
The traffic halts: people fall out
of their cars. None of their most drooling

thoughts are wild enough
to build the ant-full crystal city
she would splinter with the tone of her step.

1963

ONE NIGHT I BURNED THE HOUSE
I LOVED

One night I burned the house I loved,
It lit a perfect ring
In which I saw some weeds and stone
Beyond—not anything.

Certain creatures of the air
Frightened by the night,
They came to see the world again
And perished in the light.

Now I sail from sky to sky
And all the blackness sings
Against the boat that I have made
Of mutilated wings.

TWO WENT TO SLEEP

Two went to sleep
almost every night
one dreamed of mud
one dreamed of Asia
visiting a zeppelin
visiting Nijinsky
Two went to sleep
one dreamed of ribs
one dreamed of senators
Two went to sleep
two travellers
The long marriage
in the dark
The sleep was old
the travellers were old
one dreamed of oranges
one dreamed of Carthage
Two friends asleep
years locked in travel
Good night my darling
as the dreams waved goodbye
one travelled lightly
one walked through water
visiting a chess game
visiting a booth
always returning
to wait out the day
One carried matches
one climbed a beehive
one sold an earphone
one shot a German

Two went to sleep
every sleep went together
wandering away
from an operating table
one dreamed of grass
one dreamed of spokes
one bargained nicely
one was a snowman
one counted medicine
one tasted pencils
one was a child
one was a traitor
visiting heavy industry
visiting the family
Two went to sleep
none could foretell
one went with baskets
one took a ledger
one night happy
one night in terror
Love could not bind them
Fear could not either
they went unconnected
they never knew where
always returning
to wait out the day
parting with kissing
parting with yawns
visiting Death till
they wore out their welcome
visiting Death till
the right disguise worked

1964

IN THE BIBLE GENERATIONS PASS . . .

In the Bible generations pass in a paragraph, a betrayal is disposed of in a phrase, the creation of the world consumes a page. I could never pick the important dynasty out of a multitude, you must have your forehead shining to do that, or to choose out of the snarled network of daily evidence the denials and the loyalties. Who can choose what olive tree the story will need to shade its lovers, what tree out of the huge orchard will give them the particular view of branches and sky which will unleash their kisses. Only two shining people know, they go directly to the roots they lie between. For my part I describe the whole orchard.

FOUND ONCE AGAIN SHAMELESSLY
IGNORING THE SWANS . . .

Found once again shamelessly ignoring the swans who in-
flame the spectators on the shores of American rivers; found
once again allowing the juicy contract to expire because the
telephone has a magic correspondence with my tapeworm;
found once again leaving the garlanded manhood in danger of
long official repose while it is groomed for marble in seedily his-
toric back rooms; found once again humiliating the bank clerk
with eye-to-eye wrestling, art dogma, lives that loaf and stare,
and other stage whispers of genius; found once again the chosen
object of heavenly longing such as can ambush a hermit in a
forest with visions of a busy parking lot; found once again
smelling mothball sweaters, titling home movies, untangling
Victorian salmon rods, fanatically convinced that a world of
sporty order is just around the corner; found once again planning the ideal lonely year which waits like first flesh love on a
calendar of third choices; found once again hovering like a
twine-eating kite over hands that feed me, verbose under the
influence of astrology; found once again selling out to accessi-
ble local purity while Pentagon Tiffany evil alone can guarantee
my power; found once again trusting that my friends grew up
in Eden and will not harm me when at least I am armourless
and absolutely silent; found once again at the very beginning,
veteran of several useless ordeals, prophetic but not seminal,
the purist for the masses of tomorrow; found once again sweet-
ening life which I have abandoned, like a fired zoo-keeper
sneaking peanuts to publicized sodomized elephants; found
once again flaunting the rainbow which demonstrates that I
am permitted only that which I urgently need; found once
again cleansing my tongue of all possibilities, of all possibilities
but my perfect one.

1964

WHEN I HEAR YOU SING

When I hear you sing
Solomon
animal throat, eyes beaming
sex and wisdom
My hands ache from

I left blood on the doors of my home
Solomon
I am very alone from aiming songs
at God for
I thought that beside me there was no one
Solomon

HE WAS LAME

He was lame
as a 3 legged dog
screamed as he came
through the fog

If you are the Light
give me a light
buddy

1965

I AM TOO LOUD WHEN YOU ARE GONE

I am too loud when you are gone
I am John the Baptist, cheated by mere water
and merciful love, wild but over-known
John of honey, of time, longing not for
music, longing, longing to be Him
I am diminished, I peddle versions of Word
that don't survive the tablets broken stone
I am alone when you are gone

SOMEWHERE IN MY TROPHY ROOM . . .

Somewhere in my trophy room the crucifixion and other sacri
fices were still going on, but the flesh and nails were grown
over with rust and I could not tell where the flesh ended and
the wood began or on which wall the instruments were hung

I passed by limbs and faces arranged in this museum like hang
ing kitchen tools, and some brushed my arm as the hallway
reeled me in, but I pocketed my hands along with some vul
nerable smiles, and I continued on.

I heard the rooms behind me clamour an instant for my brain
and once the brain responded, out of habit, weakly, as if
thinking someone else's history, and somewhere in that last
tune it learned that it was not the Queen, it was a drone.

There ahead of me extended an impossible trophy: the bright,
great sky, where no men lived. Beautiful and empty, now luminous with a splendour emanating from my own flesh, the tune-
less sky washed and washed my lineless face and bathed in
waves my heart like a red translucent stone. Until my eyes
gave out I lived there as my home.

Today I know the only distance that I came was to the thresh-
old of my trophy room. Among the killing instruments again
I am further from sacrifice than when I began. I do not stare
or plead with passing pilgrims to help me there. I call it discipline but perhaps it is fallen pride alone.

I'm not the one to learn an exercise for dwelling in the sky.
My trophy room is vast and hung with crutches, ladders,

races, hooks. Unlike the invalid's cathedral, men hang with
these instruments. A dancing wall of molecules, changing nothing, has cleared a place for me and my time.

YOU KNOW WHERE I HAVE BEEN

You know where I have been
Why my knees are raw
I'd like to speak to you
Who will see what I saw

Some men who saw me fall
Spread the news of failure
I want to speak to them
The dogs of literature

Pass me as I proudly
Passed the others
Who kneel in secret flight
Pass us proudly Brothers

I MET A WOMAN LONG AGO

I met a woman long ago,
hair black as black can go.
Are you a teacher of the heart?
Soft she answered No.

I met a girl across the sea,
hair the gold that gold can be.
Are you a teacher of the heart?
Yes, but not for thee.

I knew a man who lost his mind
in some lost place I wished to find.
Follow me, he said,
but he walked behind.

I walked into a hospital
Where none was sick and none was well.
When at night the nurses left,
I could not walk at all.

Not too slow, not too soon
morning came, then came noon.
Dinner time a scalpel blade
lay beside my spoon.

Some girls wander by mistake
into the mess that scalpels make.
Are you teachers of the heart?
We teach old hearts to break.

One day I woke up alone,
hospital and nurses gone.

Have I carved enough?
You are a bone.

I ate and ate and ate,
I didn't miss a plate.
How much do these suppers cost?
We'll take it out in hate.

I spent my hatred every place,
on every work, on every face.
Someone gave me wishes.
I wished for an embrace.

Several girls embraced me, then
I was embraced by men.
Is my passion perfect?
Do it once again.

I was handsome, I was strong,
I knew the words of every song.
Did my singing please you?
The words you sang were wrong.

Who are you whom I address?
Who takes down what I confess?
Are you a teacher of the heart?
A chorus answered Yes.

Teachers, are my lessons done
or must I learn another one?
They cried: Dear Sir or Madam,
Daughter, Son.

I'VE SEEN SOME LONELY HISTORY

I've seen some lonely history
The heart cannot explore
I've scratched some empty blackboards
They have no teachers for

I trailed my meagre demons
From Jerusalem to Rome
I had an invitation
But the host was not at home

There were contagious armies
That spread their uniform
To all parts of my body
Except where I was warm

And so I wore a helmet
With a secret neon sign
That lit up all the boundaries
So I could toe the line

My boots got very tired
Like a sentry's never should
I was walking on a tightrope
That was buried in the mud

Standing at the drugstore
It was very hard to learn
Though my name was everywhere
I had to wait my turn

'm standing here before you
don't know what I bring
f you can hear the music
Why don't you help me sing

SNOW IS FALLING

Snow is falling.
There is a nude in my room.
She surveys the wine-coloured carpet.

She is eighteen.
She has straight hair.
She speaks no Montreal language.

She doesn't feel like sitting down.
She shows no gooseflesh.
We can hear the storm.

She is lighting a cigarette
from the gas range.
She holds back her long hair.

1958

CREATED FIRES I CANNOT LOVE

Created fires I cannot love
lest I lose the ones above.
Poor enough, then I'll learn
to choose the fires where they burn.

O God, make me poor enough
to love your diamond in the rough,
or in my failure let me see
my greed raised to mystery.

Do you hate the ones who must
turn your world all to dust?
Do you hate the ones who ask
if Creation wears a mask?

God beyond the God I name,
if mask and fire are the same,
repair the seam my love leaps through,
uncreated fire to pursue.

Network of created fire,
maim my love and my desire.
Make me poor so I may be
servant in the world I see,

Or, as my love leaps wide,
confirm your servant in his pride:
if my love can't burn,
forbid a sickening return.

Is it here my love will train
not to leap so high again?

o praise here? no blame?
rom my love you tear my name.

Jnmake me as I'm washed
ar from the fiery mask.
Gather my pride in the coded pain
vhich is also your domain.

CLAIM ME, BLOOD, IF YOU
HAVE A STORY

Claim me, blood, if you have a story
to tell with my Jewish face,
you are strong and holy still, only
speak, like the Zohar, of a carved-out place
into which I must pour myself like wine,
an emptiness of history which I must seize
and occupy, calm and full in this confine,
becoming clear "like good wine on its lees."

1965

HE WAS BEAUTIFUL WHEN HE
SAT ALONE

He was beautiful when he sat alone, he was like me, he had
wide lapels, he was holding the mug in the hardest possible
way so that his fingers were all twisted but still long and
beautiful, he didn't like to sit alone all the time, but this time,
I swear, he didn't care one way or the other.

I'll tell you why I like to sit alone, because I'm a sadist, that's
why we like to sit alone, because we're the sadists who like
to sit alone.

He sat alone because he was beautifully dressed for the oc-
casion and because he was not a civilian.

We are the sadists you don't have to worry about, you think,
and we have no opinion on the matter of whether you have to
worry about us, and we don't even like to think about the matter
because it baffles us.

Maybe he doesn't mean a thing to me any more but I think
he was like me.

You didn't expect to fall in love, I said to myself and at the
same time I answered gently, Do you think so?

I heard you humming beautifully, your hum said that I can't
ignore you, that I'd finally come around for a number of delicious reasons that only you knew about, and here I am, Miss
Blood.

And you won't come back, you won't come back to where you
left me, and that's why you keep my number, so you don't

dial it by mistake when you're fooling with the dial not even dialing numbers.

You begin to bore us with your pain and we have decided to change your pain.

You said you were happiest when you danced, you said you were happiest when you danced with me, now which do you mean?

And so we changed his pain, we threw the idea of a body at him and we told him a joke, and then he thought a great deal about laughing and about the code.

And he thought that she thought that he thought that she thought that the worst thing a woman could do was to take a man away from his work because that made her what, ugly or beautiful?

And now you have entered the mathematical section of your soul which you claimed you never had. I suppose that this, plus the broken heart, makes you believe that now you have a perfect right to go out and tame the sadists.

He had the last line of each verse of the song but he didn't have any of the other lines, the last line was always the same. *Don't call yourself a secret unless you mean to keep it.*

He thought he knew, or he actually did know too much about singing to be a singer; and if there actually is such a condition, is anybody in it, and are sadists born there?

It is not a question mark, it is not an exclamation point, it is a full stop by the man who wrote Parasites of Heaven.

Even if we stated our case very clearly and all those who held as we do came to our side, all of them, we would still be very few.

1966

I AM A PRIEST OF GOD

I am a priest of God
I walk down the road
with my pockets in my hand
Sometimes I'm bad
then sometimes I'm very good
I believe that I believe
everything I should
I like to hear you say
when you dance with head rolling
upon a silver tray
that I am a priest of God

I thought I was doing 100 other things
but I was a priest of God
I loved 100 women
never told the same lie twice
I said O Christ you're selfish
but I shared my bread and rice
I heard my voice tell the crowd
that I was alone and a priest of God
making me so empty
that even now in 1966
I'm not sure I'm a priest of God

IN ALMOND TREES LEMON TREES

I almond trees lemon trees
wind and sun do as they please
Butterflies and laundry flutter
My love her hair is blond as butter

Wasps with yellow whiskers wait
for food beside her china plate
Ants beside her little feet
are there to share what she will eat

Who chopped down the bells that say
the world is born again today
We will feed you all my dears
this morning or in later years

SUZANNE TAKES YOU DOWN

Suzzane takes you down
to her place near the river,
you can hear the boats go by
you can stay the night beside her.
And you know that she's half crazy
but that's why you want to be there
and she feeds you tea and oranges
that come all the way from China.
Just when you mean to tell her
that you have no gifts to give her,
she gets you on her wave-length
and she lets the river answer
that you've always been her lover.
    And you want to travel with her,
    you want to travel blind
    and you know that she can trust you
    because you've touched her perfect body
    with your mind.

Jesus was a sailor
when he walked upon the water
and he spent a long time watching
from a lonely wooden tower
and when he knew for certain
only drowning men could see him
he said All men will be sailors then
until the sea shall free them,
but he himself was broken
long before the sky would open,
forsaken, almost human,
he sank beneath your wisdom like a stone.
    And you want to travel with him,

you want to travel blind
and you think maybe you'll trust him
because he touched your perfect body
with his mind.

Suzanne takes your hand
and she leads you to the river,
she is wearing rags and feathers
from Salvation Army counters.
The sun pours down like honey
on our lady of the harbour
as she shows you where to look
among the garbage and the flowers,
there are heroes in the seaweed
there are children in the morning,
they are leaning out for love
they will lean that way forever
while Suzanne she holds the mirror.
    And you want to travel with her
    and you want to travel blind
    and you're sure that she can find you
    because she's touched her perfect body
    with her mind.

GIVE ME BACK MY FINGERPRINTS

Give me back my fingerprints
My fingertips are raw
If I don't get my fingerprints
I have to call the Law

I touched you once too often
& I don't know who I am
My fingerprints were missing
When I wiped away the jam

I called my fingerprints all night
But they don't seem to care
The last time that I saw them
They were leafing through your hair

I thought I'd leave this morning
So I emptied out your drawer
A hundred thousand fingerprints
Floated to the floor

You hardly stooped to pick them up
You don't count what you lose
You don't even seem to know
Whose fingerprints are whose

When I had to say goodbye
You weren't there to find
You took my fingerprints away
So I would love your mind

I don't pretend to understand
Just what you mean by that

But next time I'll inquire
Before I scratch your back

I wonder if my fingerprints
Get lonely in the crowd
There are no others like them
& that should make them proud

Now you want to marry me
& take me down the aisle
& throw confetti fingerprints
You know that's not my style

Sure I'd like to marry
But I won't face the dawn
With any girl who knew me
When my fingerprints were on

1966

FOREIGN GOD, REIGNING
IN EARTHLY GLORY . . .

Foreign God, reigning in earthly glory between the Godless God and this greedy telescope of mine: touch my hidden jelly muscle, ring me with some power, I must conquer Babylon and New York. Draw me with a valuable sign, raise me to your height. You and I, dear Foreign God, we both are demons who must disappear in the perpetual crawling light, the fumbling sparks printing the shape of each tired form. We must be lost soon in the elementary Kodak experiment, in the paltry glory beyond our glory, the chalk-squeak of our most limitless delight. We are devoted yokels of the mothy parachute, the salvation of ordeal, we paid good money for the perfect holy scab, the pilgrim kneecap, the shoulder freakish under burden, the triumphant snowman who does not freeze. Down with your angels, Foreign God, down with us, adepts of magic: into the muddy fire of our furthest passionate park, let us consign ourselves now, puddles, peep-holes, dreary oceanic pomp seen through the right end of the telescope, the minor burn, the kingsize cigarette, the alibi atomic holocaust, let us consign ourselves to the unmeasured exile outside the rules of lawlessness. O God, in thy foreign or godless form, in thy form of illusion or with the ringscape of your lethal thumb, you stop direction, you crush this down, you abandon the evidence you pressed on its tongue.

1965

I BELIEVE YOU HEAR YOUR MASTER SING
MASTER SING

I believe you heard your master sing
while I lay sick in bed
I believe he told you everything
I keep locked in my head
Your master took you traveling
at least that's what you said
O love did you come back to bring
your prisoner wine and bread

You met him at some temple where
they take your clothes at the door
He was just a numberless man of a pair
who has just come back from the war
You wrap his quiet face in your hair
and he hands you the apple core
and he touches your mouth now so suddenly bare
of the kisses you had on before

He gave you a German shepherd to walk
with a collar of leather and nails
He never once made you explain or talk
about all of the little details
such as who had a worm and who had a rock
and who had you through the mails
Your love is a secret all over the block
and it never stops when he fails

He took you on his air-o-plane
which he flew without any hands
and you cruised above the ribbons of rain
that drove the crowd from the stands

Then he killed the lights on a lonely lane
where an ape with angel glands
erased the final wisps of pain
with the music of rubber bands

And now I hear your master sing
You pray for him to come
His body is a golden string
that your body is hanging from
His body is a golden string
My body is growing numb
O love I hear your master sing
Your shirt is all undone

Will you kneel beside the bed
we polished long ago
before your master chose instead
to make my bed of snow
Your hair is wild your knuckles red
and you're speaking much too low
I can't make out what your master said
before he made you go

I think you're playing far too rough
For a lady who's been to the moon
I've lain by the window long enough
(you get used to an empty room)
Your love is some dust in an old man's cuff
who is tapping his foot to a tune
and your thighs are a ruin and you want too much
Let's say you came back too soon

I loved your master perfectly
I taught him all he knew

He was starving in a mystery
like a man who is sure what is true
I sent you to him with my guarantee
I could teach him something new
I taught him how you would long for me
No matter what he said no matter what you do

THIS MORNING I WAS DRESSED
BY THE WIND

This morning I was dressed by the wind.
The sky said, close your eyes and run
this happy face into a sundrift.
The forest said, never mind, I am as old
as an emerald, walk into me gossiping.
The village said, I am perfect and intricate,
would you like to start right away?
My darling said, I am washing my hair in the water
we caught last year, it tastes of stone.
This morning I was dressed by the wind,
it was the middle of September in 1965.

I STEPPED INTO AN AVALANCHE

I stepped into an avalanche
It covered up my soul
When I am not a hunchback
I sleep beneath a hill
You who wish to conquer pain
Must learn to serve me well

You strike my side by accident
As you go down for gold
The cripple that you clothe and feed
is neither starved nor cold
I do not beg for company
in the centre of the world

When I am on a pedestal
you did not raise me there
your laws do not compel me
to kneel grotesque and bare
I myself am pedestal
for the thing at which you stare

You who wish to conquer pain
must learn what makes me kind
The crumbs of love you offer me
are the crumbs I've left behind
Your pain is no credential
It is the shadow of my wound

I have begun to claim you
I who have no greed
I have begun to long for you
I who have no need

217

The avalanche you're knocking at
is uninhabited

Do not dress in rags for me
I know you are not poor
Don't love me so fiercely
when you know you are not sure
It is your world beloved
It is your flesh I wear

V / New Poems

THIS IS FOR YOU

This is for you
it is my full heart
it is the book I meant to read you
when we were old
Now I am a shadow
I am restless as an empire
You are the woman
who released me
I saw you watching the moon
you did not hesitate
to love me with it
I saw you honouring the windflowers
caught in the rocks
you loved me with them
On the smooth sand
between pebbles and shoreline
you welcomed me into the circle
more than a guest
All this happened
in the truth of time
in the truth of flesh
I saw you with a child
you brought me to his perfume
and his visions
without demand of blood
On so many wooden tables
adorned with food and candles
a thousand sacraments
which you carried in your basket
I visited my clay
I visited my birth
until I became small enough

and frightened enough
to be born again
I wanted you for your beauty
you gave me more than yourself
you shared your beauty
this I only learned tonight
as I recall the mirrors
you walked away from
after you had given them
whatever they claimed
for my initiation
Now I am a shadow
I long for the boundaries
of my wandering
and I move
with the energy of your prayer
and I move
in the direction of your prayer
for you are kneeling
like a bouquet
in a cave of bone
behind my forehead
and I move toward a love
you have dreamed for me

YOU DO NOT HAVE TO LOVE ME

You do not have to love me
just because
you are all the women
I have ever wanted
I was born to follow you
every night
while I am still
the many men who love you

I meet you at a table
I take your fist between my hands
in a solemn taxi
I wake up alone
my hand on your absence
in Hotel Discipline

I wrote all these songs for you
I burned red and black candles
shaped like a man and a woman
I married the smoke
of two pyramids of sandalwood
I prayed for you
I prayed that you would love me
and that you would not love me

IT'S JUST A CITY, DARLING

It's just a city, darling,
　　everyone calls New York.
Wherever it is we meet
　　I can't go very far from.
I can't connect you with
　　anything but myself.
Half of the wharf is bleeding.
I'd give up anything to love you
　　and I don't even know what the list is
but one look into it
　　demoralizes me like a lecture.
If we are training each other for another love
　　what is it?
I only have a hunch
　　in what I've become expert.
Half of the wharf is bleeding,
it's the half where we always sleep.

EDMONTON, ALBERTA, DECEMBER 1966, 4 A.M.

Edmonton, Alberta, December 1966, 4 a.m.
When did I stop writing you?
The sandalwood is on fire in this small hotel on Jasper
  Street.
You've entered the room a hundred times
disguises of sari and armour and jeans,
and you sit beside me for hours
like a woman alone in a happy room.
I've sung to a thousand people
and I've written a small new song
I believe I will trust myself with the care of my soul.
I hope you have money for the winter.
I'll send you some as soon as I'm paid.
Grass and honey, the singing radiator,
the shadow of bridges on the ice
of the North Saskatchewan River,
the cold blue hospital of the sky—
it all keeps us such sweet company.

THE BROOM IS AN ARMY OF STRAW

The broom is an army of straw
or an automatic guitar,
The dust absorbs a changing chord
that the yawning dog can hear,
My truces have retired me
and the truces are at war.
Is this the house, Beloved,
is this the window sill where
I meet you face to face?
Are these the rooms, are these the walls,
is this the house that opens on the world?
Have you been loved in this disguise
too many times, ring of powder left behind
by teachers polishing their ecstasy?
Beloved of empty spaces
there is dew on the mirror:
can it nourish the bodies in the avalanche
the silver could not exhume?
Beloved of war,
am I obedient to a tune?
Beloved of my injustice,
is there anything to be won?
Summon me as I summon from this house
the mysteries of death and use.
Forgive me the claims I embrace.
Forgive me the claims I renounce.

I MET YOU

I met you
just after death
had become truly sweet
There you were
24 years old
Joan of Arc
I came after you
with all my art
with everything
you know I am a god
who needs to use your body
who needs to use your body
to sing about beauty
in a way no one
has ever sung before
you are mine
you are one of my last women

CALM, ALONE,
THE CEDAR GUITAR

Calm, alone, the cedar guitar
tuned into a sunlight drone,
I'm here with sandalwood
and Patricia's clove pomander.
Thin snow carpets
on the roofs of Edmonton cars
prophesy the wilderness to come.
Downstairs in Swan's Café
the Indian girls are hunting
with their English names.
In Terry's Diner the counter man
plunges his tattoo in soapy water.
Don't fall asleep until your plan
includes every angry nomad.
The juke-box sings of service everywhere
while I work to renew the style
which models the apostles
on these friends whom I have known.

YOU LIVE LIKE A GOD

You live like a god
somewhere behind the names
I have for you,
your body made of nets
my shadow's tangled in,
your voice perfect and imperfect
like oracle petals
in a herd of daisies.
You honour your own god
with mist and avalanche
but all I have
is your religion of no promises
and monuments falling
like stars on a field
where you said you never slept.
Shaping your fingernails
with a razorblade
and reading the work
like a Book of Proverbs
no man will ever write for you,
a discarded membrane
of the voice you use
to wrap your silence in
drifts down the gravity between us,
and some machinery
of our daily life
prints an ordinary question in it
like the Lord's Prayer raised
on a rollered penny.
Even before I begin to answer you
I know you won't be listening.
We're together in a room,

it's an evening in October,
no one is writing our history.
Whoever holds us here in the midst of a Law,
I hear him now
I hear him breathing
as he embroiders gorgeously our simple chains.

AREN'T YOU TIRED?

Aren't you tired
of your beauty tonight
How can you carry your burden
under the stars
Just your hair
just your lips
enough to crush you
Can you see where I'm running
the heavy *New York Times*
with your picture in it
somewhere in it
somewhere in it
under my arm

SHE SINGS SO NICE

She sings so nice
there's no desire in her voice
She sings alone
to tell us all
that we have not been found

THE REASON I WRITE

The reason I write
is to make something
as beautiful as you are

When I'm with you
I want to be the kind of hero
I wanted to be
when I was seven years old
a perfect man
who kills

WHEN I MEET YOU IN THE SMALL STREETS

When I meet you in the small streets
of rain-streaked movies
and old-fashioned shaving equipment,
you smile at me from my blood, saying:
an obsolete wisdom would have married us
when I was fourteen, O my teacher.
    I walk through your Moorish eyes
into sun and mathematics. I polish
Holland diamonds, and deep into Russia
I codify in one laser verse the haphazard
numbers leaping from each triangular story—
oh all world-hated flashing work
I make precise
for the sake of the perfect world.

Like jigsaw pieces married too early
in the puzzle we are pried apart
for every new experiment, as if simplicity
and good luck were not enough to build
a rainbow through gravity and mist.

IT HAS BEEN SOME TIME

It has been some time
since I took away
a woman's perfume on my skin
I remember tonight
how sweet I used to find it
and tonight I've forgotten nothing
of how little it means to me
knowing in my heart
we would never be lovers
thinking much more about suicide and money

A PERSON WHO EATS MEAT

A person who eats meat
wants to get his teeth into something
A person who does not eat meat
wants to get his teeth into something else
If these thoughts interest you for even a moment
you are lost

WHO WILL FINALLY SAY

Who will finally say
you are perfect
Who will choose you
in order to edit your secrets

I sing this for your children
I sing this for the crickets
I sing this for the army
for all who do not need me

Whom will you address
first thing tomorrow morning
your dreams so bureaucratic
you refuse to appear in them

How beautiful the solemn are
Yes I have noticed you
Whoever gives you money
will be remembered for his pride

I love to speak to you this way
knowing how you came to me
leaving everything unsaid
that might employ us

When you are torn
when your silver is torn
take down this book and find
your place in my head

WAITING TO TELL THE DOCTOR

Waiting to tell the doctor
that he failed
and that I failed
I count the few remaining coins
I should have dropped at Monte Carlo
in the little wishing well
they offer you with the gun

still thinking about you
and the sparks between us
dull, milky and peculiar now
like dimes that have been dipped
in mercury too long ago

Last night I asked my brain
to put back into my loins
my love for you
Free at last I fell asleep
both of us naked and hungry
I am sure you willed me
the fullest audience with your body
on condition I die

What did you leave in my room
on my bed
against the wall
that is so cold and impossible and greedy

IT'S GOOD TO SIT WITH PEOPLE

It's good to sit with people
  who are up so late
your other homes wash away
and other meals you left
  unfinished on the plate
It's just coffee
  and a piano player's cigarette
and Tim Hardin's song
and the song in your head
  that always makes you wait
I'm thinking of you
    little Frédérique
with your white white skin
and your stories of wealth
    in Normandy
I don't think I ever told you
that I wanted to save the world
watching television
    while we made love
ordering Greek wine and olives for you
while my friend scattered
dollar bills over the head
of the belly-dancer
under the clarinettes of Eighth Avenue
listening to your plans
for an exclusive pet shop in Paris
  Your mother telephoned me
she said I was too old for you
and I agreed
but you came to my room
one morning after a long time
because you said you loved me

From time to time I meet men
who said they gave you money
and some girls have said
that you weren't really a model
Don't they know what it means
to be lonely
lonely for boiled eggs in silver cups
lonely for a large dog
who obeys your voice
lonely for rain in Normandy
seen through leaded windows
lonely for a fast car
lonely for restaurant asparagus
lonely for a simple prince
and an explorer
I'm sure they know
but we are all creatures of envy
we need our stone fingernails
on another's beauty
we demand the hidden love
of everyone we meet
the hidden love not the daily love
 Your breasts are beautiful
warm porcelain taste
of worship and greed
 Your eyes come to me
under the perfect spikes
of imperishable eyelashes
 Your mouth living
on French words
and the soft ashes of your make-up
Only with you
 I did not imitate myself
only with you

I asked for nothing
your long long fingers
deciphering your hair
    your lace blouse
borrowed from a photographer
the bathroom lights
flashing on your new red fingernails
you tall legs at attention
    as I watch you from my bed
while you brush dew
        from the mirror
to work behind the enemy lines
        of your masterpiece
Come to me if you grow old
come to me if you need coffee

DO NOT FORGET OLD FRIENDS

Do not forget old friends
you knew long before I met you
the times I know nothing about
being someone
who lives by himself
and only visits you on a raid

MARITA

MARITA
PLEASE FIND ME
I AM ALMOST 30

HE STUDIES TO DESCRIBE

He studies to describe
the lover he cannot become
failing the widest dreams of the mind
& settling for visions of God

The tatters of his discipline
have no beauty
that he can hold so easily
       as your beauty

He does not know how
to trade himself for your love
Do not trust him
unless you love him

Index of First Lines